PRAISE FOR LAURA GRIFFIN AND HER NOVELS

"I love smart, sophisticated, fast-moving romantic thrillers, and Laura Griffin writes them brilliantly."
—*New York Times* bestselling author Jayne Ann Krentz

"Gritty, imaginative, sexy! You must read Laura Griffin."
—*New York Times* bestselling author Cindy Gerard

"Top-notch romantic suspense! Fast pace, tight plotting, terrific mystery, sharp dialogue, fabulous characters."
—*New York Times* bestselling author Allison Brennan

"A gripping, white-knuckle read. You won't be able to put it down."
—*New York Times* bestselling author Brenda Novak

"An emotional, exciting page-turner. Griffin deftly balances the mystery and the love story."
—*The Washington Post*

"Griffin never disappoints with her exciting, well-researched, fast-paced romantic thrillers."
—*Publishers Weekly* (starred review)

"A high-adrenaline thriller that will keep you on the edge of your seat. . . . Griffin is a master." —*Fresh Fiction*

D0011799

Titles by Laura Griffin

Standalone Novels
FAR GONE

LAST SEEN ALONE

VANISHING HOUR

The Texas Murder Files Series
HIDDEN

FLIGHT

MIDNIGHT DUNES

The Tracers Series

UNTRACEABLE

UNSPEAKABLE

UNSTOPPABLE

UNFORGIVABLE

SNAPPED

TWISTED

SCORCHED

EXPOSED

BEYOND LIMITS

SHADOW FALL

DEEP DARK

AT CLOSE RANGE

TOUCH OF RED

STONE COLD HEART

The Wolfe Security Series
DESPERATE GIRLS

HER DEADLY SECRETS

The Alpha Crew Series

AT THE EDGE

EDGE OF SURRENDER

COVER OF NIGHT

TOTAL CONTROL

ALPHA CREW: THE MISSION

BEGINS

The Glass Sisters Series
THREAD OF FEAR

WHISPER OF WARNING

The Borderline Series
ONE LAST BREATH

ONE WRONG STEP

The Moreno & Hart Mysteries, with Allison Brennan

CRASH AND BURN

HIT AND RUN

FROSTED

LOST AND FOUND

VANISHING HOUR

HOUR

LAURA GRIFFIN

BERKLEY
New York

BERKLEY
An imprint of Penguin Random House LLC
penguinrandomhouse.com

BERKLEY and the BERKLEY & B colophon
are registered trademarks of Penguin Random House LLC.

ISBN: 9780593546697

First Edition: October 2022

Printed in the United States of America
3 5 7 9 10 8 6 4 2

Book design by George Towne

For my sisters

PROLOGUE

MOLLY DIDN'T HAVE enough water.

It was a common mistake. But that didn't make it any less dangerous on a day when the air was like a hairdryer and the slightest trace of moisture vanished from her skin in seconds.

A horned lizard scampered across the creek bed and paused beside a rock, seeming to mock her with his natural adaptations to the environment. He darted behind a boulder, and Molly stepped into the meager strip of shade provided by the canyon wall.

The sun was almost directly overhead now, which definitely wasn't part of the plan. She pulled her water bottle from her backpack, and her heart skittered.

Less than a third left.

How could that be?

She'd been careful, but not careful enough. The two-hour trek had taken twice as long as expected, and the sickening notion that she'd made a wrong turn was starting to take hold.

Trying not to panic, she set her pack at her feet and dug out the hand-drawn map. She'd pored over it by flashlight in her tent last night, memorizing every curve of the trail and every word of Camila's loopy script. Studying the landmarks, the conclusion was inescapable.

She should have reached it by now.

Molly tucked the map away. She untwisted the top off the water bottle and took a tiny pull, barely enough to wet her throat. She was angry with herself. She hadn't prepped right—everything from her shoes to her water supply was all wrong. She couldn't afford to be so careless.

Anxiety bloomed in her chest as she dug out her cell phone. She stepped into the middle of the creek bed and powered up.

No bars, of course. She would have been shocked if she'd managed to get any. She tipped her head back and gazed at the cloudless sky. A swallow flew over and swooped into a mud nest beneath a ledge.

Molly's breath caught. *There.*

She took a few steps back and stared at the twisted juniper clinging to the rocky outcropping. The tree's tortured shape was unmistakable.

She tucked away the phone and water bottle and slung on her pack. Skimming the sloped canyon wall, she spied a faint trail.

Molly scrambled up the path, grabbing tree roots and warm rocks for balance. Thorny branches snagged her shirt, but she jerked it loose as she hurried up the trail. When she reached the top, she turned around and there it was.

Panting, she stopped and took a moment to admire the axial twist, like the double helix of a DNA strand. But this life-form was even more mysterious.

Snap.

She turned and scanned the arid landscape. Green mesquite bushes fluttered in the sunlight, and a shadow shifted near a giant sotol. On instinct, she reached for the .22 in the pancake holster at the small of her back. She rested her hand on the pistol as she surveyed the brush. Mountain lions were rare in this area, but she had an irrational fear of predatory mammals. She didn't want to get between a mama and her kittens.

Snick.

"Hello?"

She listened closely, but the only sound was the faint whisper of wind through the scrub brush.

She turned to face the tree again. The Angel Tree. She didn't know who had named it or why. Heart thrumming now, she pulled out her water bottle again and took a sip to calm her nerves. The sip became a guzzle. Now that she'd reached her destination, she knew exactly how long it would take to get back. She slipped off her pack and set her gear on the ground. Then she took a deep breath and approached the tree.

It was taller than she'd expected. She studied the gnarled branches and peeling bark, noting the scattered rock piles from the hikers—pilgrims—who had come before her. Tentatively, she reached out to touch the trunk.

Nothing.

She stayed totally motionless, but nothing happened. She didn't feel a thing. A still, silent minute elapsed and then the wind gusted, kicking up a dust devil nearby. Delight zinged through her. Coincidence? Or something else? She didn't used to believe in "woo-woo nonsense," as her dad would have called it.

She didn't used to believe in a lot of things.

Once upon a time, she'd been practical. Logical. Level-headed. But desperation had a way of thwarting everything.

A warm tear slid down her cheek, and she brushed it away. Awe and reverence washed over her in a cooling wave. She took another deep breath. Now what? Should she say a prayer? Meditate? She'd never had the urge to build one of those damn rock piles, and now was no exception. But she had to do something to mark the moment.

Snap.

She whirled around.

"Hello?" she called, louder this time.

Molly squinted at the line of mesquite trees. A man stepped out, and her heart jumped into her throat. He was tall and broad-shouldered. The brim of a baseball cap cast a shadow over his face. As he moved closer, she got a better look at him, and relief flooded her.

"Oh, it's you," she huffed. "What are you doing here?"

Not answering, he took another step. She caught a flare of something in his eyes. Her gaze dropped to the leather holster at his side and she watched with disbelief as he slipped out his pistol.

She stepped back and looked at his eyes again. "What do you want?" she croaked.

His mouth spread into a bone-chilling smile. "I think you know."

CHAPTER
ONE

AVA FOLLOWED THE curve of the dirt road to the string of emergency vehicles. She checked her watch and cursed. She was later than she'd thought.

"Not good, Huck."

The black Lab nudged her arm with his wet nose.

"We're going to have to redeem ourselves."

Ava passed a sheriff's SUV and squeezed her little red car between a pair of dusty pickups from the parks department. Huck whimpered with impatience as she grabbed his lead off the seat and clipped it to his collar.

"Okay, let's do this."

Ava slid out. Huck hopped over the console and followed her. She felt dozens of eyes on her as she popped open the back hatch and retrieved her day pack. Hitching it onto her shoulder, Ava scanned the faces. None were familiar. All were skeptical. Several of the men wore the Henley County Sheriff's Office backcountry uniform of HCSO ball cap, navy T-shirt, and desert-brown tactical pants.

Ava spied some park rangers in olive green milling near

a blue tarp that looked like operation headquarters. Beneath the makeshift tent, two rangers studied a map that had been spread out across a pair of tables.

"Help you?"

She turned around as a man sauntered over. Tall, sixty-ish, paunchy. He wore a sheriff's office cap and a sweat-soaked golf shirt. He stopped in front of her.

Ava smiled. "Are you the incident commander?"

"I'm Sheriff Donovan."

"Oh." *Shit.* She thrust out her hand. "Ava Burch, West-Tex Search and Rescue."

He shook her hand and frowned down at Huck.

"We're here to help with the search," she added.

"They started five hours ago."

"Yes, I know. I was unavoidably delayed." She sensed a brush-off coming, and she glanced around. "Do you know who the IC is on this one?"

"That'd be Mel Tyndall," he said, nodding in the direction of the blue tent.

"Oh, good. I'll check in with him."

She led Huck away before the sheriff could think of any objections. She zeroed in on the park ranger who seemed to be giving orders—a wiry man with wraparound sunglasses perched atop his shaved head. Ava stepped under the tarp, and he glanced up.

"I'm Ava with WestTex SAR. Chuck Crawford said you could use a hand today?"

Dropping the name of the chief ranger in nearby Big Bend seemed to do the trick. Tyndall stepped away from the table and looked her over.

"Are you trained up?" he asked.

"Yes."

He glanced at Huck, who wore his red work vest. "Him, too?"

"Yep. He's logged more than a hundred wilderness searches."

She didn't mention that most of those had been with a different handler. But Tyndall seemed too distracted to nit-pick her credentials. He checked his watch and returned his attention to the table.

"The first teams deployed at oh nine hundred," he said. "We're just getting started on sector D."

Ava stepped closer to examine the map. It was a detailed topo of Silver Canyon State Park. A small red sticker near a campground marked what had to be the PLS, or point last seen. Sections bounded by natural barriers had been marked with letters.

"We just sent a team out to Lizard Creek Trail," Tyndall said, tapping the map.

Ava's stomach knotted as she studied the spot. Sector D was well outside of the high-probability search area. They were getting desperate.

"You up for it?" Tyndall asked.

"Absolutely."

He handed her a clipboard. "Sign in, and I'll brief you on the way over."

Ava quickly jotted her info on a card and followed the ranger to one of the dusty white pickups. She stowed her pack on the floor and hopped into the passenger seat, signaling Huck to sit on her lap.

Tyndall wasted no time pulling out and maneuvering onto the pitted dirt road that Ava had just navigated. Huck pressed his head against the glass, squirming with excitement as they passed the police vehicles.

Tyndall slid on his shades and glanced over. "You're new to the county?"

"Been here since November," she told him.

"Done any ops yet?"

"Three this spring in Big Bend."

They bumped along the narrow dirt road and hung a right onto an even narrower one. Ava visualized the state park in her head. She was familiar with it, but only from a few casual day hikes. She'd never been on a search team here.

"Silver Canyon is different," Tyndall said. "It's rugged country."

She turned to look at him. Big Bend wasn't exactly a golf resort. The sprawling national park consisted of more than 800,000 untamed acres. But Ava understood what he was getting at. Silver Canyon was a new addition to Texas's state park system, and it lacked even basic amenities.

"We've only got one paved road," the ranger continued. "It makes an outer loop. The interior roads are dirt, and they tend to wash out when we get a flash flood. The only cell service is near the entrance, so everything's by radio."

"Okay."

"Did Chuck tell you about the op?"

"Just that it's a child missing."

Tyndall nodded. "A boy, three and a half."

Ava's heart sank.

"Noah Dumfries. He's been missing since oh eight hundred. Wandered off from his family's campsite after breakfast. His mom thinks he went down to the creek to brush his teeth."

"Have they—"

"We had a canine team there all morning. No sign of him."

Ava looked out the window at the limestone canyon baking in the afternoon sun.

"He's just over three feet tall, blond hair, brown eyes. He's wearing a red Spider-Man T-shirt with blue shorts and white sneakers."

She glanced at him. "What about the parents?"

"Mom is distraught, as you'd expect. She's at the campsite with her other son, who's five, in case Noah comes back. Dad is at the ranger station. He wanted to join the search, but we convinced him to stay back."

It was standard procedure. When a child went missing

there was always the depressing possibility that the parents could have something to do with it.

"Do they have any pets?" she asked.

"No idea. Why?"

"I want to understand if he's afraid of dogs."

"I don't know. I can find out, though."

He swung off the dirt road onto what looked to be a horse trail. He bumped across the feather grass and headed for the base of a tall cliff. A wooden sign came into view.

Tyndall rolled to a halt.

"Lizard Creek Trail," he said. "The other team deployed to the east about—" He checked his watch. "Fifteen minutes ago."

"Do they have a dog with them?"

"No. It's two of our seasonal rangers."

Ava's heart sank again as she looked out the window. "Seasonal" was code for summer interns. And she knew what Tyndall was doing here. Inexperienced volunteers were being banished to the low-probability areas while law enforcement veterans conducted the real search. Ava got it—Tyndall didn't know her from anyone. And he didn't know Huck. All he knew was that she'd shown up five hours late and he'd never worked with her before. But with the clock ticking and only one other dog in the search party, it was a waste to give her a crap assignment. Especially with a missing child case. Under normal circumstances, a lost kid would have pulled in resources from all the neighboring counties. But a helicopter crash in Big Bend this morning had gotten a jump on everyone's attention, and the National Park Service had no one to spare right now.

Tyndall reached into the back of his truck cab and grabbed a radio. "How much water you have there?" He nodded at her pack.

"A gallon."

"That for both of you?"

"Yeah."

"Better take more." He grabbed a bottle of water from the back and handed it to her.

"Thanks." Huck squirmed on her lap, anxious to get started. He'd been trembling with excitement since she put on his vest.

"You and your dog are Team Six," he said. "Check in every half hour, no exceptions."

"Okay."

"And it's hot out there. Don't forget to drink."

"Got it." She pushed open the door.

"You're headed west," he continued. "Cover as much ground as you can and meet back here in four hours." He checked his watch. "We'll have someone here to pick you up."

"Got it."

"If you see anything at all, call it in. Time is of the essence."

"I know."

He looked Huck over with a frown, and she knew what he was thinking. With his thick black fur, he was going to melt in this heat. But Huck was tougher than he looked. They both were.

"How old is he?" Tyndall asked.

"Four."

"And the medal on him?" He nodded at the silver medallion on his collar.

"Saint Anthony, patron saint of the lost." She gave a self-conscious shrug. "It brings him luck."

"Luck, huh?" Tyndall squinted through the windshield at the sunbaked cliff. "Well, we're going on hour six here, so we need it."

CHAPTER
TWO

MISSING CHILDREN ARE an emergency. Always. Their little bodies are less able to regulate temperature, so they're especially vulnerable to exposure. And in a place as vast and rugged as Silver Canyon State Park, additional hazards abounded: rattlesnakes, coyotes, hundred-foot cliffs. Even the anemic little creek that Ava had been following was terrifying. A child Noah's size could drown in a bathtub.

Ava glanced up at the relentless sun that sucked moisture out of everything beneath it. She looked ahead at Huck, who trotted back and forth in front of her in his zig-zag pattern. He was working the wind, as he'd been trained, tirelessly sniffing the air with his powerful nose, which could pick up anything with human scent on it, from a candy wrapper to a dropped article of clothing.

So far, nothing.

Ava checked her watch. Two long hours since she'd left the trailhead. Sweat stung her eyes, and she wiped her forehead with the back of her arm. She paused beside a boulder and dropped her pack on the dusty ground to retrieve one of her water bottles. Huck needed some, too, but right now he was intent on his work.

She took a lukewarm sip and scanned the scrub brush lining the canyon wall. Young children had a tendency to wander aimlessly until they found a place to curl up for a nap. Some would even hide from search teams, afraid of getting in trouble for being lost. So Ava had been incessantly scanning pockets of brush.

Huck halted in front of her, his nose lifted in the air. Ava froze and watched. But then his head dropped down and he resumed his zigzags. Ava tucked the water bottle away and pushed off the boulder to continue her trek.

She watched Huck, amazed by his energy. Even in this heat, he loved working, and when he had his vest on, he didn't have an off switch. As he bounded around in front of her, she thought of the other teams, especially the canine one. She was surprised they hadn't found something close to camp.

Of course, the parents had been there, which might have been a problem. Frantic parents threw off a lot of scent, which could have overpowered Noah's smell and possibly confused the dog. Also, the temperature rising in the canyon could have wafted the scent up, well above the dog's nose. Yet another challenge here was that young children didn't throw off as much scent as adults. And still bodies—ones that were either asleep or unconscious—threw off less scent, too.

So there were all kinds of factors in play, especially in a park this size.

Ava checked her watch again and sped up her pace, unable to shake the feeling of dread that had been settling in her stomach as the hours ticked by. Scanning the canyon wall, her gaze caught on something beige and triangular.

A tent? No.

A tarp. She climbed onto a boulder for a closer look. About halfway up the slope of the canyon was a sand-colored canvas tarp that had been stretched taut to create a patch of shade. It looked like a primitive fort—just the sort of thing that would attract a kid's attention, and her pulse quickened as she climbed closer. Nearing the tarp, she spied a small yellow tent tucked in the shade beneath it.

She glanced around for Huck, but he was sniffing along at the base of a rockslide.

Grabbing hold of a juniper tree, Ava levered herself onto the ledge. She ducked under the tarp and paused a moment for her eyes to adjust. The little tent was unzipped. Hope ballooned in her chest as she pulled back the flap and poked her head inside.

Her hope disappeared as she scanned the interior. No sleeping child curled up in the dimness. The air was utterly still, and everything was coated with a thin layer of dust, as though no one had been there in weeks, maybe months. A pile of gear in the corner included a cookstove, a hiking boot, and a blue bedroll with a carabiner clipped to it. Attached to the carabiner was a black key fob.

A chill snaked down her spine. Who would leave their car key out here? The fob seemed odd. Ditto for the hiking boot. Where was the other one? And where was its owner?

On impulse, Ava took out her phone and snapped a couple of pictures. As part of her SAR training, she'd learned to document crime scenes. She couldn't pinpoint why, exactly, but that was what this felt like. She ducked out and snapped a shot of the exterior. A faint bark pulled her attention back to the mission. She couldn't afford to get sidetracked, even though this place felt creepy. She put her phone away as she skimmed the surrounding area for the missing boot, or any sign of the boot's owner. She glanced up the canyon, looking for evidence of a fire pit or any other camping equipment.

A soft whimper had her turning around.

Huck sat beside a rock pile, his ears pricked forward and his gaze fixed on hers. Ava's heart skittered. This was his sit alert letting her know he'd found something.

"Show me," she commanded, and he sprang into action,

bounding across the creek bed. She climbed down the rocks and jogged after him, frantically searching the clumps of trees. Huck darted around a giant prickly pear cactus and behind a line of mesquite trees. Amid the fluttering green leaves, she caught a flash of red.

"Please, please, please," she murmured.

Huck disappeared beneath the brush and barked. Ava spied a small white sneaker and a pudgy leg.

Huck danced in a circle, drunk on success and eager for his reward.

"Good boy, Huck! *Good boy! Good boy!*" She filled her voice with praise, even though her heart had lodged in her throat. The little body wasn't moving. *Oh God.*

But then the yellow mop of hair lifted. Relief flooded her as the boy's eyes fluttered open. His cheeks were flushed pink and his hair was matted to his head with sweat.

"Hi there." She dropped to her knees in front of him and tried to keep her voice calm even though she wanted to whoop with joy. "You must be Noah."

The radio crackled, and Noah's eyes widened as he jerked away from her.

"Base to Team Six. Team Six, check in."

Ava hit the mike. "Team Six here." She took a deep breath. "We've got him."

DETECTIVE GRANT WYCOFF got a knot in his chest as he watched the little boy.

Seven and a half hours.

Much of that during the heat of the day.

Noah sat on his mother's lap in the back of the ambulance near the command center. Ashley Dumfries hadn't stopped weeping since rescue workers had brought her son back from the trail. Now she fed him orange slices and kissed his little head as the paramedic dabbed ointment on the bug bites up and down his legs.

The kid was damn lucky, and his mom knew it. Noah had wandered an astonishing nine miles from his campsite before crawling under a tree to sleep. If not for the search dog, Noah probably would have spent the night out here. Given today's heat index and his lack of fluids, he might not have survived.

"Is that her?"

Grant turned to see Connor trudging over from the line of police vehicles. His attention was fixed on the dog handler.

"Yep," Grant said.

"She a cop?"

"Nope."

Connor's Henley County Sheriff's Office T-shirt was soaked with sweat. He twisted the top off a bottle of water and eyed the woman as he took a long swig.

"Where'd she come from?" Connor asked.

"Cuervo."

He shot Grant a look. No one really *came* from Cuervo, and definitely not her. Grant turned to look at the woman. She was talking on her phone beside her shiny red Fiat, which would have looked more at home in a European city than a West Texas desert. Her long blond hair was pulled back in a ponytail, and she wore designer jeans that hugged her curves. Her pricey leather hiking boots had red laces that matched her dog's work vest. Coincidence? Or were they color-coordinated? Maybe coordinated. Between the car and the clothes, she seemed pretty high-maintenance.

Her dog was cool, though. The Labrador sat obediently at her feet while she talked on her cell.

"No idea where she's from originally," Grant said.

"What's her name?"

"Don't know." Grant opened the built-in toolbox in the back of his truck. "Why don't you go find out?"

"Right." Connor wiped the sweat from his brow. He looked like he'd just jumped in a pool. They both reeked, and neither one of them was in any shape to hit on someone.

"So, did you hear about the wreck?" Connor asked.

"No."

"Multivehicle collision on White Bluffs Road."

"Fatalities?"

"Not sure."

Grant sure as hell hoped not. He tossed his SAR bag into the toolbox, then added his empty hydration pack. He'd been called out at six this morning on the helo crash, and he'd been running nonstop ever since. He hadn't even been by the office yet and it was almost five.

Connor eyed the dog handler again. "Well, I'm headed back to Henley."

"Need a lift?" Grant asked.

"I'm good."

"Keep me posted on that crash."

"Will do."

Connor pitched his empty water bottle into a recycle bin and walked away.

Grant pulled off his rubber boots. He'd spent five straight hours combing the banks of Lizard Creek, and he'd never been so grateful to have wasted his time.

He turned to look again at the canine team that had found the boy. The handler was off her phone finally, and Grant watched with interest as she strode up to the sheriff.

"I wrote down those coordinates for you." She handed Donovan a slip of paper. "Of the campsite?"

Donovan looked distracted as he slid the paper into his pocket.

"If you'll give me an email address, I can send along the pictures, too," she said.

"Pictures?"

"The photographs." She held up her phone. "I took a handful, just in case."

The sheriff frowned down at her. "Just in case what?"

"Just in case, you know, you guys end up needing them."

"For what?"

"An investigation."

"We won't."

She blinked up at him. "How do you know?"

The sheriff looked past her, scanning the cops and emergency workers milling along the road. Grant knew what he was looking for. A TV reporter from San Antonio had been sent out to cover the helicopter crash and then gotten wind of the lost-child story and turned up at the search headquarters. Donovan never missed an opportunity to get in front of a camera, especially when the news was good.

"Sheriff?"

"We get abandoned gear out here all the time," he said.

"What about abandoned car keys?"

Donovan glared down at her, annoyed that someone had the balls to argue with him, especially a woman.

"Talk to the park rangers," he said.

"But—"

"I'm running a law enforcement agency, not a lost and found."

He walked off, leaving her in the middle of the road with her phone in her hand. She muttered a curse, and Grant had no trouble reading her lips.

He smiled and slammed his toolbox. She glanced over at him, and her gaze narrowed. She was probably lumping him into the same category as the sheriff. She stalked back to her shiny red car and yanked open the door.

"Come on, Huck."

The dog hopped inside, and she slid in after him.

Grant retrieved his work boots from the back of his truck cab as the Fiat pulled out. He watched it speed off as he shoved his feet into his shoes. Then his phone buzzed.

"Wycoff," he said.

"Hey, you left yet?" Connor asked him.

"I'm leaving now. Why?"

"White Bluffs is a mess. I just got the call. There's a fatality."

"Shit."

"You and I are on it."

THE TOWN OF Cuervo had one stoplight, two RV parks, and three bars. Four if you counted the BBQ joint that had a beer garden in back. The town's economy had originally been based on mining and ranching, but that heyday was long gone, and Cuervo had spent the last fifty years languishing under the Texas sun.

Cuervo's fortunes were changing, though. With an uptick in tourists headed to Big Bend, more and more people were stopping in Cuervo overnight, and what had once been practically a ghost town was now a quirky way station conveniently located at the gateway to three big parks. The town's residents were an eclectic mix of river guides, rock climbers, artists, and other wandering souls who had visited the area and decided to stay. With each passing year, Cuervo attracted more people who wanted an escape from city life—or so they claimed. It was Ava's observation that most of the people who came here brought their laptops with them and were addicted to their phones. They were junkies, really, and Ava recognized the signs because she had once been one of them.

Ava rolled to a stop at the light, and Huck whimpered from the back seat as a pair of women in yoga clothes crossed Main Street with a blue-eyed husky in tow.

"Colorado," Ava said.

Huck whined and pressed his nose against the glass.

"No? Okay, Wyoming."

It was a running game she played, trying to guess where people were from. Dogs were a good indicator, and the long-haired ones almost always came from the Rockies or New York.

They cruised through town and passed the pink brick building where Ava rented an office. As if on cue, her phone vibrated in the cup holder with a call from her business partner.

"Hey," she said to Jenna. "Are you at work?"

"Just about to leave. How'd it go?"

"The callout or the hearing?"

"You had a callout?" Jenna asked.

"It came in around ten. Of course, I didn't even know till I was on the steps of the courthouse and turned on my phone."

Judge Chadwick and his absolutely-no-ringtones-or-you-will-be-in-contempt-of-court policy was presenting a challenge to Ava's SAR work. She was going to have to come up with a workaround.

"What happened?" Jenna asked. She was always intrigued by Ava's SAR calls.

"A three-year-old boy went missing out at Silver Canyon State Park."

She gasped.

"We found him," Ava said. "But he was gone for more than seven hours. Huck found him curled up under a mesquite tree."

"Oh my God, is he *okay*?"

"Dehydrated and sunburned. But fine otherwise."

"Poor thing must have been terrified."

"I think the parents were more terrified than he was."

Jenna had a four-year-old, and Ava knew she could relate.

"Well, thank God you found him. Those poor parents."

They drove by the gas station, and Huck knew they were headed home. He whimpered softly and rested his paws on the console.

"So . . . how was the hearing? I'm almost afraid to ask," Jenna said.

"Surprisingly good, actually. Chadwick granted our motion."

"No *way*."

"Way."

Ava was representing a new client in a property dispute with a neighboring ranch. Less than a year ago, it was the sort of small-potatoes case that Ava would have pawned off on a first-year associate at her law firm. But her life had taken a dramatic turn since then, and this was exactly what she'd signed up for when she accepted Jenna's invitation to go into business together. They now had the sole law firm in Cuervo, which was one of only three law firms in all of Henley County.

"I can't believe he granted it," Jenna said. "He's always such a hard-ass."

"So, speaking of locals," Ava said, "what do you know about Sheriff Donovan?"

"Jim Donovan? He's a blowhard."

Ava sighed. That had been her impression, too.

"Why?" Jenna asked.

"I don't know. I met him today and he was kind of a prick."

"Yeah, well. He's a good old boy. But he keeps getting reelected, so he must be doing something right."

Ava wasn't sure she agreed with that.

"I can't believe it about the hearing. How come you're not excited?" Jenna asked.

"I am excited. I'm beat, though. It's been a long day."

Not to mention stressful. When she'd seen that lifeless little body . . .

"Well, I'm glad you found the boy. It's freaking *hot* today."

"Tell me about it."

"Go crack open a beer and put your feet up."

"That's the plan."

"I'll see you tomorrow."

The road curved west, and Ava flipped her visor down as she squinted at the sinking sun. She passed a wide gate with a wrought iron *M* on it. Then she passed the Stoney Creek RV Park, which had been part of the McCullough family ranch until Jenna's parents got into financial straits and sold off twenty acres abutting the highway. Ava turned onto a dirt driveway and crossed a cattle guard. Huck squirmed excitedly as she navigated the familiar ruts and neared a limestone cottage. This bit of land was still part of Jenna's family's ranch, and the caretaker cottage was now a rental property.

Ava parked and got out. Huck scrambled out behind her and sprinted down the slope leading to the spring-fed creek. Ava collected her gear from the back and went inside. The place was dim and cool, but not nearly cool enough. She crossed the little living area and switched on the window AC unit. Then she went to the sink and filled a plastic pitcher with cold water before grabbing a beer and going out to the back porch.

Huck was already frolicking in the shallow creek.

Ava poured water into his bowl and lowered herself onto the porch steps. In the evenings, the cottonwoods cast shadows over the cottage and cooled things down, and Ava liked to sit here and watch the fireflies come out. She untied her boots and tugged them off, along with the thick socks that were still damp.

Huck sprinted up to her and shook water all over her legs.

"Thanks." She popped open her beer. "I needed that."

Huck scrambled up the steps to his bowl and lapped up water. Then he shook himself off again, and Ava pulled him into a hug.

"You did good today."

She kissed his wet fur and picked out some sticker burrs, then checked for ticks. It would take a good half hour to check him thoroughly. Sensing what was coming, Huck ducked away and raced back to the creek.

Ava took a long, cold swig. She tipped her head back to look at the pinkening sky. Not a cloud anywhere. The sun had been fierce today, and she felt a pang of guilt as she thought of Noah's sunburned arms. What if she'd been stuck in court another two hours and hadn't checked her phone? Just the thought made her queasy.

Music drifted over, reminding her that it was Thursday

night. The RV park would be full by tomorrow, with tourists from Houston and Dallas and even Oklahoma and Colorado crowded around the fire pits. Another weekend. Another load of work to make up because she'd canceled the back half of her day.

Her gaze fell on her dusty hiking boots perched neatly on the step. Thinking of the lone boot inside that tent, she got a knot in her stomach. The boot bothered her. The car key, too. Something was off.

She got up and went inside. Her laptop sat on the drop-leaf breakfast table that she used as a desk. Ava powered it up and clicked into her email. She'd sent herself the photos from her phone, and she opened them up now so she could enlarge the images on a bigger screen.

The boot was a Salomon—not cheap—and it was probably a woman's six or seven. An animal could have come into the tent and dragged off the other boot. But why were they left there anyway? And what about the car key?

I'm running a law enforcement agency, not a lost and found.

Sexist jerk. The sheriff had been condescending toward her all afternoon, and under normal circumstances she would have simply ignored it, but his blowing off her concerns about the campsite pissed her off.

Ava hit print. Then she opened the other two photographs and printed them as well. She kept a box of office supplies in the bedroom, and she rummaged through until she found a legal-size manila envelope—very official-looking—and slipped the printouts inside. She wrote the sheriff's name across the front, then added the word *EVIDENCE* and drew a box around it. She'd go to Henley tomorrow and deliver the photos herself. He couldn't ignore the evidence if she put it right under his nose.

At least, she hoped not.

CHAPTER

THREE

GRANT PULLED INTO the parking lot and slid into the empty space beside the red Fiat crossover. He studied the car as he got out. Texas plates, which he'd noticed yesterday. A parking decal, which he hadn't. The sticker was for space number 424, but there wasn't a four-story parking garage within a hundred miles of here.

Grant crossed the sidewalk to the Henley County Sheriff's Office, a low brick building that had been built in the seventies. It had narrow windows and boxy brick planters. The planters had probably looked good on some architectural drawing, but Grant had never seen them filled with anything but dirt.

The building's front door swung open, and the Fiat owner stepped out. She was overdressed again today, this time in a tight black skirt and a loose white blouse that tucked into a wide leather belt. She wore black sandals with skinny heels, and her blond hair was up in a bun.

She stared down at her phone and cursed, and once again Grant had no trouble reading her lips.

He walked over. "Hi there."

She looked up. Recognition flickered in her eyes, and she glanced down at the badge clipped to his belt.

"Hi. You're . . ."

"Detective Grant Wycoff, Henley County Sheriff's Office. I was with the search yesterday. You're Huck's mom."

She smiled, as he'd hoped she would.

"Ava Burch." She dropped her phone into her purse and held out her hand. Grant shook it.

"Everything all right?" he asked.

Her eyebrows tipped up. "Why do you ask?"

"People don't usually come to our office just for fun."

"Oh. Well." She glanced over her shoulder. "I had something for Sheriff Donovan. I'd hoped to catch him in person but he's in a meeting."

Grant smiled.

"What?" she asked.

"It's noon."

"And?"

"And he's in a meeting every weekday from noon to one thirty."

She rolled her eyes.

"You could come back," he suggested. "He'll probably be in after lunch."

"I can't. I have a deposition in Cuervo in"—she checked her watch—"thirty minutes."

"A deposition. So, I take it you're a lawyer, then."

The side of her mouth quirked. "You sound disappointed."

"Nope. I just didn't know Cuervo had any."

"Only two, me and my law partner." She smiled, and he felt it right in his sternum. Ava Burch was beautiful, and he didn't even care that she was probably from Dallas or Houston or some other big city.

"Who'd you leave it with?" he asked.

"What's that?"

"The thing you had for the sheriff."

"Oh." She glanced over her shoulder again. "Someone named Hildie? She seemed very"—she appeared to be searching for a word to describe their superefficient receptionist—"in charge."

"She is. He'll get it."

Hildie ran a tight ship and never misplaced a message. And she'd probably already done a search on Ava Burch's name to see who the heck she was.

Grant gazed down at her, trying not to stare at the plump pink mouth that looked especially good when she was cursing.

The phone in her purse chimed, and she pulled it out.

"Sorry. I have to take this." She stepped away, already putting the phone to her ear. "Good to meet you, Detective."

"It's Grant. And likewise."

AVA ROLLED THE windows down as she sped toward home. She'd stayed later than she'd intended, and the shadows were already long across the arid landscape. Passing the RV park, she noticed they had the **NO VACANCY** sign posted.

It was going to be a busy weekend. Schools were letting out now, and people were hitting the road for their summer vacations. She was about to find out whether renting a house a stone's throw away from an RV park was a good idea. Most likely she'd regret it, but she'd been charmed by the little limestone cottage nestled beside the creek. Plus, Jenna's mom had offered Ava a friends-and-family discount on the rent. And when Huck had taken that first running leap into the water, Ava had thought of her dad and her heart had melted a little.

She turned onto the dirt road and surveyed the parched land around her. A trio of cows vied for shade near the fence, as close as they could get to the cottonwoods along the creek.

She parked and gathered her computer bag. It was stuffed with contracts she needed to read this weekend. But for tonight she planned to toss everything into the bedroom and not think about work. Maybe she'd fire up the Weber and grill something for dinner. And then maybe curl up with a good movie.

Rummaging for her key, she eyed the front door as she mounted the steps. No barking. No scratching. She unlocked the door and stepped into the dim, quiet house.

"Huck?"

He walked over to greet her, wagging his tail as usual. But there was no mistaking the guilt in his eyes.

"What did you do? What?" He watched her as she stepped over to check the kitchen. "Don't lie to me, Huckleberry."

She peered into the bedroom. A trail of tissues littered the floor. The wastebasket lay on its side, and half a dozen shoes were strewn across the rug.

"Huck!" She snatched up a Ferragamo pump. "*No!* We do *not* eat shoes!" She spied another pump peeking out from under the bed. She grabbed that one, too.

Her favorite court shoes, shredded. Somehow, he knew.

"No, sir." She pointed a shoe at him. "*Bad.*"

Should she put him in time out? Scold him more? Guilt needled her because this was partly her fault. Her meetings had run long. She'd been away for six hours, and he was accustomed to going with her to the office when she needed to be out that long. But she'd had a hectic schedule today, so she'd decided to leave him home, which he'd obviously hated.

Part of her wanted to give him a pass. But her father wouldn't have—not in a million years.

Which was probably why she wanted to.

Huck sank to the floor and rested his chin on his paws.

"Not working. You're in trouble." She righted the wastebasket and tossed the mangled shoes in, then scooped up all the tissue shreds.

Sighing, she dropped her computer bag and purse onto the bed. She fished out her phone and—for the hundredth time today—checked her messages. No voicemail. No email. Not that she'd expected anything. But she'd clipped her business card to the envelope as a professional courtesy.

Which of course, Jim Donovan had ignored.

I'm running a law enforcement agency, not a lost and found.

Fuming all over again, Ava stripped off her work clothes and grabbed her boots from the floor of the closet.

Huck jumped up and started wagging his tail.

"This is *not* a reward," she said. But he was already practically dancing in little circles around the bedroom.

She pulled on jeans and a T-shirt and her favorite socks. She slid her feet into her boots and laced them up tight. Sunblock? No. Even her freckle-prone skin was probably fine this time of day.

Huck was trembling with glee as she retrieved her day pack from the closet and went into the kitchen. She grabbed a slice of leftover pizza from the fridge and chomped into it as she checked her supplies. She added several water bottles. Then she grabbed her phone and slid it into her back pocket as she finished off her food. Huck waited eagerly by the door, watching her every move.

It was official. She was the worst dog handler ever. He'd spent the day eating her shoes and she was rewarding him with his second-favorite activity.

She turned on the porch light, so she'd have something to come home to, and set her backpack at her feet as she locked the house. A grumbling noise had her turning around.

A black F-150 bumped up the road. Ava recognized it. Her pulse quickened as the truck rolled to a stop beside her car.

Grant Wycoff slid out. Huck barked and scrambled down the stairs.

"Stop!"

Huck halted in his tracks.

"Sit."

He sat. Of course, now that they had company, he was being an angel. Ava went down the steps to join him.

The detective smiled as he walked over, and Ava's heart gave a wild little thump. Broad shoulders, powerful build. Grant Wycoff was attractive in a badge-wearing-alpha-male kind of way—if you were into that. Which she definitely wasn't.

"Evenin'," he said with a nod. He held his hand out for Huck to sniff as he stopped in front of her.

"Hello."

She watched him curiously as he peeled off his sunglasses. His eyes were a deep, dark brown, and he had that sharp look of someone who noticed everything. In jeans and hiking boots, he appeared to be off duty, but she saw the bulge of an ankle holster above his boot.

"How'd you know where I live?" she asked.

"Stopped by your office just now. Your law partner said I might find you here."

Of course. Jenna had been trying to set Ava up ever since she'd moved to town. Jenna *did* go for badge-wearing alpha types and had never understood Ava's aversion.

Huck thumped his tail as Grant leaned down to scratch his ears.

"You heading out someplace?" he asked.

"Yes, as a matter of fact."

"I won't keep you. I just had a few questions about those photos you brought in."

She tried to mask her surprise. "Donovan showed them to you?"

"Not exactly." He straightened and rested his hands on his lean hips. "It's about the car key you saw. The one in the picture."

"What about it?"

"You remember what it was?"

"What, you mean like the make of the car?"

He nodded.

"No."

Disappointment flickered in his eyes.

"It was black. I remember that."

"You have any more pictures besides the ones you gave the sheriff?"

"No." She pulled her phone from her pocket and scrolled through. When she reached the two photos of the tent's interior, she tried to zoom in on the key fob for a better look, but the angle was bad. She wished she'd taken additional shots, but the search for Noah had been more urgent.

She glanced up. "I just got the three. Sorry."

"No problem. You remember the shape of the key fob?"

"Rectangular, I think?"

Interest sparked in his eyes. Clearly, this wasn't just an idle question.

"You could see for yourself, you know."

He nodded. "I plan to. You happen to have those GPS coordinates handy?"

"The sheriff didn't give them to you?"

"No."

She tamped down her annoyance. Donovan had probably thrown away the slip of paper she'd given him.

"Well, I recorded them on my phone," she said. "The location is about a quarter mile off the trail in Lizard Creek Canyon."

"I'll give you my number and you can text me the coordinates."

"Sure. Or we could just come with you."

His eyebrows shot up. "Come with me?"

"To the campsite." She nodded down at Huck, who was still sitting obediently at her feet. "We were on our way there, anyway, right when you pulled up."

"Why?"

She shrugged. "Just following up."

He looked skeptical of this explanation, but he didn't pursue it. He checked his watch.

"It's pretty late to get started," he said.

"Late is good. It's less hot."

"I appreciate the offer, but I can find it."

"Don't be so sure. The spot is hard to see. You're liable to miss it."

"Not if I have the coordinates."

"Even then. Trust me. I was actively searching for anything noteworthy in that canyon for hours, and I almost walked right by it."

Ava crossed her arms and stared up at him, unwilling to back down. There was some sort of battle going on in his mind. He clearly didn't want company—especially the civilian kind. But he also clearly wanted to get a look at that tent. He'd seen her pictures, and now he wanted to see it in person, which told her she'd been right. There was something suspicious about the campsite, and this detective knew it.

She nodded at Huck, who stared up at her eagerly, tail thumping.

"Look at him," she said. "He thinks he's going hiking. I can't disappoint him now."

His jaw tightened, and she knew she'd won.

"Fine." He slid on his shades. "But I'm driving."

CHAPTER

FOUR

AVA TWISTED IN her seat and glanced around as Grant neared the sign for Lizard Creek Trail.

"This doesn't look familiar," she said.

Grant looked over at her in his passenger seat. She'd put her dog in the back of the cab, but he perched his paws on the console, eager to see where they were going.

"It's a secondary trailhead," Grant said as he rolled to a stop. "Should shave about an hour off our trek."

"We won't be hiking back by flashlight, then."

"That's the idea."

Grant retrieved Ava's pack from the back and handed it to her. She slid from the truck, and Huck hopped over the console and followed her.

Grant got out and shrugged into his backpack. He scanned the area as they approached the trailhead. No other vehicles, and he hadn't expected any. This was one of the most remote trails in the park, and there wasn't much to see at the end of it. Most hikers liked to be rewarded with dramatic rock formations or sweeping views.

Ava crouched down to unzip her pack. She pulled out a little plastic bowl and filled it with water for Huck. Then she offered Grant the bottle.

"Want some?" she asked.

"I'm good."

Huck lapped up the water as Grant surveyed the contents of her backpack. You could tell a lot about a person from how they packed their gear, and Ava Burch seemed pretty squared away. Her bag had a built-in hydro pouch, but she'd also brought several extra bottles of water, which was the only way to travel out here. She also carried a first aid kit, a flashlight, a poncho, a Mylar blanket, and a pair of MREs. Plus, some nylon paracord and a heavy-duty pocketknife. She'd been well trained, obviously. But training didn't account for everything. Grant had seen plenty of cops who'd received top-notch training, but after years on the job, their innate sloppiness started to creep in.

She glanced up and caught him eyeing her stuff. "What's wrong?"

"Nothing."

The dog finished his water, and she clipped the plastic bowl to one of the side pockets. She stood up and shrugged into the backpack, then fastened the strap across her chest. "Ready?"

"Whenever you are."

The trailhead sign included a plexiglass-covered map, and they stepped over to study it.

"It's about two miles to the place where this joins the main loop," he told her.

"That should be near our destination," she said. "I'll lead since I know the way."

He lifted an eyebrow. "I thought you hadn't been here before?"

"I mean, I'll recognize it once we get there."

Grant smiled. He'd predicted she'd want to lead. He gestured toward the trail. "After you."

As it turned out, Huck led. Ava kept him off leash, which wasn't a problem since there was nobody out here. The dog trotted along at a steady pace and didn't sprint ahead. The narrow trail sloped down into the canyon, snaking between clumps of mesquite and prickly pear. Grant divided his attention between Ava's legs and the surrounding landscape.

It didn't take them long to settle into a rhythm. Some of the rocks were loose, and they had to pay attention to each step. Ava seemed absorbed with the mission and, as with the car ride, seemed content not to talk the whole time, which Grant appreciated. If there was one thing he'd grown used to since moving back to Henley County, it was solitude. He liked people well enough, but small talk made him itchy.

Grant surveyed the brown terrain dotted with scrub trees and cacti. The long shadows were a constant reminder that they had limited daylight left, and they needed to keep the pace up if they wanted to avoid hiking back after dark.

Ava glanced over her shoulder. "So, the sheriff sent you to check this out?"

"No."

She laughed. "Then why are you schlepping all the way out here?"

He waited a beat before responding. "Curiosity."

"Right."

There was much more to it, obviously, but he didn't want to go into it with her.

She glanced back over her shoulder again. "Fine. Don't tell me."

"It's an abandoned camp. I'm interested."

"Why do you say 'abandoned'?" she asked.

"You don't think it is?"

"'Abandoned' makes it sound like someone intentionally left everything."

He gave her a sharp look. "That's not what you think happened?"

"I don't know. Maybe. But . . ." Her voice trailed off.

"But what?"

"But the way the stuff was left. I don't know. I just got the feeling she thought she'd be back."

She.

Ava had taken note of the fact that it was a woman's boot. That was the first thing Grant had noticed when he looked at the photograph.

And then he'd noticed the key fob.

"So . . . you're *not* going to tell me." She glanced over her shoulder.

"Tell you what?"

She rolled her eyes and looked forward, clearly annoyed.

Grant decided small talk was preferable to dodging her questions for the next two hours.

"So, how'd you get into SAR work?" he asked.

Several moments ticked by, and he thought maybe she hadn't heard.

"You could say Huck got me into it. He loves it."

"You two didn't train together?"

"No."

Interesting. She and her dog seemed really close.

She glanced back at him and smiled. "Can't you tell I'm new at this?"

"Could have fooled me. You seemed to be doing pretty good yesterday when you found the kid."

"That was all Huck. He's amazing. And—as you can see—he lives for this stuff." She nodded up ahead, to where Huck was moving along, happily sniffing everything in his path. "I mean, he's not working now. Not in the true sense. But he just loves being out here. He's an outdoorsman. He hates being stuck inside too much."

"I don't blame him."

As they got deeper into the canyon, the limestone walls rose steeply on either side, blocking what little breeze they'd had at the trailhead. Grant's back was soaked beneath his pack. Ava kept moving at a brisk pace, but he could see the locks of hair clinging to her neck from sweat.

"Water break," he said.

Ava stopped and gave a whistle, and the dog trotted back to them as they unzipped their packs for water.

Huck sat at Ava's feet. His tongue lolled out and he was panting, but he looked happy.

"So, when did you get him?" Grant asked.

"I adopted him last fall."

"He's a rescue?"

"Sort of."

What did that mean? Search dogs took years to train. It was a huge investment of time. Not to mention money. They weren't the kind of dogs that ended up in shelters or put up for adoption.

She reached down and scratched Huck between his ears. "He spent his puppyhood in east Texas. He's still getting used to this dry heat." She glanced up. "We just moved out here in November."

"From?"

"Houston."

That explained why Grant hadn't seen her around. He was based in Henley, the county seat, and hadn't spent much time in Cuervo in recent months. If he had, he definitely would have noticed her. Even without the red Fiat, Ava stood out.

Houston also explained the fancy car and the clothes. Didn't explain the move, though. He wasn't sure why a big-city lawyer would want to live way out here.

Grant watched as Huck lapped up the last of his water.

"So, if you didn't train him, who did?" Grant asked.

"My father." She reclipped the bowl to her backpack and stood up. "Ready?"

So much for small talk.

Grant put his water away and waited as she shouldered her pack.

Huck resumed the trail, looking happy to take the lead again. He seemed to have a natural instinct for it. Probably, he was just following the smell of humans that had passed through here recently, compressing the dirt beneath their shoes and leaving their scent particles behind. Grant wasn't an expert on dogs, but he'd seen enough rescues over the years to have a healthy respect for their noses.

They continued in silence, with Grant skimming the canyon wall for that beige tarp. Now that Ava had predicted he'd need help finding it, he was determined to prove her wrong. The photograph he'd seen had shown a triangular canvas tarp, almost like a sail, stretched across a ledge to create a patch of shade for the tent underneath. Campers sometimes used that technique out here—anything to get things even a few degrees cooler. In a climate as severe as this, every bit mattered.

They trekked along as the sun sank behind the canyon and the cicadas started their low drone. They passed through some mesquite trees, then a forest of juniper. Then another patch of mesquite. The trail dipped down, then up again. Ava's pace didn't slow even as the terrain became rockier and more uneven. Sweat seeped into Grant's eyes, and he wiped his forehead with the back of his arm.

"Need more water?" he asked.

"No."

Huck trotted ahead of them, seemingly oblivious to the heat, and Grant had to admit he was impressed. He scoured the sides of the canyon, which looked smoky gray now in the fading light.

Ava halted.

Grant halted, too.

"There," she said.

Disappointment needled him as he looked around. He hadn't seen a thing. He still didn't.

"Where?"

She rested her hands on her hips. "That rockslide there."

"Where?"

"Just past the boulder."

Huck ran up to them, his attention locked on Ava's face. Grant followed her gaze to the rockslide.

Ava strode over to a boulder. With two well-placed steps, she climbed to the top of it and looked out at the canyon.

She shook her head. "No freaking way."

Huck barked and scurried around the base of the big rock. Grant walked over.

"What's wrong?" he asked.

"I remember this boulder and that rockslide and that ledge." She looked down, and the expression on her face put a ball of dread in his stomach.

"The campsite was *right there*," she said. "But now it's gone."

CHAPTER

FIVE

Tension hung in the air as they drove down the highway. The entire hike back, Grant had said hardly a word, and Ava's mind had been swirling with questions.

"Are you sure a ranger couldn't have moved it?" she asked again. It seemed like the most logical explanation.

"I'm sure." Grant cut a look at her. The truck cab was dark, and his face was lit by the bluish glow of the dashboard. "Are *you* sure we were in the right place?"

She tamped down her frustration. "I'm sure."

"How?"

"Because. I recognized the rockslide. And the ledge. And the trees nearby. Plus, we checked the coordinates. GPS coordinates don't lie."

"Any chance you jotted them down wrong?"

"No."

He darted a look at her, and she felt a surge of annoyance.

"Plus, I just know, okay? *That* was the spot. I'm certain of it."

He nodded. But she couldn't tell whether he believed her.

And for some reason it really irked her that he thought she might have led him to the wrong place. She turned toward the window and looked out at the dusky landscape. Only the slightest smudge of daylight remained on the horizon.

Huck nudged her shoulder with his nose. He always knew when she was upset.

"Someone packed all that stuff up and moved it," she said. "My guess is the park rangers. I assume you know Mel Tyndall, right?"

He had to know Mel. He was the superintendent of Silver Canyon State Park, and he also happened to be the incident commander from Thursday's search-and-rescue op.

She glanced across the dim truck cab. "Did you tell him about the tent?"

"I brought it to his attention, yeah."

"So, maybe one of his people came and got it. Or maybe he did."

"He didn't."

"How do you know?"

"Because I specifically told him not to."

She stared at him across the truck cab. Grant's jaw looked tight, and she could feel the stress coming off him in waves.

"Are you ever going to tell me what this is about?" she asked.

He didn't respond, and she shook her head and looked away.

Grant a took a deep breath and blew it out. "Two years ago, a woman went missing."

Ava turned to look at him. Her stomach tightened as she waited for more.

"She was last seen at a gas station near Cuervo." He glanced at her. "She was driving a white Ford Focus."

"So you think maybe that key—"

"Maybe."

Ava looked away. She'd been worried it was something like this, a missing person case. Why else would he be so interested in that campsite?

She'd been right. She'd *known* it was a potential crime scene the second she laid eyes on it. There was something off about it.

Who would abandon a bunch of expensive camping equipment? Not to mention a car key. And who would hike into such rugged terrain and then go wandering off without boots? Most hikers didn't carry extra shoes. In Ava's experience, they did everything possible to lighten the load. Some didn't even bring a toothbrush.

She looked at him. "So you think that campsite belonged to this missing woman?"

"It's possible."

"And that's why you told the park ranger to leave it alone?"

"I wanted to get out there and see what we were dealing with, then document everything. I brought our good camera and an evidence kit."

He nodded toward the back of the truck, and Ava craned her neck to look. On the floor beside Huck was Grant's big backpack. She'd been wondering what he'd been lugging around in that thing. He'd hiked out there prepared to collect evidence.

And now it was gone.

Ava sighed. "Well, shit."

"My thoughts exactly."

She looked at him, understanding now why he was so stressed.

"How old was she?"

"Twenty-six when she went missing."

"Is she from around here?"

"Colorado."

Ava looked ahead as the headlights blazed a path down

the endless highway. It was desolate out here. The town of Cuervo was just a few specks of light on the distant horizon.

She looked at Grant. "If that campsite is potentially related to a missing person case, then why was Donovan such a jerk about it?"

Grant frowned. "What did he say to you?"

"Nothing. That's the point. He was dismissive of the whole thing. I had to shove the evidence right under his nose, and still he ignored it. Why?"

He shook his head. "I couldn't say."

Ava narrowed her gaze at him. "Couldn't say"? As in, he couldn't say because he didn't know? Or couldn't say because he was protecting the sheriff, for some reason?

As a lawyer, Ava made a habit of choosing her words carefully. She had a finely tuned radar for evasiveness, and Grant was being evasive right now.

He didn't want to talk about his case with her. And why would he? She wasn't a cop. Her involvement was that she'd found a campsite that might or might not have belonged to a missing woman. But not every missing person case involved foul play. People went missing for all sorts of reasons—money trouble, marital trouble, addiction, suicide. The problem was especially prevalent near the national parks. Some people ventured into the wilderness and never came back. Sometimes it was planned and sometimes it wasn't. But whatever the circumstances, they almost always left behind people who wanted answers, and it fell to law enforcement to figure out what had happened. It was a painstaking task. And even when law enforcement *did* track down answers to questions, often those answers were heartbreaking.

It was difficult, frustrating work, and Ava's dad had devoted his life to it.

They neared the turnoff for the McCullough ranch, and

Huck rested his paws on the console. He was excited to get home. It was past nine, and he'd usually had dinner by now.

Grant swung onto the dirt road. As they bumped along the ruts, his headlights illuminated the little rock cottage.

He rolled to a stop and shifted into park.

Ava put her hand on the door. "It was the right spot. I'm sure of it."

"I know."

Did he really? Good. She *wasn't* wrong. And she wouldn't make a mistake about something this important.

He stared through the windshield, looking distracted now, like he had a million things on his mind.

"Well. Thanks for driving." She grabbed her pack off the floor.

"What are you doing now?"

She looked at him, startled. "Now, like, right now?"

He nodded.

"I need to feed Huck."

"Would you like to have dinner with me?"

She just stared at him. He was asking her on a date. Or at least, asking her to dinner. Was there a difference? She hadn't been on a date in so long, she hardly remembered.

She cleared her throat. "I already ate, actually." If a cold slice of pizza could be considered a meal.

"What about a drink?"

She looked at him across the dim truck cab. Those dark brown eyes were intent on her, and she felt a warm pull deep in her stomach.

The pull was a warning. She knew what it meant, and she knew the prudent thing to do would be to go inside for another evening curled up on the couch watching Netflix with a snoring dog at her feet.

"I need to feed Huck first."

He nodded. "I'll wait."

"No. I'll meet you there." Her heart skittered. "Where do you want to go?"

He smiled slightly. "You been to Dusty's?"

"No."

She'd been avoiding the place.

"Do what you need to do, and I'll meet you there in twenty minutes."

God, was she really doing this? Going out to some redneck bar for drinks with a cop? She could still back out.

"Thirty minutes." She pushed the door open and hopped out. Huck followed. "I'll see you there."

Grant watched from the corner booth as she walked in. He'd thought she wanted to change clothes, but she wore the same jeans and T-shirt from before. She'd changed her hair, though. It hung loose around her shoulders and caught glints of red from the **LONE STAR BEER** sign as she crossed the bar.

He scooted out of the booth and stood as she neared the table.

"Hi." She looked around tentatively.

"This okay?"

"Sure." She slid into the curved booth, and he joined her, taking care not to crowd her. He caught her perfume—it was feminine and sexy and probably expensive, too.

She glanced around again, skimming her gaze over everything but him.

She was nervous. He didn't know why, but he could tell that she was.

"How's Huck?" he asked.

She looked at him, and her shoulders seemed to relax a fraction.

"Good." She smiled. "Probably asleep by now in front of the AC."

"Big day for him?"

She gave a shrug. "Not really. He's used to the hiking, just not the heat."

A server walked up to their table. She had about a dozen eyebrow piercings and a cocktail tray tucked under her arm.

"Y'all want a drink?" she asked.

Grant nodded at Ava.

"Uh . . ." She grabbed the plastic sign from the middle of the table. "House margarita, please. On the rocks."

"Salt?"

"Yes."

The server looked at Grant.

"Fat Tire."

"You got it."

She turned on her heel and left, and Grant looked at Ava. Sitting this close, he noticed the faint freckles over the bridge of her nose. Her skin was pale and smooth, and anyone could take one look at her and know she wasn't from around here.

She met his gaze. A little line formed between her brows and she leaned forward to be heard over the music. "This isn't what I expected."

She smelled good, and he leaned closer. "What'd you expect?"

"From the outside it looks like a biker bar."

"They get some of that." He nodded at the **HARLEY DAVIDSON** sign over her shoulder. "Dusty draws a lot of tourists on cross-country road trips."

She smiled. "And still you hang out here. I'd think you'd want to avoid tourists."

"It's the tacos."

She lifted an eyebrow. "The tacos? Here?"

"Yep. Best you'll ever have."

She looked skeptical.

"Trust me."

She leaned back and glanced around again. Her eyes were hazel, but they looked purple in the weird light of the room.

Grant rested his arm on the back of the seat and settled in. A classic guitar riff emanated from speakers over the bar. Lynyrd Skynyrd. Dusty had eclectic tastes, and his playlist was just as likely to include Patsy Cline or Post Malone.

Ava's gaze settled on him. "So, did you call Mel Tyndall?"

"Why?"

"Just curious."

"I did."

"And?"

"And none of his rangers moved the tent."

"He's sure?"

"Yeah."

The worry line was back between her brows. "I wish I'd gotten more pictures. Of the key, especially. Then at least you'd know whether it was a Ford."

Grant believed it was. Ava had said the fob was black and rectangular, which would fit a Ford. An up-close photograph would have been good evidence to have, but there was nothing to be done about it at this point.

"Don't sweat it," he told her.

"So what happens now?"

The server was back with their drinks, saving him from having to answer. Ava's margarita came in a short, blue-rimmed glass that was deceptively small.

"Anything to eat?" the server asked.

Ava picked up her glass. "Just a drink tonight, thanks." She turned to Grant. "And you?"

"Same."

When she walked away, Ava looked at him. "What about the tacos?"

"Maybe next time."

She raised an eyebrow, and he could tell she didn't like him referring to "next time" as though he had a shot at taking her out again.

She took a sip of her margarita. Her eyes widened as she set it down.

"Damn," she said.

"Yeah, they pack a punch."

"It tastes . . . smoky."

"That's the mescal."

"I've never had it."

"It's like tequila, but they cook the agave inside a pit oven." He watched her eyes. "You like it?"

"Yeah, actually. It's different. Kinda spicy."

Grant liked it, too, but it wasn't for everyone. Connor wouldn't touch the stuff and said it tasted like an ashtray.

She took another sip and then leaned forward on her elbows, and he got the feeling she wanted to go back to grilling him about the case.

"So what's with the sheriff?" she asked. "Is he like that with everyone or is it just me?"

"Like what?" Grant asked, even though he thought he knew.

"Rude. Arrogant. Dismissive."

"That's pretty much how he is." He sipped his beer.

"You don't get along with him?"

"Why do you say that?"

"I can tell."

She was good at reading people, which probably came in handy in her job.

Grant set his beer down. "Jim Donovan and I have a cordial working relationship."

"'Cordial,' huh? Sounds like there's a story there."

There was, but it wasn't something he planned to tell her.

"Was this week your first time crossing paths with him?" Grant asked. "I would've thought you would have met him through your SAR work."

"My only other ops have been in Big Bend. He wasn't involved."

He nodded. "And how are you liking the SAR work out here?"

"You're changing the subject."

He smiled.

"I like it all right. There's a lot of attitude, but I'm used to it." She shrugged. "I'm sure you know how it is with this stuff. It's mostly men. All cops."

"All?"

"Everyone's a cop or a retired cop," she said. "Well, and sometimes there're a couple military guys thrown in. Very testosterone intensive."

He smiled again.

"But, hey, I'm fine with it. I knew what I was in for when I enrolled in the training. I've been around operations like this since I was a kid because of my dad."

"Your dad's in law enforcement?"

"He was a game warden."

Was. Some of the puzzle pieces of Ava Burch fell into place.

"That explains the search-and-rescue dog," Grant said.

"Huck is the fourth Lab my father trained. He got him as a puppy a few years before he retired."

Grant found it interesting that her dad had been a cop. Texas game wardens were sworn peace officers with state-wide jurisdiction.

"So, your father was a game warden in east Texas?"

"Yep. Angelina County." She stirred her drink. "I spent my first fifteen years in the Piney Woods."

"And the next fifteen?"

She shot him a look at the allusion to her age. "Houston." She sipped her drink. "When my parents divorced, my mom moved us there. I went to undergrad and law school at U of H."

"That's a good school. And how did you end up in business with Jenna McCullough?"

"Jenna and I worked together at a firm in Houston. She and her daughter moved out here a couple years ago to be with Jenna's parents, and she started looking for a law partner. We'd been talking about it for a while, and finally last fall, I decided what the hell, why not?"

Grant watched her eyes. There was definitely more to it than that. He didn't believe she'd moved all the way out here on a whim.

"So, how do you like it so far?" he asked.

"What, Cuervo?"

"The town, the area. This is pretty remote compared to Houston."

"That's one reason I'm here." She leaned forward. "Did you know there are only six practicing attorneys in all of Henley County? And there were none in Cuervo before Jenna set up shop."

"I didn't know that." He nodded. "Can't say I'm surprised."

"It's a legal desert. People have wills and property transactions and business matters they need help with—especially now, with all the population growth around here." She wiped salt from the rim of her glass and licked her finger, and Grant tried to focus on what she was saying. "People are moving in from the cities, buying up property right and left. More businesses are coming here. Businesses need lawyers."

"You're here to save us from encroaching civilization, huh?"

"Well. The irony isn't lost on me. I realize that as a transplant from the city, I'm part of the problem."

At least she had the self-awareness to recognize it.

She smiled at him over her drink, and he felt it—again—right in the middle of his sternum.

"I guess you're probably tired of people like me flooding into your county, right?"

"Growth isn't all bad," he said.

"Doesn't growth bring crime? I would think you'd resent it."

"It brings money, too, so it's got some upsides. Our economy was sucking wind for a lot of years, so some people welcome all the city slickers."

"Not everybody." She gave him a pointed look. "Can't say everyone at the courthouse has been welcoming. But *you*, at least, seem to have an open mind."

The server was back. "Y'all want another round?"

He looked at Ava, hoping she'd say yes. She'd loosened up, and he liked talking to her even more than he'd expected when he'd asked her out to dinner. She bit her lower lip, and he could see the debate going on in her mind.

A VA SHOULD SAY NO. That first margarita was already going to her head, and she was getting chatty with Grant Wycoff. Maybe even flirty. And nothing good could come of that.

She smiled at the server. "I'm still working on this one." She picked up the glass and rattled the ice cubes. There was at least a sip left.

The woman looked at Grant.

"I'm good."

She walked away, and Ava tried to decipher Grant's expression. He was tough to read. And he'd managed to do something she hated, which was get her to reveal things without revealing anything in return. Professionally—and personally—she almost never let that happen. Time to turn the tables.

"So, what about you?" she asked. "Have you always lived in Cuervo?"

"I don't. I live in Henley, about twenty minutes from here."

"Closer to work?"

"Work is all over the county," he said. "But, yeah, it's closer to the sheriff's office."

"It's a nice town."

He nodded.

"I've mostly spent time there at the courthouse, but it's got a good feel to it. Did you grow up there?"

Another nod. "Then I moved away for a while. I did my police training in Dallas and spent six years with DPD."

"Interesting. I wouldn't have guessed Dallas."

"Why not?"

"I don't know. Too crowded? You seem like you fit in better out here."

"Thanks. I think."

The corner of his mouth curved up in a smile, and she felt a jolt of heat.

She blamed Jenna. Jenna knew what a drought she'd been in, and she'd *sent* this man to her door. And now here she was, feeling a tequila buzz and staring at his hand wrapped around that beer bottle. He had long fingers and neatly trimmed nails. Hands were something she noticed about men, and his looked very capable.

A ringtone broke the spell, and Ava took a deep breath as Grant pulled out his phone. Yet another reminder of why she should be home right now, not having drinks with a sexy cop.

He glanced up from his screen. "I need to return this call. You mind if I—"

"Perfect timing." Ava signaled the waitress. "I need to get home anyway."

"You sure?"

"Yeah."

The server dropped off the check, and Ava reached for her purse.

"I got this," he said.

Against her better judgment, she let him pay. Then he stood up and waited for her to scoot out of the booth.

The place had filled up while they talked, but plenty of heads turned as they crossed the room. Were they staring at him or her? She didn't know—she knew only that this bar was an oddball mix of people and themes, and she hadn't decided whether she liked it.

He reached around her to open the door, and she stepped into the cool night air.

Cool.

When had that happened? When she'd walked in, the temperature had been in the eighties.

She glanced around the gravel lot, which was crammed with trucks and SUVs. A line of motorcycles filled the front row. She'd parked beside Dusty's rickety wooden sign, on the opposite side of the lot from Grant. He walked her to her car anyway.

"So what happens now?" she asked. "With the missing person case?"

"Depends," he said vaguely.

She popped her car locks. "Will you keep me posted?"

He didn't answer.

"Please?" She opened her door. "I'm interested."

"I'll tell you what I can."

"Good."

He stared down at her. His eyes were dark and luminous, and again she felt a jolt of attraction.

"Sorry to cut this short," he said.

"No problem."

And it wasn't. It definitely was *not* a problem that she hadn't given in to temptation and ordered another drink with him. He rested his hand on the top of her door and looked down at her. His gaze dropped to her mouth. Heat zinged through. He was going to kiss her. And she wanted him to. His gaze locked with hers, and the moment seemed suspended as every nerve in her body went on alert. He eased closer, and she looked at his mouth.

An engine revved beside them, and she jerked back. A motorcycle pulled onto the highway and sped away.

She looked at Grant.

"Well, good night." She stepped back, further obliterating the moment.

"Good night."

She slid into her car, and he gently closed the door. And she managed not to watch him in her rearview mirror as she drove away.

CHAPTER
SIX

THE LAST CONFIRMED sighting of Molly Shaw was at the Speedy Stop near Cuervo, where she was recorded on a security camera buying gas and food. The sighting was two summers ago, almost to the day, and Grant found this to be an odd coincidence.

If it was a coincidence.

Over the years he'd learned that many coincidences weren't really coincidences at all, but indicators of some sort of pattern—not that he necessarily knew what the pattern was, especially during the early days of an investigation.

Grant flipped through the spiral notebook that contained his notes from the interview with the store clerk, Joel Jacobson. Grant had interviewed the man several days after Molly's brother reported her missing. Matt Shaw, who lived in Denver, said his sister had recently been laid off from her job at a software company. She had been on a months-long road trip when she spent a weekend in Cuervo and then decided to stay awhile. Matt Shaw told police that he and

Molly had been keeping in touch by phone every week, but she'd missed their call on the weekend of his birthday, which didn't worry him at first. But after another week went by with no word from her, he reached out to one of her friends on social media and learned that Molly had also failed to show up for a river rafting trip.

At Matt Shaw's request, the sheriff's office sent a deputy to do a routine well check at the Happy Trails RV Park where Molly had been staying. The property manager let the deputy into Molly's rented camper, where they found some clothes and personal items—but no Molly. This came as a relief to her brother, who had described Molly as *depressed* and *possibly on a bender* following her recent divorce.

But the survey of the rented camper wasn't much of a relief to investigators. Too many things set off alarms.

Grant was the first detective to take a look at the camper, and he hadn't liked anything about it. In addition to a duffel bag, Molly had left behind some clothes, a cosmetics bag with a prescription inside, as well as a purse that contained $122 in cash. After the missing person report was filed, investigators got a warrant to run Molly's credit card, which led them to the Speedy Stop—her last known location that police could confirm.

Grant found the page where he'd jotted down Molly's purchases after viewing the gas station's surveillance footage. On June third at 6:55 p.m., she'd bought a half tank of gas for her white Ford Focus, plus a bottle of wine and a bag of Cheetos. Jacobson said he remembered the transaction for two reasons. One, Molly had stopped in during the weeks before and chatted with him. The clerk said she was always friendly. And two, on this particular occasion she tried to pay with a one-hundred-dollar bill, but Jacobson couldn't change it.

As Grant reviewed his notes, the same thing jumped out at him about Jacobson's statement as had jumped out at him then. Namely, why couldn't he change the hundred? A transaction of around thirty-eight dollars would have yielded only about sixty-two dollars in change, which should have been no problem. Grant had pressed the clerk on this point, and he'd admitted that it wasn't that he *couldn't* change Molly's hundred, but that he hadn't wanted to. Evidently, he'd gotten in trouble with his boss once for taking a counterfeit hundred-dollar bill, so now he made a habit of refusing them.

Another thing Grant noticed was the purchases themselves. Wine and Cheetos. The kind of snacks someone would more likely buy before an evening at home, not a camping trip. None of the investigators looking into Molly's disappearance had turned up anything indicating that she had plans to go camping around the time of her disappearance.

Grant finished off the last of his lukewarm coffee and stood up. The bullpen was fairly empty at the moment, with most of the Saturday shift out on patrol. Across the sea of cubicles, he saw Hildie's platinum blond helmet at the reception desk. He walked over. She had her headset on, and she signaled him to wait as she wrapped up the call. Then she moved aside the mouthpiece.

"Hey, Hildie. What are you doing in on a Saturday?"

"Izzy's on vacation."

"Oh yeah?"

"She and Will took the kids to Disneyland."

"Nice. Listen, I need to check out a box. You mind?"

"Sure thing."

She opened her top drawer and grabbed a set of keys attached to a Dallas Cowboys key chain. She got up, and Grant followed her down a short hallway, where she unlocked the door and switched on the lights.

The Henley County evidence room was a dim, windowless space crammed with endless rows of floor-to-ceiling shelves. It reminded Grant of the library at his college, except instead of books, the shelves were filled with card-board evidence boxes stacked four high in places.

"You have a number for me?" Hildie asked.

Grant rattled off the case number from memory. Hildie turned down the row on the end, and Grant followed her. They passed a long evidence locker made of chain-link fencing. All sorts of oversize evidence had been locked up behind the wire mesh—a blue dirt bike, a rusted pitchfork, a fifty-five-gallon drum with a false bottom that had been used to smuggle bricks of coke.

They reached the end of the row and Grant recognized the spot.

"These two boxes?" Hildie asked.

"There's three."

Grant grabbed the two big banker's boxes and left the small one for Hildie. They carried everything to the front of the room and set it down on a table.

"Thanks," he said.

"Let me jot it down, and you're good to go."

She logged into the computer workstation beside the door. Grant rattled off the number again, and she entered the digits.

"The Molly Shaw case," she said.

"You remember it?"

She raised an overplucked eyebrow. "Of course I do. She's Shelby's age."

Hildie had raised three daughters as a single mom while working for the sheriff's office. She paid close attention to crime in their area, but particularly anything involving young women or girls.

Hildie left him alone with the dusty cartons. Grant grabbed a pair of latex gloves from the box on the table and tugged them on. Then he took out his pocketknife, sliced through the tape, and lifted the lid.

Box one contained the small black duffel bag recovered from Molly's rented camper. Inside were clothes, mostly—

T-shirts, shorts, underwear, plus a striped bikini and a Colorado Rockies baseball cap. Grant poked through everything but saw nothing new. He moved on to the second big box, which contained the black purse Grant remembered, with the cash inside. Six twenties and two singles. Alongside the purse was the clear makeup bag with the zipper on top. Inside were some cosmetics and a box of migraine medicine. Grant checked the box. The prescription label said it originally contained twelve tablets. Only one was missing.

The meds bugged him and always had. Grant's mom got migraines. She took prescription pills for them and never went anywhere without a stash. She kept backup doses in her purse, her car, even Grant's dad's car. She never wanted to be caught unprepared when one of her headaches came on.

He replaced the box of pills in the cosmetics case and put the lid on the box again. Sliding it aside, he opened the third box, this one containing a binder and files. He thumbed through the stack of manila folders, then opened the big white binder. The missing person report was on top. Grant skimmed the details and spotted nothing new. During the early days of the investigation, he'd committed the details to memory.

He flipped to the interview reports, which included his conversation with the gas station clerk. Next in the binder was the interview with Molly's friend Olivia Mann, who had said Molly was a no-show for their all-day rafting trip on June twelfth. When she'd come in for the interview, Olivia had brought along a Polaroid of Molly, which Grant had clipped to the paperwork.

He stared down at the photo now. Molly had curly brown hair and a wide smile, and a dusting of freckles covered her nose.

Out of nowhere, he thought of Ava's freckles.

Where the hell had that come from? He'd almost kissed her last night, and now he was thinking about her at work.

He was thinking about her at home, too. Really, he hadn't *stopped* thinking about her since he'd seen her standing in that park with her phone in her hand, cursing the sheriff behind his back.

Grant studied the Polaroid some more. Molly had her arm looped around Olivia's neck. Both women wore sunglasses and had their heads tipped together as they smiled for the camera. Two years ago, Olivia had told him that she'd met Molly through some rock climbing friends. Grant wondered if Olivia even still lived in the area. So many people—like Molly—came out here and made an impulsive decision to stay. Many of them just as impulsively decided to leave, too.

Grant flipped past the friend interview and some other paperwork to the very back of the binder. He checked the binder pocket for the thumb drive he'd put there, but he didn't see it. He checked the front pocket, but it wasn't there, either. He'd used the thumb drive to store a copy of the gas station video.

Grant stepped over to the workstation, but the computer had gone to sleep. He leaned his head through the door and spied Hildie.

"Hey, Hildie, you happen to know who checked this case out last?"

She turned around in her chair. "You did."

"Are you sure?"

She pushed back her chair and walked over, clearly annoyed as she logged back into the system.

"Your name is the last one listed." She pulled up the record. "June twenty-first of last year."

"You sure?"

"Yes." She frowned. "What's wrong?"

"Nothing. Thanks."

She rolled her eyes and went back to work, and Grant combed through all three boxes, but couldn't find the thumb drive. Maybe he'd retrieved it for some reason and

left it in his desk. He hadn't touched this case in almost a
year.

Guilt needled him. This was how cases went cold. Investigators got busy with other things, and then memories
faded and witnesses slipped away. It was much easier to
work a case when the trail was new and events were fresh
in people's minds.

Grant flipped to the back of the binder and found the
object of his search today—Connor's notes on the park
ranger interviews. Connor had talked to someone at all
three parks in the area and, according to the notes, all three
had checked their systems but had no record of Molly Shaw
or a vehicle with her license plate camping at their park
overnight. Every vehicle that spent the night in a park had
to pay a fee and get a sticker.

Grant pulled out his phone.

"Hey, what's up?" Connor said when he answered.

"I'm looking at paperwork from the Molly Shaw case.
When you contacted the parks, did you call or go by?"

"I called." His words were muffled, as though he had a
mouth full of food. "Why?"

"No reason."

"Bullshit. You don't ask anything for no reason." Connor finished whatever he'd been chewing and slurped a
drink. "What's the deal?

"Something came up with the case."

"You mean the campsite in Silver Canyon?"

"Yeah." Grant paused. "How'd you hear about it?"

"Tyndall called Donovan when I was in the office this
morning. Donovan was bitching about you wasting our
time on a 'damn tent.'"

"It was more than a tent."

"Yeah, I figured, if it got your attention."

Grant gritted his teeth and looked at the evidence boxes
spread out on the table. He should have checked back in on
this case before now. But like everyone else in their office

lately, he'd been overwhelmed with work, and it never seemed to let up.

"You going out there?" Connor asked.

"Where?"

"Silver Canyon State Park."

"Yeah, probably."

"I'll go with you."

Grant hadn't expected that. "You're off this afternoon."

"So?"

"So, it's Saturday."

"Pick me up on your way," Connor said. "You can tell me about this lead."

Connor rode shotgun with Grant to park headquarters, which was a converted ranch house surrounded by hundred-year-old oaks. They'd recently built a parking lot right in front of the building, but Connor was glad they'd kept the trees. The lot was crammed with pickups and SUVs today, and Grant had to drive all the way to the edge to find a space.

"By the way," Connor said as he slid out of the truck, "her name's Ava Burch."

"What about her?"

He watched Grant's reaction over the roof of the truck. "She's the woman from the search-and-rescue op. The one with the dog."

Grant locked the doors with a chirp, and they started across the lot.

"I know, I met her." He glanced at Connor. "How do you know her?"

"I saw her at the Coffee Cup this morning having breakfast with Jenna McCullough, and I stopped to say hi."

"Yeah, they're law partners."

"Ava Burch is a lawyer?"

"Yep. Moved here last fall from Houston."

Clearly, Grant had done way more recon on this woman than he had, which told Connor what he needed to know. She was off-limits, which was fine. Ava Burch was attractive, but she seemed fairly high-maintenance.

"That's weird," Connor said.

"What is?"

"What's a Houston lawyer doing way out here?"

"Same thing as Jenna. Practicing law."

Jenna hadn't moved all the way back here to practice law. She'd moved because her dad was sick, and the family business was failing. She'd wanted to help her parents and probably get away from her asshole ex-husband, too.

But Connor didn't say all that. Maybe some people were buying Jenna's cover story.

Grant opened the door, and a waft of chilly air hit them as they stepped inside. Tourists milled in the lobby, checking out displays showing the park's previous history as a cattle ranch.

Connor peeled off his shades. "Didn't realize this place was so popular."

"Summer season."

They passed a tiny gift shop, where people were picking out postcards and T-shirts, and walked through a door marked **EMPLOYEES ONLY**. Grant waved at the ranger manning the chest-high reception desk. She had long blond braids, and she sat on a stool in front of a computer.

"Hey, Courtney. Is Mel in?"

"Nope." She looked from Grant to Connor. "He's on the south side dealing with a hit-and-run."

"Maybe you can help us."

"Sure. What's up?"

"I don't think we've met," Connor said with a smile. "Connor Burke, Henley County Sheriff's Office." He reached across the counter and shook her hand, which she seemed to find amusing.

"I'm Courtney. What can I do for you guys?"

"We're looking for a record of someone camping here two summers ago," Grant said.

She lifted an eyebrow. "You're looking for Molly Shaw."

"You heard about that?"

"Mel was on the phone this morning talking to someone."

Connor was pretty sure he'd heard the other side of that phone call.

"What do you want to know? I'm sure we already checked our records for her the summer she went missing."

"You mind checking again?" Grant asked. "I've got another name for you to run, too."

"Sure." Courtney turned to her keyboard. "Okay, shoot."

"Try Molly Lithwick. Or just Lithwick."

Connor sent him a questioning look.

"It's her married name," Grant said. "She changed back to Shaw after her divorce, but maybe she was using an old ID."

"Nope," Courtney said. "Nothing with Lithwick."

Grant slid a slip of paper across the counter. "Let's check her vehicle again just to be sure."

Courtney entered the license plate in the system and shook her head. "Nope. Sorry."

"Someone could have dropped her off," Connor said.

Grant nodded. "What about people sneaking in? Avoiding the camping fee? Y'all had any problems with that?"

Courtney tipped her head to the side. "Not as much as some places. This used to be a ranch, so we're surrounded by a pretty good fence. And if the rangers see a car overnight without a sticker, they'll ticket it. But there was this one spot we were having a problem with. You know Ocotillo Pass? It's on the far west side?"

"What about it?" Grant asked.

"We had a section of fence down. Someone had cut through with wire cutters, and we got wind of some people sneaking in over there. Mel sent a crew out to repair it, and we haven't had a problem since."

"When was this?" Connor asked.

"The repair? Sometime last summer. August, maybe?"

Grant looked at him. "So, a long time after Molly went missing."

"Maybe she came in that way. But what happened to her car?"

Grant ignored the question, probably because he didn't want to discuss the case in front of a ranger. The whereabouts of Molly's white Ford had been one of the biggest mysteries of her disappearance. It was one reason Donovan had no patience for pursing the investigation. In the sheriff's mind, her missing vehicle was a sure sign that she'd taken off somewhere of her own free will. Unless they turned up concrete evidence that something had happened to her in Henley County, Molly Shaw was some other jurisdiction's problem.

"Let's try something else," Grant said. "Can you run a search of those tickets?"

Courtney looked puzzled. "Tickets?"

"You know, parking violations, speeding, public intox. Whatever citations you have from the week we're looking at."

She nodded and turned to her computer. "That's the week of June third, right?"

"Yeah."

She tapped some keys and shook her head. "No one named Shaw or Lithwick got a ticket then for illegal camping. Or for anything, actually. That week we had some speeders, some noise complaints, a report of possible poachers on the west side."

"Poachers?" Grant asked, clearly interested. Connor was interested, too.

"Yeah. Looks like . . . June fifth. Some campers reported a shot fired near one of the bluffs." She looked at Grant. "We've got a small herd of pronghorn that moves through that area, and we've had problems with poachers over there for years."

Connor looked at Grant. They were thinking along the same lines.

"Did someone check it out?" Connor asked.

"We sent a game warden out there. Let me see. . . . Looks like no tickets were issued."

"I need a copy of that incident report," Grant said.

"Sure."

He leaned over the counter to peer down at her screen. "And where was this, exactly?"

"The west side of the park. Over near Diamondback Gorge."

CHAPTER
SEVEN

THE DINNER BELL was packed with the usual Sunday regulars, plus a fair number of tourists who'd probably read about the place online. Ava had learned to spot the tourists because they always looked unimpressed by the restaurant's Formica tables and torn leather booths. Actually, they always looked unimpressed by everything until they tasted the food.

Jenna sawed through her Sunday special: chicken-fried steak smothered in gravy.

"How's your mom this week?" Ava asked.

Through some unwritten rule, they never discussed Jenna's parents at the office. It was a touchy subject, and they typically saved it for moments when they were away from both their receptionist and Jenna's daughter, Lucy.

"She's okay," Jenna said.

"Just okay?"

"It was a rough weekend. He took the car out again."

Jenna's father, Hank, had started sneaking away from the ranch when his wife was distracted.

"Where'd he go this time?" Ava was almost afraid to ask. Last time, he'd driven sixty miles to Marfa.

Jenna sighed. "The grocery store."

"That's not too bad."

"He bought twelve jars of pickles."

"Twelve?"

"Yep. Kosher dill. Came home and put them in the pantry with the nine jars of mayonnaise he bought last trip." Jenna dipped her biscuit in gravy. "You know, the weird thing is he doesn't even *like* pickles. I've never seen him eat a pickle in my entire life. But, hey, now we're all stocked up for the next decade."

Ava didn't know what to say. She never knew what to say, so she mostly just listened. She still hadn't decided which was worse—to lose your dad abruptly, out of the clear blue, or to lose him by inches slowly over time.

"My mom is really pulling her hair out. She tries to be patient, but every day it's something."

"What about the residential place in Henley?" Ava asked.

"We're talking about it. She still thinks she can do everything herself, especially with me here. Honestly, this whole thing might have been easier if I'd never moved back. Then I could just say, 'Mom, let's be real. You're in over your head.'"

"You can still say that."

"I know, and I do. But she seems to think we can handle it. A year ago, I was inclined to agree with her, but now it keeps getting worse."

"I'm sorry."

"Thanks. But enough about *my* crap. What's up with *you*?" Jenna smiled and sipped her tea from a straw. "You still haven't told me what the sexy sheriff wanted with you Friday night."

"He's a sheriff's *detective*. The sheriff is a jackass."

Jenna rolled her eyes. "Stop stalling. What happened?

He seemed like he was on a mission when he came by the office looking for you."

"He wanted to interview me about a campsite I stumbled across on the SAR op Thursday."

"Why?"

"He thinks it's possible that it could be related to a missing person case from two years ago."

Jenna's eyebrows shot up. "The Molly Shaw case?"

"You remember it?"

"Sure. Everyone does. That was right after I moved here. It was all anyone talked about for weeks."

The case had certainly dominated the local news. Grant had been stingy with details, but it had taken Ava all of two minutes on the Internet to figure out the missing woman's name based on the timing Grant had mentioned.

"So, they just now found her campsite?" Jenna asked.

"They don't know, really. It appeared to be a tent that had been left there quite some time ago. There were some personal items inside. Anyway, we went out to take another look, and the whole thing had been cleared."

Jenna frowned. "What do you mean, 'cleared'?"

"Cleared away. Removed. Everything was gone."

"So, maybe the campsite wasn't abandoned. Maybe some hiker came back and packed up and moved on."

Ava had run that scenario through her mind over and over, but she couldn't get past the fact that everything about that tent had seemed old. Dusty. Neglected.

Then last night she'd sat down at her computer and examined every pixel of the photographs she'd taken, and she'd noticed the corner of an *Outside* magazine sticking out from under the bedroll. With a little legwork, Ava discovered that the issue with that cover was from twenty-six months ago. It had been on newsstands and at outdoor recreation stores eight weeks before Molly Shaw went missing. No way that timing could be a coincidence.

"So, wait. Back up," Jenna said. "Did you just tell me

you went *hiking* out to this place with Grant Wycoff?" She leaned forward. "Um, hello? Bury the lede much?"

Ava focused on her food. She'd ordered the veggie platter under the assumption that it would be lighter than the rest of the Dinner Bell's menu.

"Ava."

"Yeah?" She forked up some butter beans.

"What's the deal with Grant?"

"Nothing."

"Nothing."

"Yeah, nothing," Ava said. "He needed some help, and I helped him. End of story."

"So . . . you just went hiking into the backcountry with one of the hottest men in the entire county and that's it."

"Pretty much. We grabbed a drink after."

Her eyes bugged out. "*What?* Where?"

"Dusty's Cantina."

Jenna leaned back against the booth and tipped her head back to look at the ceiling. "I swear to God, Ava. I've been sitting here an hour and you're just now telling me you went on a *date* this weekend?"

"It wasn't a date." She scooped up a giant bite of mashed potatoes.

"You had a drink together at Dusty's. That's a date."

"Not really," she said around a mouthful of food.

"Well, it's the closest damn thing you've had to a date since you rolled into Cuervo. Unless you have a secret life you're not telling me about."

Ava stabbed the last butter bean on her plate.

"Well, at least you finally mentioned it. So, how did it go?" Jenna watched her with keen interest as she polished off her biscuit.

"Good. Sort of."

"Why 'sort of'?"

The server came by to collect their empty plates. "Y'all want some dessert today?"

"Two peach cobblers. One to go," Jenna said with a smile. "My dad loves your cobbler."

"Sure thing. And you?" She looked at Ava.

"I'm fine, thanks."

The server walked away, and Jenna leaned forward on her elbows, clearly intent on getting the full story. "Keep going. It was 'good, sort of'?"

"We had one drink and chitchatted, but then he got a call from work and had to leave. Which just goes to show why you should never date someone who's a cop."

"Give me a break."

"It's true. Law enforcement is a marriage wrecker," Ava said. "Have you seen the divorce stats? Not to mention alcoholism, suicide, PTSD."

"Oh, and all those lawyers you dated in Houston had such great work-life balance."

Jenna had a point.

"Half the male lawyers I know are divorced," Jenna continued, "and the other half are cheating on their wives."

"It's not that bad."

"Well, almost. My point is, both professions are filled with workaholics, so you shouldn't be so hard on Grant. But since you went on a date with him—"

"It wasn't a date."

"—I should probably give you the backstory."

"What backstory?"

"It's no big deal, really."

"There's a backstory with this guy, and yet you sent him to my house? Thanks a lot, Jen."

"It's nothing bad, it's just . . ." Jenna's eyes sparked and she leaned back. "Oh, damn. Guess it'll have to wait."

Ava turned around, and her stomach did a flip-flop. Grant was crossing the restaurant, and his gaze locked on Ava as he made a beeline for their table.

She turned around and Jenna was grinning.

Grant stopped beside their booth. He was dressed like a

civilian again in faded jeans, a T-shirt, and a Rangers baseball cap.

"Ladies." He nodded at Jenna and then zeroed in on Ava. His look was intense, and there was no doubt he'd walked over here specifically to talk to her.

"Hey, Grant. Good to see you." Jenna sipped her tea through the straw and sent Ava a smug smile.

"Hi. What's up?" Ava's voice sounded casual but all she could think about was how the last time she'd seen him he'd almost kissed her.

"Having some dinner?" he asked.

"Just finishing."

The server was back. Grant stepped aside as she placed a bowl of cobbler in front of Jenna and then put down a cardboard to-go box.

"Well, I've got to run." Jenna reached for her purse and pulled out some cash.

"What about your dessert?" Ava asked.

She set some bills on the table and grabbed the to-go box. "That's for you." She scooted out of the booth and smiled at Grant. "Nice to see you again, Grant."

"Don't run off on my account."

"Oh, I'm not. I promised Lucy I'd watch *Paw Patrol* with her." Jenna turned to Ava and smiled. "See you tomorrow, Av."

She hurried off. Ava looked at Grant.

"Mind if I . . . ?" He gestured toward the empty seat.

"Not at all."

As he sat down, he removed his baseball cap and set it on the edge of the table. His thick brown hair was flattened to his head, and she couldn't help but smile.

"What?" he asked, combing his fingers through his hair.

"Nothing. What's up?"

"I was on my way to your house when I saw your car."

She reached for her tea. "Oh?"

"I wanted to ask about Huck."

She didn't know what she'd expected him to say, but that definitely wasn't it.

"What about him?"

"I've been reading about scent dogs. How they can get scent off an object someone touched and then track the same scent down miles away."

She nodded. "Some can."

"Can Huck?"

"He's got a pretty good nose. Why?"

His brown eyes were intent on hers. "I've got some personal items that belonged to my missing person."

"Molly Shaw," she said.

He nodded, not looking terribly surprised that she'd figured out the missing woman's name after he refused to tell her anything.

"These items have been put away in an evidence box, so they haven't aired out," he said. "I've got clothing, sandals, a baseball cap with some sweat stains on the inner headband. Is that the kind of thing you could use for scent tracking?"

Now she understood where he was going with this.

"Theoretically, yes," she said, "but it's been a long time."

"I realize that. But if I could narrow the search down to a limited area—"

"It's not really the area that's the problem. It's the time that's elapsed. From a chemical standpoint, live people are completely different from dead people. For the kind of search you need here, you want a cadaver dog."

He just looked at her.

"Huck isn't trained for that." At least, Ava didn't think so. She'd never had a chance to ask her dad the specifics of Huck's training, so she was going with what she'd seen him do with his past dogs while she was growing up.

"So . . . he can't sniff out human remains?" Grant asked.

"I mean, he *could*, theoretically. All dogs are interested in things that give off scent, and some breeds are better than others. What I mean is, that isn't his specialty area."

Disappointment flickered in his eyes. "I was afraid you'd say that."

"Sorry."

Ava meant it, too. She really would have liked to help him. She knew how frustrating it was for investigators trying to get answers in a missing person case. Those cases had a way of wearing on you. They could get under your skin, even become an obsession. She'd seen it happen with her dad.

"I take it Henley County doesn't have a cadaver dog?" she asked.

"No."

"Couldn't you bring one in? If you've narrowed down the search area, it seems like bringing in a cadaver team would be pretty straightforward."

Grant's mouth tightened. "You'd think so, wouldn't you?"

In other words, there was some sort of bureaucratic red tape standing in his way. Or maybe Donovan was, for some reason. Or maybe there was some kind of turf war going on between law enforcement jurisdictions. Ava had been involved in only four SAR operations, and every single one had been fraught with politics.

Another problem was resources. Rural sheriff's offices—just like parks and wildlife departments—were stretched thin, and the problem was only getting worse. Ava's father had chosen his career because he cared about wildlife and wanted to enforce the fishing and gaming laws so there would be something left for future generations. But as the years ticked by, he started spending more and more of his time dealing with drug runners and meth labs popping up throughout the region. Budgets were tight, positions got axed, and fewer and fewer people ended up with more responsibility. The job was a grind, and many people burned out.

Grant raked his hand through his hair again and sighed.

She felt a twinge of sympathy. "You look like you've had a long day."

He gave a short laugh. "Yeah."

"Want some cobbler?"

His gaze dropped to the dessert. It smelled of peaches and cinnamon, and the dollop of whipped cream was already melting into the streusel.

"You don't want it?" he asked.

"I'm stuffed from my veggie platter."

He winced. "Veggie platter? I didn't even know they had one."

"They do, and if you thought it might be low in saturated fat, you'd be mistaken. It's fried okra, mashed potatoes, and butter beans."

"I always go with the chicken-fried steak here." He nodded at the cobbler. "You sure you don't want this?"

"Go for it."

He picked up the spoon and took a bite. He didn't comment, but she guessed it was good because he finished it off in less than two minutes.

In the meantime, Ava paid the dinner check. She snuck a glance at her phone as she tucked her wallet back into her purse. It was barely six o'clock. Was he going to ask her what she was doing now?

"Are you ready?" she asked.

He stood up and waited for her to precede him out of the restaurant, and once again they attracted glances from people. It had to be him. Ava had been here eight months, and people didn't notice her that much. Her car, yes. That had attracted some looks when she first moved to town.

They stepped outside, and everything was bathed in sunlight. Despite the heat, it was a beautiful time of day—the golden hour, as she'd come to think of it. She glanced across the lot and spotted his car parked two down from hers.

"So, what are you up to now?" he asked as they crossed the lot.

"I need to take Huck for a walk and work off my veggies."

He glanced at her. "Is a potato even a vegetable?"

"It's an edible stem of an annual plant. So technically, it qualifies, although some would argue it belongs in the bread group."

He smiled.

"What?" she asked.

"You sounded like a lawyer just then."

They reached her car and his expression turned serious as he looked west, toward the distant mesa that marked the boundary of Silver Canyon State Park. Somehow, she knew he was thinking about his cold case.

"So, how did you manage to zero in on a place?" she asked.

"I did some poking around over at the park headquarters. Turns out, the week Molly Shaw went missing there was a report of a gunshot fired in an area known for poachers. They've had some issues with people shooting pronghorns."

They reached her car, and Ava shielded her eyes from the sun as she looked up at him. "Poachers?"

"Yeah."

"Well, that changes everything."

"Why?"

She smiled. "Because Huck is a game warden dog. He's trained to sniff out guns and ammo. Poachers are his specialty."

CHAPTER

EIGHT

GRANT STUDIED THE map spread out on his tailgate. Cell phone maps were worthless out here—a fact that had led to countless problems with tourists flocking in from the cities.

"The gunshot was reported by a couple driving along here." Grant traced the dirt road with his finger. "They both insisted it came from the west, somewhere near here"—he pointed to the trailhead where they were standing—"on the opposite side of the gorge."

"What were these people driving?"

"A Jeep," he said.

"Noises can play tricks, though. Especially in a canyon."

"I know. But they both seemed sure."

Ava leaned back and looked around. "Where'd Huck go?"

"He's sniffing over there by that agave."

She returned her attention to the map, frowning down at it. "What were these people doing way out here, anyway? We're really far off the main road."

"The wife's a nature photographer and she'd been staking out various bluffs, hoping to get a glimpse of the pronghorn herd."

"I didn't even know there were any around here. I've never seen one."

"Yeah, they're shy."

Ava leaned closer, and Grant caught a whiff of her perfume. Or maybe it was her body lotion. Whatever it was, it had been driving him crazy since he'd first noticed it.

"What time of day was this?" she asked.

"Three fifteen."

"Heat of the day. I'm surprised anyone was out here."

"Some people avoid peak times. They come here for the solitude. They want to be remote."

"Well, 'remote' is right. Do you realize it's more than five miles as a crow flies from the campsite I found?"

"Six, actually." Grant had measured it on the map. "Seven miles if you follow the trail."

"What trail?"

"It isn't labeled. But one of the park rangers said people hike through here sometimes." He ran his finger along the base of the gorge. "See? Cut through this and come down. . . . It's about seven miles."

"Well, that's a fourteen-mile round trip from the campsite. Do you know if Molly Shaw was a big hiker?"

"She was athletic, I know that. She grew up in Colorado, where she was an avid skier and rock climber. Plus she did some mountain biking."

"Okay, so we can assume she could handle it." Ava stared down at the map. "You think we should follow that trail in the gorge?"

"Let's stay up high so we get some breeze. Unless Huck seems to want to go down there." Grant glanced around. "Where is he?"

Ava gave a sharp whistle, and Huck loped over from the

clump of plants he'd been exploring. Ava crouched down and scratched his ears.

"You ready to work? Huh, boy?" She shrugged off her backpack and pulled out the dog's work vest. Huck practically vibrated with excitement as she put it on him and clipped the straps.

"Seems eager," Grant said.

"Oh yeah. This is his very favorite thing. Except of course, the chew toy he gets when he makes a find. That's heaven for him."

She patted the back pocket of her jeans where she had a pitiful-looking yellow rope toy. Huck nudged her pocket and whimpered with impatience.

Ava stepped away and looked at Grant. "You want to start here?"

He glanced at the arid landscape dotted with desert plants. About twenty yards to the east was a deep gorge. "It's as good a place as any."

Ava made a clicking noise, and Huck went stock-still. She gazed down at him, her expression deadly serious. His big brown eyes were fixated on her face as he waited for whatever she was going to say.

"Huck, *find gun*."

Huck dashed off. He got about twenty yards away and started sniffing the ground in a zigzag pattern.

Ava fell in behind him. Grant followed her.

"Find gun? That's his command?"

She glanced at him over her shoulder. "Gun covers everything—guns, ammo, spent shell casings. Anything with the slightest hint of gunpowder."

"Even if it's been here awhile?"

"Even then. Fresh is always better, but he's really sensitive. I mean, *this* is his main skill set. It's what he's really trained for. He's spent months and months learning to locate people hiding illegal hunting activity, whether that's a deer carcass or a box of shotgun shells or a rifle that's stashed under a log somewhere."

Grant could hear the pride in her voice. "How long was he on the job?"

"Two years before my dad retired."

"And they didn't want to keep the dog?"

"I'm sure they did, but Huck's his. *Was*." She cleared her throat. "My dad bought him from a breeder and paid for all his training."

"He didn't train him himself?"

"Well, he did, but it's still an investment. You have to go to group sessions with other handlers. There's a ton of practice involved. Really, it takes years for a dog to get good at it."

Huck settled into his pace, ranging from side to side along the edge of the gorge. Ava walked along behind him, and Grant followed her. When they'd stopped at her house for Huck, she'd changed into jeans and hiking boots and put her hair up in a ponytail. She'd also grabbed her gear and stocked up on water bottles.

"So, not to be morbid," she said, "but what are you hoping to find, exactly? Human remains?"

"I'm not sure," he said, opting for honesty. "Maybe a shell casing or a slug. Any brass at all would be useful. If someone fired a shot in this area just two days after Molly Shaw went missing . . ." He trailed off, realizing it probably sounded far-fetched. But over the years Grant had seen cases break wide open based on thinner leads than this.

Ava glanced at him over her shoulder. "You think there's a chance she might have come out here and taken her own life?"

The possibility had been in Grant's mind since the beginning, for a variety of reasons.

"I don't know," he said. "But this reported gunshot is a lead, and we need to follow up."

"I get it. It's good that we're here. Just, you know, keep in mind that it's been a while."

"I know."

Guilt gnawed at him. This lead should have been uncovered two years ago, and he couldn't believe they'd missed it.

Grant went over the incident report in his head as they walked along. He'd read through it three times and even screenshotted it for future reference. He couldn't believe they'd missed it earlier, and he blamed himself. This park's incident reports—and those of *every* nearby park—should have been checked two summers ago. But at the time, they'd had no particular reason to think Molly Shaw had gone missing in the backcountry of a park. Her friends had said she liked to drink—sometimes way too much—and Grant believed she could just as easily have disappeared from a bar parking lot.

"Huck, *no*."

Ava jogged up ahead, and Grant followed her.

"What's wrong?"

"He's into something. *Huck!*"

He poked his head up from the pile of rocks he'd been sniffing. Ava stopped beside him and looked around. "Okay, keep working, boy."

Huck loped off.

"I freaking hate that this place is called Diamondback Gorge." She let out a sigh. "I keep thinking he's going to stick his nose into a snake pit."

Grant had been thinking about that, too.

Ava pulled out a bottle of water from her side pocket and offered it to him.

"I'm good."

"It's hot. Drink."

He took the bottle and twisted the top off. After a sip, he handed it to her, and she stopped to take a long gulp. Little locks of hair had come loose from her ponytail and clung to her neck.

Grant turned away, scanning the other side of the gorge. It rose up higher on the far side, and a row of mesquite trees lined the top of the bluff.

"How deep is this gorge?" she asked.

"Here, about fifty feet. A hundred feet in other places."

"Is there ever any water in it?"

"Mostly it's dry as a bone, but every now and then we get a flash flood. It's been a long time since we've had one with this drought. At least three years."

Ava took another swig, and he tried not to stare. Her skin was smooth and flushed and dewy with perspiration, and he couldn't stop wondering what she looked like in bed.

"More?" she asked.

"No, thanks."

She tucked the water bottle away and they continued on their trek.

"Oh, I meant to tell you!" She looked back at him. "I can't believe I forgot."

"What?"

"So, I was examining those photos last night. The ones of the campsite. I noticed something important. If you enlarge one of the images you can see a small corner of a magazine sticking out from under the bedroll. You can see the edge of this yellow *O*, so I started researching *Outside* magazine."

"April two years ago."

She halted and turned around. "You noticed it?"

He nodded.

She sighed. "Of course you did. You're a detective." She turned and kept walking. "Here I was thinking I'd come up with some clever lead for you."

"It is a clever lead. It corroborates your first impression that the campsite looked old."

She nodded. "Someone could have had an old issue of the magazine with them, but what are the odds?"

"Low."

"Of course, that tees up a whole bunch of other questions."

"I know."

She shot him a worried look over her shoulder. "Namely, why was it moved now, two years later, after sitting there all that time? And even more importantly, *who* the hell moved it?"

Grant had some ideas, and none of them was good.

"Any theories?" she asked.

"I don't know."

"Oh, BS. You have theories, you just don't want to tell me." She shot him an annoyed look. "I know how this goes."

"How what goes?"

"You law enforcement guys are a tight-lipped bunch."

Grant couldn't argue with that. He made a habit of keeping the details of his cases guarded, especially when it came to civilians. Henley was a close-knit community, and people were always approaching him and leaning on him for information of one kind or another. Some of that was just small-town nosiness, but some of it wasn't. Over the course of his career, he'd seen more than a few cases go sideways because some detail that should have been kept quiet ended up out there in public.

She glanced back at him again, smiling. "What, no comment?"

"No comment."

She snorted.

Grant scanned his gaze over the opposite bluff. It caught the western sun, making a bright white wall of limestone.

Ava halted. "Look!"

Grant's heart lurched and he followed the line of her gaze. Across the gorge was a rocky outcropping.

"Are those pronghorns?" she asked, her voice filled with wonder.

"Yep."

Huck barked and trotted back toward them.

"I've never seen them before," she said. "Oh, look, there's a *baby* with them."

Grant squinted at the cliffside and sure enough, a little fawn was picking his way up the steep rock face.

"I can't believe they can climb that," she said. "How many are there out here?"

"The herd's about twenty." He glanced around, looking for more but he saw only three.

Huck barked again and sat down, his ears pricked forward. He stared at Ava.

Grant's stomach tightened as he watched the dog.

"Ava."

She turned around.

"I think he's trying to tell you something."

"Oh! That's his sit alert." She rushed toward him, and Huck jumped to his feet.

"Huck, *show me*."

A FEELING OF DREAD settled over her as she watched Grant work. He knelt beside a yellow evidence marker taking an up-close picture of the brass shell casing. Then he stood and exchanged words with Mel Tyndall. As soon as Grant had radioed headquarters, the superintendent had driven out here with a Nikon camera that belonged to the park. While Grant had photographed what might or might not be evidence, Mel had combed the area with a metal detector.

Ava crouched beside Huck's bowl and added another splash of water, which he lapped up eagerly. After a gleeful game of tug-of-war with his favorite toy, he'd poked around the area some more and then decided to rest.

Grant glanced over his shoulder at Ava. They seemed to be wrapping up. Mel stowed the metal detector in the back of his truck cab and then hitched himself behind the wheel.

"Finish up, Huck."

He licked the bowl clean, and Ava clipped it to the pocket of her pack as Grant walked over.

"Mel's offering us a ride."

Ava tried to read his expression in the fading light. "What do you think?"

"I'm good if you are."

"I'm fine. So is Huck," she said.

"You got a flashlight?"

"Two. And, honestly, I'd rather walk back than drive. Maybe he'll find another one."

Grant turned and waved. Mel tipped his hat and pulled away, and Ava watched the taillights fade.

"He turn up anything with the metal detector?" Ava asked.

"Two bottlecaps and an aluminum can." Grant sighed and rested his hands on his hips.

"Probably not evidence," she said.

"Probably not."

She nodded at the Nikon slung over his shoulder. "He let you keep the camera, though?"

"I'll get it back to him tomorrow. I need to download everything first."

They started back the way they had come, and Huck dashed ahead, his energy renewed from all the excitement.

"He's better than a metal detector," Grant said.

She felt a surge of pride. "I know, right? His nose is very discerning."

She glanced around the dusky landscape. The sky had gone from orange to pink to light purple, and they didn't need the flashlight yet, but it wouldn't be long.

She glanced back at Grant. "So, you think that spent brass is related to your case?"

"Maybe. We'll send it to the lab, get some details."

"How long does that take?"

He scoffed. "You never know. But usually too long for me. I'm pretty impatient."

They hiked along in silence as dusk settled over the mesa. The warm air smelled of dust and juniper. Ava scanned the path ahead for Huck. He still wore his vest, and he zigzagged ahead of them, working the air with his nose.

A chorus of crickets started up. Ava glanced around nervously as she imagined a den full of rattlesnakes watching them from the shadows.

She halted, and Grant grabbed her backpack as he bumped into her.

"You okay?"

"Yeah, sorry," she said. "Could you unzip me and get that flashlight?"

Grant unzipped her pack and retrieved the heavy-duty Maglite.

"I've got a backup, too, in the inner pocket."

He dug around for it and handed her the smaller flashlight, then zipped the pack closed. The weight felt much lighter, and she realized he'd grabbed the remaining water bottles, too, and added them to his own pack. The sweetness of the gesture put a warm tingle inside her.

"Thanks," she said.

"Sure."

They continued on, and Ava's flashlight beam glinted off Huck's reflective orange collar.

"Rattlesnakes are more active at night, aren't they?" she asked.

"Yeah."

They kept walking as she listened for any tambourine-like noises.

"We're probably good, though," he said. "You've got your boots on. And your fancy jeans."

"These jeans aren't fancy."

"You have rhinestones on your pockets. That's fancy."

She felt another warm tingle. He'd been looking at her pockets.

"It's not me I'm worried about," she said. "Huck doesn't have any protection."

"You want me to call Mel to come back and get us?"

"No. It's probably fine. Huck's all over the yard every night, and we haven't had any snake problems yet. I think the name of this gorge just freaks me out."

Their flashlight beams bobbed in the darkness as they walked. Wind whispered through the scrub trees, bringing another waft of juniper.

"Water?" he asked.

"Sure."

She stopped and waited as he pulled the bottle from his pack. He twisted the top off and handed the bottle to her, and she took a long gulp. Then she passed it back. He took a swig.

A wind gusted up, and she tipped her head back to look at the sky.

"Whoa."

"What?" He looked up.

The sky was an inky dome with about a billion pin-pricks of light. "The stars here. I never—" She looked at him, and he was watching her intently with those brown-black eyes.

Anticipation zinged through her. He was going to kiss her.

She'd thought that the last time, too, but this time she knew it. His gaze dropped to her mouth, and she felt the heat from his body as he eased close.

His fingertips brushed the side of her neck, and butter-flies filled her stomach as he gently tilted her head back.

And then his mouth sank down on hers, and the world shifted.

His lips were warm and firm, and she leaned her head back to get a better angle as his tongue found hers. God, he tasted *good*. He was sharp and manly with the faintest hint of cinnamon, and she slid her hands over his shoulders and pressed against him as she took a good long taste. His hand slid down around her waist, then to her lower back, holding her against him as she sank into the kiss.

She couldn't get enough of him—his taste, his lips, his body. She ran her fingers into the thick softness of his hair where it curled at the back of his neck, just beneath his baseball cap.

Ava tipped her head back and his warm mouth slid over her throat. The stubble of his beard rasped her skin, and a million nerve endings fired to life. It had been way, way too long since she'd felt a man's beard on her skin, and she was suddenly starved for more.

She found his mouth again, tangling her tongue with his as she pulled him even closer. She felt the straps of his backpack under her fingertips, and remembered they were weighted down with gear. He was still holding the water bottle they'd been drinking from.

"Ava," he said against her mouth.

She started to ease away, but then she changed her mind and pulled him back, needing just a little more.

"Ava." He pulled back and stared down at her, his gaze intent.

"What?" she asked hoarsely.

"He's barking again."

"What?"

"Huck."

Panic hit her as she glanced around at the darkness. Her flashlight lay at her feet. She snatched it up as Huck trotted over and sat down.

He pricked his ears forward, and Ava's stomach knotted.

She stepped over to him. "Show me."

Huck jumped up and bounded away. Ava jogged after him, dodging around weeds and scrub brush.

"What is it?" Grant asked behind her.

"I don't know."

Huck disappeared behind a boulder, and she nearly crashed into it.

"Huck, wait."

What was she thinking? She never told him to wait. But then, she'd never followed him to a find in the dark before. She could barely see anything.

She spotted a flash of orange as Grant's flashlight beam found Huck's collar and stayed locked on it.

"Where is he going?" she muttered.

"Over there." Grant strode past her.

She heard a clatter of rocks as Huck disappeared over a cliff. Ava's stomach dropped.

"Huck!"

"There's a trail. He's fine."

She jogged to catch up with Grant, frantically aiming her light at the ground.

Grant paused beside a crooked juniper tree. "Watch your step here. It's steep."

She followed behind him as he picked his way over a trail that led down, down, down into the gorge.

Diamondback Gorge.

Ava looked ahead, desperate for the reflective orange of Huck's collar.

Up ahead, Grant cursed.

"What is it?" she asked.

He dropped into a crouch beside a pile of rocks. Huck barked and Ava reached for his collar to pull him away.

"Grant, what is it?" she asked as Huck strained against her hold.

Ava shined the flashlight over the pile. She couldn't make out what she was looking at, and she leaned closer. Amid the heap of rocks was a glimpse of fabric and . . . hair?

"Grant, is that—"

"Yes." He stood up. "It is."

CHAPTER
NINE

GRANT MADE HIS way through the crowd of people clogging the sidewalk in front of the sheriff's office. A local reporter had caught wind of the recovery operation, and by midmorning news vans were arriving from as far away as Austin.

A young woman in high heels caught Grant's eye. She pushed through her colleagues and shoved a microphone at him.

"Detective, have the remains been identified?"

"No comment."

Grant reached for the door and caught sight of another woman, also in heels, standing at the corner of the building. He changed directions and slipped through the mass of reporters to join her.

Ava looked wary as she watched him approach. She was dressed up again today in one of those tight-fitting skirts and loose blouses, and her hair was up in a bun. He hadn't seen her since midnight, when he'd put her and Huck into a sheriff's office SUV and told a deputy to drive them home.

Grant had wanted to do it himself, but he'd needed to stay and manage the recovery operation. Because of the condition of the remains, they'd had to call in a forensic anthropologist from the university in Alpine.

"Hey," she said as he stopped in front of her. "You look very official today."

"So do you." He guided her closer to the eaves where there was a patch of shade. "You headed to court?"

"I've got a hearing at one." She blew out a sigh. "What time did you get home last night?"

"Late."

So late it had been eight in the morning. He'd grabbed a quick nap and then cleaned up and put on his official uniform so he could stand behind Donovan at a press conference.

"I saw the news briefing," Ava said.

"What'd you think?"

"He did a remarkable job of talking for twenty minutes while saying nothing at all."

Grant nodded. "It's a talent."

"I know."

Ava looked at her watch, and Grant thought she seemed nervous. Was it the kiss? It had been good. Better than good. But Grant hadn't had time to think about it again until he'd been standing in a steaming hot shower this morning and trying to wake up.

Ava cleared her throat. "So, I had a bit of a break, and I wanted to see if you had time to grab lunch at the Coffee Cup."

"I'd like to, but I have a meeting in a couple minutes."

She nodded and looked away, and he noticed the worry line between her brows.

"Ava, are you okay?"

"Yeah."

"You sure?"

She finally made eye contact. "Yeah, just . . . last night was a first for us."

A first.

And then he got it. Her other SAR operations had resulted in live finds. Finding a body was different. Disturbing. The experience stayed with you long afterward.

"Sorry you were out there," he said.

"I'm not. I'm glad we could help." She glanced toward the station, and Grant turned to see a deputy from El Paso County, along with a big German shepherd, approaching the building. The crowd of reporters parted, and the frantic *click click click* of cameras left no doubt that the dog would feature prominently in the next news broadcast. The media loved dogs.

"Guess you finally got your cadaver team," Ava said.

"Yeah."

"Anything new?"

"I don't know, actually. I'll probably find out at the meeting."

She checked her watch. "I'll let you go. I need to go grab some lunch before they get crowded. Keep me posted, okay?"

"I'll try."

He gazed down at her hazel eyes that looked tired today—and he knew his did, too. He had a sudden urge to kiss her forehead. But he had a feeling that wouldn't go over well when they were standing in front of the sheriff's office with a bunch of reporters around.

He touched her elbow instead. "Thanks for the lunch invite. Rain check?"

"Sure."

She took out her sunglasses and slid them on, effectively ending the conversation. "Good luck this afternoon."

Grant watched her cross the street to the town square. When she stepped into the café, he turned away.

His gaze landed on a woman standing beside a blue SUV parked directly across the street. She was staring right at him.

Shit.

"We're in the conference room in ten."

Grant turned to see Connor walking over from the side parking lot. He had a Whataburger cup in his hand. Like Grant, he was in his official uniform, which they both hated. One of the perks of making detective was being able to wear street clothes most of the time.

"I'll be there," Grant told him.

"You coming in now?"

"In a minute."

Grant checked for traffic, then strode across the street toward the woman. Her long dark hair was in a braid, and it had a lot more gray than he remembered.

He stopped in front of her and tipped his hat. "Ms. Spencer."

"You remember me."

"Yes, ma'am."

Desperate parents had a way of sticking in people's minds. Last summer Rachel Spencer had made sure every law enforcement officer in three counties had her number programmed into their phone.

She stared up at him, and the mix of fear and hope in her eyes put a knot in his chest.

"What can you tell me?" she asked.

The answer he needed to say got stuck in his throat.

She huffed out a sigh. "Just be straight with me. It's been a long year."

Grant nodded. "I've been in touch with the agent in charge of your daughter's case," he said.

"Agent Woods."

"Yes, ma'am." Woods was with the FBI's El Paso field office, which was the closest one to Big Bend National Park, where Rachel Spencer's daughter was last seen. The FBI was assisting NPS investigators with the case. Henley County had been involved with the search only because the park rangers needed extra boots on the ground.

"Agent Woods reached out to me early this morning," Grant told her.

She gave a watery smile. "Probably because I called her at six a.m."

"You did?" He couldn't hide his surprise.

"I follow all the local law enforcement agencies on Twitter. I got in my car as soon as I heard about the recovery operation."

Grant glanced at the sheriff's office and hoped the reporters didn't catch sight of Rachel Spencer and figure out who she was.

"If there's anything pertinent to their investigation," Grant said, "we'll be sure to let them know about it, ASAP."

Her eyes swam with tears as she looked up at him. "Please, just . . . is it Brittlyn?"

The whispered words were like a dart in his chest. And Grant knew what he should do here, but he couldn't bring himself to tell her nothing.

He cleared his throat. "At this time, I have no reason to think so."

It was the closest he could get to candor. Hell, he shouldn't have said even that much.

She pressed her hand to her heart and stepped back.

"Are you all right?" he asked.

"Yes, just . . ." She shook her head. "I thought I'd feel relieved, hearing that. But I don't. I don't at all." She took a deep breath and seemed to compose herself. "When is the autopsy?"

"It's scheduled for late this afternoon."

She nodded and looked around. "I guess I'd better find a place to stay before y'all run out of rooms."

Grant knew it would be futile to try to convince her to drive back to San Antonio and wait for a call from Woods. That wasn't happening. This was a woman who'd spent the entire last summer camping out near the headquarters of Big Bend National Park after her daughter went missing.

Even after they suspended the search, she stayed out there, waiting for news and handing out flyers to tourists. Deputies over in Brewster County tried to avoid her because she was constantly popping up and hounding them for updates.

Grant had never been one to dodge her. He felt obligated to talk to her whenever their paths crossed. But he dreaded the conversations. Nothing in the world made him feel quite as inadequate as talking to a distraught parent and having no answers whatsoever.

"Well." She took a deep breath. "Thank you for telling me what you can."

He nodded.

"Here's my number, if anything comes up." She handed him a slip of paper. "You can call me anytime."

He took the paper, even though they both knew that if anything did come up, his first call would be to Woods.

"Day or night. I mean it."

He nodded again.

"I'll let you get back to work."

T HE COFFEE CUP was busy with the usual tourists and courthouse employees, plus a handful of reporters who had already sniffed out the best java in town. Ava stood in line for a plain drip coffee and a ham sandwich, then found an empty high-top table beside the window.

She blew on her coffee as she watched the crowd milling in front of the sheriff's office.

"Okay if I sit here?"

She turned to see a woman standing at her table. Short. Fiftyish. Salt-and-pepper hair pulled back in a braid.

"Sure." Ava scooted her sandwich over.

"They're not usually this crowded." She hitched herself onto the empty stool and placed a to-go cup in front of her. "I noticed you talking to Grant Wycoff a minute ago."

Ava's guard went up.

"He's a good one."

Ava stared at the woman, not sure what to make of that.

"Sorry." She smiled. "I'm Rachel Spencer."

Ava studied the woman's face before replying. No makeup, lots of freckles, sun-browned skin. Despite the odd introduction, something about her seemed trustworthy. Something in her eyes, maybe.

"I'm Ava," she said. "How is it you know Grant Wycoff?"

The woman looked out the window toward the mob of reporters still milling around the flagpole.

"My daughter went missing last summer, and he's been helping with her case."

Ava felt a pang of sympathy. "I'm sorry."

She turned to Ava and nodded, and Ava realized it *was* the eyes. They were deep and brown and held a world of pain.

"I heard about the recovery operation." She looked down at her untouched coffee. "Well. I had to come." She pulled a flyer from her purse and set it on the table. "That's Brittlyn."

Ava slid the paper closer. It had the words HAVE YOU SEEN ME? printed across the top. The color photo beneath showed a smiling girl standing on a balcony. Or was she a woman? Based on the birthdate beneath the photo, she was nineteen at the time she went missing. *Nineteen.* Ava studied the picture with an ache in her chest. Brittlyn's hair was long and blond, and her chocolate-brown eyes resembled her mother's.

Ava glanced up at Rachel Spencer and understood what she was doing here. This woman was desperate for information. If the sheriff's office wouldn't give it to her, she was going to hit up anyone else she could.

Ava recalled her dad's missing person cases, how family members would call at all hours and track him down at work or even at home.

Rachel Spencer gazed down at her daughter's photo.

"What happened with Brittlyn?" Ava asked.

"You didn't hear about her?"

"No. I'm sorry. I just moved here in November."

She nodded. "This was last summer. June." She paused and seemed to collect her thoughts. "She was camping with friends in Big Bend National Park. She went rock climbing one day and didn't come back. We thought she must have gotten lost or injured."

Ava watched her, waiting for her to continue.

"For the first ten days, everything was full throttle. We had search teams, dogs, even helicopters. But then it went from rescue to recovery, and everything changed. The volunteers went home. No more helicopters. The extra sheriff's people went back to their home counties." She shook her head. "Everyone gave up, but we still didn't know anything." She gave Ava an urgent look. "That's the hardest part. Not knowing. I feel like I could handle it if I just had some *fact* to hold on to. But all I have is guesswork. Nobody can tell me anything tangible."

Ava didn't know what to say, so she just listened. Brittlyn's mother looked down at her coffee. She still hadn't had any. She glanced up and regarded Ava with a curious look.

"So, you're not from around here?"

"I'm from Houston, actually."

She looked out the window. "Has the detective told you?"

"Told me what?"

"He hasn't, then."

Ava waited for her to elaborate.

"I'm not surprised. They don't like to talk about it. None of them do."

"Talk about what?" Ava asked.

Rachel took a sip of her coffee, then set it down. Her gaze locked on Ava's, and she leaned forward slightly.

"An unusual number of girls have disappeared from around here."

Dread settled in Ava's stomach.

"First that climber. Then the woman from Denver. Then Brittlyn."

"A climber disappeared?" Ava asked.

"Deanna Moore. She went missing in Big Bend three years ago. It was in June, too. Yet another thing no one wants to talk about."

"I hadn't heard."

"Of course you hadn't. Missing girls are bad for business. The parks don't like to talk about it, and you sure as hell won't hear anything from the sheriff's office."

Ava took a sip of coffee and watched her, wondering how much of this was real and how much was based on the understandable frustration of a distraught mother searching for her child.

"So, Deanna went missing in Big Bend, just like your daughter?" Ava asked.

"Different part of the park, but yes. They had the helicopters and search teams then, too. The whole nine yards. But then they found her."

"They did?"

"At the base of a cliff. One-hundred-foot drop."

Ava shuddered.

"Accidental death, they said."

"Who said?"

"The medical examiner." Rachel Spencer shook her head. "Not that I *believe* that, but that's the official report."

Ava wanted to ask why she didn't believe the medical examiner, but something held her back.

"That was three years ago," she continued. "Then there was Molly Shaw. Then there was Brittlyn. It's a pattern, but no one wants to talk about it. No one wants to acknowledge what most likely happened. They just keep talking about *scenarios*. That's the term the FBI agent used. 'We've explored every scenario of how and why the target came to be missing.' She actually *said* that to me." Anger flashed in her eyes. "Can you believe that? She called Brittlyn a 'target.'"

Ava stared at the woman, unsure of what to say. Her frustration was like an aura shimmering around her.

"What do you think happened?" Ava asked, bracing herself for the answer.

The woman's jaw tightened as she looked down at her coffee. "I don't know. But I'll tell you what *didn't* happen. Brittlyn didn't run off with a boyfriend. Or OD on drugs. Or commit suicide. Not Brittlyn. I know my daughter. And she would never do that." Tears fill her eyes. "She would never do any of this to me. Brittlyn is *kind*. And sensitive. She loves people and nature and animals. She would never leave me searching and worrying and wondering like this. Something happened to her. Just like Deanna Moore and Molly Shaw."

Ava's stomach knotted with worry as she watched Brittlyn's mom. Ava felt for this woman. And she also felt for the police investigating her daughter's disappearance. Missing person cases were difficult as a rule, but wilderness disappearances were especially hard. And in a place as vast and rugged as Big Bend, the challenges were only magnified.

It sounded like this FBI agent wasn't a very good communicator—at least, not as far as victims' families were concerned. But Ava had no doubt the agent wanted to find answers.

Rachel Spencer sipped her coffee and put it down. Then she gazed through the window at the crowd in front of the sheriff's office.

"Lord, I hate dealing with these people," she said.

"How come?"

"I don't trust them. Well, not most of them, anyway. They just want to close the case, whether they get it right or not."

"Why would they do that?" Ava asked, although she could think of a few possibilities.

"Plenty of reasons. PR. Economics." She leaned forward. "Having a string of women go missing isn't good for tourism around here. Not to mention it makes the sheriff look incompetent. Which he *is*."

Ava's eyebrows tipped up.

"Do I sound cynical? Well, I am." Her face softened. "But Grant Wycoff is better than most. At least he has the guts to talk to me. All the other cops that helped look for Brittlyn run the other way as soon as they see me coming."

"That must be frustrating," Ava said.

"It is. Incredibly. But I'm not going away." She smiled slightly. "Maybe that's why Grant talks to me. He recognizes a determined woman when he sees one." She looked out at the sheriff's office again. "He knows I'm going to keep turning up like a bad penny until I get answers."

CHAPTER
TEN

Connor spotted Grant in the parking lot as he was leaving work. Grant was in an official SUV, so it looked like he was still on duty. He pulled up alongside Connor and rolled down the window.

"Didn't see you inside," Connor said.

"I was talking to Donovan."

That explained the closed door to the sheriff's office.

Connor rested his hand on the top of the door. "What happened with the autopsy?"

"You have time for a ride? I'll tell you."

Connor glanced at his truck on the far end of the row. He'd put in a fifteen-hour day already. But the only thing waiting for him at home was an empty fridge. He walked around the SUV and got in.

"Where're we going?" Connor asked as Grant pulled out of the lot.

"The Richter place. Someone took a baseball bat to Scott's truck."

"No shit? The new one?"

"Yeah."

Connor had seen the pickup in town just the other day. Extended cab, lift kit, chrome rims. It was a sweet ride. Or it had been.

"I hear he's going through a divorce," Connor said. "Maybe his wife did it."

"Yeah, I heard they're back together. My money's on the girlfriend."

"Scott has a girlfriend?"

Grant shot him a look, and Connor got his point. Scott always had a girlfriend. Connor had never figured out why his wife put up with it, and he'd been glad to hear that she'd finally kicked him out.

"So . . . you're thinking the divorce didn't take, and now the girlfriend's pissed off?"

"Something like that," Grant said.

"What a mess. I'm surprised he reported it."

"Probably needs the paperwork for his insurance."

Connor looked at Grant across the truck cab. Even in the dim light of the dashboard, he could see that he was whipped. Grant had been up all night managing the body recovery and then he'd been through two press conferences, three team meetings, and an autopsy. Connor had offered to go with him to the autopsy, but Grant had said he was fine on his own, and Connor had secretly been relieved. He hated those things.

"So, what happened?" Connor asked.

Grant stared at the road for a moment before responding. "It's Molly Shaw."

"That's confirmed?"

"The ME has the dental records."

"Shit. Is Donovan going to hold another press conference tomorrow?"

"He wants to wait a day."

Connor turned to him. "For what?"

"He wants to hold off announcing the manner of death."

"Everyone already knows the manner of death. The body was buried under a shit-ton of rocks."

"He thinks he can stall the media, maybe buy some time before this turns into a circus."

"That's not happening."

"I know."

Grant turned onto the highway leading out to the Richter place. Connor watched him, waiting to hear the rest. He had an idea now what Grant and Donovan had been talking about in their closed-door meeting. Grant often disagreed with the sheriff's decisions, but he had the sense not to do it in front of the whole team.

"So, manner of death, homicide," Grant said. "Cause of death, gunshot wound."

"You were right, then."

Grant looked at him. "About what?"

"Those people in Silver Canyon park. They didn't hear poachers—they probably heard a murder."

Grant's jaw tightened, and Connor knew what he was thinking. He was still pissed off—at himself and probably the sheriff, too. If they had run a more thorough investigation two years ago, they would have uncovered this incident report before the case went stone cold.

But they hadn't been thorough. They hadn't even been adequate. Donovan had been dragging his feet on this thing from the get-go.

"You know, these last two years, I kept thinking she was a suicide," Grant said.

"How come?"

"Her brother told me that's what he thought happened." Grant glanced at him. "When he originally contacted us looking for his sister, he said she'd gone into a depression after her divorce. Then when she told him about the road trip she had planned, she asked if she could borrow a pistol from him. Said she wanted it for protection. He told me he almost didn't lend it to her because he worried she might be suicidal."

"But he lent it to her anyway?"

"Yeah." Grant sighed and shook his head. "Guy's been racked with guilt this whole time, thinking he maybe lent his sister the gun that she used to take her own life somewhere. Now, we've got to tell him she was murdered."

"From his perspective, not sure which is worse," Connor said.

Grant didn't comment.

"So, gunshot wound," Connor said. "Any idea the caliber?"

"Not yet. The ME recovered a slug and sent it to the lab."

Connor looked at Grant's tense profile. "What else?"

"What else what?"

"There's something else bothering you about the autopsy. What is it?"

Grant glanced at him. "She was shot in the back."

Connor just looked at him.

"Close range, right between the shoulder blades."

"Damn."

Connor stared ahead at the highway and pictured Molly Shaw. She was five-three. Petite. Pretty. The Polaroid in the case file showed a smiling woman mugging for the camera with her friend.

The idea of someone walking up behind her and putting a bullet in her back made Connor's skin crawl.

"She also has bone fractures consistent with a sixty-foot drop," Grant said.

"So . . . she was pushed off that cliff?"

"Possibly. It's unclear whether this was before or after she was shot in the back."

Connor cringed. "So, he shot her, pushed her into the gorge, and then went down there and buried the body under rocks. Wonder why he did all that."

"Probably to delay the body being found, by either people or scavengers." Grant looked at him. "It worked, too.

Here we are two years later just now getting our shit together."

Connor blew out a sigh. "This sucks."

"Yep. Time since death is hard to determine, at this point, because the body is mostly skeletonized. But the ME said the remains have been there at least a year and likely more, which checks out with Molly's disappearance two summers ago."

"And we don't know whether she encountered her attacker on the trail while she was hiking, or whether this was someone she was camping with, maybe a friend or a boyfriend." Connor raked his hand through his hair. "We need to figure out what she was doing and who she was with those last few days before she went missing."

Connor looked across the truck cab. Grant was tense and had been for days.

"At least we recovered a slug and a shell casing," Connor said. "That could give us a lead, if we're lucky."

Grant slowed as he reached the turnoff for the Richter place. The unhappily married couple lived at the end of a dirt road with their two young kids.

Grant made the turn and then glanced at Connor. "We just opened a homicide investigation two years after the fact. We have no suspects, no eyewitnesses, and the trail is fucking ice-cold."

"In other words, you're not feeling very lucky about this one."

"Not even a little."

AVA ANSWERED THE door with her hair wrapped in a towel.

"You've been dodging me," Jenna said.

"What do you mean? I'm right here."

"It's gossip time." She held up a bottle of red wine. "And I came bearing alcohol, so you can't turn me away."

Ava stepped back to let her in. "When have I ever turned you away?"

Jenna swept into the little house, and Huck circled her excitedly.

"Well, hello there, sweet boy. You've been busy, haven't you?"

Ava stepped into the kitchen and took a pair of wine-glasses down from a cabinet.

"Hope I'm not interrupting any plans," Jenna said.

"Oh yes, big night. I just washed my hair."

She lifted an eyebrow. "Late date this evening?"

"No."

"You sure?"

"Yes." Ava twisted the cap off the wine and poured two servings.

Jenna picked hers up and watched Ava over the rim as she took a sip. She set the glass on the counter.

"So, I can't believe you haven't tracked me down for the rest of the story," Jenna said.

"What story?"

Jenna shot her a look. "Please. This is me you're talking to. And I didn't mean to leave you hanging on the subject of our sexy sheriff."

"He's a detective."

"Whatever. There's a bit of backstory you should be aware of before you take the plunge with him."

"I'm not *taking the plunge*—"

"Ah-ah-ah." Jenna held up her hand. "I know you're at least thinking about it, so I just wanted to let you know—full disclosure—that while Grant Wycoff is very hot and very eligible, he also once left a woman at the altar."

Ava blinked with surprise.

"I know." Jenna made a face. "Doesn't sound like him, does it?"

"How on earth would I know what sounds like him? I barely know the man."

"Well, I've known him almost my whole life, and I was surprised by it." She took a sip of wine and set down her glass. "Basically, he was all set to marry his high school sweetheart—the Pearl of the Prairie, no less—and he broke the engagement and moved away to Dallas."

"The pearl . . . what?"

"Pearl of the Prairie." Jenna rolled her eyes. "It's like our homecoming queen. Very big deal. Anyway, he went off to Dallas and enrolled in their police academy and then spent almost six years there before moving back home. Which, of course, stirred the pot all over again."

Ava did a bit of math in her head. "And . . . this was, what? Five years ago that he moved back? Sounds like old news."

"Well, except that his fiancée was Missy Donovan."

"Donovan as in—"

"As in Jim Donovan, yes. It was a pretty big deal at the time. I was shocked to hear Grant moved back to town and had the nerve to apply for a job with the sheriff's office."

Ava sipped her wine. She set the glass down and leaned back against the counter. "I don't know. It doesn't seem that shocking to me." She folded her arms. "I mean, if he wanted to move back and stay in law enforcement, where else was he going to work?"

Jenna smiled. "Well, you're very reasonable, aren't you? When he did it, the whole county was in a tizzy about it."

"Why? Did he and Missy get back together or something?"

"God, no. Now she's married to Rod Crowly. They've got kids together."

"Who's Rod Crowly?"

"Crowly Motors out on Highway 90. You've seen it. He's the only truck dealer between here and Alpine. Makes a fortune."

Ava took another sip of wine, and Jenna made a pouty face.

"You know, as a gossip, you're really not much fun."

Ava shrugged. "I don't see what the big deal is."

"Well, you went to high school in Houston, so you have a different perspective. Henley is a small town, that kind of stuff's a big deal. Anyway, I just thought you should know in case you're starting something up with him."

"I'm not starting something up with him."

"No?"

"No."

Huck erupted in barks and scrambled for the door. Ava glanced out the kitchen window to see a flash of headlights. Jenna crossed the tiny living room and peered through the curtains.

She turned to Ava and smiled. "You are *so* full of shit."

"What?"

"I'm out."

"What? Why?"

"I'll leave you the wine." She reached for the kitchen door.

"What are you doing?"

"Sneaking out the back."

"But—"

"Hope you shaved your legs." Jenna grinned and slipped out.

Ava whirled toward the front door. "Huck, *no*. Stop scratching."

A sharp knock sounded at the door as she tugged on Huck's collar. Then she remembered the towel on her head. She yanked it off and rushed into the bedroom to run a brush through her hair as Huck went crazy pawing at the door. Ava glanced down at her clothes. She was wearing a pink tank top and cutoff shorts, but with Huck barking she didn't want to take the time to change. She crossed the living room again and checked the peephole.

Grant stood on her front porch. He was dressed in his

casual cop attire tonight—a navy golf shirt and jeans, with his badge and gun at his hip.

Ava felt a flutter of nerves as she pulled open the door.

"Hi." She caught Huck's collar as he lunged.

"Hi. Sorry to drop by without calling." He reached down to pet Huck's head. "You got a minute?"

"Sure." She stepped back to let him in, tugging her besotted dog with her. "Everything all right?"

"Yeah, I just had something to ask you." He stepped inside and looked around, and she saw his attention get hung up on the pair of wineglasses. He darted a glance at the bedroom, then looked at her. "This a bad time?"

"No. Jenna was just here. She . . . had to go suddenly."

His brow furrowed. "Everything okay?"

"Yeah. Huck, *chill.*"

"He's fine." Grant leaned down to pet him again, and Huck wagged his tail.

Ava sighed. "Would you like some wine? I'm having some."

"No, thanks."

Ava put Jenna's glass in the sink as Grant stepped into her kitchen. The space was small, but it seemed especially tiny with a six-three man standing in the middle of it. He glanced around, and she felt a flurry of nerves as she suddenly remembered how his mouth had tasted.

"Nice place."

"We like it." She picked up her glass and leaned back against the counter. "Sure you don't want a drink?"

"I'm on duty still."

Of course he was. Ava took a sip.

"It's about the SAR op," he said, getting down to business.

"You mean Thursday?"

"Yeah."

"What about it?"

"After you discovered the campsite, who did you mention it to?"

She set her glass down. "Let's see. Mel Tyndall, when I came back to base. And Sheriff Donovan."

"Who else?"

"No one."

"Are you sure?"

"Well, I mean, you heard about it because you were standing around. Some other SAR people probably did, too. But as far as specifically telling anyone about it, just Tyndall and Donovan."

"Did you discuss it with anyone else, like maybe Jenna or someone, in a public place?"

"Jenna and I talked about it at dinner Sunday."

"That's it? You're sure?"

"Yes. Why?"

"I'm trying to get a sense of who knew about it," he said.

"You mean who knew about it *before* it disappeared the next day," she said, seeing where he was going with this. "You're trying to figure out who moved it."

He didn't confirm or deny her reasoning, and she felt a twinge of annoyance. He was so damned closed off about everything, as if she weren't completely involved in all of it.

"So, you think whoever moved it might have been trying to conceal evidence? Like . . . they heard about the campsite that potentially belonged to Molly Shaw and had to go get rid of it, for some reason?"

Grant tipped his head to the side, as if considering it. But he still didn't confirm that that was what he was investigating.

"I'm on your team, you know." She stepped closer. His shoulders tensed, and she felt a rush of warmth as she eased closer. She glanced down, and her bare feet were almost touching his scuffed brown work boots, and there was something impossibly tempting about her shiny red toenails right next to his big leather boots.

She looked up at him. His eyes were bloodshot from lack of sleep, and she knew he'd had a long, hard day. A thick layer of stubble covered his jaw, and she remembered how it had felt against her skin last night.

She eased closer and felt him tense again. She was making him uncomfortable, and she realized he truly was here on business. He was thinking about that kiss, though. She knew it. His gaze dropped to her mouth and then came back up again.

She felt a little thrill as he rested his hand on her hip. She wanted to kiss him again. Right now. Here. And he wanted it, too.

He looked down at his watch. "I need to go. I have another stop to make." He stepped away, and she felt her cheeks flush with embarrassment.

He crossed the cabin to the front door, and Huck trailed behind him, wagging his tail. Grant reached for the door, and she walked over to grab Huck's collar so he wouldn't follow him out.

"Thanks for the information," he said.

"Anytime."

He gave her a strange look as he stepped onto the porch. "Everything okay?"

"Everything's fine. Good luck with your case."

GRANT STARED AT the door with a sour ball of dread in his gut. He wanted food. And a beer. And about twelve uninterrupted hours with Ava in her bedroom, followed by twelve uninterrupted hours of sleep. But none of that was happening, and instead he had to deal with reality.

Grant got out of his truck and approached the door to room 103. He lifted his hand to knock, but the door swung open before his knuckles touched the wood.

"Hi."

"Hi."

"I heard you pull up." Rachel stepped back and ushered him inside.

The motel room smelled like mildew—which was something of a feat given that this area had been in a drought for years. Grant noticed the brown water stains on the ceiling. Maybe that had something to do with it. His gaze skimmed over the bed and the table. A map was spread across it with a coffee cup perched on the corner. Beneath the table was cardboard box stuffed with file folders.

He turned to Rachel. She was watching him with a wary look.

Grant cleared his throat. "I attended the autopsy late this afternoon."

She nodded, and Grant could see she was holding her breath.

"The remains recovered from the park were positively identified. It's not Brittlyn."

She didn't move or speak or even blink.

"They're certain," she stated.

"Yes, ma'am. They actually had two doctors involved due to the, um, age of the remains. A medical examiner and a forensic anthropologist."

"It was all bones, then."

Grant tried not to wince. He really, really didn't want to get into this with her. The last thing he wanted to do was talk about how the body was almost completely skeletonized— but not quite—and how human skin responds to an arid climate. Grant was pretty sure he'd never eat beef jerky again.

"The forensic anthropologist is an expert on bones, yes." He cleared his throat. "They used X-rays and dental records to make the identification."

She turned away, hugging her arms to her body. She wore jeans and an oversize T-shirt, and her hair was still in the long braid. It was after eleven, but the double bed was still neat as a pin. It looked to Grant like she'd been camped out at the table all night, drinking coffee and poring over her files.

Frustration washed over him. Where the fuck was Agent Woods right now? She was a professional investigator trained by the most elite law enforcement agency on the planet. She'd been to Duke Law School, for crying out loud. And Grant was willing to bet her files on Brittlyn Spencer's disappearance weren't half as full as the those of this fifty-three-year-old social studies teacher from San Antonio.

Rachel turned around. She took a deep breath and squared her shoulders.

"Thank you for telling me tonight, not making me wait."

He nodded.

"So . . . if it isn't Brittlyn, I assume it's Molly Shaw?"

"I'm sorry, I can't—"

"It's okay. I can guess." She waved her hand. "Who else's dental records would y'all have on hand for comparison?"

Grant just looked at her, deeply regretting that this woman had had a crash course in investigative procedures during the past year.

Brittlyn's disappearance had upended her life, derailed her job, destroyed her marriage. Her entire world had fallen away, and the only thing left was the unrelenting search for her daughter.

"And Agent Woods? What does she think?" Rachel asked.

"About . . . ?"

"This development. Molly Shaw. I assume it's a homicide?"

"At this time I can't—"

"I know, I know. You can't officially tell me yet. But we *know* it's a homicide, right? I mean, I heard one of the park rangers talking about the pile of rocks she was buried under, so—"

"Ma'am, I need to caution you about sharing details like that. It could hurt our investigation."

She looked down. "I know. I understand. I'm just saying this to you." She met his gaze, and the pain in her eyes put a tight knot in his chest. "The last thing in the world I want to do is mess anything up for y'all. I just hope that the FBI is *realizing* what all this means, in context. I hope investigators are *zeroing in on the pattern here*." She stared up at him. "Are you?"

"Again, I can't—"

She held up a hand. "Please do *not* say the words 'cannot discuss an ongoing investigation' to me. I swear to God, I'll throw up."

"I understand your frustration."

Her eyes widened. "No, you don't. You couldn't possibly." She took a deep breath and seemed to compose herself. "But I really do appreciate your talking to me tonight."

"Of course."

"Not 'of course.' No one else will even give me the time of day—not the sheriff, not the FBI. It's unprofessional."

He stared at her, ashamed of his colleagues because he knew she was right.

"Anyway, thank you," she said. "Call me as soon as you have any more news you can share."

Grant had no idea when that would be, but he gave a confident nod.

"I will."

CHAPTER

ELEVEN

AVA TIPPED HER head back and watched the boy scale the wall with dizzying speed.

"Welcome to Elevation. Can I help you?"

She glanced at the young woman behind the counter.

"I'm here to watch," Ava told her. "Do I need a wristband?"

"Watch all you want. If you decide to climb, we can check you in."

"Thanks."

The climbing gym didn't look like much from the road, but the giant warehouse was a popular summer destination, apparently. Ava skirted around a group of kids donning orange helmets and stepped into the main room. The cavernous space had eight separate rock walls of various heights, all peppered with brightly colored climbing holds. At the center of the gym was an enormous purple-and-yellow boulder surrounded by foam mats. Ava walked around the fake rock and approached the highest climbing wall, where a man with a long brown ponytail crawled up like a spider.

"You want to try it?"

Ava turned around to see a woman in an orange Elevation T-shirt watching her from beside a rack of helmets. Ava studied her face and glanced at her name tag to be sure.

"Just visiting today." Ava walked over. "Are you Skye Jennings?"

"That's me."

"I'm Ava Burch. We spoke on the phone?"

"Oh yeah." She frowned and glanced at her sports watch. "You're early. Let me get a break and I'll be right with you."

She crossed the gym and talked to a tall guy at one of the other walls. Then she grabbed a thermos off the floor and returned to Ava.

Skye Jennings had the short, compact build of a gymnast. She wore her dark hair in a loose bun, and her sun-browned skin suggested that she preferred to climb outdoors rather than in a gym.

"Thanks for meeting with me," Ava said.

"Sure. I only have a few minutes, though. We've got a summer camp coming this morning and we're about to get slammed."

"I'll make it quick." Ava smiled.

Skye led her across the gym to a stack of folded floor mats. She took a swig from her thermos and gave Ava a once-over, probably not sure of what to make of Ava's tailored jeans and silk blouse. Everyone else in here was wearing shorts or yoga pants.

"So," Skye said. "How did you find me, anyway?"

"Your name was mentioned in several newspaper articles," Ava told her. "The one about Molly Shaw and also the one about the candlelight vigil for Deanna Moore. I just had a few questions I wanted to ask."

"But you're *not* a reporter? I really don't want to be quoted again."

"I'm not a reporter, I promise." Ava had assured her of that over the phone. Molly Shaw's death had just hit the news, and Ava guessed reporters had been trying to get quotes from locals. "I'm friends with Rachel Spencer. I'm sure you've heard about the search for her daughter, Brittlyn, who went missing last summer. I'm helping her gather information."

Skye's expression turned somber. "I didn't know Brittlyn. Just Deanna and Molly."

"That's fine. I just wanted to ask a little about them."

She nodded.

"So . . . the news article mentioned that you knew Molly from Elevation?"

"She was a member here," Skye said. "She joined up, let's see, the spring after she moved here? This was a couple years ago."

"And I know Deanna was a climber, too. Was she a member here as well?"

"Not Deanna."

"No?" Ava was surprised.

"Deanna was way beyond what we have here. She did big walls in, like, Zion and Yosemite. Our setup here is really more for recreation."

"I see." Ava adjusted her assumptions. When she'd discovered that Skye worked at a rock climbing gym and that she was friends with both Molly and Deanna, she had assumed all three women were connected through the gym. "So . . . if you didn't meet Deanna here then where—"

"We were in a climbing club together. That's how I ended up in the search party over in Big Bend when Deanna went missing. We'd been camping there together the week before."

Ava tugged a notepad from her purse. "Would you mind

if I write this down? I want to make sure I get the details right."

"Sure." Skye watched as Ava jotted down some notes. "Like I said, I never knew Brittlyn, though. She wasn't in my circle of friends."

"Okay. What's your circle of friends like?"

"You know, outdoor types. Climbers, river guides, mountain bikers. People into extreme sports. There's a lot of us around here."

"And Molly hung out with y'all?"

"Sometimes. I met her at work and introduced her to some of my friends."

Ava stopped writing. "Molly worked here?"

"No. Sorry. I meant my other job. I also worked at Whitehorse Ranch back then. That's where I first met Molly. I'm the one who convinced her to join the gym."

"And Whitehorse Ranch is . . . where, exactly?"

"It's a few miles west of here. You may have seen the sign."

"Is it a cattle ranch or—"

"No." She smiled. "It's a wellness retreat. Think of a dude ranch, but with yoga and meditation. Molly and I cleaned cabins there. Deanna worked there for a while, too, but she was in the kitchen."

Ava jotted it down. "And this was, what, two summers ago?"

"Deanna was there when I hired on, so . . . a little over three years ago? Then Molly started the following spring. She originally came out here on a road trip and she decided to stay in Cuervo, but she was low on money. The ranch had an opening in housekeeping. The pay wasn't great, but the tips were pretty good, so it wasn't a bad gig."

"Do you still work there?"

"Not since they gave me full-time hours here." She glanced over her shoulder. "Speaking of, my manager needs me back. I have to go."

"I understand."

"I wish I could help more, but I didn't know Brittlyn at all. I really feel for her mom, though."

"Me, too."

Skye looked over her shoulder again but seemed reluctant to leave.

"I watched what Deanna's parents went through when we were searching for her," she told Ava. "All the waiting and worrying. We searched the park for an entire week. It was agonizing. Thank goodness for dogs."

"Dogs?"

"Yeah, you know, it was a search dog that found her at the base of that cliff. I thought it would be one of the drone cameras because they were using so many, but it ended up being a dog." Skye shook her head. "The whole thing was a nightmare for everyone, especially her parents. I can't imagine how Brittlyn's family must feel after all this time."

Ava didn't have to imagine it. She'd met with Rachel Spencer twice now, and she knew that the pain of having a child missing dominated every aspect of Rachel's life. Her search for Brittlyn had become an obsession.

Skye grabbed her thermos. "I have to go."

"Thanks for making time for me."

"Sure. Tell Brittlyn's mom I'm praying for her."

"I will."

She started to walk away, then turned back. "You know . . . for what it's worth, I never bought the story about Deanna."

"The story?"

"The story that she fell. I know it's in the official report and everything, but to me it doesn't make sense."

A feeling of dread settled in Ava's stomach.

"Why not?"

"Just . . . everyone who knew Deanna knew she was super careful. I mean, she could handle these monster walls out west. And she was extremely safety-conscious, always dialed in. It's just never made sense to me that she slipped and fell."

"What do you think happened?"

"I don't know," Skye said. "But not that."

IT WAS STRAIGHT-UP noon when Grant stepped into the law offices of McCullough & Burch. He was greeted with the clatter of cowbell and an overexcited dog. Huck rushed up to him and danced around at his feet. Today he had on rainbow fairy wings with glittery silver straps.

"*No*, Huck. You have to lie down."

A little girl got up from the coffee table where she had a coloring book and crayons spread out. She had curly brown hair and wore a pink princess dress over her T-shirt.

"Hello, there," Grant said.

"Hello. My mom's not here and Samantha's at lunch."

He cast a glance down the hall and noticed the closed door. "Do you know if Ms. Burch is here?"

"Are you a policeman?" she asked, staring at his badge and gun.

"I work for the sheriff's office."

She looked blank.

"It's a type of policeman."

"Oh. Is Ava in trouble?"

"Nope. I'm Grant, by the way. Ava's friend."

"I'm Lucy. Ava's talking on the phone. That's why her door is closed."

Huck nudged him with his snout, and Grant reached down to scratch his ears.

The girl smiled. "He likes you."

"Yeah, we're buddies. We've done some hiking together."

"Phone calls usually take a while. You can sit on the sofa if you want." She went back to the coffee table, and Huck followed. "Or we have a Keurig for guests."

Ava's door opened and she poked her head out. "Lucy—

Oh. Hi." She stepped into the hallway, and Grant could tell he'd caught her totally off guard.

"Got your message," he said. "I was passing through town, so I thought I'd just swing by."

"Oh. Good." She stepped into the reception room. Today she wore white jeans and a silky gray top that shimmered when she moved. "Lucy, hon, did you get some lunch?"

"Mom's bringing me nuggets."

Huck did a few circles and plopped down beside her, maybe sensing there was a nugget in his future.

"This is Lucy, Jenna's daughter. Lucy, did you meet Mr. Wycoff?"

"His name is Grant."

Ava looked at him and smirked. "Grant, can I offer you some coffee? Or a bottle of water?"

"I'm fine, thanks."

She leaned around him. "Lucy, we're going to sit in the conference room, okay?"

"Okay."

Ava led him down the hallway. The first open door was a conference room, and she gestured for him to go in.

"Have a seat. I'll be right back."

The conference room had a large window that looked out on Main Street. The blinds were mostly shut, but Grant adjusted them anyway, just for the hell of it. He didn't need anyone speculating about what he was doing at a law office in Cuervo.

"Thanks for stopping by," Ava said as she stepped into the room and closed the door. She looked good, and he couldn't believe he hadn't found a way to see her since three days ago when he'd gone by her house.

"No problem." Grant pulled out one of the six leather chairs and sat down. "What's up?"

She dropped a file folder and legal pad onto the table. The top sheet of yellow paper was filled with notes, and Grant felt a prickle of foreboding. Ava's message hadn't said what she wanted to talk about, only that it "pertained to the case"—which he assumed meant Molly Shaw.

"Sure you don't want coffee?"

"I'm good. What's up?"

She was nervous. He could tell. And his sense of foreboding grew stronger.

"Well." She sat down across from him and scooted up her chair. "I've been doing a little research."

"About?"

"Molly Shaw."

"Why?"

She drew back, looking surprised that he would ask.

"Well, because I thought it might be helpful." She smiled. "During law school, I got really good at online research. There are all sorts of search tools available to lawyers."

Grant just looked at her.

"Anyway, I found a few interesting facts that I thought I'd pass along." She cleared her throat and flipped through several pages on her legal pad.

"First off, I know you're looking for people who spent time with Molly right before her disappearance."

"Why do you say that?"

She glanced up. "What, that you're looking for people who spent time with Molly?"

"Yes."

"Well . . . isn't it obvious? If you're investigating her death, you want to put together a timeline of who—"

"So, you just came up with that?"

"Yes." She looked at him for a long moment. If she registered his annoyance, she didn't show it. She glanced down at her notes again.

"I came across the name Skye Jennings. She and Molly Shaw were members of the same climbing gym here in Cuervo. It's called Elevation."

"How do you know this?" Grant asked.

"Skye was quoted in one of the news articles from when

Molly went missing." Ava opened the manila folder and
flipped through a stack of printouts. She tugged out a
printed article from the *Henley Herald*, their semiweekly
paper. "See?" She passed him the story and tapped on a
passage highlighted in yellow. "The reporter quotes her
here, along with some others, and she says she knows Molly
from her climbing gym. So, I got to thinking about rock
climbing. It's an interesting connection, don't you think?"

Grant skimmed the article.

"I mean, Molly Shaw liked to rock climb. Deanna
Moore *died* while she was rock climbing."

Grant looked at her.

"And here's the thing. Skye was friends with both of
them." She opened the file again and pulled out another
news article, this one in the *El Paso Times*. **CANDLE-
LIGHT VIGIL HELD FOR MISSING CLIMBER**, read the
headline. The photo showed a trio of young women holding
candles. It was dark outside, and their faces were lit from
below. Ava tapped the girl in the middle.

"This is Skye. She's quoted in this article as well. So,
obviously, she's someone you want to talk to."

"Why 'obviously'?"

"What do you mean?"

"I mean, why do you assume I want to talk to this
woman?"

Ava blinked at him like he was slow on the uptake.
"Well, because. She was friends with both victims."

"Deanna Moore was the victim of a fall. Her death was
ruled an accident by the medical examiner."

"Well, some people think that's debatable."

"Who?"

"Rachel Spencer, for one. She feels adamant that Deanna
Moore's death wasn't an accident." Ava leaned back in her
chair. "And there's been chatter online—"

"I've heard it. I know about the chatter. And speculation.
But as an investigator, I deal in facts."

"Why are you getting defensive?"

"I don't need random civilians meddling in my case."

"Rachel Spencer is the mother of a missing woman. She's not random, she's directly involved." Ava paused. "And if you're familiar with the chatter, then you must know that people are speculating about Molly's and Brittlyn's disappearances being connected. And that Deanna Moore's death may be connected, too."

Grant just looked at her, trying to rein in his temper. He'd been hearing this gossip for years and it had only flared up again with the discovery of Molly Shaw's remains. None of the speculation was new, but he wasn't sure why it ticked him off to hear it coming from Ava.

"Listen, I appreciate what you're trying to do."

She rolled her eyes. "Please don't tell me you're too stubborn to accept help."

"I accept help all the time. I'm part of a *joint task force* investigating Molly Shaw's death that includes people from four different law enforcement agencies. What I don't need is help from armchair detectives."

Her lips clamped into a thin line.

"Fine." She snatched up the news clippings and returned them to the folder, then slapped it shut. "Here's the research I did." She slid the folder toward him. "Go through it yourself. See if you don't think Skye Jennings is someone you should interview. See if you don't notice some interesting *connections* between these three cases, starting with the fact that Molly Shaw and Deanna Moore both worked at the same place."

Grant glanced down at the folder. "Where'd you hear that?"

"From Skye. That's where she met both of them."

"How do you know?"

"Because I *talked* to the girl. I asked her if she met Deanna at the same climbing gym where she met Molly, and she said no, Deanna didn't climb there. But it just so happens that all three of them worked at Whitehorse Ranch at one time or another. Deanna and Molly didn't overlap, but Skye overlapped with both of them."

Grant just looked at her.

"You didn't know about Whitehorse Ranch?"

"No."

"It's a nearby dude ranch. Or something like that. I haven't had a chance to look into it yet."

"No, I know about the ranch. I just didn't know they had worked there."

She took a deep breath. "Just read the file, okay? I took notes on all of it."

"Why are you spending your time on this?"

"Because I'm invested, all right? I traipsed all over that damn park searching for any sign of a missing woman. And then I talked to Brittlyn Spencer's mom. And I think she's right. There something weird about three young women, three summers in a row, disappearing from the parks in this area. I think Rachel Spencer is onto something. Maybe they're all connected."

Grant just looked at her, the knot in his chest tightening.

Ava pushed her chair back. "Read the file for yourself. I hope it helps."

She stood up. Grant stood, too, and gazed down at the thick manila folder. She'd compiled a lot in the few short days since Molly's remains had been discovered.

"Go on, take it," she said, opening the conference room door. "No sense wasting good research."

Grant picked up the file because he agreed. And also because he wanted it out of her hands. Ava's research project ticked him off. He wasn't sure why, exactly, but it did, and he wanted her to drop the whole thing.

He tucked the folder under his arm. "All right, well, I'll let you get back to work."

"You're welcome," she said pointedly as he stepped through the door.

CHAPTER

TWELVE

CONNOR SPRAYED DOWN the floor mat and tossed it onto the sidewalk to dry.

"We haven't even talked about motive." He looked at Grant.

"I know."

Grant sat on the picnic table near the car wash station, wolfing down a cheeseburger. He'd hit a drive-through on his way back in and gotten lunch for Connor, too, but Connor hadn't touched his yet. He wasn't ready to eat until he washed the vomit out of the SUV he grabbed from the motor pool today. Someone must have used it to transport a drunk last night and then clocked out without cleaning up the mess.

"What about the ex?" Connor asked.

"What about him?"

"Well, they'd just gotten divorced, right? Maybe he had a beef with Molly—she cheated on him, he got ripped off in the divorce, whatever—and he tracked her down here seeking revenge," Connor said.

"And then somehow located her in a fifty-two-thousand-acre park?"

A couple of uniformed deputies walked by, and Connor shot them a look, wondering if either had been driving the puke-mobile recently.

"Hey, either of you guys have this ride last night?"

They stopped and turned.

"No. Why?" the younger one asked—a rookie named Diaz.

"You know who was on graveyard last night?"

"No idea. Why?"

"No reason." He saluted them. "Carry on."

The rookies walked off, and Connor focused on Grant again.

"So . . . maybe Molly and her ex went to Silver Canyon park together," Connor said. "Maybe he told her he wanted to reconnect and patch things up or some BS, and then he got her alone in the middle of nowhere and killed her."

Grant shook his head. "Doesn't add up." He sipped from his straw, and Connor suddenly felt thirsty. "If he wanted to kill her, why not go after her when she was in Denver instead of driving all the way here and hunting her down in the back of beyond? Also, Molly's brother doesn't think the ex is a suspect. He says Molly told him they had an 'amicable divorce.'"

Connor snorted. "No such thing. When everything's amicable, people don't split. What do you know about why they got divorced?"

"Her brother said it was financial stress. And they were having fertility problems, too, which was why Molly went into a depression. He said she was in a real funk and thought a road trip through the Great American West might help her hit reset."

A lot of people came out here thinking the exact same thing. Some of them liked it so much they ended up staying, too. But their problems had a way of following them here.

"The other thing is, if Molly's ex did it, that doesn't explain the others."

Connor hosed down the splatter on the door. How had some deputy not noticed this before he turned in his vehicle?

Connor looked at Grant. "So, you definitely think Molly and Brittlyn are connected," he stated.

"I do."

"Shit."

"Yeah."

Connor slammed shut the door and rolled up the hose.

"And possibly the climber, Deanna Moore."

Connor stopped what he was doing. "The climber?"

"You've heard the rumors."

"Yeah, *rumors*. Since when do we care about Twitter rumors?"

"I took another look at Deanna Moore's autopsy report."

Connor's stomach sank. There was something to this, then. Grant was a good investigator. In fact, he was gifted. If he'd spotted something worth worrying about, then Connor was worried.

"What is it?"

"The report says she had all these bone fractures consistent with a fall or drop from a high elevation. Seventeen bone fractures, including her skull."

Connor grimaced. "Damn."

"Yeah. But one in particular stood out to me. Her arm was fractured. A spiral fracture on the right humerus."

"You've lost me."

Grant had the courtesy not to look annoyed that he wasn't following.

"So, back when I worked for Dallas PD, I was with the special victims division," Grant said. "We handled a lot of domestics. I remember seeing several kids and women with spiral fractures. You know, they turn their back on someone and he grabs their arm and wrenches them around."

"So, you're saying she struggled with someone before she fell?"

"Or before she was pushed. That's what it looks like to me."

"I don't know," Connor said. "Why wouldn't the ME call it out, though? He ruled it 'accidental.'"

"Hell if I know. For that matter, how can he be so sure it wasn't a suicide? Point is, I'm not putting a lot of stock in the ME's opinion over there, at least on this particular case. Maybe he took the path of least resistance and wrote it up as an accident."

"Why? It's his job to get it right."

"Yeah, well. You may remember that the sheriff was running for reelection that year," Grant said. "That search was all over the news and there was a lot of pressure to wrap up the case."

"Sounds familiar."

"Yep."

Donovan was facing reelection in the fall, and his campaign had already ramped up. Connor didn't like to think about politics affecting the sheriff's decisions.

He tipped his head back and sighed. There was something deeply depressing about questioning the integrity of the people above him.

"You know, I hate this crap," Connor said.

"Same."

Grant offered him the food bag. Connor opened it up and grabbed some French fries. He was suddenly hungry now that he'd gotten rid of the vomit smell.

"So, how's Ava?" he asked as he chewed.

Grant just looked at him.

"I don't know," he said after a long moment.

"Why not?"

Grant shook his head. "I've been buried with this thing. I've hardly been home in four days. Not a lot of time left over for other stuff."

"Other stuff like . . . a life?"

"You know what I mean. It's not a good time to start something."

"When is it ever?" Connor grabbed some more fries. "We're always buried with one thing or another. It never stops. If you like her, you should just go with it."

Grant tipped his head to the side and looked at him. "When was the last time you dated someone again?"

Connor smiled.

"No, remind me. Was it, like, three years ago?"

He wasn't far off, but Connor just shrugged. "We're talking about you, not me. If you don't make your move, someone else will."

Grant's gaze narrowed, and Connor laughed.

"Relax. I'm not talking about me. But someone."

T HE ORNAMENT ON the wrought iron gate was a rearing horse, and Ava eyed it with interest as she turned onto the driveway.

She had planned to simply drive past and take a look. But the wide-open gate seemed to beckon her, and she decided she had time for a quick stop.

The dirt road sloped down and curved around a high stone bluff. She rounded a bend, and the view opened up. Across a grassy plain was a line of trees, and she could see red tile rooftops peeking through the foliage.

Ava followed the narrow road to a long, low-slung ranch house made of Texas limestone. A wrought iron arch with the horse logo marked the entrance to a gravel lot beside it. Ava selected a shady spot beneath an oak tree and parked next to a white pickup with oversize tires.

She checked her watch. Almost two. She had a conference call in an hour, but she'd keep this brief and be back to the office by three, no problem.

The building's rustic wooden door was shaded by an overhang. Ava mounted the stone steps and looked for a bell or knocker. She didn't see one—only a black handle made from a horseshoe.

She stepped inside. The interior was cool and dim and smelled of sandalwood. Ava took off her sunglasses and scanned the space and was startled to see a young woman watching her with a smile.

"Namaste," she said.

"Hello." Ava smiled back. "I heard about your retreat from a friend and thought I'd stop by to get some info."

The woman's serene expression didn't change. She had dark corkscrew curls and wore a pale blue scarf that matched her eyes. Her desk was made from the cross section of a tree, and a silver laptop sat open in front of her.

"Do you have a brochure or something?" Ava glanced around the reception room, noting the conspicuous lack of furniture. There were no chairs for visitors, only a small glass coffee table with an incense stick smoldering in a bamboo tray.

"We're paperless. But I'd be happy to share an overview, and you can visit our website to learn more." The woman flowed to her feet—*flowed* was the only way to describe it—and held out her hand. "I'm Kyra, by the way."

Ava shook her hand and noticed she wore all white. Her formfitting top, her yoga pants, even her flip-flops were white.

"Nice to meet you. I was on your site yesterday, actually." It had been long on photos and short on information. "I didn't notice any prices, but maybe I missed something?"

"Oh no. That's intentional. Each guest's stay is custom-tailored to their spiritual goals. What sort of retreat are you thinking about?"

"Well—" She scrambled to remember the misty photos of stones and sunrises and beautiful people meditating. "I was thinking one of the yoga ones? Or—I don't know—what else do you offer?"

"We have a variety," Kyra said, "all lasting between four and thirty days. There's Chakra Awakening, Mindful Meditation. We also offer Week of Fasting, Fruits and Fertility, the Sunrise Retreat. Those are just some of our most popular ones. And we can combine several to fit your goals. Except the fasting program, obviously."

"And prices?"

"It varies. But we start at five hundred."

Ava nodded.

"That's per night."

"Per *night*? Even the fasting one?"

She looked apologetic. "I know it sounds expensive. But all of our experiences are designed to increase strength and focus, and bolster positivity. You should read our testimonials." She tilted her head to the side. "Would you like to see our meditation pavilion?"

"Sure."

"Just fill out this form." She grabbed an iPad from the bookshelf behind her, swiped at the screen, and handed over the tablet. Ava filled in her name and left the other fields blank, but Kyra didn't seem to notice when Ava handed it back.

"Right this way," Kyra said.

"Thanks."

The woman led her through a heavy wooden door and stepped outside onto a patio.

Ava stopped short. "Whoa."

"I know, right?" Kyra smiled at her over her shoulder. "The view never gets old."

The green took her breath away. There was so *much* of it. Ava walked to the edge of the patio and stared out at the verdant lawn sloping down to a tree-lined creek. Since moving out here she'd gotten used to dusty browns and grays, plus bright blue skies and canyons that could glow

pink at sunset. But green—rich, vivid *green* in abundance—
was rare around here.

"What creek is that?" Ava asked.

"That's Juniper Creek. It's spring-fed and it runs through
the property."

That explained the water, which had been scarce here
during the drought. In addition to a scenic focal point, the
creek was evidently providing irrigation, because the lawn
looked like a golf course.

"And how big is the property?" Ava asked.

"Four hundred fifty-two acres."

"Wow."

"This way," Kyra said, leading her down a flagstone path
to a pointy white tent in the center of the lawn. People stood
beneath the tent with their hands uplifted in a way that
made Ava think of a religious revival. But on closer inspec-
tion, she realized they were doing yoga. Tadasana pose?
Ava couldn't remember. She hadn't touched a yoga mat in
years.

Ava skimmed her gaze over the people. The vast major-
ity were women, but there were a few men mixed in. Everyone moved in sync, and she could tell they were mostly
young and exceptionally limber.

"Have you participated in a wellness retreat before?"
Kyra paused beside a cobalt blue planter overflowing with
yellow zinnias.

"No." Ava smiled at her. "I've always wanted to, though."

"This group is Chakra Awakening."

Ava watched as everyone glided into another pose. The
instructor had her back to Ava as she led the group through
their movements. The woman wore all white, like Kyra, and
her thick auburn ponytail trailed down her back. She pivoted to the side, and Ava noticed her basketball-size bump.

"She's pregnant."

"What?" Kyra followed Ava's gaze. "Oh yeah. That's
Willow, one of the owners. She trained in India."

Ava winced as the woman twisted herself into a pretzel.

"Would you like to see the stables? We're known for our equestrian programs."

"Sure. But then I need to get going."

The stables were painted red, like the nearby barn. Ava noticed a smaller red barn just down the road. A white van with the horse logo on the side pulled up to the barn as an automatic door whisked open.

"Two barns?" Ava looked at Kyra. "How many horses do you have here?"

"The smaller one is a hay barn." Kyra opened the gate just enough for Ava to squeeze through, then resecured the metal latch. Ava kept her eyes peeled for some stable workers or ranch hands, or any other man that might have interacted with Deanna or Molly here on the property. But so far almost everyone she'd seen had been female.

"We've got nine horses altogether," Kyra said. "Mares mostly and a couple of foals. Oh, and Starlight. He's a gelding."

A chestnut horse grazed in a paddock. Ava walked to the fence, and he lifted his head to look at her.

"He's beautiful," Ava said, reaching her hand through the slats. "Here, boy."

A chime emanated from the pocket of Kyra's yoga pants, and she pulled out a phone. "I'm sorry, I have to take this. You mind?"

"No problem. Is there a restroom I could use?"

"Sure." She nodded toward a row of small stone buildings. "Right there, near the casitas."

"Be right back." Ava walked off, glancing around as she went. She wanted some time to herself without a guide. She surveyed the row of casitas, each with a small front porch and a wooden rocking chair. Were these the cabins Molly had cleaned as part of the housekeeping crew?

Ava headed for the restrooms and picked the side marked with a *W* made from horseshoes. She had a bit of a compulsion about restrooms. Many of her clients were caring for aging parents, and she always advised them that if they were choosing a nursing home, they should check out the restrooms. You could learn a lot about a place based on the condition of the bathrooms.

Ava opened the door. A woman at the sink jumped and turned around.

"Oh, excuse me," Ava said.

The woman pressed her hand to her chest. "Dang, you scared me." She tucked an airplane-size liquor bottle into the zipper pack clipped around her waist. "I thought you were one of the staff."

"Nope. Just visiting." Ava stepped to the other sink and started washing her hands, watching the woman in the mirror. She had short brown hair and flushed cheeks and wore an oversize T-shirt instead of a strappy sports bra, which seemed to be the uniform here.

"I swear, I don't know how I let my sister talk me into this," she said. "Meat free. Sugar free. Alcohol free. *Fun* free." She screwed the top on her thermos.

"Which package did you get?" Ava asked.

"Meditation." She rolled her eyes. "I thought it would be restful. Ha. Thank God it's only four days."

Ava glanced down and noticed the sticker burrs clinging to her leggings.

"You look like you'd be able to handle the yoga part," the woman went on. "At least you're in shape." She dabbed a paper towel across her forehead. "But do yourself a favor and read the fine print."

Ava smiled. "Thanks for the tip."

She scooted around Ava and tossed her towel in the trash can. "Good luck!"

As the door whisked shut, Ava checked her watch.

Crap. How had she been here half an hour already? She hurried back to find Kyra leaning against the fence and stroking Starlight's nose.

"Ready for the tour?" she asked brightly.

"I'm sorry, but time got away from me, and I have to get back. Maybe another time?"

"Sure."

"You have a business card or something? I could call you if I have any questions?"

Kyra smiled. "No cards, sorry."

"Oh, that's right. Paperless." Ava dug into her purse. "How about I give you one of mine and you can write down your email for me in case I have any questions?"

Kyra took the card and read it. "You're an attorney?"

"That's right."

"I didn't know Cuervo had any."

"We do now. You know anyone who needs legal advice?" She lifted an eyebrow. "Maybe."

"Here's a few extra. Feel free to hand them out." Ava smiled. "I just moved to the area, and I'm taking new clients."

G RANT STEPPED ONTO the porch of Cuervo Outfitters and put on his sunglasses. Another wasted stop. The last few days had been filled with them, and the lack of progress was making him antsy.

He descended the steps and caught sight of Ava striding down the sidewalk across the street. She had an armload of groceries and a cell phone pressed to her ear.

Today she wore another slim-fitting skirt, this one long, and her hair was in a knot on top of her head. He'd learned that this was her courthouse attire.

Grant's pulse picked up as he watched her. Ava stood out here—everything about her—and he noticed all the heads turning as she balanced the groceries on her hip and pulled open the door to her little red car.

If you don't make your move, someone else will.

His gut clenched as he thought of Connor's words. What

was that about? Since when did he take relationship advice from Connor? The man hadn't dated in years, let alone been in a serious relationship.

Ava ended her call, and Grant watched as she tucked her phone into the top of her blouse. Did she have a pocket, or did she slide it right into her bra?

He crossed the street as she loaded the grocery bags. She caught sight of him over the roof of her car, and interest flared in her eyes.

Or maybe that was his hopeful imagination.

"Hey," he said, stopping beside her.

"Hi there. I was just about to call you."

"Oh yeah?"

"I had a conversation yesterday that I thought you'd be interested in."

His gaze narrowed. "Oh yeah?" he said again, but with a different tone. Why did he suddenly get the impression that her "conversation" had something to do with his homicide investigation?

The investigation she'd said she wasn't meddling in anymore.

"Does this conversation pertain to my case?" he asked.

She gave a nonchalant shrug, which he took to mean yes. "Maybe, maybe not."

"I thought you said you were dropping that?" he asked.

"I don't remember saying that."

Grant looked away, trying to swallow his annoyance. Their last conversation had ended on a sour note over this same issue, and he didn't want another day of radio silence as he tried to think of an excuse to talk to her so he could smooth things over.

Hell, he hated playing games. He looked her in the eye.

"How about dinner tonight?" he asked. "You can tell me about it."

Wariness flashed across her face, but she didn't reply.

"Do you have plans?" he asked.

"No."

"So . . . you want to have dinner, then?"

She just looked up at him, clearly debating something in her mind as she bit her lower lip.

He smiled slightly and leaned closer. "It's a simple question."

"No, it's not."

Grant braced himself for rejection. He didn't usually have to work this hard. Really, he never did. He stared down at her, waiting for her answer. His attention dropped to the phone she'd tucked into her lacy white bra, and God help him, he'd never wanted a woman to say yes so badly.

"Do you like chili?" she asked.

"Chili?"

"You know. Meat, veggies, spices."

"Sounds really good."

"I was planning to have chili tonight if you'd like to join me. At my house," she added.

He'd figured that, but his pulse picked up anyway. The last time he'd been to her house, all he'd been able to think about was her bedroom just off the kitchen. But work had interfered, like it always did.

Ava looked at him, and heat sparked in her eyes, as if she knew the direction his thoughts had taken.

"I'd love to come," he said. "Can I bring anything?"

"Just yourself."

"I have a task force meeting at six. It'll probably take about an hour."

"That's fine. I have some errands to run, and I won't even get home till six, anyway. How about eight?"

He nodded.

She slid behind the wheel and looked up at him. "Eight o'clock. Don't be late."

CHAPTER
THIRTEEN

A VA PUT THE call on speaker and pulled on an oven mitt. "Thanks for calling me back," she told Rachel.

"No problem. What's up?"

Ava opened the oven and checked the cornbread. Not quite done. She glanced at the clock and felt a flutter of nerves.

"Well, I wanted to run something by you," she said to Rachel. "Do you have a minute?"

"Yeah."

"I was wondering if Brittlyn ever mentioned anything to you about a wellness retreat? Maybe working at one or attending one?"

"What's a wellness retreat?"

"It's kind of like a health spa. Located on a ranch, in this case. They offer yoga, meditation, juice cleanses, that kind of thing."

"Sounds expensive," Rachel said.

"It is."

"Brittlyn never mentioned anything like that to me. Why do you ask?"

Ava glanced at the map spread out on her coffee table. She'd been reading up on some of the local lore surrounding area landmarks.

Ava cleared her throat. "Well . . . this may sound a little far-fetched. It's just a thought."

Rachel sighed. "My daughter's been missing for almost a year, Ava. She vanished into thin air. Over the last twelve months I've consulted psychics and palm readers. I've researched portals and cryptozoology. Nothing is too far-fetched for me." Her voice got quieter. "When you think your child's been murdered . . . there's no alternative you won't consider."

Ava felt a sharp pang of empathy. "I'm so sorry for what you're going through."

"Thank you. Now, tell me your thought."

"There's this ranch in the area that does wellness retreats. They offer all these different packages that are designed to 'uplift the mind' and provide 'spiritual clarity.' Some of them are supposed to recharge your life energy and provide other benefits."

"Well, Brittlyn's not into all that woo-woo stuff. She's about the most down-to-earth girl you could ever meet."

"I hear you. But one of the programs—the Sunrise Retreat—is a weeklong experience that culminates in a two-day hike in Silver Canyon State Park. The destination is a place called Sun Rock and it's supposed to be an energy vortex."

"Huh."

"Also, it isn't too far from where Molly Shaw was found. And I just thought . . . I don't know. It seemed like an interesting coincidence."

No response. Ava waited patiently, holding her breath.

"What about Big Bend? Do they do any hikes out there?" Rachel asked.

"Not that I'm aware of. I'm still reading up on the different programs. Another thing I learned is that Molly and Deanna both worked at this place. Molly was a housekeeper and Deanna worked in the kitchen. Did Brittlyn ever mention taking a job while she was out here? Maybe to earn a little extra money?"

"No. But that doesn't mean she didn't." Rachel sighed. "It's one of my biggest regrets about all this."

Ava waited for her to explain.

"Brittlyn went off on this big road trip, and she didn't tell me everything she was up to. I know there were some drugs, some boys. But when she called on the phone, she mostly talked about the hiking and camping. I should have asked for more details about who she was with and what she was doing." She sighed. "But I can make some inquiries. I'll get in touch with a few of her friends and ask if they know anything about a wellness retreat."

"Ask them if Brittlyn ever mentioned Whitehorse Ranch. It's about fifteen minutes west of Cuervo."

"White*horse* Ranch?"

"That's right."

"Brittlyn loves horses, ever since she was a girl. Anything to do with horses would have caught her attention for sure." Excitement filled her voice now. "That's really the name of it?"

"Yes. Their logo is a rearing horse."

"I'll reach out to a few people and ask about it."

Her voice sounded so hopeful, and Ava wondered if she'd made a mistake here. Maybe she should have vetted this idea more before bringing it up with Brittlyn's mom.

"I know what you're thinking, and don't," Rachel said.

"Don't what?"

"Don't regret telling me this. That's why I'm here—to follow up on leads that are either too vague or too out there for the police to deal with. These sheriff's offices around here are overworked and underfunded, and they can't

follow up on everything. Not like I can. I've come to terms
with that fact. Makes me sick, but I've come to terms with
it. In a perfect world, they'd have unlimited resources to
devote to Brittlyn, but that's not the world we live in, is it?"

Ava stared down at the map she'd been studying of Silver
Canyon park. Brittlyn had last been seen hiking in Big Bend.
But what if she'd ended up in Silver Canyon somehow?

"Rachel, do you mind if I ask . . ." She trailed off, not
sure how to phrase it tactfully.

"Ask me anything."

"Do you have a hunch, or maybe a mother's instinct,
about what might have happened with Brittlyn?"

The phone went quiet, and Ava regretted asking. But
Rachel knew her daughter better than anyone. Certainly
better than the West Texas cops investigating her bizarre
disappearance.

"I pray that I'm wrong, but . . . I think a predator could
have taken her. The human kind."

Ava closed her eyes.

"I think about it all the time. I dream about it. I hope I'm
wrong, but the possibility haunts me every minute."

She didn't know what to say to that.

"I'll let you go now," Rachel said. "I've got some calls to
make."

They hung up, and Ava stared down at her map for a
long moment.

Then she remembered the cornbread.

"Crap!"

She rushed into the kitchen and yanked open the oven.
The cornbread hadn't burned, thank goodness. It was a rich
golden brown with a nice split across the top, like her mother's always had. Ava set the cast-iron skillet on the stovetop
and glanced at the clock.

Her stomach knotted.

There was no getting around it. She'd been ignoring it

for twenty minutes, then forty minutes, then an hour. But the cold reality was staring her in the face now. He was late, and Ava knew what that meant. He probably wasn't coming.

And worse, he hadn't even called.

The knot in her stomach tightened. She took the lid off the pot and stirred the simmering chili.

Why had she done this to herself? She should have known better.

She *did* know better.

And yet still, she'd rushed home from work and showered and put on *makeup*, damn it. She'd squeezed into her favorite jeans and cleaned her house and made her mother's chili recipe. She'd even caved in to Lucy's begging and let her and Jenna take Huck home so Lucy could give him a bath and play with him tonight.

Ava stirred the chili as thoughts swirled through her head. *You know how this goes. He's not coming. He got "tied up" or "lost track of time" or "something came up."*

A sour stew of anger and hurt and embarrassment churned inside her.

Klink.

Ava froze. What was that? She stepped to the window above the sink and peered out. Maybe it was an armadillo poking around again? But she saw nothing out there, only shadowy bushes and the glow of light spilling from the front porch.

Ka-thunk.

Ava's pulse skittered. She hadn't imagined it—there was definitely something outside. If Huck were here, he'd be going ballistic right now. She'd gotten used to his protection, and she felt weird to be in her house all alone.

Ava crossed the living room and parted the curtains to look outside. The line of cottonwoods down by the creek formed a dark silhouette against the moonlit sky. Ava unlocked the door and stepped onto the porch, but then thought better of it. She went back inside and grabbed the Smith & Wesson pistol from the top of her closet. Then she switched off the porch light and stepped out.

It took a moment for her eyes to adjust as she scanned the grassy slope leading down to the creek. She strained to listen for a critter or maybe a couple of deer moving through. But all she heard was the faint rustle of wind in the scrub trees.

She walked down the steps and tipped her head back to look at the sky. It was dark at last. They days had gotten long as they approached the summer solstice. The half-moon cast a silvery glow over everything, and the soft scent of juniper wafted over her.

The pistol in her hand felt cool and heavy, and she thought of her father. The Smith & Wesson was his, like Huck had been. Ava stared up at the sky, picking out Ursa Major and Scorpius, and she remembered her dad teaching her the constellations back when she was a little girl, and he could do no wrong.

Something came up. I couldn't get away.

A bitter lump lodged in her throat. She understood exactly how her mother had felt all those times. Ava remembered the tight set of her mother's mouth as she switched off the stove and told Ava and Abby to go ahead, have dinner, don't wait for your father. She pictured her mother pulling the turkey from the oven and lighting the birthday candles and serving the Christmas coffee cake. It was always the same, just the three of them, and when her mother finally decided she'd had enough and left him, it wasn't even that different. It was a change of geography, yes, but Ava's dad had been absent from their lives for years.

She'd sworn to herself that she'd never let a man take her for granted. All her life, she'd watched her mother do it. She'd seen how it chipped away at her confidence, little by little, until there was almost nothing left. Ava wasn't sure what finally pushed her mom over the edge and prompted her to leave, and her mom had never talked about it. But Ava had her suspicions.

A screech pierced the air, followed by a *thunk*.

Ava whirled around. That had come from the fence, up by the driveway. Using her phone as a flashlight, Ava walked across the grassy yard, scanning the bushes for any sign of an animal. She neared the fence and there it was again: *screech-thunk!*

The gate stood open.

Ava glanced around nervously before tromping across a patch of knee-high grass. She swung the metal gate shut and secured the latch. She scanned the area, and her gaze lingered on a dark clump of trees in the distance and the faint yellow light of the McCoulloughs' front porch. Maybe Jenna had been down here. Or Lucy with Huck.

Ava turned and looked down toward the water. The RV park was quiet. Had some trespasser come up from the creek and cut through here?

A predator could have taken her. The human kind.

A chill snaked down Ava's spine as she trekked back to her house. She scanned the bushes and shadows around her. She aimed her light at the path as she neared the porch steps.

Shoeprints.

Ava's pulse quickened as she stared down at the impressions in the dirt. Taking care not to step on them, she followed the prints from the patch of grass and across the dirt driveway to where they disappeared into the grass again.

The prints were moving *toward* the house, and Ava felt a flurry of nerves as she approached it. Gripping the pistol in her right hand, she held the phone in her left and aimed the light along the ground as she circled the cottage.

More shoeprints.

Ava glanced up at her bedroom window, and a slimy ball

of dread filled her stomach. Had someone been standing here, watching her? Had someone tried to break in? She studied the window casing but saw no pry marks or damage.

She aimed her light at the prints again. Tapping on her camera feature, she snapped a picture.

Large shoes, maybe a man's ten or eleven. Textured tread. Ava breathed in and out and tried to keep her nerves steady as she photographed the prints from various angles, but her throat was dry as sand and her hands were shaking.

Someone had been here, *right here*, creeping around her house. What were they doing? And where had they gone? Maybe they were still out here, hiding in the shadows and watching her.

"Hey."

Ava gasped and whirled around.

CHAPTER
FOURTEEN

A SHADOW LOOMED BEHIND her.

"Oh my *God*, put that down!" a voice said.

"Jenna?"

Ava turned the light toward her, and Jenna flinched.

"What the hell are you doing out here with a gun?"

Ava tucked the pistol in the waistband of her jeans. "Sorry."

"Seriously, Ava. What the hell?"

"I heard a noise out here. And I came out and found the gate open and shoeprints around the house."

"Shoeprints?"

"Yeah. See?"

She shined the phone flashlight at the prints, and Jenna stepped closer.

"Well?"

"Well, yeah. They're shoeprints." Jenna's brow furrowed and she looked at her. "Whose are they?"

"I don't know."

Jenna cast a glance toward the creek bed. "Probably some pervert from the RV park."

"You think?"

"Or maybe a thief. My dad's truck was broken into last month."

"It was?"

"Yeah, sorry. I meant to tell you. They didn't steal anything, but they busted the window and searched the glove box."

Ava took another glance at the shoeprints. Then she and Jenna walked around the house and mounted the front steps.

"I wish you'd told me when it happened," Ava said.

"I'm sorry. I meant to. I don't know why I forgot."

Jenna followed her into the house. Ava put the pistol away and returned to the living room.

"Someone was skulking around here, looking in the windows," Ava said.

"Did they try to break in?"

"Doesn't look like it. But still, it's creepy."

"You want to call the cops?"

Ava shrugged.

Jenna glanced around the cottage. Her gaze landed on the drop-leaf table near the window, which was set for two. Ava had put a little votive candle in the middle.

Jenna looked at her. "Date tonight?"

"He's not coming." She went into the kitchen and turned off the stove.

"Why not?"

"I don't know. He probably got tied up at work."

Jenna's eyebrows arched.

Ava looked her friend over and noticed she was wearing her favorite white jeans and a stretchy black top.

"Where are *you* headed?" she asked.

"Henley. I'm meeting a high school friend for drinks. I stopped by to see if you wanted to come."

"No, thanks."

"You sure?"

"Yes."

If it was a male friend, Ava didn't want to be a third wheel. And if it was a female friend, Ava didn't want to smile and make chitchat and listen to gossip about people she didn't know. She was in a mood now. Two hours ago she'd been humming in the shower, and now she just wanted to eat ice cream and go to bed.

Jenna stepped closer and leaned her hip against the counter. "What did Grant say when he called?"

"He hasn't."

"No?"

"No."

"How late is he?"

"An hour and a half."

Jenna bit her lip. "Well. I'm sorry. That's shitty. But when he *does* call, you should tell him about the footprints."

"Maybe."

"Or I could call Connor."

"Don't bother. I'll talk to Grant."

Jenna turned away from the pathetic dining table and surveyed the living room. "What's all that?"

"Maps."

"I can see that. What are they for?"

Ava sighed and stepped over to the coffee table. "Silver Canyon State Park." Ava sank onto the sofa. "Are you aware that there are vortexes all over this area? There are two in Silver Canyon and one near Big Bend."

"Are you talking about that New Age crap? Crystals and earth energy?"

"It attracts a lot of people here."

"I've heard." She shrugged. "What about it?"

"I don't know. I think it's interesting."

"Why?"

"Molly Shaw was found near one of the locations."

"She was?"

"Yeah."

Jenna stepped over and frowned down at the map. "Where?"

Ava tapped her finger on the map. "Have you ever been to this spot? It's a giant boulder about thirty feet tall called Sun Rock."

"Never heard of it. There's a *Moon* Rock on the north side of the Bensen Ranch next door to here. It's near a cave filled with bats. We used to have keg parties out there."

"But you've never been to Sun Rock?"

"No. It looks really remote. That's, like, the dead center of the park."

"It's a five-hour hike from the nearest trailhead. You've heard of Enchanted Rock just outside Austin?"

"Yeah."

"Well, like Enchanted Rock, Sun Rock was thought by Native American tribes to hold special powers. Some people believe these rock formations are a portal to another world." Portals were yet another one of the theories Rachel Spencer had been researching in the months since her daughter's disappearance.

Ava traced her finger over the shortest route to Sun Rock from the trailhead. It wasn't even marked on the map. So, was there a trail there that the map wasn't showing, or did people simply know how to find it?

"Ava?"

She glanced up.

"Are you okay?"

"What do you mean?"

"I'm worried about you. You seem preoccupied lately with this whole Brittlyn Spencer thing."

"I am. I've been talking to her mom."

"Well, do you think that's healthy?"

"Healthy how?"

"You know, getting pulled into this woman's obsession with finding her daughter."

Ava stared up at her.

"I don't think it's good for you," Jenna went on. "And you're spending a ton of time on it, canceling meetings and disappearing from the office in the middle of the day."

Ava blinked up at her, unable to believe what she was hearing. She would have thought Jenna, as a mother, would understand where Rachel Spencer was coming from.

"Don't get defensive," Jenna said.

"I'm not."

She rolled her eyes. "Oh, come on. I can see you're pissed. I just don't want you to get completely sucked into this woman's orbit. I mean, vortexes and earth energy? Since when are you interested in that?"

Ava's phone chimed in her pocket, and she pulled it out. Grant.

"See?" Jenna said. "I knew he'd call."

Ava glared up at her.

"I'll let you take that."

"I'm letting it go to voicemail."

"Oh, don't be that way." Jenna walked to the door. "He's probably on his way over here right now."

"He's not."

"How do you know?"

"Because I know how this goes. My dad was just like this."

"Don't forget to tell him about the shoeprints."

Jenna walked out, leaving Ava to stare at her phone. Finally, she picked up.

"Hi," she said.

"Hi."

Her heart sank at the regret in his voice.

"I hate to do this," he said.

"Don't worry about it." She got up and locked the door behind Jenna.

"Something came up, and I can't get away."

"Not a problem."

"I'm really sorry."

"I understand. Really. You're tied up."

He went quiet on the other end of the line, and she let the silence hang there awkwardly.

"You're mad," he said.

She hadn't been. But him *saying* she was mad completely pissed her off.

"Ava?"

"I'm not mad. I'm fine."

"You're lying."

She battled the urge to throw her phone against the wall.

"Can we take a rain check?" he asked.

"No."

"No?"

"Grant . . . let's not do this, okay? You're busy, I'm busy. Both of us have a lot going on with our jobs, and I think we should let this go."

"I don't."

"I'll see you around, all right?"

"Ava—"

"Goodbye."

G RANT STARED DOWN at his phone. *Fuck.*

Now what? What he needed to do was hightail it over there and talk to her in person, but he couldn't get away and by the time he could she'd probably be dug in and refuse to talk to him. It sounded like she already *was* dug in.

He should have called earlier, before she'd had a chance to cook and probably get her house ready. But he'd been focused on a lead and time had gotten away from him.

His phone lit up with a call, but it wasn't Ava.

"I'm here," Connor told him. "What do you want me to do?"

"Hang tight. He just showed up, and I'm about to go in there."

"You think he'll talk to you?"

"I don't know. Keep your phone on. I may need a hand."

"Roger that."

Grant ended the call and slid from his truck. He and Connor were in their personal vehicles tonight to keep a low profile. Grant crossed the parking lot, eyeing the gray Chevy as he approached the entrance. The door opened and a pair of women stepped out. One staggered slightly and smiled at Grant as he caught the door and held it open.

"Thanks," she said, leaning on her friend.

Grant looked at the other woman as she rolled her eyes.

"She okay?" he asked.

"Yeah. Don't worry, I'm driving."

Grant watched them cross the lot. The friend seemed fine, so Grant let it go and stepped into the bar.

The Cattleguard was just as dark and dingy as Grant remembered. Same neon signs, same outdated jukebox. The TV above the bar looked new, but that was about it. The place wasn't much to look at, but they had cheap drafts and did a steady business with ranch hands, river guides, and travelers on a shoestring budget.

Grant spotted the guy at the bar. Long hair, goatee, trucker cap. Grant walked over and leaned a hand on the bar as the man picked up his beer.

"Trent Gilchrist?"

He stopped mid-sip. "Yeah?"

Grant shifted so the badge on his hip was visible. "Grant Wycoff, Henley County Sheriff's Office. You got a minute to talk?"

"What, you mean here?"

"We could go to my office if you prefer."

He darted a look at the bartender, who was pretending not to eavesdrop. Then he looked at Grant.

"Here is fine."

"Let's go outside." Grant nodded toward the door leading to the patio in back.

"Okay." He caught the bartender's eye. "Hey, keep my tab open, will you?"

"Sure. Anything for you?"

"Just a water," Grant said.

The bartender filled a glass and passed it across the bar, and Grant followed Trent Gilchrist to the beer garden out back. Swags of white lights hung between the ramshackle building and a giant oak tree in the middle, and picnic tables were scattered beneath. It wasn't crowded, but Gilchrist led him to a table in the shadowy corner where they wouldn't be noticed. He was feeling shy, apparently. Grant often had that effect on people.

Grant took the seat with his back to the fence so he could face the patio and keep an eye on the door.

Gilchrist sat down opposite Grant. He had the tanned skin and the sinewy forearms of a seasoned river guide.

"What's this about?" he asked Grant.

"Molly Shaw."

He heaved a sigh looked down at his beer.

"You don't look surprised," Grant said.

"I'm not, really. I saw what happened on the news." His brow furrowed as he looked at Grant. "You're talking to people who knew her?"

"I hear you two dated a while back."

He frowned. "I wouldn't say 'dated' really."

"No?"

"Who told you that?"

"One of Molly's friends."

He didn't want to give him Skye's name and run the risk of her getting any blowback. Investigators wouldn't even know about Skye—or Trent Gilchrist, for that matter—if it weren't for Ava, and it irked Grant that he was using this lead. But he needed every lead he could get with this case, even if it came from a civilian who shouldn't be involved.

"We hung out," he said. "It wasn't anything serious."

"Was it a sexual relationship?"

He hesitated a beat. "Yeah."

"When did it start?"

He glanced at the sky, as if trying to remember. "I don't know. Like, not long after she moved here?"

"And how'd you meet?"

"Through friends."

"Who?" Grant had this already from Skye, but he wanted to establish a baseline with this guy.

"Some of the other guides I hang out with."

"Okay."

"It didn't last very long," he added.

"What happened?"

"I don't know. It fizzled."

"Why?"

He sipped his beer, then put the glass down and stared at it a moment before making eye contact. "Molly was kind of a roller coaster. You probably know that already if you talked to her friends. She came out here after her divorce and she was pretty depressed."

"Did she talk about it?"

"Not really. But she'd go on these benders. Couple days of drinking. Then she'd sober up and want to do big hikes or climbs or whatever."

"So, you two broke up?"

"I wouldn't say 'broke up' because we weren't together, really. We just stopped seeing each other."

Grant watched him, trying to gauge his truthfulness. Gilchrist was twenty-five but he looked even younger and had a talent for seeming genuine.

"Do you remember the last time you saw her?" Grant asked.

"I don't know. All this was more than two years ago."

"I'm sure you've had time to think about it in the months since she went missing."

Hostility flared in his eyes. Good. Grant wanted to needle him.

"Think hard, Trent. When was the last time you saw her?"

"I don't know. Our friend Nico's birthday, maybe? We got together with some people for drinks over at Dusty's Cantina in Cuervo. You know the place?"

Grant nodded. "When was this?"

He took off his cap and raked his hand through his long hair. "Sometime in April, I think? The spring before she went missing?"

Grant just looked at him expectantly.

He sighed and pulled his phone from his pocket. "I've got it here somewhere." He scrolled through text messages. "Okay. Yeah. Nico's birthday is April fifth. We went out again this year." He looked up from his phone. "So, you know, it would have been sometime around April fifth that year, but I don't know the exact date."

"And you're sure? The last time you saw Molly Shaw was in April before she disappeared?"

"I'm sure. It was at Dusty's. That was the last time."

Grant watched his eyes. They were bloodshot, like he'd gotten high before coming here. But his story didn't waver, and Grant knew for sure that this kid had thought through all this before, probably back when Molly went missing and investigators were going around asking questions about her. Grant was surprised he hadn't come across Trent's name back then.

Better late than never.

Grant sipped his water and let an awkward silence settle over the table.

"So, about Molly's divorce. What did she say about it?"

Trent's eyebrows arched. "What do you mean?"

"Did she talk about her ex-husband and why they split?"

"Not really. I mean, I know they tried to have a baby and couldn't, and she still wanted to get pregnant."

"Yeah?"

He nodded. "She was pretty hung up on it. It kind of spooked me."

"How's that?"

"Well, I was, like, twenty-three at the time. Definitely not down for being a dad, you know? I wanted to get some distance."

"So, it didn't just fizzle?"

"No, it did. But that was part of why."

Grant watched him until he shifted uncomfortably and picked up his beer.

Grant checked his watch. "Did she ever talk about her job with you?"

"What, the ranch?"

"Yeah. Whitehorse Ranch."

"No."

"She didn't tell you about it?"

"No. But she cleaned hotel rooms. What was there to tell?"

Grant nodded. "Do you have any idea if she had any problems with anyone around here?"

"She never said anything like that."

"You have any idea why anyone might want to hurt her?"

"No."

"One more thing. Did Molly ever mention talking to her ex at all? Or him still being in the picture?"

He shook his head. "No. Is he a suspect?"

Grant didn't answer. Instead, he pulled out a small spiral notebook and pen.

"That about covers it for now." He slid the notebook across the table. "Give me your number in case there's anything else."

Gilchrist just looked at him. Then he took the pen and scribbled a number down.

"Thanks." Grant stood up.

"I hope you find out what happened to her. She was a nice girl."

CONNOR SAT IN the parking lot with his laptop open, reading Trent Gilchrist's rap sheet. He had a public intox arrest and a couple of other misdemeanors. But no assaults and nothing that suggested he was a prime candidate for shooting a woman in the back and then pushing her off a cliff and hiding the body.

Connor glanced up as a car pulled into the lot. His heart lurched at the sight of the familiar white Camry. It slid into a space between two pickups.

What was Jenna doing here? This place was a craphole. He watched as she crossed the parking lot. She wore a low-cut black shirt and tight jeans. Connor got a sinking feeling in his stomach as she pulled open the door and walked inside the bar.

His phone buzzed.

"Yeah?"

"He's paying his tab," Grant said. "Keep an eye on the door."

"I see him." Connor shut his laptop and moved it to the passenger seat. "What now?"

"Tail him. We need to find out where he's living. His driver's license is showing an old address."

"Okay, he's getting in his truck."

"Stay back. Don't let him see you."

Connor waited until the truck pulled onto the highway to start his engine.

"How'd it go?" he asked Grant. "Anything interesting?"

"Yeah."

"You think he's a suspect?"

Connor drove across the parking lot and rolled to a stop at the highway as the pickup's taillights faded into small red dots.

"Grant?"

"Maybe. I need to check some stuff out."

"Like what?"

"Like some of the things he told me don't add up."

A VA LAY ON the couch, flipping through channels as she thought about her failed dinner date. Her phone chimed. She reached for it on the table, and the number on the screen surprised her.

"Abby, hey. What's up?"

"Sorry to call so late."

"Is everything okay?"

"Yeah."

Ava's stomach clenched as she waited. Something had to be wrong. Her sister didn't call often, and certainly not after eleven at night. Ava had talked to her mom just this morning, but maybe something had happened.

"Is Mom all right?" Ava asked.

"Yeah, sorry. Mom's fine. I didn't mean to freak you out, I just—" She paused.

"Abby, spit it out."

"I'm going to the storage unit tomorrow."

"*Our* storage unit?"

"Yeah."

Ava and her sister had rented a storage unit back in October, shortly after their father's funeral. After packing up his apartment, they'd moved all his stuff there and decided to sort through it at a later time, when they didn't feel so overwhelmed. They still hadn't done it, and Ava felt guilty every time she thought about it.

"Is that okay with you?"

Ava reached for the remote and turned down the volume. "Sure. Why wouldn't it be?"

"I don't know. We said we'd go through it together. But I have some time this weekend, so I thought I might get started."

Ava sat there silently in the dark.

"Ava? Are you mad?"

"Why would I be mad?"

"I don't know. That I'm starting without you. I just . . . I keep thinking about him all the time, and I thought going through his stuff might help."

Ava didn't respond. She thought about him all the time, too, but the last thing she wanted to do was sort through a bunch of boxes in an airless storage unit.

"Abby . . . I can't get there this weekend."

"I don't expect you to. That's not why I'm calling. I just wanted to, you know, clear it with you."

"I worry about you doing this all by yourself. If you'll wait until later in the summer—"

"I don't want to wait. And I don't mind doing it by myself. I feel like it's time. That stuff's been sitting there long enough. Anyway, I won't throw anything away. I just want to sort it into categories, and maybe bring some of the pictures home."

"That's fine."

"If I see anything I know you'd want, I'll send it to you."

Irritation surged through her. "You don't need to do that."

"I want to."

"That's a lot of trouble, Abby. Are you sure you want to do this alone? I can come help if you'll just wait until I can get there—"

"I'm sure. I'm ready now. I know you're not, but I am."

A tight knot formed in Ava's chest as she sat there in the darkness. She felt angry, but she wasn't sure why.

"Ava?"

"I have a question for you. About Dad."

"Okay."

"Did he cheat? Is that why she finally left?"

Her sister didn't respond, and Ava held her breath as the silence dragged on.

Abby sighed. "I thought you knew."

"I didn't. I *suspected*." Furious tears burned her eyes. "Who was it?"

"I don't know. Mom would never say. I always figured it was someone from work. Who else would it be?"

Ava sat forward, feeling sick suddenly. How long had Abby known this? It sounded like a long time. Her mom and her sister had kept her in the dark for years.

Or maybe she'd kept herself in the dark by not asking.

Ava cleared her throat. "Yeah, well, I guess it doesn't matter now."

"It matters," Abby said. "But Mom let go of this a long time ago. So did I. You should, too."

Ava sniffed.

"You'll feel better."

Ava's throat burned, but she made her voice sound normal. "Well. Thanks for the heads-up about the storage unit."

"Sure," Abby said. "And you're really okay with this?"

"Of course. Do what you need to do."

CHAPTER
FIFTEEN

A VA SCOOTED OUT of the booth and offered a handshake to her newest client.

"Thank you for understanding, Mr. Shaffer. I'm sorry I have to run, but I'll call you tomorrow."

"Call my mobile number. I've got a fence to work on in the morning." He settled his cowboy hat on his bald head.

"Will do."

He nodded and walked out of the diner, and Ava tucked a tip under her unfinished mug of coffee. She checked her phone as she walked outside into the sweltering sun. Another message had just landed, this one marked **ASAP**.

Ava glanced up and down the street. Where had she parked? She'd been doing errands all afternoon, and she'd stopped three different times. She spied her car in front of Henley Hardware, where she'd gone looking for some security locks for her windows.

Ava responded to the text from her team leader as she hurried down the sidewalk: **ETA 30 min**.

She popped her locks and slid behind the wheel, then plugged her phone into the charger before pulling out.

She passed the sheriff's office, which looked quiet today now that most of the big-city reporters had left. The NBC guy from San Antonio was still lurking around town—Ava had seen him at the Coffee Cup yesterday. But everyone else had moved on, at least temporarily, as breaking news in their home communities edged out a West Texas cold case.

Ava rolled to a stop at a red light and cast a glance at the clock. Thirty minutes was way optimistic. She still had to race home and change clothes, plus get her gear together.

Ava glanced at the nearby parking lot and spotted a sheriff's SUV pulling out.

Grant.

Crap.

She trained her gaze on the stoplight. Had he seen her? She'd dodged two calls from him earlier, and she really didn't want to talk to him. The light turned green, and she darted a look from the corner of her eye as she went through the intersection. He lifted his hand from the wheel in acknowledgment, and she pretended not to notice.

Ava kept driving and checked her side mirror. He was right behind her now. She glanced at the phone in the cup holder, wondering if he'd call again. The sign for the highway came into view, and Ava put on her turn signal. Grant did, too. She cast another glance at her phone.

A siren whooped, and she felt an instinctive burst of panic as she glanced in the mirror. The SUV's red-and-blue grille lights flashed on.

What the hell? She was going *under* the speed limit, for crying out loud.

Another *whoop.*

"You've got to be kidding me," she muttered, veering onto the shoulder. She checked the clock on her phone as she rolled to a stop.

Grant parked behind her as she glared at the side mirror. Then he pushed open his door and took his sweet time getting out. He wasn't even in uniform right now, and he had the gall to pull her over.

Ava shoved open her door and got out. "Are you really doing this?"

He walked up to her, adjusting the HCSO cap on his head. "Looks like it."

"Seriously? A traffic stop? How about a voicemail, like normal people?"

He stopped in front of her and rested his hands on his hips. "You don't answer your voicemail."

"Oh my God. Can't you take a hint? I *don't* want to talk to you! And pulling me over is *an abuse of power.*"

"Your plate's missing."

She blinked up at him. "What?"

"Your license plate." He jerked his head toward the back of her car.

She ducked around him and walked to the back bumper.

"My plate's gone," she sputtered.

"That's what I said."

"But . . . how?"

He walked over to stand beside her.

"And *who?* Who on earth would take my license plate?"

"Probably a thief."

She turned and glared at him.

"A car thief," he said. "That's the reason plates usually get stolen. They swipe something off a car that looks like the one they've stolen so the car doesn't come up hot if someone runs the plate." He frowned down at the empty rectangle where her license plate used to be. "Course, not a lot of cars around here look like yours. None, in fact. More likely, they slapped it on a vehicle they want to use to commit a crime."

"*Crap.*"

"You can file a report."

"I don't have time for a report." She stomped her foot. "I'm late for a callout."

His brow furrowed. "A callout?"

"We've got a Silver Alert in the park, and I have to go grab Huck and get over there."

"I didn't hear about it."

"Well, you probably will soon. It just got confirmed. Can I file a report later?"

"Sure."

"*Thank you!*" She reached over and squeezed his arm, then instantly regretted it.

She glanced around, flustered, and strode back to her door. "Thanks for not making me sit here for paperwork."

"Come in tomorrow, and we'll get it taken care of."

She slid behind the wheel. "I will."

He rested his hand on the top of her door. She made the mistake of looking up, and instantly wished she hadn't. Those deep brown eyes of were way too sincere.

"I'm sorry about last night, Ava."

"It's fine."

"No, I mean it."

"It's fine. Huck enjoyed your homemade cornbread."

He made a pained face. "Damn. That's harsh."

She smiled.

"After your op wraps, any chance I can get you to have dinner with me?" he asked.

She looked ahead at the highway. Her feelings were still raw from last night when he'd completely blown her off.

"I can cook for you and return the favor," he said.

She glanced up at him, and he was watching her with that charming half smile.

"You can stand me up, if you want," he said. "Even things out."

"*I* would at least have the courtesy to call you."

"I'm sorry about that, too." He paused. "Have dinner with me tonight. Let me make it up to you."

Butterflies swarmed in her stomach. What exactly would him making it up to her entail? She had a feeling she'd be better off if she never found out.

Ava's thoughts were all jumbled. Last night, she'd sworn off him for good, and now she was thinking of going to his house.

She couldn't focus on this now. And she didn't have to. She had the perfect excuse to put him off.

"I'll think about it," she said briskly. "I don't know how long I'll be tied up with this."

"Fair enough."

She fastened her seat belt, and he started to close her door for her.

"Be safe out there," he told her.

"I will."

T HE CRACKLE OF the radio had Ava halting in her tracks.
  "Base to Team Four. Team Four, copy."

Courtney stopped and pulled the radio from her belt. "Team Four here. We're just finishing the loop and then we're headed back."

"Anything to report?"

Courtney looked at Ava. The park ranger's cheeks were flushed, and her olive green uniform was soaked with sweat. Dirt and leaves clung to her braids, and tiny cuts covered her arms from ducking through mesquite thickets. Ava's arms were similarly scratched up.

"Negative," Courtney replied.

That one word pretty much summed up their afternoon.

"We're almost to the trailhead," Courtney continued. "Should be back to base, oh, about twenty minutes."

"Copy that, Four."

Courtney reattached the radio to her belt as Huck circled back to Ava, panting and looking thirsty. Ava shrugged out of her pack. She unclipped Huck's bowl and filled it with water. As he lapped it up, it occurred to her that her dog had probably had much more to drink today than the target they were searching for.

"This sucks," Courtney declared.

Ava eyed the park ranger as she tipped back her thermos. Courtney was the only other woman on this SAR op, so Mel had paired them up together.

"I wish people would *listen* to our advice," Courtney said. "It's printed on every park map, too: Bring water. Bring a map. Hiking not recommended after ten a.m. during summer months."

Walter Masterson had headed out at eight o'clock this morning equipped with only a small canteen of water, a pair of binoculars, and a pocket field guide to birds of North America. He also had his cell phone with him, according to his wife, but had been keeping it turned off because cell reception in the park was nonexistent except near the ranger station.

One small canteen.

For a three-hour hike.

Walter's wife, Helen, had driven him to the trailhead in their Jeep Wrangler with plans to pick him up at eleven. Then she'd gone to Cuervo for groceries and unloaded them into their Winnebago, which was parked at Silver Canyon's main campground. She'd returned to the trailhead promptly at eleven, but Walter was a no-show.

By 11:15, Helen was getting worried. By 11:40, she was on the phone with the rangers, and by noon she was hysterical.

Walter was never late, Helen had told them, and she felt sure her seventy-nine-year-old husband must have injured himself on the trail.

Courtney tore open a pouch of orange powder and poured some into her water bottle. Then she offered the pouch to Ava.

"Want some?" Courtney asked.

"What is it?"

"Tangerine-flavored sports powder. It's got electrolytes in it."

"I'm good," Ava said. She kept her water straight so she could share with Huck.

Ava reached down and picked some sticker burrs from his fur as he finished his water.

"He's got a lot of stamina," Courtney said. "I'm surprised the heat doesn't bother him with all that thick fur."

"He loves it out here."

Courtney zipped her water into her backpack and heaved it on again. By some unspoken agreement, they'd been keeping their breaks short and pushing it hard.

Like children, missing elderly people were cause for alarm. Not only were they extremely vulnerable to heatstroke, but some had memory issues and could become confused and disoriented.

Ava and Courtney resumed their trek with Huck in the lead. They were following the creek bed that was all but dried up. The water was just a faint trickle that disappeared completely in places.

"I worked an operation once where the guy had been a POW," Courtney said.

Ava glanced at the ranger over her shoulder. "Here in Silver Canyon?"

"This was in Big Bend. They called us in from everywhere because the guy had Alzheimer's. Turned out, he'd been hiding from the search party, thinking they were enemy soldiers out to get him."

"You found him?"

"Yep. Dehydrated as hell, but he was alive."

Ava watched Huck sniffing the wind in front of them. Luckily, Walter didn't have memory issues, according to his wife. What he did have, though, was COPD, which was a major concern because the medicine he took made him especially prone to dehydration.

One canteen of water. Ava felt sick every time she thought of it. It was after six o'clock now, and with every minute that ticked by, Walter's chances diminished.

Courtney stopped and turned toward the canyon wall.

"There's the trail," she said.

"Where?"

"See the post there?"

Ava spotted the wooden marker. The faint trail ascended gradually to the top of the canyon where her car was parked at the gravel lot beside the trailhead. Guilt needled her as she surveyed the route. Returning to her car felt like giving up hope.

Ava wiped the sweat from her brow and glanced around. Huck was about ten yards ahead of her now, sniffing a barrel-shaped cactus with long needles. A hummingbird hovered over the scarlet cactus flowers.

Ava looked ahead at where the canyon curved slightly. It was a shallow canyon—only about twenty feet deep. Not like some of the treacherous gorges she had explored before.

"I think we should try that area again," Ava said.

"They cleared that sector earlier."

Courtney's voice was neutral, but Ava still sensed some disapproval there. She'd gotten more than a few hostile looks from the rangers when she arrived because the search op was already well underway.

"Did they have a dog with them?" Ava asked.

"No," Courtney said. "It was Team Two, I think."

Ava looked at the hummingbird again, thinking of the pocket field guide.

"Fine." Courtney reached for her radio. "I'll call Mel, tell him we'll be a while longer."

Ava pushed ahead, following Huck along the creek as Courtney paused to make the call. Ava scoured the scrub brush, looking for any sign of a person—hopefully, sleeping— in the shade.

Courtney caught up to her. "We're good. He wants a dog to recheck this sector."

Ava stopped and squinted ahead.

"What's that?" she asked.

"Where? Oh, you mean the windmill?"

"I didn't know there was a windmill out here," Ava said.

"It's one of the original structures on the property. It's really old, actually. Think it's been there since the eighteen hundreds."

Ava adjusted her pack and trudged forward. A windmill suggested water. And birds liked water, so maybe Walter had seen something that caught his interest.

"It's not on the map, is it?" she asked Courtney.

"Nope. But, you know, our maps really need to be updated. They're lacking quite a few landmarks."

"Why?"

She shrugged. "We've only been a park about ten years, and the original ranch has lots of little spots that need attention, so they're not ready to showcase them yet."

Ava looked back at her. "What other landmarks aren't labeled?"

Courtney sighed. "I don't know. Plenty of stuff. The windmill, the stables. There's even an old mine shaft on the west side of the park. It's pretty cool, but it's not on the official map we give visitors."

"What about Sun Rock?" Ava asked. "I saw the site marked, but I didn't see a trail."

"That's on purpose. It's kind of like the mine shaft—if there's no trail there, maybe people won't come."

"Why don't they want people to come?"

"Well, with the mine shaft, it's a safety thing. Sun Rock—" Courtney shrugged. "Some people are superstitious about it."

"Who?"

"The park board, for one. I asked Mel about it once, and he said it doesn't attract the kind of visitors we want."

"What kind of visitors does it attract?"

"Devil worshippers and satanists."

"Satanists?"

"There are some old legends about the place. That people used to do animal sacrifices out there. Or even child sacrifices."

"You can't be serious."

"It's just talk. But the place is kind of, I don't know, mystical. I think it's the petroglyphs. Some ancient tribes did some rock art there—which is yet another reason they don't want to put in a trail. They don't want people flocking there and damaging it."

"Have you ever been out there?"

"Sure. All the rangers have at one time or another."

"But there's no trail?"

"Not really. You have to go through Diamondback Gorge and then climb up a mesa and cross over. It's a five-hour hike from the closest trailhead, and the last part is pretty much vertical."

"Wouldn't it be safer to build a trail?"

"Sure, but you know, 'If you build it, they will come.' They've got this old-fashioned mentality here." She rolled her eyes. "One of the joys of working at this park."

Ava glanced at her. "You don't like it here?"

"No, I do. It's good, mostly. I would rather be at Big Bend, obviously, but the National Park Service is tough. It's really hard to get hired full-time, and even if you do, it's not like you can pick your assignment. I could end up in Alaska freezing my ass off."

"That sounds like heaven right now."

Courtney smiled and used a yellow bandanna to mop the sweat from her brow.

"What about you?" she asked Ava. "Someone said you're a lawyer? It's such a trip that you're out here doing this."

Ava gave her a sidelong glance.

"Don't get me wrong," Courtney said. "I'm glad you're here. It's good to have another woman on the SAR team. All the other volunteers are men. It's kind of testosterone overload."

"I get it," Ava told her. "I've been in courtrooms like that."

"So, how'd you become involved in this?"

"My dad was a game warden."

"No kidding? Where?"

"East Texas. He worked at several of the parks out there until he retired a couple years ago." Ava's stomach clenched as she thought of everything she was leaving out of that story. The cancer. The chemo. The sudden revelation at the end of his life when it was too late for anyone to do anything. Her dad's illness had been like their whole relationship—filled with missed opportunities—and every time she thought about it, she got a hot, tight knot in the center of her chest.

Ava cleared her throat. "My dad was the one who trained Huck," she said.

"He's a really good dog. You're lucky to have him."

"I know."

"Well-trained dogs are hard to come by. We had a Belgian Malinois back a couple years ago, but it didn't work out."

"Too hot?" Ava asked.

"He was too aggressive. He bit a volunteer."

Ava spied Huck up ahead, sniffing excitedly around a rockslide. Her stomach clenched as she remembered the last time she'd seen him with a pile of rocks.

"He found something." Ava hurried toward him, holding her breath as she scanned the area. In the fading light it was hard to see.

"What? What is it?"

Ava didn't answer because she didn't know. She stopped beside Huck, skimming her gaze over the rocky ground.

Something shiny glinted up at her.

"Is that . . . ?" Ava crept closer to the object. But Courtney was a step ahead of her, dropping to her knees to examine it.

"Glasses," she said.

"Are they Walter's?"

"I don't know. I can check." Courtney pulled out her phone as Ava did a slow 360, searching the trees and rocks nearby.

"Look." Courtney held up her phone and showed a photograph of Walter that his wife had provided the searchers. "Rectangular lenses and clear frames, just like these."

Ava's pulse thrummed as she looked around. Huck started barking up ahead, and she broke into a jog.

"He found something," she told Courtney.

"Where is he?"

Huck loped up the trail and sat down, pricking his ears forward.

"Show me."

He ran ahead of her, darting around an enormous agave plant at the base of a boulder. Ava jogged behind him, skimming the creek and the base of the canyon and the cacti and scrub trees all around.

Huck plunged into a thicket of junipers and Ava ducked in after him, stabbing herself in the neck with a twig. Cursing, she batted at the branches and peered into the shadowy brush.

Courtney came up behind her, huffing and puffing as she swatted at leaves and branches.

"Where'd he go?" Courtney gasped.

Huck gave another high-pitched bark, and Ava's heart skittered again. He'd found something. She could hear it in his voice.

Ava plowed through the trees, cursing again as the branches scratched her arms and cheeks. *Please be alive. Please . . .*

She thought of Helen, looking pale and blanched under

that blue tent, twisting a tissue in her hands as she told Mel about her husband's many medications.

Ava tripped forward, catching herself on a rock as Huck jumped into her path.

"Show me, Huck."

He lunged forward, then danced back and lunged forward again.

"Where, boy? Where?"

And then she saw it. A flash of white peeking out from beneath the shadow of a rock overhang.

"There he is!" Courtney darted around Ava and dropped to her knees beside the lifeless body. Unlike little Noah, this body didn't move.

Ava rushed to Courtney's side and unzipped her pack.

"He's unconscious," Courtney said tightly.

"Any pulse?"

"I can't tell." Her voice had an edge of panic as she gently rolled the man onto his side. "His skin's dry. That's not good."

"He moved," Ava said. "Did you see that? His leg twitched."

Ava whipped out a bottle, and Courtney grabbed it.

"Walter, can you hear me? We need you to sip some water." She looked at Ava. "Call it in, then help me get some water in him."

Ava's hands were shaking as she unclipped the radio from Courtney's belt.

"Hurry," Courtney whispered. "We don't have much time."

CHAPTER
SIXTEEN

AVA AIMED HER flashlight at the path as she trekked up the incline. She was in shock. Still. The team of paramedics had come and gone, but the evening's events kept tumbling through her head.

Huck growled at her side, and she glanced up as a man emerged from the shadows in front of her. She halted.

"Good work today."

Mel Tyndall. She barely recognized him in the dark without his usual wraparound sunglasses.

"Thank you," she said.

He stopped in the middle of the trail and looked down at Huck.

"He's got quite a nose on him, doesn't he?"

"He does, yes."

Mel looked her over. "WestTex SAR is lucky to have you two."

"Thank you."

"Y'all have a good night, now."

"We will."

He stepped around them, and Ava felt a renewed surge of euphoria as she hiked to the top of the canyon. The dizzying realization that Huck had saved a life—*again*—kept swirling through her mind.

Walter had been birdwatching off the trail when he tripped on a rock and lost his glasses. Practically blind, he'd spent hours crawling around searching before giving up and taking shelter under a tree. As the sun had moved, he had moved, too, finally ending up under a rock ledge as he tried to escape the blistering heat.

Huck had found him just in time. Another half hour, and he might have slipped into a coma or died, according to the paramedic. After getting him to sip some water, Courtney and Ava had applied instant cold packs to his neck and armpits until the medics arrived. The team had carried him out of the canyon on a stretcher to a waiting ambulance, where they'd promptly hooked him up to an IV.

And reunited him with his wife.

Now both Walter and Helen were at the regional hospital, recovering from their ordeal.

Ava reached down to scrub Huck's head between his ears. He'd been prancing around for the last half hour, basking in the praise from the SAR guys and emergency responders.

"Maybe we'll celebrate tonight. What do you think?"

Ava's phone chimed. She pulled it from her pocket, and her heart gave a happy little thump as Grant's number showed up on the screen.

Definitely not good for her to get so excited to see his number.

"Hey, what's up?" she said.

"I heard about the op."

She felt another surge of euphoria. "Wow, news travels fast around here."

"Congratulations," he said.

"Thanks."

"You sound happy."

"I am. It's been a good day." She reached the top of the trail and glanced around. The gravel lot was empty, except for her Fiat and a couple of park vehicles. "Where are you, anyway? I saw Connor here earlier."

"I got sidetracked. Had to drive to El Paso."

Some of her euphoria faded. It sounded like dinner was off, which definitely, *definitely*, shouldn't have mattered at this moment. But his words had been floating in the back of her mind for hours.

Let me make it up to you.

"So, how's tonight looking?" he asked.

Ava stopped in her tracks. "Tonight?"

"You're finishing up there, right?"

Taillights glowed on one of the pickup trucks as a park ranger pulled out of the lot.

"Yes."

"How about dinner at my place in half an hour? I'll cook for you this time."

Her stomach fluttered.

"I need to change," she said. "I'm all gross."

"Don't change."

"And I have to run Huck home."

"He's invited, too."

Ava glanced around the lot, debating with herself. Courtney, smiling broadly, walked over and gave her a fist bump.

Ava muted the phone. "You headed out?"

"Yeah. Thanks for all your help." She crouched down and looped her arm around Huck's neck. "And thank *you*, buddy. We need to make you a ranger." She stood up and grinned. "Good work today."

"You, too."

Courtney strode off toward her pickup truck, and Ava turned to face her car, which was parked right beside the trailhead.

"You there?" Grant asked.

"Are you sure you want both of us?"

"Yes."

"Okay, well . . ." She couldn't believe she was going to go over there straight from an op. But what the hell? She was in too good a mood to care what she looked like right now. She'd helped save a man's life today, and every time she pictured the pure relief on Helen's face, she felt a rush of happiness.

What she *should* do was go home and clean up and spend a quiet evening lavishing attention on her dog.

But she was going to do what she wanted.

She was going to have dinner with Grant. And she was not going to think about his job or her emotional hang-ups or the fact that getting involved with him would be a bad idea.

"Text me your address," she said.

"Texting it now."

"Is it hard to find?"

"Not at all. It's on the east side of Henley, just before Dovetail Road."

"Do I need to stop and get anything?"

"No. See you in a few."

He clicked off before she could change her mind, and Ava slid her phone into her pocket.

Huck paced back and forth beside the car, whimpering and looking anxious as she unzipped her backpack and dug out her keys.

"I probably should have said no, huh?"

She set her backpack by the tire and popped the locks. Her T-shirt was glued to her back with sweat, and she couldn't believe she'd just agreed to go to his house like this. But she had a spare shirt in her car. And some wet wipes, too. She kept a gym bag full of gear in her cargo space.

Huck bristled and made a low grumble.

A chill shot down Ava's spine as she glanced around the shadowy parking lot. "What is it, boy?"

Huck growled deep in his throat.

Ava darted a glance around and lifted the hatch of the car.

Sssssssssst.

She froze. A thick brown snake was coiled in the cargo space. Her heart did a flip-flop as the snake lifted its head.

Huck lunged.

Ava screamed and grabbed his vest. She dragged him back just as the snake shot forward.

Ava leaped to the side and slammed the hatch down. Shrieking, she checked the ground around her feet and Huck's paws. Had it jumped out? Where was it?

Huck barked and strained against her grip.

"No! Huck, *no!*" She pulled him back, looking frantically around.

Oh my God, oh my God, oh my God.

Courtney came running across the parking lot. "What happened? What's wrong?"

"A rattlesnake's in my car!"

Courtney turned to look at the Fiat. "Are you sure?"

"Yes, I saw it! I heard it, too! It tried to bite us. Huck, *no!*"

He was going crazy now, barking and straining against her grip. She reached down with her left hand and grabbed his collar.

"*Don't* open that hatch." Courtney jogged toward her pickup truck. "And move away from the vehicle. Are the other doors closed?"

Ava darted a panicked look at the doors and windows. Had she left something open? How had it gotten in there? Still gripping Huck's collar, she pulled him away and side-stepped around the car to check the other doors. Everything was closed up tight as a drum.

And yet there was a freaking *rattlesnake* inside.

Ava's heart thundered. Her knuckles burned as she clenched Huck's collar.

"*Hey.* Stop it, Huck."

He seemed to calm down a fraction.

"Sit."

He sat, then turned and whined at her.

Courtney strode toward them with something long and metal in her hand. She wore thick leather gloves now, too.

Ava's stomach dropped. "Are you crazy? Don't tell me you're going to try to catch it!"

"What else are we gonna do with it?"

"Nothing! Shouldn't we call someone?"

Courtney shot her a look. "Like who? Parks and wildlife?"

Ava's jaw dropped as Courtney approached the back hatch. The snake's silhouette hovered in the window, and Ava's stomach clenched.

"Courtney, seriously. That thing is ready to strike."

"Damn. He's big."

The wariness in her voice made Ava sick to her stomach.

"Courtney, *please* don't do this. We can call someone out here."

Huck barked and lunged again, and Ava tightened her two-handed grip on his collar.

"Put him in my truck," Courtney said, not taking her eyes off the window. "It's the safest place for him."

Ava glanced at the pickup with the driver's-side door hanging open.

"Come on, Huck. Let's go."

Ava walked him to the truck and commanded him to get inside.

"Get my .22 while you're over there. It's in the glove box."

Ava closed the door on Huck, then went around to the other side and grabbed the small black pistol from the glove box.

She jogged across the lot.

"Be careful. It's loaded." Courtney looked at Ava. "Can you pop the hatch with your keys?"

"Yeah."

Courtney held the snake hook in her hand as she edged close to the car. "Okay, stand back. On the count of three, I want you to pop the hatch."

Ava gripped the key fob in her left hand and the gun in her right. "Are you sure about this?"

"Yes."

She sounded firm now. Adamant. And amazingly calm.

Ava lifted the pistol and aimed it at the back of the car. "Stand aside, Court."

"I am." She held the long hook. "Okay, one . . ."

Ava trained her focus on the snake, which had its head raised like it was ready to strike.

"Two . . ."

She took a deep breath.

"Now."

Ava popped the lock and lifted the hatch.

The snake sprang forward and landed on the ground with a dull *thud*. Ava jumped back.

Courtney looked calm and focused as she reached the hook forward and deftly lifted the snake.

It flopped to the ground, hissing, and Courtney lurched back.

"Careful," Ava murmured.

Huck's muffled barks from the truck didn't drown out the persistent *hiss*. It got even louder as the snake wrapped itself into a coil again and thrust out its forked black tongue.

"Damn. He's ticked off," Courtney said. "Wonder how long he's been in there."

Ava's stomach roiled at the thought.

Courtney moved forward again. She lifted the thick viper and walked across the lot with it dangling from her hook.

"Where are you—"

"The canyon." She headed away from the trail and reached a rocky slope. Ava followed, keeping the pistol ready in case the snake tried to strike again.

Courtney lowered the hook and backed away as the snake quickly slithered into the shadows.

Ava stared, slack-jawed, at the empty patch of rocks. Sweat streamed down her back and arms, and her heart felt like it might pound right out of her chest. Holy crap. What had just happened?

"Crotalus atrox."

She turned to Courtney. "What?"

"Western diamondback." She rested her hook on the ground. "Causes the most fatalities of any snake in North America."

CHAPTER
SEVENTEEN

AVA SURVEYED GRANT's house as she pulled up and cut the engine. It was just as he'd described—a brown A-frame with green shutters. Ava grabbed her backpack off the floor and got out. Huck hopped down, and she locked her car with a chirp as the cabin's front door opened.

"I was getting worried," Grant said as Huck rushed up to him.

Ava was late, but she didn't apologize as she walked over.

"Any trouble finding it?" he asked.

"No."

He stepped back to let her in, and Ava set her backpack down beside the door. He led her down a dim hallway into a living room with floor-to-ceiling windows. The door to the deck stood open, and a cool breeze wafted inside.

"I'm getting the coals going," he said. "Want a drink? I've got beer, wine. A batch of margaritas in the fridge."

"Just water for now, thanks. I need to hydrate."

Huck had already trotted out to explore the deck, and

Ava followed him. She needed some space to breathe. She didn't want to be inside right now with the kitchen lights blazing down on her. After spending half an hour at the ranger station on the snake report, she'd barely had time to clean up in the bathroom and put on a fresh T-shirt. At least it had long sleeves, which covered the scratches up and down her arms.

Ava stepped to the deck railing, and her breath caught as she took in the view. The cabin perched at the top of a gentle slope down to a rocky canyon. On the far side of the canyon, a line of trees was silhouetted against the purple sky.

Huck started down the wooden staircase.

"No."

He looked back at her.

"Stay here."

He seemed to sense not to push it. He walked back up and started sniffing around the Weber grill at the end of the deck.

Grant came out and handed her a glass of ice water.

"Thank you."

He set his beer bottle on the railing, and she looked him over as she took a sip. He wore a gray T-shirt with faded jeans and flip-flops, and she realized she'd never seen him look so civilian.

"You like steak?" he asked.

Just the word put a pang in her empty stomach.

"Sounds great."

"I've got steaks, potatoes, and salad. Potatoes are in the oven, but I just started the coals, so it'll be a while. You want to look around?"

"Sure. Give me the tour."

He led her to the weathered wooden stairs leading to the yard, and Huck happily trotted at her heels.

Ava followed Grant down, admiring his muscular shoulders and the way his hair curled at the back of his neck.

He'd cleaned up after work, obviously, and she felt self-conscious again about her wilted appearance. But he didn't seem to care, at least.

A short distance from the house was a fire pit surrounded by several tree stumps and a pair of Adirondack chairs.

She glanced at the properties on either side. They had fire pits, too, but the houses were dark.

"Where are your neighbors?" she asked.

"No idea. They're snowbirds."

She looked at him. "Really?"

"They get out here a couple months a year, but the rest of the time their places sit empty."

"What a waste of a nice view."

He lifted his beer bottle and pointed it down the row. "Family on the end there, they have their place listed on a couple of rental sites. They get some pretty good traffic."

Ava eyed Huck as he sniffed around the fire pit. He seemed to understand he was on a short leash tonight.

"Ava."

She looked at Grant.

"What's wrong?"

"Why do you ask?"

"You seem tense," he said.

"I do?"

He eased closer and gazed down at her with those bottomless brown eyes. "Yeah, you do."

"Long day," she said. "I don't really want to talk about it now."

His brow furrowed. He reached out and tucked a lock of hair behind her ear, and she felt a jolt of attraction.

"Later?" he asked.

"Maybe." She sipped her drink and looked away. "Is that a creek there?"

His hand dropped and he followed her gaze. "It was. Hasn't been any water in it for years now."

She walked to the fire pit and set her drink down on the arm of the Adirondack chair. Fireflies blinked in the distance, and she had a sudden memory of Fourth of July picnics with her cousins. They'd play in the woods near her aunt and uncle's house while their mothers made brisket. When it got dark, they'd go to the lake and shoot fireworks off the dock.

"Is your family here?" She turned to look at him.

"Some of them." He walked over to stand beside her. "My parents, plus my sister's family. My older brother lives out in Los Angeles. He's an attorney."

"He is?"

"Yep. He's the academic in the family. Loves to debate people. You'd like him."

Ava tried to envision Grant's brother. She pictured someone who looked like Grant, but in a designer suit and sunglasses, and just the image made her smile.

"What?" he asked.

She shook her head. "Does he like it out there?"

"Loves it."

"Do you miss him?"

He hesitated a moment before answering. "I miss him a lot. We were really close as kids, but—" He shrugged. "I don't see him very much anymore."

Ava wondered if Abby felt the same about her. They had been close growing up, but Ava hadn't seen her sister in months. Or even talked to her, really—just the occasional phone call. Maybe it was natural. People grieved in different ways. Ava had always heard that, but she'd never realized what it meant until recently.

She glanced at Grant. He was watching her closely. He wanted information. That was his nature—he was an investigator. And he didn't like that she was holding back.

Ava looked away. She understood this man much better than she should, given the short time they'd known each other.

"So." She sipped her water. "What was in El Paso?"

"Long story."

She lifted an eyebrow and looked at him. "The Molly Shaw case?"

He gave a brief nod but didn't elaborate.

Well, at least he was making progress, even if he wouldn't tell her what the progress was.

Still, curiosity burned inside her.

"Have you been to Whitehorse Ranch yet?" she asked.

"No." He frowned. "Why? Have you?"

"I stopped by to look around."

"You drove out there?"

"Sure, why not? They're open to tourists."

"You weren't there as a tourist."

His clipped tone told her he didn't approve of her continued interest in his investigation—just in case she wasn't already aware of how he felt.

I don't need random civilians meddling in my case.

"Rachel Spencer has been looking into whether Brittlyn ever worked there," she said, ignoring his look of disapproval. "So far, she hasn't uncovered anything, but she thinks it's possible."

He stepped closer. "You need to be careful, Ava."

"Why?"

"Rachel Spencer . . ." He shook his head and looked down. "Well, she's a little obsessive."

"Oh? And how would you be if your teenage daughter disappeared?"

"I'd be a maniac."

She nodded. "So cut her some slack. She's determined to turn over every stone. Two other women who went missing from this area just so happened to work at Whitehorse Ranch. That makes it a stone. And while we're on the subject, Rachel Spencer is not the only one who thinks the place is worth checking out. I've been talking to some people—"

"Who?"

His sharp tone made her draw back.

"A local rancher named Lisa Felding. You know her?"

"She was the Henley County barrel racing champion twenty years ago. What's she got to do with anything?"

"She runs a dude ranch now. Her place has been losing tourists—particularly women—to Whitehorse Ranch. She says her customers are flocking there because they claim they can cure whatever ails you—anxiety disorder, insomnia, infertility, compulsive eating. Oh, and they claim to help people 'achieve spiritual clarity.'"

"Do they?"

She shrugged. "She thinks Willow and Adam Shelton are quacks taking people's money. She's reported them to the Better Business Bureau."

"Willow and Adam are . . . ?"

"The couple who own the place."

"So, she's losing money to them. Sounds like sour grapes."

"I agree." Ava sipped her water. "But the two things aren't mutually exclusive. Could be sour grapes *and* there's something shady going on. Also, I talked to Skye Jennings again and asked her some more questions about the ranch. She said one of the reasons she left was that she didn't like working for Willow and Adam. She said they're really controlling and the whole place has a 'cultish vibe.' That's how she described it."

"What's your point?"

"Just that two women who went missing and were later found dead have a link to the ranch. I think you should check it out."

"I will. But I've been sidetracked with something else."

Ava watched his expression carefully. "The thing in El Paso."

He looked away, and Ava's pulse picked up.

"You have a suspect, don't you?" She leaned around to see his face. "Don't you?"

"Let's talk about something else." He swigged his beer.

"Fine. Don't tell me."

He wasn't going to—she knew from the resolute expression on his face. Part of it was his being protective. He didn't want to encourage her interest in the case. But it was professionalism, too, and she grudgingly admired that.

She looked back at the A-frame cabin glowing behind them. "Want to check on the coals?"

"Sure."

They headed back to the house. He caught her hand in his, and a ripple of warmth went through her. He held her fingers loosely, and she cast a sideways glance at him as she picked up the unspoken message: no more work talk tonight.

"You ready for a drink yet?" he asked.

"Sure. A margarita sounds good."

Huck was poking around the base of the deck, probably looking for critters. Ava gave a soft whistle and he followed them up the stairs.

"You're good with him," Grant said over his shoulder.

"Ha."

"You are."

"Sometimes."

Grant opened the glass door, and she followed him into the kitchen. She smelled the potatoes baking. He opened the fridge and took out a salad kit and a package of bacon-wrapped filets.

"Those are huge," she said.

"I figured you'd be hungry."

"There's no way I can eat all that."

"You can give your leftovers to Huck."

"No way. And he already ate." Ava had fed him in the parking lot of the ranger station after filling out paperwork.

Grant pulled a silver drink shaker from the fridge and

set it on the counter. Ava handed him her empty glass, and he added ice cubes.

"On the rocks," he said. "You want salt on the rim?"

"No, thanks."

He shook the drink and poured, then handed her the glass and watched as she took a sip.

"That's good. Mescal?"

He nodded.

She took another sip. It was cold and tart and felt heavenly going down her throat.

"I'll check the grill," Grant said. "Can you make the salad?"

"Think I can handle that."

He headed outside, and she opened several cabinets before locating a ceramic bowl. She emptied the kit into it and then cut up the tomato sitting on the counter. She stashed the bowl in the refrigerator and paused for a moment to study the photograph taped to his fridge. It showed freckle-faced kids, a boy and a girl, grinning for the camera and holding up a crab trap with several big blue crabs inside it.

Ava dimmed the kitchen light so it wouldn't create a glare and joined Grant on the deck.

"Are those your sister's kids on the fridge there?" she asked.

"Belle and Baxter," he said, placing the grate on top of the coals. "They're five."

"Twins?"

"Yep."

"Oh my gosh. I can't even imagine."

"She just had another one, too. Three months old."

Ava couldn't fathom it. She'd seen how hard it was for Jenna juggling work and motherhood, and that was just with one. She couldn't imagine three.

Ava leaned against the railing and watched as Grant arranged the coals. He hung the tongs on the grill handle and wiped his hands on his jeans.

Ava turned around and looked at the stars. The cabin faced northwest, toward the distant Davis Mountains, which were home to the McDonald Observatory.

Grant came up behind her, and she felt the heat of his body as he rested his hands on her waist.

"See the Milky Way?" He pointed.

"You know, I never saw it before I moved out here. Too much light pollution in east Texas."

"We're a designated Dark Sky Community."

She gazed up at the stars, liking the hint of pride in his voice. He felt good about his home, and she wasn't sure why that appealed to her so much.

She leaned her head back against him, and his arms slid around her. His body was warm and solid, and his closeness made her feel loose and giddy in a way she hadn't felt in a long time.

He pressed a kiss to the top of her head, and she squeezed his forearms against her.

"I thought you wouldn't come tonight." His voice was a low rumble beside her ear. "I'm really glad you did."

"Why?"

He laughed softly. "Haven't you figured it out yet?"

She turned around, and he was watching her with a look that was both amused and puzzled.

"Figured out what?"

His eyes turned serious, and he traced a finger along her jaw. "I like you a lot, Ava."

Her pulse thrummed as she stared up at him.

"Ever since that first day, I can't stop thinking about you." He shook his head. "I was so pissed off at myself yesterday when I forgot to call you because I knew I blew it. I fucked up my chance."

He looked down at her, and his expression was so *earnest* she didn't know what to say. He truly was sorry. And he truly seemed scared—this big, tough man *scared*—that he'd lost his chance with her.

The backs of his fingers rested against her neck, and she felt the warmth of it down to the soles of her feet. He was disarming her. Taking away her defenses one word at a time.

"Let's forget it," she said quietly.

His fingers slid up to stroke the side of her face, and he bent down to kiss her.

It was like they'd never stopped. Like a perfect continuation of the kiss in the canyon the other night, underneath all the stars. His mouth was warm and firm, and she immediately slid her hands around his neck and combed her fingers into the thick softness of his hair. He tasted good again. And he smelled even better—like soap from his shower and smoke from the grill. She pressed against him, and heat zinged through her as she felt his hands slip into her back pockets.

His kiss was firm and confident, like he knew exactly what he wanted and how to get it. And she wanted it, too. She pressed against him, loving the hard feel of his chest and the warm pressure of his hands holding her against him. His mouth slid to the side of her neck and she felt the cool breeze against her damp skin.

"God, you taste good," he murmured.

His warm breath tickled her ear, and she found his mouth again. She wanted to taste him. She wanted more of that sharp, masculine flavor that she'd been missing since the last time. Their tongues tangled together, and she stroked her fingers over the stubble along his jaw.

She ran her hands over his shoulders, his arms, then beneath his T-shirt to feel the warm skin above the waist of his jeans. She rocked her hips against him, and he made a low groan in his chest and kissed her harder.

A soft crackle snapped her attention to the grill as a column of sparks flew up.

"The coals," she said.

"They'll keep." He reached back and opened the door

behind him, then held her gaze as he pulled her into the dim house.

She kissed him as he walked backward across the room, pulling her with him.

"Sofa?"

She eased away and looked up at him. The intensity in his eyes sent a surge of lust through her.

"Bed," she whispered.

For an instant he looked shocked. But then he scooped her off her feet, and she yelped with surprise as he carried her into the bedroom. He set her down on the bed, and her heart skittered as she glanced around his private space.

A faint bark jerked her back to reality.

He leaned over her, resting his knee on the bed and his hands on either side of her shoulders. "You good with this?"

"Yes, but Huck—"

"I know." He kissed her forehead. "Be right back."

He left the room, and she propped herself on her elbows to look around. She was in the middle of his king-size bed. He had a blue plaid bedspread and a TV on the dresser and a stack of books on the nightstand. The bathroom door stood ajar, letting a wedge of light into the room.

She was really here, in his bedroom.

She was really doing this.

Nerves flitted through her stomach as she unlaced her hiking boots and tugged them off. She tucked her socks into the boots and dropped them beside the nightstand.

She heard the scratch of Huck's paws on the wood floor as he preceded Grant into the room.

"Huck, lie down." She pointed to the floor beside the bed.

He ignored her and started sniffing around the dresser, and she sat forward.

"He's fine," Grant said, resting a knee on the bed.

Huck did some circles on the rug at the foot of the bed before plopping down with a sigh.

"See? He's good."

Ava eased back on her elbows again and looked up at Grant as he leaned over her, smiling.

"Are you sure the coals are okay?"

"Yes." His expression turned serious. "Are you sure *you're* okay?"

She nodded.

"I don't want to rush you."

She grabbed the front of his T-shirt and pulled him down for a kiss. And then his weight settled between her legs, and she had the sudden feeling that all was right with the world.

His body felt good. Solid. She moved her hands over his shoulders and traced the muscles through his T-shirt.

She wrapped her legs around him, and his hand slid up to cover her breast.

He stroked her nipple through her shirt. "You are so beautiful."

She laughed and tipped her head back.

"Why is that funny?"

"Just—" She shook her head. She knew better than to argue with someone giving her a compliment, but she really couldn't think of a time she'd felt less sexy going to bed with someone.

She traced her hand over his face, stroking the dark stubble along his chin.

"Thank you," she said.

He kissed his way down her neck, sliding his hands under her shirt, and she sat forward so he could pull it over her head. He tossed it away and then sat back on his knees on the bed, frowning as he caught sight of her bare arms.

"What happened?"

"Thorns." She reached back and unfastened her bra, hoping to distract him.

It worked like a charm, and his gaze heated as he watched

her slide the bra off and drop it on the nightstand. He pulled his shirt over his head, then scooted up beside her and slid his hand over her ribs to cup her breast.

He dipped his head down, and Ava's body clenched as his hot mouth closed over her nipple. She gasped and squirmed as he stroked her with his tongue, and she draped her arms over his shoulders. His palm glided down her body and came to rest at the top of her jeans. He looked up at her, then unbuttoned her jeans and eased the zipper down, and she closed her eyes, buzzing with anticipation as her jeans and panties slid down her legs.

And then his warm hands moved up, lingering on her inner thighs before sliding over her hips. Ava watched the top of his head. She had a freckle beside her hip bone and he paused and pressed his lips to it.

"Grant."

He moved up to her breasts again, plumping them in his hands and kissing them as her body started to throb everywhere—places he'd touched, places he hadn't touched. She arched against him, combing her fingers into his hair.

And then he touched her. She gasped and leaned back as every nerve ending came alive under his exploring hand.

She started to feel intoxicated. He knew exactly how to touch her, exactly how to take her right to the edge until her entire body hummed with yearning. He looked up from her breast, watching her face as he teased her with his mouth and his fingers. He knew he was making her crazy and he was enjoying it, and all she could do was close her eyes and tip her head back as it went on and on until she was burning up, moving closer and closer to the point of no return. And then he pressed his thumb against her and she thought she'd combust.

"Oh my God, *wait*. Please."

He moved up her body, settling his weight on her, and the rasp of denim between her legs made her want to scream.

She reached for his zipper, and he helped her get it down as he kissed her.

"Hurry," she said against his mouth.

The bed shifted as he rolled onto his back and got rid of his clothes. Then he leaned over her—naked now—and reached for the nightstand drawer. She ran her hands over his beautiful abs as he fumbled with the condom.

"Hurry," she whispered again, wrapping her leg around him.

"I'm trying."

"Try harder."

She arched against him, and then he suddenly lunged over her, pinning her wrists to the bed as he smiled down at her.

"You're bossy," he said.

"I'm impatient."

He bent down and kissed her deeply and thoroughly, and the playfulness faded away as she wrapped herself around him. She needed him. Now, no more teasing. She wanted them fused together.

He pulled back.

"Ava."

She opened her eyes. He gazed down at her, watching her intently as he positioned himself and slowly filled her. She closed her eyes and tipped her head back, gasping at the hard heat of him. And then he started moving, thrusting into her with a sultry rhythm, and it was exactly what she wanted. She squeezed her legs around him as tightly as she could.

"Yes."

Every nerve ending ached and throbbed as he drove into her again and again, and she clutched his shoulders and held on. And then the dam started to break, and she felt wave upon wave of searing pleasure as the climax crashed over her. Her body quaked and shuddered, but he kept going, and she held on until he made a deep groan and came, too.

He collapsed on top of her. She kept her eyes closed, luxuriating in the heavy weight of him pressing her hips into the mattress. But then she realized he was propped up on his elbows so he wouldn't crush her. She ran her fingers into his hair and then let her arms go lax at her sides.

She opened her eyes as he rolled onto his side, breathing hard.

Ava stared up at the ceiling, catching her breath. She hadn't expected that. But why not? He was intense about everything. Why not sex, too?

She turned to look at him beside her on his back with his arm flopped over his face.

"For the record, I fully intended to feed you first." He turned and looked at her.

She smiled. "What, and then you were going to carry me off to bed?"

"Yes."

The mattress shifted as he got up and went into the bathroom. She sat up to admire his muscular body as he came back and slid into bed next to her.

She scooted closer and rested her head against his chest. Her skin was damp with sweat, and his room felt drafty, but heat emanated from him.

Ava gazed up at his ceiling, and butterflies filled her stomach as she thought about what she'd done. Twenty-four hours ago, she'd been furious with this man. And hurt. And embarrassed at being stood up.

And now she was naked in his bed. She lay beside him, absorbing the heat of him as she listened to his steady breathing. She wondered what he was thinking, but she didn't want to interrupt the moment to ask. The room was so peaceful and quiet.

Too quiet.

She shot up. "Where are the steaks?"

"Huh?"

She jumped out of bed and snatched a shirt off the empty

floor. Yanking it over her head, she hurried across the house. The kitchen was empty. She whirled around. The living room was empty, too.

Except for a mutilated foam tray in the middle of the rug.

"Huckleberry!"

She swept around the couch and found him lying on the floor, head on his paws, staring up at her.

"No!"

Grant walked into the room, zipping his jeans.

"Ugh!" She grabbed the drool-covered bits of foam off the floor. "I can't believe he did that."

"He's a dog."

"He ate our dinner!"

"What'd you expect? We weren't paying attention to him."

"I expect him to behave! Look at him." She gestured to Huck, watching them lazily from the floor. "He's in a filet mignon coma. He's not even sorry."

"Why should he be sorry? He got steak for dinner."

She turned to look at Grant as he stood there, pants undone and shirtless, laughing down at her.

"Sorry about the filets."

"Don't be." He pulled her against him. "I'm sure as hell not."

CHAPTER

EIGHTEEN

S TILL WEARING GRANT'S T-shirt, Ava sat on a barstool in
his kitchen as she finished her cheesy baked potato.

Grant topped off the margarita in front of her, then returned the shaker to the fridge. He leaned against the counter
in the kitchen and watched her across the bar.

"So, are you ever going to tell me?" he asked.

"Tell you . . . ?"

He crossed his arms over his beautifully sculpted chest.
"The thing that was bothering you earlier."

She took a sip of her drink. "Someone put a snake in
my car."

He leaned forward. "Come again?"

"A western diamondback."

"You're serious."

She nodded.

"Where was this?"

"At the park. I went to open the back hatch, and it was
coiled up there, ready to strike. Huck tried to lunge at it,
and I slammed the hatch shut."

"How the hell did it get in there?"

"The doors were closed, and the windows. I'm pretty sure I locked it, but I could have left it unlocked." She slid her plate away. "Someone definitely *put* it there, though. It didn't just slither inside."

Grant reached for his phone on the counter.

"What are you doing?" she asked.

"Calling Mel Tyndall."

"It's almost midnight."

"He's up."

"Grant, *don't*, okay? I already filed a report at the ranger station. Let me finish telling you what happened."

The muscles at the side of his neck tightened. He looked to be struggling for patience as he set down his phone.

"This was after the search-and-rescue op when everyone was leaving," she said. "I was with Courtney—one of the park rangers—and she had a hook in her truck. I opened the hatch for her, and she collected the snake with the hook and let it go in the canyon."

Grant stared at her, his jaw clenched.

"It was about six feet long, I think." A sour ball formed in Ava's stomach as she remembered the forked black tongue and the steady hissing. Just thinking of it made her queasy.

"Do you have any idea who would do something like that?" he asked.

"No. Maybe someone playing a prank?"

"A western diamondback isn't a prank. It's a lethal weapon."

She slid off the stool and picked up her plate. "I know that. I'm saying I don't have any idea why someone would do it."

"You should have reported it to the sheriff's office."

"Well, I am right now. Sort of." She smiled at him as she carried her plate to the sink.

"This isn't funny, Ava."

"I know, okay?" She turned to face him and sighed. "And while we're on the subject of police reports, there was someone skulking around my house last night."

"What? When?"

"Around nine thirty. Just before you called me to cancel."

"That was probably when your license plate was stolen," he said.

"I realize that now." She crossed her arms. "I went out there to look around—"

"Why'd you go out there?"

"Because I thought it was an armadillo or something. The gate was open, and I found shoeprints under my window."

Grant raked a hand through his hair. "Why am I just now hearing about all this? So, in the last day, someone's been prowling around your house, someone stole your license plate, and someone put a deadly snake in your car. Why?"

Ava hesitated. "I'm thinking, I must have pissed somebody off."

"Who?"

She rolled her eyes. "I'm a lawyer. The list of possibilities is long. Maybe someone on the other side of a custody battle, or a property dispute, or a lawsuit I filed for someone." She shrugged. "Or maybe somebody just doesn't like me."

Grant gave her a long, hard look, and she felt her shoulders tightening. She hadn't wanted to get into this right now, but now that they had he seemed determined to pin down every detail.

"Your house doesn't have a security system," he said.

"No. But I've got Huck. And my Smith and Wesson."

"Do you know how to use it?"

She gave him a *get real* look. "My dad was a game warden, Grant. I'm probably a better shot than half the cops around here."

He looked away, the muscles in his jaw bunching. He was angry. Not at her, but at someone, and not knowing where to direct his anger was probably part of what was putting him on edge.

She was on edge, too. It made her sick to think about how close she *and Huck* had come to being bitten by a venomous snake.

Ava crossed her arms. Just a few minutes ago she'd been relaxed and happily invigorated from sex, and now she was tense again.

"I didn't tell you this to upset you," she said. "I told you because I thought you'd want to know."

"I do."

She sighed and glanced at the clock on the microwave. "I should probably go."

"Why?"

"It's late."

"Stay."

She just looked at him, and his expression softened.

"Don't go yet." He stepped closer, and she watched him warily.

"I don't want to stay if we're going to argue."

"We won't talk about this anymore."

"Yes, we will."

"We won't, I promise." He slid his hands around her waist. "Stay with me."

G RANT BUCKLED HIS belt and looked at Ava fast asleep. His phone vibrated on the dresser, and he grabbed it and slipped out, easing the bedroom door shut behind him. He walked into the kitchen to take the call.

"You on your way?" Connor asked him.

"Almost."

"Fucking feds."

"Since when is the DEA doing a sting tonight? Did you know about this?"

"No, and neither did Donovan," Connor said. "Diaz heard it was all on the down-low but then something went sideways with one of their CIs. Now two of their suspects are on the run, and there's a BOLO across six counties. We're setting up checkpoints."

Grant glanced down the hall and thought of Ava warm and naked in his bed.

"Fuck," Grant muttered.

"Yeah, ditto. See you in a few."

He slid his phone in his pocket and walked down the hall, dreading waking Ava up to tell her he had to leave.

He eased the door open.

She sat on the side of the bed, fully dressed, tying her hiking boot.

She glanced up. "Hey."

"What are you doing?"

"You have a callout, don't you?" She tied her other boot.

"I have to go in. But you can stay here."

"I need to go."

"But you were sound asleep. It's three in the morning."

"It's fine." She grabbed her bra off the nightstand and stuffed it into her pocket.

"Ava, I want you stay."

"I need to get home. Come on, Huck."

She walked past him, and her dog trotted after her.

Grant followed them down the hall to the front door, and Ava scooped up her backpack.

"Would you just . . . wait a second?" He strode into the kitchen and grabbed his keys off the bar.

Ava waited in the open doorway with her dog at her feet. She turned and walked to her Fiat, which was parked beside his car, and Grant's gut clenched as he thought about the western diamondback someone had *put in her car.*

"Wait."

She stopped and looked back at him. He switched on his phone flashlight and aimed it at her windows. He scoured the seats and the cargo space but saw nothing except a black gym bag and a six-pack of Evian water.

Ava opened the door and Huck jumped in. She turned to look at Grant.

"I wasn't expecting a call tonight," he told her.

"No worries."

That was crap. But the last time he'd told her he knew that she was upset, it seemed to piss her off more, so he held his tongue.

She tossed her backpack into the passenger seat as Huck watched from the back, his paws resting on the console.

Grant hated her going home to an empty house tonight, and he didn't care how good a shot she was.

He rested his hand on her shoulder and kissed her. "I'll call you later."

"You don't have to."

"I want to."

"Grant." She looked away, then back at him. "It's okay if we just let this be . . . you know."

"What?"

"What it is."

"What's that?"

"One night."

He stared down at her in the darkness. "I'll call you," he said, and kissed her again.

She slid behind the wheel and started her car.

Grant closed the door and stepped back as she backed out.

Cursing, he turned and walked to his truck.

CHAPTER
NINETEEN

CONNOR SMELLED FOOD. He'd skipped breakfast, and his stomach rumbled as he followed his nose across the bullpen to the conference room, where he was surprised to find Grant alone at the long table. He had his laptop in front of him and a pile of foil-wrapped tacos at his elbow.

Connor stepped into the room. "Dude, are those Juanita's?"

"Yeah," he said, not taking his eyes off his screen.

"Can I have one?"

Grant looked at him for a long moment, then slid a taco across the table. "Sausage and cheese."

"Sweet."

Connor grabbed the warm foil bundle and unwrapped it. Juanita's food truck on the square attracted customers from miles around. Most days, she sold out of anything with meat in it by noon, and it was already one o'clock.

Connor chomped into the taco and looked at Grant. "I thought you went home," he said, chewing.

"I'm working on the case."

"Molly Shaw?"

Grant glanced at him.

Of course Molly Shaw. He'd been obsessing over it since before the bones were even identified. But that was standard for Grant. When he got his head in a case, he was laser focused.

Connor dropped a chunk of sausage and scooped it up. "So, how'd it go in El Paso yesterday?"

"It was interesting."

"Oh yeah?"

Connor had meant to ask earlier, but they'd been buried in shit work all night. Every badge in six counties had been out looking for the two suspects that had slipped through the feds' fingers. They hadn't found them, and Connor figured they were deep into Mexico by now.

Grant continued to stare at the screen, entranced.

Connor leaned forward. "Interesting . . . as in you located Olivia Mann?"

Grant looked up. He glanced at the clock on the wall and then scrubbed his hands over his face.

He looked like shit. They both did. After their middle-of-the-night callout, they were running on fumes. Not to mention the last two weeks had been crazy, too.

Grant checked the paper coffee cup in front of him, but it was empty, and he pitched it into the nearby trash can. He sighed and looked at Connor.

"Yes, I found her."

"And did she know anything?"

"Yeah. A lot."

Connor was surprised. He'd figured if Grant had turned up any good leads, he would have called him last night or at least responded to his text messages. But he'd gone radio-silent, so Connor had assumed El Paso had been a bust.

Grant shut his laptop and looked at him across the table. Connor could tell by Grant's eyes that he had something good.

"I hadn't talked to this girl in more than eighteen months," Grant said. "Last time I touched base with her, she was still in Cuervo. Now she's living with her sister."

"What'd you learn?"

"It's like I thought. Trent Gilchrist lied."

"About what?"

He folded his arms across his chest. "I told you how he said the last time he saw Molly Shaw was a couple months before she went missing, around April fifth."

"The friend's birthday thing."

Grant nodded. "He wouldn't move off that story. I really pinned him down on it."

"Okay."

"So, Olivia—she was one of the friends who was with them that weekend—she remembers the get-together. It was the usual suspects, she said, all hanging out. But get this. She *also* distinctly remembers hanging out with their group, including Trent *and* Molly, a couple times after that. She said they got together at a bar and also she had a party with everyone on Memorial Day."

"Huh."

"So, Trent Gilchrist flat out lied to me. I knew it at the time. I could see it in his face."

Connor looked at the files spread out in front of Grant. He had the murder book open, too. The thick white binder was packed full of reports and case notes. Sitting beside it was a Polaroid of Olivia and Molly that Olivia had given to Grant when he first interviewed her two years ago about her friend's disappearance.

Two long years.

"Okay, playing devil's advocate," Connor said. "Maybe he didn't lie. Maybe Olivia remembers it wrong. I mean, we're talking about some casual get-together, and it's been more than two years since it happened."

"It wasn't just a casual get-together. It was a Memorial Day party that she and her roommate threw at their duplex in Cuervo. She ordered a keg for it. Hell, she even has pictures on her phone."

Connor's eyebrows arched. "She still has pictures?"

"Yeah. I'm telling you, this is nailed down. Trent and Molly and a bunch of their friends were at a party together a few days before Molly went missing. And Trent lied about it."

"So . . . maybe he's the one who's forgetting something."

Grant leaned back in his chair and cast a frustrated glance at the ceiling. He didn't like when Connor challenged his logic, but this was their thing. They poked holes in each other's theories, over and over, until they figured out what made sense and where the weaknesses were in a suspect's story.

"Okay," Grant said. "I could maybe buy it that Gilchrist is forgetful, even though—let's get real—who forgets when they last saw a woman if she goes missing soon after and a bunch of cops start poking around asking questions about her? At the time Molly disappeared, he had to have thought all this through. But, still, even if you *could* buy that, Olivia mentioned something else about Gilchrist that we weren't aware of."

Connor waited.

"He knew Brittlyn, too."

"Brittlyn Spencer?"

"Yep. They had a thing together."

"When?"

"Not long after she came here and fell in with the rock climbing crowd. They hung out with some of the same people."

Connor crushed his foil wrapper into a ball. "Shit."

"Yeah, I know."

"Why didn't we figure this out before?"

"We didn't know about Brittlyn then. I mean, I haven't even talked to Olivia Mann since *before* Brittlyn went missing in Big Bend. I didn't know the two of them had mutual friends until just now."

Connor tipped his head back. "Every time I feel like we're making progress on this case, I realize how behind we are."

"Tell me about it." Grant watched him with a grim look. "So, we now have this guy who was involved with both Molly *and* Brittlyn."

"And he just lied to a cop about the last time he saw Molly. We need to haul him in here and take his bullshit story apart."

Grant's face darkened.

"What's the problem?" Connor asked.

When Grant didn't answer, Connor guessed what the problem was. Donovan. He'd been the problem with this case from the beginning. Connor didn't know why, but the sheriff was dragging ass on this thing, and had been since day one.

"Donovan wants to wait," Grant said. "He wants more corroboration before we bring him in for a formal interview."

"Why?"

"Case he lawyers up."

Connor shook his head, understanding now why Grant looked like he was ready to punch someone today.

"Okay, so . . . we need to find another way to go at this guy," Connor said. "We need leverage. What else do we know about Trent Gilchrist?"

"We know his address, thanks to you."

Connor had tailed the guy from the dumpy bar in Cuervo to an even dumpier apartment complex in Henley the other night. He was living with a woman who was presumably his girlfriend.

"I ran the girlfriend," Grant said, opening one of the manila file folders in front of him. "Sylvia Armondo, thirty-one."

"He likes older women, apparently," Connor said. "Does she have a sheet?"

"Nope. Squeaky clean," Grant said. "She has a five-year-old son and a job at one of the motels here in town."

"Any 911 calls to her apartment?"

Grant shook his head.

"And what else do we know about his employment?"

"He does raft tours with Cuervo Outfitters. Been doing it for years."

"Anything else?" Connor asked hopefully.

River guiding was somewhat seasonal and didn't pay much. Some of the people who did it had a side hustle, like selling dope. It was a pretty easy gig to fall into because they worked only a stone's throw from the border and interacted with tourists all the time. If he and Grant could turn up a side gig like that, it would give them leverage in an interview.

"Didn't find anything," Grant said. "Yet."

Connor blew out a sigh. "So, we have our first genuine suspect, and Donovan won't even let us bring him in. What the hell are we going to do with him?"

"Investigate," Grant said, "but keep a low profile. I want to know everything about this guy. Everything. I want to turn his life inside out."

A N ATTRACTIVE COWBOY held the door for Ava as she stepped inside.

"Ma'am," he said, tipping his hat to her.

"Thank you."

He let the door swing shut behind him, and Ava watched him through the window as he strutted away. She thought of the cowboy from *Thelma & Louise* and suddenly understood why so many of the guests here were women.

"May I help you?"

Ava turned around. Kyra was seated in front of her laptop, just like last time. Again, she wore white head to toe, but instead of a scarf holding her hair back, she had it up in a white scrunchie.

Ava smiled and stepped forward. "Hello again."

The room chilled a few degrees as Kyra regarded her with a cool look.

"I had a few more questions, if you have a minute."

"I don't, actually." Kyra smiled thinly. "I have a staff meeting at three, but I'm sure you can find whatever you need on our website."

"This shouldn't take long." Ava stepped closer, glancing down at the iPad on the edge of the desk. "It's about the Sunrise Retreat. I'm thinking about putting a deposit on that one, but I wanted to get some more detail."

Kyra pulled the iPad into her lap. "I'm sure you can find answers to all of your questions on the website." She gave another fake smile. "And if there's anything further, there's an email link right at the bottom."

Ava gazed down at the young woman who'd been so sparkly and outgoing only a few days ago.

"Who told you to tell me that, Kyra?"

Her smile faltered.

"Was it Willow?"

She stared up at her.

Ava unzipped her purse and pulled out a flyer Rachel had given her. She'd given Ava a thick stack of them, actually, from a box she kept in her car. Ava unfolded the flyer and put it on the desk where the iPad had been and then turned it so Kyra could read the words at the top: HAVE YOU SEEN ME?

"Do you know this girl, Kyra?"

She barely glanced at the picture. "No."

"Are you sure?"

"Yes."

Ava drummed her fingertips on the desk, watching Kyra's eyes.

"How long have you worked here?" Ava asked.

"Why?"

"Just wondering."

She hesitated a beat. "Two years."

Not long enough to have known Deanna, but long enough to have known Molly. And Brittlyn Spencer, too, if she had ever worked here.

Definitely long enough to have seen Brittlyn's smiling face all over the news when she went missing last summer.

Unless this girl lived under a rock, she couldn't have missed it. But maybe that's what this place was like—living under a rock.

"Look again, Kyra. Are you *sure* she's not familiar at all?"

"I'm sure," she said, not even looking.

Ava watched her steadily. "I don't believe you."

Kyra's cheeks flushed, and she darted an anxious look at the door.

Ava suddenly got a feeling of déjà vu. She'd spent a summer during law school working at the public defender's office in Montgomery County. More than a few of the people in and out were abused women, many of them single moms trapped in bad relationships because they needed food or rent money. Kyra's body language right now reminded her of those women.

Kyra darted another look at the door. "I have a meeting to go to."

Ava picked up the flyer and tucked it into her purse. "At this moment police know of two women connected to this place who suddenly went missing and were never heard from again." She leaned closer. "Personally, I think it's three."

Kyra stood up, flustered now.

"You should think long and hard about your job here, Kyra." She took out a business card and set it on the desk. "Call me if you want to talk."

Ava turned and walked out, and immediately the hot, dry air sucked the oxygen right from her lungs. She crossed the parking lot to her car, glancing over her shoulder. Through the trees, she could see another yoga class meeting in the shade of the Meditation Pavilion. They were led by a white-clad instructor—not Willow this time, but a tall brunet with hair to her waist.

Ava slid behind the wheel and stared at the limestone ranch house. She started up her car and cranked the AC to high as she wended her way across the property to the main gate. She noticed a road veering off to her right. On impulse, she turned down it. The rutted road curved around, and the stables came into view.

Ava rolled to a stop in the shade of a leafy pecan tree. Several horses stood in the paddock. One was Starlight and the other was a palomino.

Brittlyn loves horses, ever since she was a girl.

Rachel Spencer's words came back to her as she eyed the big red barn behind the stables, and the smaller one behind it—the hay barn. Just the other day, Kyra had offered her a tour of those stables, and Ava wished now that she'd taken her up on that offer when she had the chance.

A rap on the window made her jump.

A man in a big white cowboy hat stood beside the car, smiling down at her.

She clutched her hand to her chest, catching her breath as she rolled down her window.

"Afternoon," he drawled, tipping his hat.

"Afternoon."

"Help you find somethin'?" He rested his arm on the roof of her car and leaned down. He wore a blue chambray shirt, faded jeans, and a big silver belt buckle that looked like a rodeo prize.

Ava pasted a smile on her face. "I stopped by to get some information about your retreats."

He nodded. "Did you get it?"

"Yes, I did. Thank you. I was just leaving."

His mouth curved into a sly smile. "Gate's back that way," he said, nodding toward the main road.

"Oh. My mistake. Must have taken a wrong turn."

"No problem. Need me to show you out?"

She smiled sweetly. "I think I can find it."

CHAPTER
TWENTY

GRANT TRACKED MEL down in his office. He was seated behind a metal desk heaped with paperwork and had the phone pressed to his ear. Grant leaned against the doorframe and waited a moment while he wrapped up the call.

"I know why you're here," Mel said as he hung up. "Have a seat."

Grant took a seat and eyed the man across the desk. He'd worked with Mel on numerous cases, from drug trafficking to people who had driven into the park with a bottle of whiskey and a desire to end it all. Mel was good at his job, and Grant respected his work ethic.

The park superintendent leaned back in his chair and sighed. He was tapped out. Grant could see it. They dealt with deaths in the park on occasion, but a murder investigation was different, and Mel and his staff had been working overtime.

Throw in a pair of urgent search-and-rescue operations and everyone was hitting their limit.

"So. Ava Burch." Mel rubbed his hand over his shaved head. "I hear you're friends with her."

Grant nodded, not surprised he'd heard. Park rangers gossiped as much as cops.

"We forwarded her report to your office."

"I read it," Grant said. "That's why I'm here."

"You're here to butt in."

He didn't argue.

Mel sighed and reached for a coffee cup on the edge of his desk. He took a sip and winced, then put the cup down.

"You've had a record number of thefts at the park this year," Grant said. "You guys need security cameras in the parking lots."

"Tell me something I don't know."

"You have them at the entrances, though, correct?"

He nodded.

"I need to see the footage from yesterday, from six a.m. on. All three gates."

Mel sighed. "Don't y'all have your hands full right now? I wouldn't think you'd have time to mess with a car break-in."

"That's not what this is."

Mel just looked at him. He'd been a diligent worker all the years Grant had known him, coming in early and staying late whenever any kind of emergency cropped up. So Grant was willing to cut him some slack right now. But he wasn't about blow off what happened to Ava.

Mel seemed to read the determination on Grant's face. He sighed.

"I'll get someone to pull it up for you," he said. "It's going to be a bitch going through it all, you know."

"I know."

"I can spare one guy, but that's it. We've been slammed all weekend, and my overtime budget's about to pop."

"No need to spare someone. I can do it myself."

"You sure?"

"Yeah. But there's one more thing."

"What?"

Grant leaned forward. "Tell me about your staff."

He looked genuinely surprised by the question.

"Anyone with a history?" Grant asked.

His look of surprise turned to wariness as he grasped what Grant was asking.

"I told you before. My guys didn't touch that abandoned campsite."

Grant nodded. "I hear you. But I'm covering the bases."

Grant was almost 100 percent certain that the abandoned campsite had belonged to Molly Shaw. And someone had heard about its discovery and moved it just hours before her remains were recovered nearby. The timing made Grant think that campsite might have yielded evidence that Molly's killer didn't want investigators to find. That fact was way too important to overlook, and Grant was done pussyfooting around. Everyone with any connection to that SAR op—including the rangers here—needed to be looked at.

"We vet our people," Mel said. "You know that."

"I know."

"Everyone's record is clean."

Grant nodded. "What about everyone's reputation? I know you hear things. Anyone have domestic problems? Drug problems? Anyone known to have a short fuse?"

Mel's expression hardened. Grant was asking him to give up dirt on the people who worked for him. And Grant was asking as a detective investigating a homicide.

So far, Grant's prime suspect was a raft guide with no known connection to this park or its staffers. But Grant believed there *was* a connection, even if he didn't see it. He couldn't shake the certainty that whoever had killed Molly had some sort of inside access to this place.

And now—coincidentally—the SAR volunteer who had played a critical role in finding Molly's remains had been targeted here in the park. If there hadn't been a ranger trained to handle rattlesnakes nearby, ready to spring into action, Ava could have been hurt or killed. Not to mention the dog that—coincidentally, again?—had discovered the victim's body out in the middle of nowhere.

It wasn't everybody who had the skills to handle a western diamondback and place it inside a car. The sheer brazenness of it told Grant they were dealing with someone seriously sick.

Or seriously motivated.

Either way, he wasn't about to dismiss what happened to Ava as a prank.

Mel watched him and rubbed his hand over his bald head. "I'll give it some thought."

"Thanks."

"And I'll go through my personnel files, see if anything jumps out." He stood up, and Grant stood, too. "Meantime, we'll let you get a look at that camera footage."

"Appreciate it." Grant held out his hand, and Mel shook it. "I know you're stretched thin around here, same as we are."

Mel sighed. "You know, it wasn't long ago our biggest problems were parking violations and campers who couldn't hold their liquor. Now it's kidnappings and homicides. What the hell happened?"

When Grant didn't answer, Mel shook his head.

"It's all these damn city people moving here," he went on. "We used to be dying for tourists to discover us. Now I'm wishing they'd all go back home."

AVA CUT UP a hot dog and sprinkled the chunks over the mac and cheese. She hadn't made this meal in years, but desperate times called for desperate measures.

The door swung open, and Lucy burst in.

"Grant's here!" She rushed to the counter and grabbed the plastic box of cupcakes. "Can I have a snack?"

"Those are for after dinner." Ava set down her knife and

looked through the open door to see Grant coming up the path with Huck.

"Please, please, please."

Lucy gave her a pitiful look, as though she hadn't eaten in years, even though her lips were still blue from a Popsicle.

"One cupcake." They were mini ones, so it wouldn't spoil her dinner. At least, Ava didn't think it would. She wasn't an expert on four-year-olds' appetites.

Grant's tall form filled her doorway, and her heart did a little dance. She hadn't seen him since leaving his house in the dark.

Lucy strode up to him. "Do you want a cupcake?" she asked, proudly showing him the box.

"Those look good."

"There's three each, but Ava said she probably won't eat all of hers, so you can have one."

Grant looked at Ava across the messy living room. A game of Sorry was spread out on the table, and Lucy's dress-up costumes littered the floor. Grant had on the same clothes as last night, which she took to mean he hadn't been home yet.

"I think I'll pass, but thank you," he told Lucy.

She dropped to her knees beside the coffee table and opened the box as Huck looked on.

"You got a minute?" Grant asked Ava.

"Sure." She wiped her hands on a dish towel. "What's up?"

Grant stepped onto the front porch, and she joined him, closing the door behind her.

"I hear you came into the office," Grant said.

"I wanted to get that report filed on my stolen license plate." Ava searched his face, looking for clues as to why he seemed tense. "Any news?"

"No."

He gazed down at her, eyes intent, and nerves fluttered through her as she remembered that same look last night.

"I stopped by to check on you," he said.

"I'm fine. Just watching Lucy for a while. Jenna took her dad to the doctor."

"On a Sunday?"

"He had a dizzy spell earlier. They want to get him checked out, make sure it's nothing serious."

Grant looked down at her, not speaking. He had something on his mind, and she wondered if he planned to tell her.

"You want to show me where you found those shoeprints?" he asked.

"Sure."

She led him down the steps and around the side of the house. "They started here," she said, pointing. "Looked like he crossed the driveway and came around back." She walked to the back of the house.

Grant crouched beneath the window and studied the dirt where it was still possible to see faint impressions made by a man's shoe. The long evening shadows made the texture stand out, and Ava knew it wasn't lost on Grant that the prints were right beneath her bedroom window. The prospect of someone out here spying on her made her queasy every time she thought about it.

"My best guess is the plate was stolen when I was in the shower and Huck was at the main house with Jenna. Otherwise, I would have heard barking."

Grant took his phone from his pocket and snapped some photos from various angles.

"I took some pictures the other night, but it was dark by then."

He looked up at her. "I'll make a cast of these."

"You really think that's necessary?"

Without answering he stood up and walked back to his truck. He opened the chrome toolbox and dug around. He took out a jug of quick-set plaster and a bottle of water.

"So . . . do you still think it was maybe a car thief?" she asked as he poured water into the jug and screwed on the top.

"Maybe."

In other words, whatever his theory was, he didn't want to share it. She had no doubt he *had* a theory.

He shook the plaster, then walked back to the shoe-prints.

Ava leaned against the house and watched him work. His movements were brisk but meticulous, as though he had years of experience doing this. Which he did. And it suddenly occurred to her that Grant had an entire set of skills that she'd only glimpsed.

He checked his watch and stood up.

"How long does it take?" she asked.

"About twelve minutes."

She walked over to him and gazed up at his deep brown eyes. The stubble on his face was even darker now, and she wanted to run her fingers over it.

The "one night" plan was going to be harder to stick to than she'd anticipated, and she was glad Lucy was here right now.

"What?" he asked gruffly.

"Nothing." She cleared her throat. "You look tired. Have you had a chance to go home yet?"

"No."

"I'm sorry I kept you up late."

"I'm not."

She turned away, shielding her eyes from the setting sun as she looked west. "Any new leads today?"

"Yes."

She turned toward him. "Anything you care to share?"

He just looked at her, and she blew out a sigh. He didn't want her involved, so the last thing he was going to do was give her updates about the investigation.

How would he react if she told him she'd returned to

Whitehorse Ranch today? Or that she'd been researching the owners, Willow and Adam? Or that she'd spent three hours at her office this morning, hunting for information about the property?

She knew exactly how he'd react. He'd tell her to back off.

But she wasn't going to. She was going to keep at it, doing what she did—which she happened to be good at—on the chance that it might yield a lead for the police. She had a valuable set of skills, just like Grant did. And she knew he wanted her to stay away from this case, but she couldn't do it, especially not after she'd come to know Rachel Spencer.

She was invested now.

They stood together quietly as the cast finished setting. Then he carefully lifted it and transferred it to a cardboard box for transport. She followed him back to his truck, where he placed the box in the back of the cab and stowed his supplies in the toolbox.

He looked at her and nodded toward the house. "So that pistol of yours, where do you keep it?"

"In my closet."

"Out of reach of Lucy?"

"Yes. Always."

He stepped closer and gazed down at her, and a warm ripple of sexual awareness went through her.

He hadn't asked what she was doing later or suggested they get together when she was finished babysitting. He was giving her space, like she'd indicated she wanted.

Her gaze dropped to his mouth, and she had a fleeting memory of how he tasted.

He slid his hand around her waist and kissed her. It was hard and brief, and then he let her go and opened the door to his truck.

"Call me if you need me," he said.

"I will."

CHAPTER
TWENTY-ONE

CONNOR STEPPED INTO the air-conditioned courthouse and immediately spotted Jenna across the crowded lobby. She stood near the elevators, gazing up at the building directory. Last time Connor had seen her she'd been dressed for a night out, but this morning she wore a conservative white button-down and black pants with low heels.

Connor peeled off his sunglasses and walked over.

"You lost?"

She turned to look at him. She had on those cat-eye glasses that made her look—in his humble opinion—like a really smart, really sexy librarian.

"Oh. Hi," she said.

"Looking for someone?"

She turned to the directory again and sighed. "Matt Collier, an assistant district attorney. I have a meeting with him in two minutes."

"He the new one?"

"Yes."

"Well, he's bound to be in the annex. I'm headed over there if you want to walk together."

"Sure."

They headed down a hall that was crowded with people.

"They're busy today," Connor said.

"Mondays are like this. Some of the judges front-load their week so they can work Fridays remotely."

They neared the door to the annex, and Connor reached around her to open it. He caught a whiff of her perfume and noticed that her crisp white shirt had lavender pinstripes.

"So, how's your father?" Connor asked.

She glanced up, looking startled. "Okay. Why?"

"Just asking."

A man in a suit strode toward them, and Jenna flagged him down.

"Oh, hey, Ross, you know where Matt Collier's office is?"

"End of the hall. Last door on the left."

"Thanks a bunch."

"Sure." He looked at Connor, then back at Jenna. "I'll see you around."

They continued walking, and Jenna gave Connor a sideways glance. "So, I guess you've heard about my dad, then?"

"Yeah."

It seemed to be a sore subject, and Connor didn't want to push it. They reached the end of the hall, and she stopped in front of a closed door. She turned to face him.

"Sorry if I seem defensive. People are always asking about him, and I never know what to say."

"It's okay."

A worry line appeared between her brows. "He has good days and bad, you know?"

Connor nodded. He *did* know. His grandfather had had Alzheimer's, and it had been hell for his mom.

Jenna was watching him now with a tense expression. His gaze dropped to her mouth. And then to a dark red dot on her collar.

"What's wrong?" she asked.

"You have something on your shirt there."

She looked down and gasped.

"Is that blood?"

"Strawberry." She rolled her eyes. "Pop-Tart goop. Ugh! Now I'm really going to be late." She glanced around. "Where's the restroom?"

"Back the way we came."

"Damn it. I've got to run, okay?"

"Sure."

She rushed away, and he watched her for a moment before crossing the hallway to the office he'd come to visit. He entered a tiny waiting room that had a pair of empty chairs and a coffee table covered with magazines. He stepped up to a desk where a gatekeeper sat typing away at her computer.

"May I help you?" she asked without looking up.

"I'm looking for Libby Bowers."

She glanced up. "Libby Bowers?"

"Yes. Is she in?"

"One moment, please."

She picked up the phone just as the woman in question walked out of an office with a load of folders in her arms. Her face brightened the instant she saw him.

"Connor. Hi." But then her smile disappeared and she looked wary. "What brings you here?"

"I had a quick question. You got a minute?"

"Barely. Can you walk and talk?"

"Yep."

"I'm on my way to a hearing upstairs."

Connor held the door for her as she stepped into the hallway. Libby watched him with a curious look. She had curly dark hair that she'd chopped since the last time he'd seen her.

He nodded toward her stack of files. "Need a hand with those?"

"I've got it," she said as she started walking.

"So, how have you been?" he asked.

"Fine."

If she was annoyed that he hadn't called or texted her in more than a year, she didn't let on.

"What about you?" she asked.

"Busy."

"Yeah, I bet you guys are slammed with the murder case." She sent him a sidelong look. "It's been a zoo around here. I've never seen so many reporters in town."

"Yeah."

"It's really awful what happened to that hiker." She shuddered. "God. It's crazy to think about, isn't it? I've camped in that park before. How's the investigation coming?"

"Slow," he said, hoping honesty might buy him some goodwill.

They exited the annex and stepped back into the main courthouse.

"So, I'm investigating a person of interest at the moment," Connor said. He didn't specifically say it had to do with the Molly Shaw case, but she'd probably assume. "I understand you dealt with him a while back, when you first joined the prosecutor's office."

"Who?"

"Trent Gilchrist."

She frowned. "That had to be, like, four or five years ago."

"Six, actually. You remember the case?"

She stopped beside the elevator bank. "Why don't you just look it up?"

"I did. Looks like he copped a plea."

"Sounds about right."

"The records are pretty sparse, though. I want to know more about what happened, and I saw your name in the file."

Now she looked peeved. "That was a long time ago, Connor."

"I know."

"I barely remember the case. I'd have to check the files."

He'd known that, too.

Connor eased closer and lowered his voice, not that anyone around them was paying attention. "We're taking a hard look at this guy, Libby. If you have anything at all that might help us, I'd really like to hear it."

She laughed softly and shook her head as she looked away.

"You've got a lot of nerve, you know that?" She smiled at him. "You ghosted me more than a year ago and now you show up at my office to pump me for information?"

Connor gave her a calm, steady look, hoping she wouldn't be able to resist doing him a favor.

She rolled her eyes. Then she shifted the files in her arms to look at her watch. "Even if I did want to help you, I don't have time for this right now." She glanced at the elevators as the doors slid shut. "I'm supposed to be in court."

He just looked at her, waiting.

She heaved a sigh. "Call me at twelve thirty. I should be on a lunch break."

He smiled. "Thanks, Libby. I really appreciate it."

She jabbed the elevator button. "Yeah, I bet you do."

J ENNA POKED HER head into the room. "You're here finally."

Ava glanced up from her computer. "What do you mean? I've been here."

"Not much lately."

She was referring to the previous week when Ava had spent much of her time either doing search-and-rescue work or surreptitiously investigating Grant's homicide case.

Jenna stepped into Ava's office and pulled the door shut behind her, a signal that she wanted to talk without Samantha eavesdropping.

"What's wrong?" Ava asked, noting Jenna's worried expression.

"Nothing," she said. "You want to have lunch?"

"I can't. I'm prepping for a mediation at two." She picked up the shiny red apple on her desk. "This is lunch today."

"Which case is it?"

"The Kosenski thing."

"Remind me again?"

"It's a custody battle. Dad doesn't like mom's new boyfriend and is demanding full custody of the kids. Mom says he can't even handle weekend custody and the whole thing is a stunt to get out of paying child support."

"Is it?"

Ava tipped her head to the side. "It's partly financial. And there's some jealousy in there, too, I think."

"So, you're repping the mom, I take it?"

"Yeah. She can't afford for it to go to court, so we're hoping the mediation will do the trick."

Jenna nodded, still looking tense.

"How's your dad?" Ava asked.

"You're the fourth person to ask me that today."

"Well, he spent Sunday in the emergency room. Word gets around."

Jenna came to stand beside the desk. "He's fine." She checked her cell phone. "At least, he was an hour ago when I talked to my mom."

The tests yesterday had come back normal, and the doctors attributed Hank's dizzy spell to low blood sugar and not a mild stroke, as they'd been worried about. But Jenna still didn't seem totally convinced.

"You want to sit down?" Ava asked, even though she was behind on her work. She could tell there was something on Jenna's mind.

Jenna moved a stack of unread ABA journals and took a seat.

"I'm sorry you've been stressed about your dad," Ava said.

"Me, too. But what about you? I never heard about your weekend. How was Saturday?"

"Good. Huck had another big rescue."

She waved a hand. "You told me that part. I meant Grant."

"Grant?"

"Oh, come on. Your car was gone all night, Av."

"Not *all* night."

Jenna rolled her eyes.

"I went over there for dinner," Ava said, knowing it was futile to dodge her questions.

"And?"

"And . . . we had nice time."

She leaned forward. "Nice as in . . . ?"

"Yes."

Jenna squealed.

"Shush!" Ava motioned toward the door. Samantha was just down the hall, no doubt listening intently now.

"Finally. *God.*" Jenna leaned forward and lowered her voice. "I've been rooting for you two."

"There's nothing to root for." Ava glanced at the door again.

"What does that mean?"

"It was a onetime thing. No big deal."

Jenna regarded her with a skeptical look. "How's Grant feel?"

Ava remembered his arms around her near the fire pit.

I like you a lot, Ava.

"I don't know," she lied. "It's not like we had a big heart-to-heart after."

And then she felt guilty, like she was being dismissive of his feelings. Which was ridiculous because he wasn't even here to get his feelings hurt.

"Anyway, he had to go in the middle of the night. Which is exactly what I knew would happen," she said. "That man's job runs his life."

Jenna arched an eyebrow. "What about your job?"

"My job is fine. Much more manageable now that I'm not toiling away for a bunch of oil companies. Now I can actually go home at night."

"No, I mean your other job, the SAR work. Whenever they call you, you have to haul ass to the middle of nowhere to search for some idiot who's lost in the wild with a dead cell phone and a half bottle of water."

"That's volunteer work," Ava said.

"So? It's still unpredictable and demanding, like Grant's is. I'd think you'd be more understanding."

"Why are you on Team Grant all the time? Do you two have some past I don't know about?"

Jenna rolled her eyes again. "No. I'm on Team *Ava*. I just want you to be happy."

"Did a man in your life make you happy?"

"No."

"So quit wishing me the same fate."

"I don't wish—"

A knock sounded at the door and Samantha leaned her head in.

"Sorry to interrupt," their receptionist said. "You have a visitor, Ava."

Ava checked her watch. *Crap.* She was supposed to be prepping for her mediation right now.

"Who is it?" Ava asked.

"A Ms. Napoli? She said you know her."

Ava and Jenna exchanged blank looks. They didn't have any clients named Napoli.

"Kyra Napoli?" Samantha continued. "A young woman? She wants to talk to you, and she says it's urgent."

TWENTY-TWO

G RANT CUT THROUGH the bullpen to his desk, and Connor waved him over. He was on the phone, but he ended the call as Grant walked up.

"Hey, good news."

Grant could use some good news. He'd spent his entire day so far on leads that didn't go anywhere.

"I talked to someone I know in the D.A.'s office," Connor said.

"Who?"

"Libby Bowers. You know her?"

"Vaguely."

"She handled a case about six years back involving Trent Gilchrist."

That got his attention. Grant grabbed a rolling chair from the neighboring cubicle, pulled it over, and sat down.

"This the public intox?"

"The vandalism." Connor's eyes sparked, and Grant could tell he'd turned up something good.

"He vandalized a car, right?"

"Busted out the window of a Ford Mustang," Connor said. "He was nineteen at the time. Copped a plea and got the full two-thousand-dollar fine, plus community service. That seemed a little harsh, so I looked up the case and came across Libby's name. She was a new hire at the time handling some of the crap cases."

Connor had probably dated her once. Or hooked up with her, more likely.

"So, she reviewed the case for me," Connor said, "and sure enough, there was more to it."

"He was trying to steal the car," Grant guessed.

"That's what I suspected, too, but nope. Turns out, the car belonged to his ex-girlfriend. She'd just broken up with him and he got drunk and went on a tear."

Grant just watched him, absorbing the implications. "So, he knew this woman whose car he vandalized. How did we miss this?"

"It's not in the arrest report. But Libby remembered hearing about it during the plea negotiations. Gilchrist was all torqued up because this woman had broken up with him, so he started blowing up her phone and showing up drunk at her house and harassing her. Then one night he took a hammer to her Mustang."

Grant sat back in his chair. "Hot temper."

"Yep. When prosecutors found out about the harassment stuff, they decided to push the case to make a point with him."

"But this isn't in the paperwork?"

"Not really. Libby got the details from her notes."

"Damn, Connor."

He smiled. "I know."

"So now we know he lied to police and he has rage issues when it comes to ex-girlfriends."

Grant wanted to haul this guy in, ASAP.

"The problem is Donovan," Connor said, clearly reading his mind.

Grant clenched his teeth and looked at the sheriff's office at the other end of the bullpen. He wasn't there. Why should he be? It wasn't like they had a high-profile homicide case in their lap or anything.

"Where is he?" Grant asked.

"Some fund-raising lunch, I heard. Damn campaign stuff."

Grant's phone buzzed and he pulled it from his pocket. Ava.

"I need to take this," Grant said, standing up. "I'll talk to Donovan."

Connor nodded and watched with blatant curiosity as Grant stepped into a conference room to take the call.

"Hey," he said, closing the door behind him.

"Are you at work?"

Grant caught the tension in her voice. "Yeah. What's wrong?"

"A woman just showed up at my office. Kyra Napoli. She works at Whitehorse Ranch."

Grant bit back a curse. He should have known she was still investigating his case.

"She has a friend there, a woman named Camila." She paused, and Grant's stomach tightened with dread. "Camila left the ranch Saturday to do an overnight hiking trip in the park and—"

"Which park?"

"Sorry. Silver Canyon State Park. But she didn't come back and she's not answering her phone."

"She was supposed to be back when, yesterday?"

"Yesterday by four. But no one's seen or heard from her since Saturday morning."

"Has your friend notified the park yet?"

"She just did. We called them together. Now she's on her way to you. I figured you'd want to talk to her."

"I do. Where are you right now?"

"In my car."

"You got a callout?"

"No, but I'm expecting one any minute. I canceled my afternoon and now I'm on my way home."

Grant checked his watch. It was after three. This woman was almost twenty-four hours overdue, at this point.

"Yep, there it is," Ava said. "I just got the message. They're launching a search."

A VA CAST A nervous look at the lavender sky. This was the worst light for searching. All the sharp shadows had faded, and everything looked flat and gray.

Today's plan was aggressive. Mel had divided the searchers into nine teams of two to maximize coverage. Once again, Ava had been paired with Courtney, which suited her fine. They'd established a rhythm together and had already cleared one entire sector before taking on another, which put them ahead of all the other teams.

Ava paused and sipped some water from her hydration pack. She was traveling light this time, as was Courtney, in an effort to speed their progress and scour as much ground as possible. To amplify their efforts even more, Courtney was combing the canyon base while Ava covered the upper rim.

A short whistle split the air. Ava changed directions and tromped over to the edge of the bluff.

"How's it going?" Courtney called up.

"Same."

"I'm about to check in. Have you seen anything up there?"

"No, nothing."

The words echoed down the canyon, and a knot of frustration formed in Ava's chest. Despite their swift pace, they hadn't found so much as an orange peel to suggest that Camila had ever passed this way.

Courtney stopped and took out her radio, and Ava resumed

her trek. She focused on Huck ranging in front of her, working the air with his powerful nose.

Glancing north, Ava scoured the horizon, wishing she could see Sun Rock, the object of Camila's trek. But it was on the other side of a mesa from here, inside a different team's sector.

Ava's curiosity festered. After all the research she'd done on Sun Rock, Ava wanted to see the damn thing and find out for herself whether the thirty-foot boulder lived up to all the hype.

Of course, it wouldn't. How could it? But she would have liked to see the petroglyphs, at least.

Ava scanned the scrub trees ahead of her. She paused beside a giant yucca plant, careful to stay away from its daggerlike leaves. The yucca's flowers were edible, as were its stalks. Did Camila know this? Had she learned which plants were edible and how to suck water from a prickly pear ear? Or was she just as clueless and overconfident as so many of the urbanites who came here from Dallas and Atlanta and even New York? Just yesterday, Ava had stood in the grocery store line with a woman from Brooklyn.

Unfortunately, Ava knew precious little about the target of her search today. She hadn't spent much time with Kyra before snatching up the phone to notify Mel Tyndall and then sending Kyra off to the Henley County Sheriff's Office to file a missing person report.

Ava pictured the photo of Camila that Kyra had pulled up on her phone. The smiling young woman, bridle in hand, had been standing beside a black horse at the ranch. According to Kyra, Camila worked in the stables and took guests on trail rides. She'd been on staff for years, Kyra said, although she didn't know exactly how many. Kyra didn't even know where Camila was from originally.

Ava couldn't get over the coincidence that yet another missing woman had a connection to Whitehorse Ranch.

What was going on there? On the surface everything looked healthy and wholesome. All those white-clad yoga girls and those long-legged cowboys tipping their hats and *ma'am*ing her. Ava felt sure it was supposed to be charming, and she *had* been charmed in that brief moment when that cowboy politely held the door for her. But looking back it seemed creepy. Ava could see now why Skye described the place as having a cultish vibe.

She looked at Huck, zigzagging ahead of her with a seemingly endless energy. She scanned the shadows beneath a clump of mesquite trees, like the ones where she'd found Noah and Walter. Was Camila hunkered down in the shade somewhere, nursing a broken ankle? Was she rationing her water supply? Or had she passed out from dehydration?

Or had something more sinister happened to her? Rachel Spencer's words came back to her.

I think a predator could have taken her. The human kind.

Ava shivered, despite the heat. She cast another look north, toward Sun Rock, once again wondering what was so compelling about the spot that a hardworking stable hand would use two of her rare days off to hike out there and camp.

Ava's gaze landed on a distant tree, a twisted juniper silhouetted against the sky. The shape resembled a DNA helix, and a chill went down Ava's spine as she realized it was familiar.

She halted.

The Angel Tree. Also known as Lucifer's Staff.

It was one of three vortexes in this region. If you traced a line from Enchanted Rock just outside Austin to Sun Rock, the line passed directly over this tree, supposedly.

Huck jogged up to the tree's base and started sniffing around. Ava rushed forward to call him off, but then stopped

herself. She was being ridiculous. There was nothing
magical—black magic or otherwise—about the tree or this
place or anything else in this park.

As Huck sniffed, Ava glanced around. Little rock piles
were everywhere, diminutive monuments built by numerous pilgrims who had passed this way.

Had one of those stacks of stones been left by Camila?

Or Molly?

Or Brittlyn?

Maybe even Deanna Moore had heard about this place
from her thrill-seeking friends and come out here before
that fateful day when she went rock climbing in another
nearby park and fell to her death.

Ava's stomach knotted and she glanced at the sky. She
checked her watch and made a clicking sound.

"Huck, let's go."

She and Courtney were meeting in five minutes to begin
their hike back to the trailhead.

Something whisked past her ear and hit the juniper tree
with a *thwack*.

Ava stared at the quivering feather lodged in the trunk.

Not a *feather,* but—"

Hisssss . . . thwack.

She dropped to the ground with a shriek. An *arrow*!
Someone was *shooting at her*!

"Huck!"

He raced over, and she grabbed him by the neck and
dragged him to the ground with her. But he wriggled away
and danced around by her side.

"Courtney!"

Grabbing for Huck again, Ava commando-crawled away
from the tree.

Where was the shooter?

She glanced around frantically, grabbing fistfuls of
Huck's fur as she tried to drag him down.

"Huck, *get down*!"

Hisssssssss . . . thwack!

Her heart lurched. She stumbled to her feet, grabbing Huck's collar as she made a dash for the ridge. She tripped to her knees, diving behind a prickly pear cactus near the edge. The slope was steep, but at least it wasn't a sheer cliff. She scrambled over the edge of the canyon, grabbing bushes and rocks to break her momentum as she slid down the slope. Fire tore up her arm as she caught something sharp.

"Huck! Come on!"

He was right beside her, hastily picking his way down the slope with much more agility than she could manage.

"Courtney!" She searched the base of the canyon for the park ranger. Where the hell was she?

Ava fell back on her butt—*hard*—and slid straight into a bush. She grabbed a branch to haul herself up, then tripped the rest of the way down the slope to the canyon floor.

"Ava!"

She whirled around as Courtney jogged up to her.

"Someone's shooting at us!"

"What?"

She grabbed Courtney by the back of her shirt and sprinted for the base of the cliff, where the dark shadows would make it harder for someone to see them from the ridge.

"Ava, what the hell? I didn't hear anything—"

"They have a crossbow!"

"But—"

"Come on!" Ava ducked down and jogged along the cliffside, desperate to put as much distance between them and the shooter as possible.

"Use your radio," Ava yelled. "Call for help!"

Courtney tried the radio, but all she got was static.

"I can't get anything. We need to be out in the open."

"Hell no!" Ava grabbed her shirt again just in case she

thought she was going to run into the open to use the radio.
"Keep going."

They jogged as fast as they could along the uneven terrain with Huck galloping alongside them, probably thinking this was some sort of game.

Someone had shot at them. *Shot at them!*

Ava tripped on a rock, and fire shot up her leg as she
went down on one knee. She managed to get to her feet as
Huck barked and Courtney grabbed her arm.

"Are you okay?"

"Yeah. Keep moving."

"Ava, seriously, what the *hell* is going on?"

"We were up on that ridge, and someone shot an arrow
at us." Her chest constricted as the words rushed out. "And
then another and another."

"Are you sure it was an *arrow*?"

"I saw it! One landed on the tree."

Courtney gave her a panicked look and attempted the
radio again.

More static.

"We need to get to the trailhead. It'll work there."

"How far?" Ava asked, gasping for breath. Darts of fire
blazed up from her ankle.

"Half a mile. Maybe more. Can you make it?"

"Yes. Let's go."

CHAPTER

TWENTY-THREE

DONOVAN WAS IN his office.

"About time," Grant muttered, cutting across the bullpen. The sheriff had picked a hell of a day to be off campaigning.

Grant rapped his knuckles on the door and stepped into the room as Donovan glanced up and reached for his phone.

"Whatever it is, I don't have time right now, Wycoff. I'm dealing with a drug bust, an injury accident, and a missing hiker in the park."

Grant had taken the missing person report himself while Donovan was glad-handing donors at a Rotary Club luncheon.

Grant took a seat. "Well, I'm working on a homicide, so I was hoping you could squeeze me in."

The sheriff's face hardened, and his eyes turned icy. Missy had the same gray eyes. She could look just as mean, too, when she got her back up about something.

Grant sometimes couldn't believe that this man had come close to being his father-in-law. The broken engagement with

Missy had been a shit show, but their marriage would have been worse.

"Close the door," Donovan snapped.

Grant reached over and shut the door.

"I don't like your attitude lately, Wycoff. You walk around here like you've got a pole up your ass."

He was right that Grant had an attitude lately. He was pissed off, and he wasn't much good at hiding it. But he was the best investigator Donovan had, the workhorse of the department, and Grant knew the sheriff wasn't going to fire him.

"Open your desk," Grant said.

His gaze narrowed. "Why?"

"Just open it. Hildie found something interesting in there the other day."

He opened the desk and frowned down.

"See that blue thumb drive?"

"What about it?"

"It contains the surveillance footage of Molly Shaw walking into a Speedy Stop," Grant said. "It's the last known video of her alive. That was stored in the case file. Why is it in your desk?"

Donovan shut the drawer. "I didn't want someone passing it on to the media so they could drag it out every time there's a slow news day."

"When did you put it there?"

"Two fucking years ago. So what? I don't need a bunch of reporters drumming up drama around here." He leaned forward. "Until a few days ago, Molly Shaw could have been sunning her tits in Mexico, for all we knew. She wasn't our problem."

"Well, she is now. Seeing as how we found her bones in Henley County."

"If you have a point to make, make it. I don't have time for this."

Grant struggled to rein in his temper. Arguing with

Donovan wasn't going to get him what he wanted—especially if Grant won the argument. He needed to at least attempt to acknowledge the man's authority.

"The point I'm making—sir—is that the time for minimizing this case has passed. If we want to avoid a media circus, we're better off solving it."

Donovan's eyebrows arched. "You don't think I know that?"

"We've zeroed in on a person of interest," Grant said. "Trent Gilchrist. Connor's been working on a new lead, and now we're ready to call him a suspect."

"What lead? I didn't hear about it."

Of course not, because he'd been gone all day.

"Connor dug up something in his past. A car vandalism charge from when Gilchrist was nineteen. We learned from someone in the prosecutor's office that there was more to it. The car belonged to Gilchrist's ex-girlfriend, and he was on a rampage."

Donovan sat back in his chair. "This is from the prosecutor?"

"An assistant who helped with the case," Grant said. Donovan seemed to be listening now. "So, now we have Gilchrist caught in a lie about when he last saw Molly Shaw—a lie we can prove with photographs. And we have him in a romantic relationship with Brittlyn Spencer, which he didn't tell us about. In addition, we now know of a history of violence against an ex-girlfriend. And he may even have a connection to Deanna Moore, too. That's one of the things I'd like to ask about in an interview."

"*That* is not our fucking case. And anyway, it was ruled an accidental death."

"I'm aware of that, but—"

"I don't want to hear a word about Deanna Moore. The whole damn Internet is spreading rumors about it, and I won't have my office spreading them, too."

Grant nodded. "All right. There're plenty of other things I need to interview him about."

Donovan regarded him for a long moment. He stuck his chin out, which generally meant he was coming around to the opposing point of view.

"So, you want to bring him in here," Donovan stated.

"I want to get him in an interview room, sweat him down. This kid's only twenty-five. I think in less than an hour I can get him to crack."

"Fine. Do it."

Relief flooded him. Grant felt like he'd been working this case with one hand tied behind his back.

"But bring him in the back door and keep a low profile," Donovan said. "I better not see it on the news."

Grant stood up. When he had what he wanted, it was best to leave. "Thanks. I'll keep you posted."

The sheriff turned away, and Grant walked out of the office, nearly bumping into a sweat-soaked deputy with a bottle of water in his hand. He was one of six people they'd sent over to help the search-and-rescue operation.

"How's it going at Silver Canyon?" Grant asked him.

He wiped his forehead with the back of his arm. "We're done for the night."

"Did they find her?"

"Still looking. They've suspended everything till morning, though. One of the volunteers got injured."

Grant's blood ran cold. "Who?"

"I don't know her name. Some woman with a search dog."

HUCK JUMPED UP and ran across the room, and only then did Ava hear the truck rumbling up the drive. She peered through the curtains and unlocked the door.

"Hi," she said as Grant stepped past her into the house. "You got my message?"

He nodded, but the grim look on his face told her he'd

heard more about what happened than her pithy voicemail telling him she'd turned her ankle.

Grant crouched down to look at her foot, which was wrapped in an Ace bandage. She'd changed into shorts when she got home and had been trying to keep her foot propped up, but she was a bundle of nervous energy and couldn't sit still.

"You been to the ER?" he asked.

"It's fine. Just bruised, not broken."

He stood and rested his hands on his hips as he frowned down at her.

"A paramedic at the park checked it out," she said. "He was able to fully rotate it, so he said put some ice on it and elevate it, everything should be fine."

"I think you should get it x-rayed."

She huffed out a breath, annoyed. "I broke my ankle once and it swelled up like a ham. This is just a bruise, trust me."

"Why are you downplaying this?"

She gaped at him. "Downplaying?"

"Yes."

"Someone shot an arrow at me *and* my dog! I'm not downplaying anything—I'm pissed!"

Huck leaned against her uninjured leg, clearly agitated by her raised voice.

"Sit down. We're upsetting Huck." Ava hobbled to the sofa and sat, propping her foot on the coffee table.

Grant perched on the arm of the chair beside her, his brow furrowed with worry as she arranged a drippy ice pack on top of her ankle. His gaze went to the pistol on the end table beside her, and his expression hardened.

"So, I take it you heard all about the crossbow," Ava said.

"Mel told me about it, yeah."

Mel Tyndall had personally driven out to the site with another park ranger, and they hadn't managed to recover a single one of the three arrows. But they'd come back with a slew of questions.

"I saw the arrows with my own eyes," she said. "It wasn't my imagination."

"I know."

The two simple words took some of the sting out of her mood. Grant believed her. And he hadn't had to cross-examine her first.

He got up and went into the kitchen. She stroked Huck's head, trying to calm him, as she watched Grant opening and closing drawers until he found a box of plastic baggies. He filled a bag with ice cubes and then used the mallet she'd left on the counter to break them into chips. He came back and lowered himself onto the arm of the chair, then lifted the melted ice pack and gently arranged the new one on her foot.

"Thanks."

He looked at her. "Why don't you stay at my place to-night?"

Nerves filled her stomach. She was tempted.

"Will you even be there? I thought you were working."

"I've got some stuff I have to take care of," he said vaguely. "I'll likely be out really late."

"I'd just as soon stay here, then."

"You don't have a security system, Ava."

"Do you?"

"No, but no one expects you to be there."

"We're fine here. Really."

He looked at her, his face taut. He glanced over at her laptop computer, which was sitting open on the coffee table. The screen was open to the home page for Whitehorse Ranch, and once again she knew what he was thinking. He wanted to wall her off from his investigation, but it was too late for that.

"Any word on Camila?" she asked.

"No."

"I talked to Kyra again, and she told me some interesting things about Whitehorse Ranch."

Grant lifted an eyebrow.

"They made her sign an NDA when she took the job there," Ava said. "She's not supposed to talk about her work, or anyone she meets there, or what techniques they use to 'heal' people. So, I asked her if I could take a look at this document to see if it was legally binding, and she said they never gave her a copy after she signed it. Supposedly, they run a 'paperless office' and don't like to print things out. Kyra also mentioned all the ranch's records are digital only, and they're on a computer in an office that only Willow and Adam have access to." She paused, trying to gauge his reaction. "Does that strike you as suspicious?"

"Maybe they're being eco-friendly."

"That's what they claim, but to me as a lawyer, it's a red flag. In my experience, people who try to avoid leaving a paper trail are usually trying to hide something."

He didn't respond to that, so she shifted topics.

"I also found out more about what Camila was up to in the park this weekend," she said. "She was doing a Sun Solo."

His eyebrows tipped up. "A what?"

"It's a trek to Sun Rock and an overnight campout there. It's supposed to be done alone to allow for meditation and self-reflection along the way."

When he didn't respond, she kept going.

"Sun Rock is an energy vortex, according to local legend. It's a popular hiking destination in June. Supposedly, its power peaks at noon on the day of the summer solstice, which is next week."

She didn't have to tell him that June was the month that three other women—and now Camila—had gone missing. She also didn't have to tell him that three of those women had a confirmed connection to Whitehorse Ranch.

Grant sighed, and she could tell he didn't like this entire topic. He wanted her to drop the whole thing.

"So, I've been checking out your theory," he said.

"Which one?"

"About Willow and Adam Shelton."

Ava watched him closely. That he was taking her seriously came as a relief. But she sensed there was a catch.

"And?"

"And there are some problems with it."

"Okay."

He leaned his palm on his knee. "The last confirmed sighting of Molly Shaw was at the gas station near Cuervo on June third two summers ago. We believe she was shot inside the park on the afternoon of June fifth." He paused. "Willow and Adam Shelton were out of the country for the first two weeks of June."

Ava's stomach clenched. "Are you sure?"

"They were at a yoga retreat in Fiji."

"Fiji?"

"Yes, Fiji. On the other side of the world. Their social media accounts are covered with pictures—time-stamped—from that entire two-week period. So, whatever happened to Molly, they were six thousand miles away. I called the place where they were staying, just to confirm."

Ava blew out a breath. Disappointment washed over her as she stroked Huck's head.

"I'm not saying you're not right about the ranch," Grant said. "That couple could be running a shady operation over there. But in terms of killing Molly, they're not looking like promising suspects."

"Who is?"

He hesitated a beat, and she thought he might be about to open up, at last.

"We're working on that," he said.

His phone buzzed. He pulled it from his pocket to check the screen, and Ava had no trouble reading his expression.

"You need to go," she guessed.

He didn't respond, and her heart deflated just a little.

He looked up from his phone. "I'd feel better if you were at my house tonight."

"I'd rather be here."

He glanced at her foot.

"We're good. Really."

He sighed and then tapped at his screen. "I'm texting you my garage code in case you change your mind. The inside door to the house is unlocked."

"I won't change my mind but thank you."

He leaned over and kissed her. It was gentle and sweet, and she resisted the urge to pull him down onto the sofa with her. She wanted his weight on her again and she wanted to feel his skin under her hands. She'd gone so long without that kind of intimacy. She hadn't missed it at all, but now she was craving it. Which was a problem. Wanting this man—*craving* time with him—was a recipe for disappointment.

He pulled away slowly, and the heat in his eyes was unmistakable. "I wish I didn't have to leave," he told her.

"I know."

G RANT CLIMBED INTO the back of the surveillance van. It was disguised as a utility truck tonight, which made it only slightly less conspicuous in the parking lot of this low-rent apartment complex. He quietly slid the door shut and took a seat.

"Any activity?" he asked Connor.

"Nada."

Connor was dressed in street clothes and had his sneakers propped on a milk crate directly behind the driver's seat. He lifted his binoculars and peered through the windshield at unit 209, which belonged to Sylvia Armondo.

"She know we're out here?" Grant asked.

"No idea."

Connor lowered the binoculars and reached for the fast-food cup beside him. After getting the green light from Donovan, they'd set up a stakeout of Trent Gilchrist's apartment so they could catch him coming home and bring him in for questioning. But it had been nearly ten hours, and the man hadn't shown his face. Connor had parked in a shadowy corner of the lot beside a pair of dumpsters, so at least the van wasn't visible from most of the units. But even if Sylvia hadn't seen them out here, a neighbor might have noticed them and mentioned something, and she could have given Gilchrist a heads-up.

"I spoke to the manager over at Cuervo Outfitters," Grant said. "Gilchrist had a raft trip today, but they came in at four."

"Maybe he's out drinking with his buddies."

"Maybe."

Grant eyed the light in the second-floor unit where Gilchrist lived when he bothered to come home. Anger simmered inside of him. His blood had been on a low boil since Mel Tyndall had told him what happened to Ava. Grant wanted to go up to that apartment right now and question Sylvia Armondo about her boyfriend's activities today and whether he happened to own a crossbow.

"I heard about Ava."

He looked at Connor. "Who told you?"

"Courtney. She told me about the snake, too." Connor shook his head. "That's fucked up, man. Who would go after a woman with a rattlesnake? And a crossbow?"

"Assuming someone went after her."

Connor's eyebrows shot up. "You don't believe her?"

"No, I definitely believe her. I'm saying maybe she wasn't the intended target."

"Then who . . ." Connor trailed off and seemed to grasp his implication.

Grant held out his hand and Connor passed him the binoculars. He peered through the lenses at unit 209. The flicker of bluish light told him Sylvia was still waiting up for her boyfriend.

"You think it's the dog," Connor stated.

"I don't know. He's new on the scene and he's good. He's been part of two successful rescue missions recently, and he just sniffed out a body under a pile of rocks." Grant lowered the binoculars. "Maybe there's something else in that park that someone doesn't want him to find."

Connor pursed his lips and stared straight ahead, as if considering the idea.

"So, you don't think Ava's the target?"

"Could be they both are."

The dog wouldn't be part of the SAR team without Ava. Grant thought that was the most likely reason behind all the shit that had been happening. Ava and her dog were—*literally*—digging up secrets that someone wanted to remain buried.

Then again, maybe Ava's other theory was right—she might have pissed someone off through her legal work.

But Grant didn't really think Ava's work as a lawyer was putting her at risk. More likely, her going around asking questions about a murdered woman was rubbing someone the wrong way. And that person now had her in his crosshairs.

Grant's chest felt tight just thinking about it. He wasn't used to getting emotional about a case. He cared, always. He put his heart and soul into his job. But the consuming anger gripping him since Ava had been put in danger—that was new. He felt like his emotions were controlling his thoughts, and not the other way around.

"Grant."

He looked at Connor.

"You look like shit, man. Go home."

"I'm fine."

"I got this. Really. You were up all night."

"So were you."

Connor raised an eyebrow in a way that made Grant

think Connor knew Ava had spent the night at his house. Or at least tried to, before he got called out of bed for a manhunt.

Grant looked through the windshield at the second-floor unit just as the light went out.

"Looks like she's going to sleep." Connor lifted the binocs. "He probably told her he's going to be home late."

That assumed he was coming home at all. If Gilchrist had his radar up—and he definitely should—maybe he'd figured out investigators were casing his place and waiting for a chance to grab him. They could be here all night, and he might never show up.

"Diaz is relieving me at five a.m." Connor looked at his watch. "That's four hours from now. I got this. Really. You should take off and get some rest."

Grant checked his watch. He was tempted to take off, but not so he could rest. He still had a ton of video footage to wade through from the park's surveillance cams. He was on the lookout for any sign of the dinged Chevy pickup belonging to Trent Gilchrist going in or out of the park before Ava's rattlesnake incident.

Or before tonight, when she'd been targeted yet again.

"Seriously, I got this."

Grant looked at him. "You sure?"

"Yes. Go."

Grant nodded. "Let me know if anything happens."

"I will. But I got to be honest, I'm not feeling it tonight. He could be getting wasted with his buddies. Or maybe he has a side chick."

"Or maybe he knows we're waiting for him." Grant looked at the dark apartment window. "What's your gut telling you?"

"You don't want to know."

"Yeah, I do."

Connor shook his head. "I'm thinking our primary suspect might have skipped town."

CHAPTER TWENTY-FOUR

CONNOR OPENED THE window of his truck, hoping the blast of air would wake him up. Diaz had shown at five a.m. sharp to take over surveillance. He'd looked showered and annoyingly cheerful with a supersize cup of coffee in his hand. Meanwhile, Connor smelled like BO and fast food and had a crick in his neck from sitting in the back of the van all night. He pinched his neck now, trying to work out the knot as he sped down the highway and the first rays of sunlight peeked over the canyon.

He neared the Desert Rose motel just as the neon sign switched off. Two patrol units were parked there, and Connor tapped his brakes. A uniformed deputy stood in the middle of the lot, talking to a heavyset man in a trucker cap. Near the entrance, another deputy talked to a skinny guy in a purple golf shirt. Whatever was going down, they looked like they had a handle on it, but Connor slowed anyway and skimmed the parking lot for Trent Gilchrist's gray Chevy pickup. No gray truck, but he spotted a familiar white Camry.

"Shit," he muttered.

Connor pulled into the lot and parked alongside one of the patrol units. He got out, and the deputy with the clipboard—Jack Pullan—caught his eye and stepped away from the man he was interviewing—probably the night manager, based on the logo on his shirt.

Connor scanned the row of motel room doors facing the highway. The nearest motel room had a black sedan in front of it. The passenger-side window was busted out, and a pile of glass glistened on the asphalt.

"Jack." Connor nodded at the deputy. "What do y'all got?"

"Vehicle smash-and-grab. Looks like they made off with some cash and a couple laptop computers."

Connor looked down the row of cars to the white Toyota Camry parked at the end.

"Anyone injured?" Connor asked.

"Nah, it happened quick. By the time someone's alarm went off and people came outside, they were long gone."

"How many cars hit?"

"Three." He turned and gestured his clipboard at the Camry. "The one on the end there had an alarm that started wailing, and that's when the manager came out."

Connor stared at the Camry across the lot. It was difficult to tell from this distance, but he was pretty sure the driver's-side window was busted out. The other burglarized vehicles looked to be the black sedan and a dark red minivan. A shiny black pickup near the motel lobby appeared untouched. The red light of the vehicle's alarm system blinked conspicuously from the dashboard.

"We're getting statements now, but we should be good."

Connor looked at the deputy. "What's that?"

"We've got it covered. We have everyone's statement, we just have to get the lady in 112 there to sign off." He nodded at the motel room where the minivan was parked.

"What about the Camry owner?"

"She didn't want to give a statement."

"No?"

"Yeah, she said she's in a hurry, has to get on the road."

The motel room door near the Camry opened, and Jenna stepped out. She wore jeans and a tight black shirt, and her hair was in a messy bun at the top of her head.

Connor walked over. She spotted him over the roof of her car and visibly flinched. Then she muttered something and pulled open the door. Her makeup was smeared and her eyes looked bloodshot.

"You okay?" Connor asked as she tossed her purse into the car.

"Fine."

"Careful there." He nodded at the pile of glass at her feet. When he looked up at her, she turned away and he noticed the hickey on the side of her neck.

"Jack tells me you didn't give a statement?"

She looked at him. "Jack?"

"Deputy Pullan." Connor nodded at him.

"I don't have time." She checked her watch and glanced away again. "I've got stuff this morning."

Connor looked at her for a long moment, then peered inside her car. "Anything stolen?"

"Not really."

He arched his eyebrows. "Not really?"

"Just some sunglasses and a charger."

"You sure you don't want to—"

"No. I just want to get home."

"Why don't I drive you?"

She frowned. "What? Why?"

"Because you shouldn't drive right now."

"I'm fine."

"Jenna, you smell like a distillery."

She jerked back. "I'm *fine*, all right? And I need my car this morning. I'm not leaving it here."

She started to get in the car, and he blocked her way with his arm.

"I'm not letting you drive right now, Jenna. If you need your car then I'll drive it."

Her jaw dropped open with shock.

"Hold on." He strode back to Pullan, who was watching him warily as he handed off his clipboard to a woman in a tracksuit who was probably the minivan owner.

"Get Rodriguez to finish up here," Connor told him. "I need you to follow me."

He looked surprised. "You want me to—"

"I'm driving this woman home, and I need you to follow me."

"Roger that."

Connor walked back to Jenna, who was watching him with her arms crossed.

"This is totally ridiculous. I'm fine."

He held his hand out for her keys. She gave him an icy look before plunking the key ring into his hand and stalking around to the passenger side.

Connor grabbed a Dairy Queen napkin from the cup holder and swept glass chips off the seat before sliding behind the wheel. His knees were in his chest, and he racked the seat back as Jenna slid into the car and yanked the door shut.

Connor adjusted the rearview mirror and watched as the deputy on the other side of the parking lot got into his patrol unit.

"This is *such* a waste of time." Jenna crossed her arms with a huff. Then she fastened her seat belt and crossed them again.

Connor put the car in reverse and looked over his shoulder to back out. He noted the car seat in back and the Goldfish crackers scattered all over the floor.

He pulled onto the highway and adjusted the mirror again. The deputy was following behind him, as directed. He was talking on his radio, probably relaying his plan to dispatch, and Connor knew that even if this kid didn't know Jenna McCullough it wouldn't take long for this little incident to make its way through the grapevine.

Beside him, Jenna fumed and stared out the window. Wind whipped through the car, and loose strands of hair swirled around her head.

"I'm fine to drive," she said tightly.

"Oh yeah? Want to take a Breathalyzer?"

She muttered something and looked away.

"What?"

No answer. He'd never seen her so pissed. No doubt if her sunglasses hadn't been stolen, she'd put them on right now to freeze him out even more. A Taylor Swift song came on, and she switched off the radio.

Connor looked at her. "You know, we've had a lot of assaults at that motel. Not to mention drug deals."

She didn't say anything.

"You need to be careful."

"*You* need to mind your own business."

"What happens to Lucy if you get hurt, Jenna?"

She whirled toward him. "*Don't* talk about her."

"Okay, let's talk about you. I'm worried about you."

"Oh my God."

"What?"

"I do not need a fucking lecture from *you*, of all people."

Connor glanced at her, stung by her tone.

But okay, fair enough. He'd done plenty of reckless shit over the years, especially in his early twenties.

"I'm not trying to lecture you."

"Yes, you are. You know what? Just don't talk." She held up her hand. "I have a splitting headache and I don't want to listen to it."

He gritted his teeth and focused on the road. The next fifteen minutes went by in silence as she stared out the window, her arms crossed tightly.

The McCullough ranch came into view. Connor slowed at the turnoff. The gate with the *M* was closed.

"Keep going," she said.

Connor drove on, passing the sign for Stoney Creek RV

Park, which had once been part of the ranch before Jenna's
dad lost a fortune to some credit card scammer targeting
senile old people. It was the second plot of land the Mc-
Culloughs had been forced to sell in the years since Hank
McCullough's diagnosis.

At least, it was the second one Connor knew of. They
may have sold off other chunks of land he hadn't heard
about. As far as Connor was concerned, anyone who ripped
off old people should rot in jail for life.

"Here," she said.

Connor braked and turned onto a dirt driveway with a
simple metal gate. Jenna reached across him and tapped the
remote control clipped to the sun visor. The gate swung
open.

Connor drove through quickly to give the patrol car time
to follow him.

They bumped over the rutted road, and the ranch house
came into view. It was a low one-story made of Texas limestone and surrounded by oak trees. Right out of a story-
book, really. At least, Connor had always thought so
growing up. The McCulloughs were believed to be wealthy
and connected back then. But cattle ranching had lost much
of its luster in recent years.

"Park behind the truck," she said.

He rolled to a stop behind the dark red pickup belonging
to Jenna's father.

He cut the engine and looked at her. "I wasn't trying to
lecture you."

"Keys?"

He held them out, and she snatched them from his hand
and got out.

He slid from the car and looked at her over the roof as
she hitched her purse onto her shoulder, still not making
eye contact.

He wanted to say something to let her know that he
wasn't some hypocritical asshole who cared about whatever

she'd done last night. He didn't. Not really. Mostly, he cared about her not hating him for driving her home.

He closed the door, and she clicked the locks with a chirp, even though it didn't matter with the window wide open.

"Thanks for the ride," she said.

"Sure."

She walked up the steps without a backward glance.

TELL ME YOU'VE got something," Ava said when she picked up the phone.

"I do."

She leaned back in her chair. "Thank God. I've been tearing my hair out here. How can a simple background check be so hard?"

After days of looking for information on Adam and Willow Shelton, Ava had decided to call up the private investigator used by her former law firm in Houston. Darcy was expensive, but she got results. Ava had hired her in the past to track down everything from deadbeat dads to long-lost heirs who had inherited mineral rights they didn't know about.

"Well, I'm not surprised you've been tearing your hair out on this one," Darcy said. "Adam and Willow Shelton aren't their real names."

"I knew it!"

"I just emailed you a driver's license photo."

Ava pivoted to her computer and clicked open the email.

"You get it?" Darcy asked.

"Opening now." Ava held her breath as she clicked into the file.

"*That's* Willow?"

The woman in the photo had bleach-blond hair with dark roots and heavy black eyeliner. The second attachment showed a man with a stringy brown mullet and a goatee.

"Okay, you're looking at James and Whitney Shelton of Toledo, Ohio."

Ava clicked open the bookmarked website for White-horse Ranch. The About Us section had a photo of Willow—in all white, of course—with natural makeup and wavy auburn hair. Her husband stood behind her in his white Stetson hat with his arms draped around her. Ava hadn't realized it at the time, but this was the charming cowboy who'd offered to help her find the exit when he'd come across her snooping around the stables.

"You said Toledo, Ohio?" she asked Darcy.

"Yep."

So his Texas drawl was probably as phony as his name.

"Do they have a rap sheet?" Ava asked.

"Not that I could find."

Ava was surprised. And disappointed, because she'd wanted to have something concrete to share with Grant to help bolster her theory. Camila's disappearance had added urgency to her search for answers about Whitehorse Ranch.

"But I found something else you might be interested in," Darcy said. "They filed for bankruptcy twice before evidently moving to Texas to make a fresh start about four years ago."

Ava grabbed the spiral notebook off the corner of her desk. "Where'd they move? Here?"

"Their first Texas address was in Dallas. But let me get back to that in a minute. You wanted a title search of the property in Henley County. I ran down that shell company you gave me, Bennett Enterprises, LLC."

Ava gripped her pencil and waited.

"Turns out, the person behind that entity is Eleanor Bennett. She's the niece of the original landowner, John Henry Bennett, who died with no kids."

"Wait—she *is* the niece? As in—"

"Yeah, she's still alive. She's ninety-three and living in a nursing home in Flower Mound, Texas."

Ava's pulse picked up. "That's just outside Dallas."

"Yup. I called over there to talk to her and inquire about possibly purchasing her property, and I learned that Eleanor's business affairs are handled by a family friend, who happens to have power of attorney."

Ava's heart skipped. "No way. Whitney Shelton?"

"Nope."

Ava sighed.

"James Shelton. They even gave me his contact info."

"Oh my God. How did they get their claws into Eleanor Bennett?"

"I'm not sure. But they did somehow."

"Any relation to her?"

"None that I could find. But interestingly, Whitney Shelton used to work at a nursing home in Toledo, so maybe this is a thing she's done before. She probably knows some of the ins and outs of how those places work."

Ava leaned back in her chair, her mind swirling. "So . . . let me get this straight. This lady is in a nursing home, and meanwhile this couple has taken over her languishing ranch and are using it to mint money."

"Well, I didn't get to the ranch part yet. I don't know what all they've got going on there beyond what I gleaned from the website."

"That's okay. I've had an up-close look at the operation," Ava said. "It's right down the road from me."

"Oh, hey, but on the subject of family relations, I *did* learn something about James Shelton," Darcy told her. "His father—Reverend Mark Shelton—did six years in prison for defrauding the parishioners at his church in Ohio."

"No kidding?"

"I found a news clip about it in the local paper. I'll text you the link."

"Thanks."

"You want me to keep digging?"

It was Darcy's subtle way of asking if Ava wanted her to keep racking up billable hours. Ava was tempted to tell her to continue, but she really couldn't afford to pour more money into this. At least for now.

"I think I can take it from here, now that I have legit names to work with," Ava said. "This is a huge help."

"Glad to hear it."

"Go ahead and send me an invoice. And thanks."

"Anytime."

Ava glanced through the blinds as a dark red pickup slid into the parking space beside her car. It looked like Jenna was in her dad's truck today.

She returned her attention to her computer and studied the two versions of the Sheltons displayed on her screen. The contrast was jarring. Ava considered herself more cynical than most people, and even she had bought into their cowboy-and-earth-mother shtick at first. The pastoral setting and all those Instagram pictures made the fantasy seem, if not real, then at least possible.

Ava studied the Whitehorse Ranch photo of the attractive young couple. Willow smiled serenely and cradled her baby bump. This picture had to have been posted several months ago. And Ava thought it was no accident that she wanted to show off her pregnancy. She was the very embodiment of health and fertility—and she was using that as a marketing ploy. In talking to Kyra yesterday, Ava had learned that the ranch's Fruits and Fertility retreat was by far their most popular offering, accounting for more than half of the guests. Based on the testimonials, women came from all over the country seeking help on their baby quest. They were willing to pay big bucks, too.

The more Ava learned about the operation, the more outraged she felt. Desperate people forked over huge amounts of money on the basis of vague promises. Then while at the ranch, they were isolated from loved ones and manipulated into believing the cure for whatever health issue they were facing was totally attainable, if only they demonstrated enough desire and commitment. And, hey, if their custom-made treatment program didn't work? That was on them.

As part of the housekeeping staff, Molly easily could have caught a glimpse of the inner workings of Whitehorse Ranch. Maybe she'd been onto their scam—and Ava had no doubt that it truly was a scam now. Someone could have figured out what Molly knew, or maybe she threatened to expose them, and they decided to get rid of her. And maybe something similar had happened with Deanna and Brittlyn. The women could have been eliminated because they knew something about the operation that the Sheltons didn't want them to know or they were viewed as threats to the moneymaking operation.

Ava glanced at her phone, wishing for a text from Grant or Courtney. She was dying for an update about the SAR operation. And she wanted to tell Grant all this new intel about the Sheltons.

Of course, Ava's theory had one small problem. Adam and Willow—aka James and Whitney—had been in a different hemisphere when Molly was murdered.

Ava grabbed her phone and pulled up Willow's Instagram feed. It was filled with peaceful, meditative photos of rocks and sunrises and beautiful people meditating on the dew-covered lawn overlooking the creek. She scrolled through the posts until she got to June two years ago. Those pictures showed more beautiful people meditating, but these people sat under slender palm trees with turquoise water stretching endlessly before them. For two solid weeks, Willow had posted photos of her and her husband in Fiji, looking healthy and in love as they sampled tropical fruit and practiced yoga on the beach at sunrise.

No doubt about it—the Sheltons had an airtight alibi. But Ava couldn't shake the feeling that somehow they were responsible for Molly's death.

Ava downed her last sip of coffee, then pushed back her chair and gingerly got to her feet. Huck looked up sleepily from his bed on the floor beside her desk.

Ava's ankle was still sore, so she was keeping it wrapped in a bandage. She didn't have to be in court today, so she'd dressed comfortably in jeans and a loose white blouse, and she wore a Converse sneaker on her uninjured foot.

She limped to the door and stuck her head out. The office was quiet except for the steady clacking of Samantha at her computer in the reception room, which told Ava that Lucy was home with her grandmother.

She crossed the hall to Jenna's office and tapped her knuckles on the door before easing it open and leaning her head in. The room was dark except for the bluish glow of the computer.

Jenna glanced up and winced.

"What's wrong?" Ava asked, stepping inside. The room smelled of sausage.

"Close the door."

Ava shut the door behind her and leaned against the doorframe. Jenna's hair was up in a baseball cap, and she had an Egg McMuffin spread out in front of her.

"What's up?" Jenna asked, returning her attention to her computer screen.

"Is that Pedialyte?"

She glanced at the bottle at her elbow. "Yeah."

"Late night, I take it?"

Jenna sighed. "I don't want to talk about it."

"Are you okay?"

"Yeah. Just hungover."

Ava watched her, waiting for more about last night. Or possibly an explanation for why she was just now rolling in at eleven o'clock. Or maybe a question about Ava's bandaged foot. Or the ongoing search for the missing hiker.

Finally, Jenna looked up from her screen. "What is it?"

"You missed the meeting with the Frasiers."

She gasped. "Shit! Was that today?"

"Nine o'clock."

"Oh, damn. They came in?"

"Right on time," Ava said. "I tried to call you, but you didn't pick up. So, I told them your daughter woke up sick today and you needed to reschedule."

She buried her head in her hand. "Thank you for covering. Were they mad?" She snatched up her phone and scrolled through it. "*Damn it*. I can't believe I forgot. I'm redoing their wills."

Ava stepped to the sofa and lowered herself onto the arm. "Jenna, what's going on with you?"

She looked up from her phone. "What do you mean?"

"You've been going out by yourself a lot. Meeting guys. Coming to work hungover."

Jenna put down her phone.

"I know you're stressed about your dad, and you've been blowing off steam or whatever, but do you think maybe you should talk to someone?"

She laughed. "What, like a therapist?"

"Yeah."

"Are you serious right now?"

"I'm just saying, I know you've got some unresolved feelings about everything going on with your dad."

Jenna's expression turned sour. "That's really rich, coming from you."

"Why?"

"*I* have daddy issues? Do you even hear yourself?"

Ava bristled. "What's that supposed to mean?"

"Forget it. I don't want to do this."

"No, tell me. What is it you want to say?" Ava braced herself. Evidently, this was something Jenna had been keeping bottled up.

"Ava, *you* are the one with unresolved stuff about your dad, not me."

"That's not true."

"You barely heard from the man for fifteen years. And then you *turned your entire life upside down* the minute he died. You adopted his dog and quit your job and moved all the way out here and started doing search-and-rescue work."

Ava drew back, shocked. "You *wanted* me to move here. You practically begged me!"

"That's not my point. My point is your father neglected you and your mom and your sister for decades, and now you've upended your entire life for the man, and you still haven't dealt with all your hang-ups about him."

Anger swelled inside her chest. "How the heck would you know? I hardly ever talk about my dad to you."

"That's the point! And what about Grant?"

"What about him?"

"Ava . . ." She squeezed her eyes shut and pinched the bridge of her nose. "Oh my God."

"What?"

Jenna glared at her. "A perfectly nice, perfectly hot, perfectly unmarried man is totally into you, and you won't even give him a chance just because his damn *job* reminds you of your father."

"That's not why."

"No? Then what's the problem?"

Ava just looked at her, feeling flushed with anger now as she absorbed all these accusations. Jenna didn't know crap about Grant or how he felt about her. And she knew even less about Ava's history with her father. Ava barely talked about her dad to anyone, and she certainly didn't tell people she'd been neglected.

"You're trying to make this about me when it's not," Ava said. "You're upset you blew that meeting, and now you want to blame me for your crappy day."

Jenna pinched the bridge of her nose again. "That's BS. You know what? I don't want to talk about this anymore." She grabbed her purse off the floor. "I'm going to go for a walk and get some air."

"No, no, no. It's your office. I'll go."

Ava got to her feet and slipped out before she said anything she couldn't take back.

CHAPTER
TWENTY-FIVE

GRANT STRODE ACROSS the bullpen just as Connor stepped out of the break room.

"Where is he?" Grant asked.

"Room three." Connor nodded over his shoulder at the closed door. "He's been in there twenty minutes."

Grant looked at the room where Trent Gilchrist was waiting to be interviewed. He'd been picked up at his apartment this morning.

"Hey, did you hear about Ava's car?" Connor asked.

Grant frowned. "What about it?"

"Well, not her car—her license plate. It turned up on an abandoned vehicle in New Mexico."

"When?"

"Sometime overnight. The vehicle was stolen. Hidalgo County Sheriff's Office says it was used in a couple of gas station robberies off I-10."

"Any connection to everything else going on here?" Grant asked.

"Don't think so. Sounds like it's just random bad luck."

Well, not completely random. Living next to a public campground ramped up the odds of Ava's car being targeted. Grant needed to talk to her about getting a security system above and beyond her dog.

But right now he had a murder suspect to deal with. Grant turned his attention to the door again, rubbing the stubble on his chin as he thought about strategies.

"Gilchrist give you any trouble?" he asked Connor.

"Nope. He's nervous, though."

"Who brought him in?"

"Me and Diaz."

"How'd it go down?"

"No problems," Connor said. "He got home about ten. I went over there, and we just knocked on his door, totally low-key. His girlfriend and her kid weren't there, and he'd just gotten out of the shower. We made sure to tell him this is a voluntary conversation. We just want to talk to him."

"He ask for a lawyer?"

"Nope," Connor said. "But I wouldn't be surprised. He's dealt with lawyers before, so we need to be careful not to push him too much or he might shut us down."

Grant stepped over to his desk and grabbed a thick folder that contained paperwork and notes. Very little of it had to do with Gilchrist, but Gilchrist didn't know that.

"You want me to sit in?" Connor asked.

"You have a good rapport with him?"

He shrugged. "I chatted him up on the way over here. He seems okay with me."

"Then, yeah. Let's try to keep him comfortable, at least at first, so he won't clam up."

Connor nodded. "You take the lead."

Grant opened the folder and skimmed some notes as he thought through his strategy. He needed to get this right. Donovan was breathing down his neck about this whole thing. But more important, Camila was still missing, and her disappearance could be linked to Molly somehow. Grant took a deep breath and opened the door.

Trent Gilchrist sat behind the table with his arms folded over his chest. He wore a faded blue T-shirt and cargo shorts and worn Teva sandals that had been repaired with duct tape.

"Hey, Trent." Grant pulled out a chair.

"Hi."

He had one of those carefully blank expressions, but Grant could tell he was anxious. Grant put his folder down and took the chair closest to the wall, leaving Connor the chair by the door.

"You met Detective Burke?"

He nodded.

"We appreciate your help today," Grant told him. "Okay if we record this conversation?" He nodded at the video camera mounted on the ceiling behind him.

"Sure, whatever."

"You're free to leave at any time."

"I know."

"So." Grant leaned back in his chair. "You been on the river lately? Looks like you got some sun."

"Had a couple trips the last few days." His attention shifted from Grant to Connor and then went to Grant's thick folder.

"How was it?" Grant asked.

"The usual."

"What time'd you get back yesterday?" Grant opened the folder and thumbed through, as if he didn't care much about the answer.

"The usual. Around four fifteen. It's about a five-hour run."

Grant closed the folder. "And then what?"

"What do you mean?"

"What'd you do after you left work?"

"Met some friends over at Miller's."

Miller's was a barbecue joint in Cuervo that had a beer garden in back. It was a step up from the Cattleguard, where Grant had met him earlier, but not by much.

"Y'all eat there?" Grant asked.

"We had some ribs."

"And after that?"

"Not much." He shrugged. "Drove to Henley to shoot some pool."

"All the way to Henley?"

"Some friends from Alpine met up with us."

So, two bars and two groups of friends. The story would be easy to verify. But Gilchrist could have peeled off from the group at some point and gone to the park.

Grant planned to save that for later, though.

"Last time we met I asked you about Molly," Grant said, watching his expression.

Again, carefully blank.

"You told me you two weren't ever really dating, but you stopped seeing each other."

"Yeah?" He sounded puzzled, like he was waiting for the question.

Grant opened his folder again. "That was around, let's see, early April, you said. You saw her at a birthday party for your friend Nico."

"That's right."

"When was the next time you saw her?"

"What do you mean?"

"After the birthday thing in April."

He looked down at the folder, frowning now. "I told you. That was the last time I remember seeing her."

Connor tensed beside him. It was slight, but Grant caught it. This guy was hedging now, and there had to be a reason.

"You don't remember seeing her after that?" Grant asked.

"No."

"You two didn't spend the night together after the birthday thing?"

"No."

"Did you see her after that in a group?"

"I don't know. Maybe."

"So, you *maybe* saw her in a group?"

He raked his hand through his long hair. "I mean, *possibly.* It was two years ago, so I could have maybe seen her at a bar or something."

Grant smelled blood in the water. This lie was at the crux of everything, and he needed to drill down. But he needed to drill very, very carefully or the hole Gilchrist was digging for himself would collapse and he'd stop talking.

Or worse, demand a lawyer.

"So, all right." Grant nodded. "Two years is a long time, I know. It's hard to remember. But you think you could have seen Molly out with friends someplace? You guys had a lot of mutual friends, right?"

"Right."

Grant caught the relief in his voice as Grant fed him this excuse.

"I talked to a few of them," Grant said, "and they mentioned a Memorial Day party at Olivia Mann's place. You remember it?"

"Memorial Day?" He looked worried now.

"Yeah. The last Monday in May. You and Molly were there together with some of your other friends. You did some shots together?"

"Oh. Yeah." He rested his arms on the table. "I remember that now. I think I was pretty wasted though, to be honest."

Connor darted Grant a look. Now Gilchrist was giving himself an excuse about why he'd lied before. And Connor looked worried because Grant was letting him do it.

"What about a few days later?" Grant asked.

His eyebrows arched. "Later?"

"A few days after Memorial Day. You think you might have seen Molly then?" Grant opened the file again and flipped through some pages. "It's been two years, I know, but any chance you saw her someplace after that party on Memorial Day, the one where you were wasted?"

Gilchrist just looked at him. The tension in the room was thick now as Grant edged closer and closer to the last day they could confirm that anyone had seen Molly alive.

Grant tipped his head to the side. "You think it's possible?"

The room went quiet as Grant stared across the table. The silence was taut. Mesmerizing. The suspect was utterly still, and Grant held his gaze, wordlessly coaxing him through the moment so that he could get the answer he needed before this guy ended the conversation.

"Trent?" Grant leaned forward. "I'm sure you're aware about the cameras in Silver Canyon State Park."

He blinked. "Cameras?"

Grant flipped through his file to a computer printout. He ran his finger down the page and tapped it. "Dome security cameras with 360-degree visibility, one at each park entrance." He skimmed a page in front of him, then closed the file. "Every car coming and going is recorded."

"Every car?" Connor asked, chiming in for the first time.

Grant nodded, not taking his eyes off Gilchrist. "License plates, too." He drummed his fingers on the folder. "Anyway, back to Molly. Think back, Trent. Is there any chance you saw her after Olivia's party on Memorial Day? You think it's possible you saw her later that week?"

The suspect's gaze darted to Connor, then went back to Grant again. His Adam's apple bobbed as he swallowed.

"I think . . . it's possible."

* * *

THE SHERIFF LOOKED up from his computer when Connor and Grant entered his office.

"What'd you get?" Donovan asked.

"He lied," Connor told him, still feeling the buzz of a successful interrogation. "And he admits it."

"Close the door."

Grant closed the door and leaned against the wall, and Connor grabbed the chair across from Donovan.

"I *knew* he freaking lied to me," Grant said. He was still amped up from the interview, although you never would have known it a minute ago. Grant had looked almost bored as he listened to Gilchrist's story.

Connor knew Grant was a good interrogator, but that interview had been perfect.

"Tell me what happened," Donovan said.

"He went from, 'The last time I saw her was April, months before she disappeared' to 'Oh yeah, I may have actually driven her to the park,'" Connor told him.

"He now says he dropped her off inside the park on Friday, June fourth, the day before we believe she was shot," Grant said.

"Dropped her off?" Donovan looked skeptical.

"Yeah, I think he's lying about that, too," Connor said.

"He says Molly talked to him at a Memorial Day party and asked if he could give her a ride out there," Grant told him. "She was going camping, she said, and didn't want to pay the overnight vehicle fee."

"Or so he claims," Connor added.

"Does he say he dropped her off there all by herself?" Donovan asked.

Grant nodded. "That's his story."

"And where'd he pick her up?"

"At the Happy Trails RV Park in Cuervo, where she was

renting a camper. He says her car was parked right by her place when he picked her up, by the way."

"So, what happened to the car, then?"

"I don't know. Maybe someone moved it so people would think she left town and wouldn't look for her too hard."

"How?" Donovan asked. "Didn't you say her car key was at this abandoned campsite?"

"*A* car key was there. She could have had a spare key inside the camper she was renting. Or someone could have hot-wired the car. Either way, getting rid of the vehicle bought them a lot of time. We spent months under the assumption that she could have taken off of her own free will."

"So, this guy picked her up and drove her to the park, at her request, and just dropped her off," Donovan said.

"Again, that's what he *claims*," Connor said. "But this means we now have our primary suspect admitting he lied to us about the last time he saw the victim *and* admitting he drove her into the park where we found her body. Next thing we need to find out is whether he has a nine-millimeter pistol."

Donovan frowned. "A nine? Where'd you get that?"

"The ballistics results came in this morning," Grant said. "I meant to tell you. The shell casing and slug we recovered came from a nine. And I already ran his name. Gilchrist hasn't got a concealed carry permit, but that doesn't mean he doesn't own a pistol."

Donovan folded his arms over his chest, still looking unconvinced. "How'd you guys get him to admit all this now?"

"Grant did it," Connor said. "It was masterful. I mostly just listened."

"I let him know we had video footage from the surveillance cameras at each park entrance," Grant said.

Donovan looked surprised. "Do we?"

"Yeah. I've been wading through it since yesterday. But

it only goes back thirty days. The stuff from two years ago is long gone."

"But Gilchrist doesn't know that," Connor said, smiling at Grant. "I'm telling you, that was genius. You should have seen the look on his face when he realized he'd been filmed driving into the park with her." Connor looked at the sheriff. "He was total deer-in-the-headlights, and then he just started talking."

"He says he drove her to the Diamondback Gorge trailhead, let her out by the sign, and left," Grant said. "He says he was inside the park less than thirty minutes. And that Molly paid his entrance fee."

"Any witnesses who can corroborate this?" Donovan asked.

"No one at the trailhead, but he says he talked to the park ranger who sold him the day pass at the gate. Says it was a guy, probably midtwenties."

"That description applies to about half the people working there," Connor pointed out.

"He insists all he did was drop her off," Grant said. "She said she wanted to be alone, supposedly, and planned to be gone two nights and she'd get someone else to give her a ride home. He swears all he did was drive her there as a favor and then he left."

"What else is he going to say if he thinks we can prove that he drove her into the park where she was murdered?" Connor asked.

Donovan looked at Grant. "You buy his story?"

Silence settled over the room. Connor turned to Grant, surprised he'd even hesitate.

Grant sighed. "I think I believe him."

Connor leaned forward. "You've got to be kidding me."

"I think he was telling us the truth."

"*Why* would you think that after he lied to us repeatedly?" Connor looked at Donovan. "I don't buy it for a red-hot minute."

"Slow down. Let's walk through it," Grant said. "We got him to start talking because he thinks we have him on camera driving into the park with Molly. By that logic, we have him on camera going out, too."

"We don't," Connor said.

"But he *thinks* we do. If he was lying, if it was any more than a quick in-and-out drop-off, we'd be able to prove he was lying with a video." Grant shook his head. "I think he was being straight about what happened."

"I don't," Connor said.

"What's he say about Saturday, the day of the reported gunshot?" Donovan asked.

"That's the other thing," Grant said. "He claims he was working that day, doing an all-day raft trip."

"He remembers his work schedule two years later?"

"He says he always works Saturdays in the summer. Without exception. Those are the best shifts with the best tips, and he's been doing this for years, so he gets his pick."

"Shouldn't be too hard to corroborate the alibi, at least," Donovan said. "Which raft company does he work for?"

"Cuervo Outfitters," Grant replied. "I can go talk to the manager over there, get him to look it up."

Connor shook his head. "Let me go on record as saying I think this guy's still full of shit. He's been lying from the beginning."

Silence settled over the room as Donovan looked at Grant. Connor couldn't tell what the sheriff thought about Gilchrist's story. He looked skeptical of it, but Connor also knew he put a lot of stock in Grant's opinion.

"Go check it out," the sheriff told Grant.

"What about Gilchrist?" Connor asked. "What do we do with him in the meantime?"

"Nothing. Kick him loose. But let's keep an eye on him. We might learn something based on where he goes next."

Connor couldn't believe this. "You really want us to release him?"

"What would we arrest him for?" Donovan asked.

"Lying. Obstructing our investigation."

Donovan waved him off, like he was shooing a fly. "Then he'll lawyer up for sure, and next thing we know, this whole thing will be all over the news. Better if we keep him relaxed. If his alibi falls apart, we'll bring him in again."

"So, just to be clear—you want someone to tail him around?" Grant asked.

"Yeah, but keep it low profile. We don't want him nervous." Donovan looked at Connor. "Got that?"

The phone rang, and Donovan reached for it, effectively dismissing them.

Connor followed Grant out of the office, frustration churning inside him at the thought of kicking this suspect loose.

"I don't like this plan," Connor said as they crossed the bullpen. "It's risky."

"It is," Grant agreed, "but we don't have much choice. We can't charge him with murder yet. Our only evidence is circumstantial, and even that looks pretty weak right now."

Connor stopped beside his desk and glanced at the interview room where Gilchrist was still sitting, probably trying to memorize his bullshit story.

"You still have a pretty good rapport with him," Grant said. "You brought him in, so I think you should drive him back. Keep it casual. Chat him up and let him know we appreciate his help and all that—like he's got nothing to worry about."

"And what about you?"

Grant checked his watch. "I'm going to talk to his boss and find out if he lied to us again."

CHAPTER
TWENTY-SIX

A VA LEFT THE office to get some coffee and clear her head. She drove to the Dinner Bell, even though it was only a three-block walk. Stepping out of the restaurant with her lidded cup, she felt anxious and unsettled as she limped down the sidewalk to her car.

Ava didn't like conflict with people, even though her choice of profession might suggest otherwise. Her years-long friendship with Jenna was based on respecting each other's boundaries. In all their strategic discussions about Ava's moving out here, they'd never once talked about grief, and Ava had hardly mentioned her father. But was that what this move was really about—Ava trying to run away from her feelings?

Oftentimes, Ava was glad she'd come here. She felt like this place fit her perfectly, and she was grateful to be running a small-town law firm and helping real people instead of faceless corporations. On days when she got up to watch the sunrise with Huck and drank coffee during her trafficless commute, she felt focused and energized—as though she was *meant* to be here, and she'd found her calling.

Other times she looked around at the parched landscape and wide-open spaces, and she felt like she'd landed on the moon.

Ava tweaked her ankle and gasped as pain pulsed up her leg. Her car was just a few feet farther, but she needed a moment. She sipped from her to-go cup and glanced at the nearby store window. Cuervo Outfitters. The crowded window display included everything from high-end coolers to backpacks and camp stoves. Ava noticed the little patch on the backpacks—a black bird against a sky blue circle. A crow, or *cuervo*, for which the town was named. She tried to place where she'd seen the logo before. She took out her phone and scrolled through the photos.

There.

Ava stared down at the picture she'd taken of the abandoned tent. She zoomed in on the corner of the photo with the cookstove and bedroll. Right there on the bedroll was that same little blue circle with a black crow.

Someone exited the store. Ava glanced up at the sign again and then stepped inside.

The place was crowded, with racks of T-shirts competing for space with camp chairs and hammocks. Ava took a moment to let her eyes adjust as she scanned the store's interior, which felt blessedly cooler than outside. To her left was a display of fishing rods. To her right was a wall lined with colorful kayaks and canoes. At the back of the store, near a row of mountain bikes, Ava spotted a woman in an olive green park ranger uniform. It was Courtney, and she had her arms filled with hydration packs. She was talking to a tall man in a baseball cap, and something about him seemed familiar.

Courtney's face looked intent as she talked with the guy, and Ava wondered if there was news about the search-and-rescue operation.

"May I help you?"

She turned around to see a smiling young woman with long dark hair. Her sky blue T-shirt had the crow logo on the front.

"I noticed your sign outside," Ava said. "It says you do rentals?"

"Yep."

"Is that, like, tents and sleeping bags, or does that mean kayaks and mountain bikes?"

"Both," she said. "What is it you're looking for?"

"Well . . ." Ava hadn't really thought through what she wanted to ask. She showed the woman her phone displaying the close-up photograph of the bedroll. "I wonder, is this some of your camping equipment?"

"Yep. That's ours."

"So, would someone have bought this here or rented it?"

"We put our patches on the rental gear. You know, to mark it as ours."

"I see."

Maybe Molly had told the person she'd rented gear from something about her travel plans and if she planned to go with anyone. Her backpack had never been recovered. But if she'd rented it here, it would lead investigators directly to this store, and so would the rest of her equipment. Maybe that was the reason someone had cleared the campsite after hearing that it had been discovered.

"So, I assume you keep a record of every person who rents from you?" Ava asked.

"Well, we don't rent to a lot of individuals. It's mostly commercial."

"How do you mean?"

"You know, like hotels or dude ranches or guided tours," the girl said. "Outfits like Lucky Seven Ranch, Dark Sky Tours, places like that."

Ava's pulse picked up. "What about Whitehorse Ranch?"

"They're one of our biggest customers."

"Really? I would have thought they'd have their own gear for their guests."

She shrugged. "People prefer to get it through us. Then they can add an upcharge. Plus, we refresh our stuff every year, so they get the latest technology with all the bells and whistles."

Ava glanced at the display beside her. "What kind of bells and whistles do you need on a bedroll?"

The girl smiled. "None for that. But we rent hydration packs, GoPro cameras, tracking devices."

"Tracking devices?"

"Yeah, like emergency beacons. You can signal for help if you get lost or injured. Or someone can signal *you* if you go missing while you're out. We attach them to our backpacks as a safety measure." She lowered her voice. "It's also a theft deterrent so people don't walk off with our stuff."

"So"—Ava's pulse was thrumming now—"you're saying someone could locate a person with one of these beacons if they were, say, lost in the backcountry of a national park?"

"Yeah. You just need to log in to the software and ping it." She looked over Ava's shoulder. "Sorry, could you excuse me for a moment? I need to check out a customer."

"Sure."

The girl walked off and Ava stared after her. Her heart was racing. She couldn't wait to tell Grant about this lead. Someone who wanted to get rid of Molly could have located her while she was trekking in the backcountry and killed her with no witnesses. Same for anyone else using one of these backpacks. If that person was doing a *Sun Solo*, they were guaranteed to be alone. It was the perfect window of opportunity for a killer.

Ava glanced around the store, but Courtney was gone now. Ava wanted to get an update on the search for Camila. But first, she needed to call Grant.

She stepped out of the store and dialed his number. The call went straight to voicemail, and she cursed.

"Grant, it's me," she said after the beep. "Call me when you get this. It's important."

Ava scanned the sidewalk for Courtney as she limped toward her car. No Courtney, but the baseball cap guy she'd been talking to in the store was crossing the street. She watched him from behind. Realizing where she'd seen him before, Ava halted in her tracks.

Her blood ran cold.

"Oh God."

She scrolled through her phone until she found Courtney's number. The park ranger picked up on the first ring.

"Hey, it's Ava. I just saw you in Cuervo Outfitters."

"You did? Sorry, I didn't see you. How's the ankle today?"

"Fine. Better. Listen, how is the search going?"

"Still no sign of her," Courtney said. "The good news is, we've been inundated with volunteers. Mel sent me to town to get stuff for all of them, and we're expanding the foot search this afternoon. I'm on my way back to the park now with ten more CamelBaks."

"So, that guy I saw you talking to in the store a minute ago. Is he your boyfriend?"

"Used to be, but now we're just friends. He was asking how the SAR op is going. Why?"

Ava squeezed her eyes shut. "He works at Whitehorse Ranch?"

"Yeah."

Her pulse was going double time now as her mind whirled with possible scenarios.

Ava cleared her throat. "Weird question, but did you happen to talk to him about that other SAR op we did recently, the one where we found Noah Dumfries?"

"Uh . . . yeah. I went out with some other rangers that night and bumped into him at a bar. Why?"

"Nothing, I just . . . I thought I recognized him. What's his name?"

"Peter Shelton. He goes by Pete."

"Peter *Shelton*?"

"Yeah. What's wrong?"

"Nothing. Sorry. I have a call coming in and I need to go. I'll see you later."

She hung up and frantically dialed Grant again.

"Pick up, pick up, pick up, damn it."

Voicemail.

"Damn it!"

Ava gripped her cardboard coffee cup as she waited through Grant's message.

"It's me again," she said. "I need you to call me *right now*. I think I know who killed Molly. It's a long story, but I just ran into Courtney in Cuervo Outfitters, and she was telling me about this ex-boyfriend she talked to after the search-and-rescue op where I found Molly's campsite, and I figured out who—"

Beep.

"Crap!" Ava glared down at her phone as the call cut off. She started a text message.

Something hard jammed into her side and a hand clamped around her arm.

"That's a gun," a voice said into her ear. "Don't say a fucking word or you're dead."

Ava's heart seized. The barrel of the gun dug into her side as the man pressed up behind her, clutching her upper arm in a steely grip.

"Walk," he ordered. "And don't say a word."

She didn't move.

"Now."

She lurched forward clumsily, gripping her coffee and her phone as she cast a frantic look around. The sidewalk was empty now—*empty!*—on both sides of the street as they passed her car. She shuffled forward, exaggerating her

limp as she tried to buy time to figure out how to get free
of his tight grip. He was pressed up behind her now, propel-
ling her forward with his big body. If only someone would
step out of one of the stores and see her—

Suddenly, he spun her to face a pickup truck parked
along the street. "Get in."

Panic shot through her. If she got in that truck, she was
dead, she knew it. She had to make a run for it now, even if
he shot her. But the grip on her arm was like iron, and she
couldn't run even if she wanted to.

"Open the door," he said.

This was her chance. He couldn't open the door himself
because he held her arm in one hand and his gun in the
other.

Ava tucked her phone into her front pocket and reached
forward like she intended to follow orders. With her other
hand, she popped up the lid off her coffee cup.

She flung the coffee over her shoulder and screamed.

CHAPTER

TWENTY-SEVEN

Grant pulled onto Main Street as he listened to Connor's account of the drive back with Gilchrist.

"So, that was it. He really didn't say much," Connor reported. "Mostly small talk about his job and stuff."

"What time did you drop him off?"

"About five minutes ago. A deputy is keeping an eye on him from the Taco Bell across the street."

"He in uniform?"

"Street clothes. And he's driving his personal vehicle, so it's pretty low profile."

"Let me know if he goes anywhere."

"Will do."

"I'll let you know what I get from his boss."

"Thanks."

Grant hung up. He'd missed two calls from Ava and one from Donovan. Ava had left two voicemails, so he called her back first, but she didn't pick up. He listened to her message.

Call me when you get this. It's important.

The urgency in her voice put a knot in his stomach.

He played the second message. *I think I know who killed Molly. . . . I just ran into Courtney in Cuervo Outfitters. . . .*

"Damn it, Ava."

He tried her again, but again she didn't answer.

Grant clenched the wheel as he drove down Main Street, scanning the cars. Ava's red Fiat was parallel-parked near the store.

Grant whipped into an empty space and jumped out. No sign of her on the sidewalk. He went into the store, nearly colliding with some guy carrying a fishing pole.

"Sorry." Grant scooted past him and pulled off his shades to scan the store's interior. No Ava. He walked outside again and spotted a woman in a Cuervo Outfitters shirt near the door, arranging clothes on a clearance rack.

"Excuse me."

She looked up.

"Did you by chance see a woman come by here a minute ago? She's about five-four. Blond. Maybe she had a dog with her?"

She darted a nervous look at his badge and gun. "Um, yeah. A woman like that was here. She didn't have a dog, though."

"Where'd she go?"

She turned to look down the sidewalk toward Ava's car. "Um, she was limping a little. I think someone gave her a ride?"

Grant's pulse jumped. "Who?"

"I don't know." She looked at him. "I saw her talking to Pete and—"

"Pete who?"

"I don't know his last name." She bit her lip. "He comes in here a lot, though. He works at Whitehorse Ranch."

Grant stared at her. *Shit.*

He turned and strode back to Ava's car, trying her phone number again. No answer.

His gaze fell on a paper cup on the sidewalk near the space where Grant had just parked.

Grant got a sinking feeling in his stomach as he crouched to examine the spilled coffee on the pavement.

He dialed Ava yet again and this time waited through the recording.

"Ava, it's Grant. Where the hell are you?"

AVA'S CHEEK WAS on fire. The pain started at her right cheekbone and radiated behind her eye.

The hot coffee had done nothing more than piss him off, and he'd shoved her into the truck and punched her in the face before climbing over her.

The blow stunned her. Her vision had gone blurry, and before she knew what was happening, he was speeding down Main Street.

Now he drove down a narrow country road. She didn't recognize this area, but they were near the ranch. Maybe it was a back access route.

Ava's heart thudded wildly against her ribs. She resisted the urge to touch her cheek to feel how swollen it was. Tears stung her eyes, but she forced them back. She couldn't get emotional. She had to find a way out of this.

She eyed the man in the seat beside her. The cowboy getup was gone. He wore jeans again, but instead of a Stetson and boots, he now wore a baseball cap and worn sneakers. She looked at the edge of her phone sticking out of his back pocket. If only she'd hit send on that text before he'd plucked it from her hand. If only she'd explained everything in that message to Grant. If only someone had seen her being shoved into his truck. *If only, if only, if only . . .*

He reached for the tallboy beer in the cup holder and took a swig. Maybe she'd get lucky, and he'd get pulled over. Unfortunately, she hadn't seen a single other car—let alone a sheriff's unit—in miles.

Think of a plan. Talk your way out of this.

She glanced at the gun on the dashboard, and a sour ball formed in her stomach.

"We have an open container law in Texas," she said. "Do they have one in Ohio?"

He slid a look at her.

"You and your brother and Whitney should familiarize yourselves with the local laws when you move to a place."

He took another sip and burped. "You're one nosy bitch, aren't you?" He tucked the can back into the cup holder and leaned toward her. "You're going to regret that."

Even his drawl was gone now.

Ava looked out the window as an endless barbed wire fence raced past them.

"You get pulled over, you're looking at a stiff fine," she told him. "A good lawyer could get you off, though, assuming you have no prior DUIs. Do you, Peter?"

No response.

"Now, first-degree murder is a whole different story," she said. "We have the death penalty here. We're not shy about using it, either."

He jerked the wheel right and whipped onto a dirt road. Ava braced her hand on the dashboard as he skidded to a halt.

"Get out," he snapped.

She stared at him.

"Now. Open the gate."

Her heart lurched. She looked at the metal gate in front of them. If she could manage to—

"If you run, you'll get a bullet in the back." He leaned across her, and Ava's chest constricted as he opened the door latch.

A smile spread across his face. "Don't think I won't do it. I've done it before."

* * *

G RANT WAS GETTING desperate.
      Ava wouldn't pick up her phone. She wasn't at the
Dinner Bell, and she wasn't at her office down the street.
Jenna and Samantha hadn't seen her in almost an hour.

Huck was there, though, which just ramped up Grant's
alarm. Where had Ava gone without Huck or her car? And
on a bum ankle?

Grant got her voicemail again.

"Shit."

He scanned the sidewalk as he strode back down Main
Street toward his truck. If Ava *had* gone somewhere with a
guy from Whitehorse Ranch, he doubted she'd gone will-
ingly.

He listened to her second voicemail again. He didn't
have Courtney's number, so he called Mel Tyndall.

"I need to call you back, Wycoff. I'm in the middle of—"

"Is Courtney there with you? The park ranger?" Grant
didn't even know her last name.

"Uh, yeah. She was here a minute ago."

"I need to talk to her about something important. Could
you put her on?"

Grant heard muffled conversation on the other end of the
phone as he continued to scour the sidewalks for Ava. Her
red car was still there on Main Street.

"Hello?"

"Courtney, it's Grant."

"Hey, did you hear? We found her!"

Relief flooded him. "Where was she?"

"In a cave in the western end of Diamondback Gorge.
She was passed out from dehydration, and a search dog—"

"I'm talking about Ava," he cut in. "She's missing. I
can't find her anywhere, and she left me a phone message
that she just talked to you."

"Oh. Yeah, I saw her in town, and then she called me."

"She said something about an ex-boyfriend of yours?"

"She was asking me about Pete."

"Pete?"

"Peter Shelton, my ex."

Grant halted beside his truck. A sick feeling of dread filled his stomach. "Any relation to Adam Shelton at White-horse Ranch?"

"That's his brother. Why?"

Grant jerked opened the door and jumped behind the wheel of his truck. "If you hear from Ava, tell her to call me, ASAP. And if you find out where she is, I need *you* to call me. Get my number from Mel and put it in your phone."

"Sure. Grant, what's wrong?"

"ASAP, Courtney. You understand?"

"Yeah, I got it."

Grant hung up.

WHY'D YOU FUCKING bring her here?"

"Where else was I going to take her?"

Ava pressed her ear against the door. She was in a tack room, surrounded by saddles and bridles and shovels that smelled like manure. Peter and someone else—probably his brother—were in a horse stall just outside the door.

Peter had taken her to the hay barn. After cutting across the ranch, he'd tapped a code into a keypad and driven right inside. Why a hay barn needed a secure electronic door, Ava could only guess. Maybe they conducted business here and wanted to keep it concealed from guests. Or from curious employees, like Molly and Deanna and possibly Camila, too.

Ava's hands were bound with duct tape. She lifted them to the knob and turned it slowly. Peering through a narrow crack, she saw a man from the back. He wore a straw cowboy hat, and she figured it was Adam Shelton.

The man said something Ava couldn't hear, and Peter scowled.

"Are you crazy? The park is blown now," Peter said. "The whole goddamn place is crawling with people and search dogs."

The next words were muffled.

"You know what? Fuck you."

"No, fuck *you*, Pete. This is *your* fault. *You* wanted to go after her."

"I had to."

"She didn't know anything."

"Yes, she did! She'd been asking me questions and I caught her snooping around the office!"

"You're paranoid. And it's going to bring all of us down."

Were they talking about Camila? If so, then her disappearance in the park was no accident.

Sweat trickled down her spine and she tried not to panic. She had to stay calm and think of a way out of this.

Adam said something else that she couldn't make out, and she strained to listen.

"We agreed to lie low, and now you go and bring a lawyer here."

"She won't be here for long. I'm—" Peter's next words were muffled, and Ava's heart squeezed. What were they planning? "—eastern gate. There's an old well there."

Silence.

Ava held her breath, desperate to hear more. Her pulse thrummed wildly. Was Adam going to object to this plan?

"Do what you have to," Adam said. "But keep it quiet."

"I know."

"And make it fast."

Ava eased the door shut and released the knob. She had to get out of here *now*. She crept across the tack room and tried the only other door again. It was locked from the other side, but it was one of those padlock latches. Maybe she could use a shovel and pry the board loose. She pushed the door open as far as it would go and peered through the one-inch gap.

Ava picked up a shovel with her bound hands. She slid the blade between the thin wooden door and the doorframe and watched the padlock as she tried to widen the opening. Bracing her weight on her good foot, she put more muscle into it, but the door and the frame held firm. She leaned closer and peered through the narrow gap into the dim room beyond. It was filled with hay, rectangular bales stacked halfway to the rafters. At the end of the wall of hay, she spied the back of a white car.

Ava squinted into the dimness. Something about the dusty car nagged at her. She studied the dented bumper and the Ford emblem.

It hit her like a gut punch. The car was Molly's.

CHAPTER

TWENTY-EIGHT

G RANT CALLED CONNOR as he sped down the highway.
      "You hear the news?" Connor asked when he picked
up. "They found the hiker."

"Listen, I can't find Ava," Grant told him. "There's a
chance she was kidnapped."

"Kidnapped?"

"She was on Main Street talking to someone and—"

"Wait, Main Street? Are you talking about Cuervo?"
Connor asked.

"Yeah."

"Did you hear the radio just now?"

"No."

"This just went out. Some lady called to report that she
was at the Dinner Bell and saw a man in a pickup punch a
woman in his truck, and then he drove off."

Grant's blood turned cold. "Did they get a plate?"

"No. Just that it was a white Ford pickup. We sent a unit
over there, but they didn't—"

"That's Ava. He's taking her somewhere! Where would

he take her? Not the park. The place is swarming with people. It's Whitehorse Ranch. *Has* to be." Grant stomped the gas. "I'm headed there now, and I need backup."

"You know, Trent Gilchrist hasn't moved," Connor said. "He's still at home."

"I'm not worried about him anymore. It's Peter Shelton."

"Who?"

"I'll explain later. Just get to Whitehorse Ranch."

"I'm on my way."

AVA'S HEART JACKHAMMERED as they bumped along the dirt road. It wasn't even a road, really—more like a horse trail. Her bound hands felt tingly, and her palms were sweating.

"Killing me won't help," she told Peter. "I already tipped off investigators to what you're doing here."

He stared straight ahead.

"They know about Molly Shaw, too. You're about to be arrested." She tried to keep her voice calm, but even she could hear the panic in it. "You're just making things worse for yourself, Peter. You should leave now while you still have the chance. Start over somewhere else. No one will know."

Still nothing. He didn't even look at her.

She eyed the clunky black pistol on the dashboard. It was on the left side of the steering wheel, within easy reach for him.

Her throat tightened and she turned to face the window. She had to do something. Running her mouth wasn't working. She didn't know where the eastern gate was, but they'd been in the car at least ten minutes, and they had to be getting close to the edge of the property.

He grabbed his phone from the cup holder and texted something with his right hand. Ava's phone was still sticking out of his pocket. It was turned off, though. She'd set an alarm for herself about a client meeting at two, and she hadn't heard a sound. Had Grant tried to call her? Or Jenna? They had to be getting worried by now.

Tears stung her eyes and she blinked them back. She wished someone would track her down, and maybe they were trying but this was all happening so fast. She frantically tried to think of what she could do. She'd been involved in plenty of searches, but always as the searcher and not the target. She'd tried to leave a trail, though. She'd unwound her Ace bandage and left it back in the tack room. Peter hadn't even noticed that her foot wasn't wrapped anymore. And she'd dropped a gum wrapper she'd had in her pocket just outside the hay barn. Now she lifted her hands to her face and pretended to be rubbing her bruised cheek as she undid her gold hoop earring. She'd drop it on the floor of the truck, where police might find it, or maybe a search dog.

Ava bit her lip with frustration as the landscape whisked by. Her trail of breadcrumbs wasn't going to help her if no one knew where to look.

G RANT SPOTTED CONNOR parked on the side of the road near the gate. He screeched to a stop and rolled down the window.

"Get in."

"You don't want to wait for backup?" Connor asked.

"No."

Connor left his sheriff's office SUV on the side of the road and climbed in. Grant hit the gas.

"Tell me what's going on."

"I think Peter Shelton was the guy on Main Street who assaulted that woman in his truck, and I think that woman was Ava. Earlier, she left me a message that she believed Courtney's ex-boyfriend was behind Molly Shaw's murder."

"Courtney's ex?"

"Ava didn't explain, but then I talked to Courtney, and she said Ava had just asked her about Peter Shelton, her ex-boyfriend. I think Peter has Ava and he brought her here."

Grant hooked a right onto the driveway. The gate was wide open, and he went right through. He skimmed the surrounding area as he thought through his plan.

"I've got a satellite map pulled up on my phone," he told Connor. "Looks like most of the buildings on the property are on the front ten acres."

Connor picked up the phone and studied the image. "Except this little rooftop back here. What's that?"

"I don't know. Maybe a cabin?"

They swung around a bend and neared a fork. To the left were some stables. Down the road to the right was a cluster of stone buildings with red tile roofs.

"Drop me off here," Connor said. "I'll poke around."

Grant dropped him off and then drove a bit farther and turned into a gravel parking lot. He parked right outside the door to the main building.

A tall, very pregnant woman stepped out. Willow Shelton. She wore white yoga clothes and had her hair up in a turban.

"May I help you?" she asked, looking alarmed at the sudden appearance of a police vehicle right at her door.

He flashed his ID. "Grant Wycoff, Henley County Sheriff's Office. I'm looking for Peter Shelton."

Surprise flickered across her face, but then it was gone.

"Peter isn't here," she said.

"Where is he?"

"I don't know."

"Call him."

"Excuse me?"

"Call him and ask him where he is. I'll wait."

Her cheeks flushed as she realized her predicament. She didn't want to appear uncooperative, but she definitely did not want to make that phone call.

"I don't understand." Her brow furrowed with fake confusion. "I just told you he's not here, and now you want me to call him?"

"Grant!"

He turned to see Connor jogging over from the horse corral. Grant left Willow standing on the doorstep, pretending to be confused.

"I talked to a girl in the stables," Connor said. "Peter Shelton's here. She just saw him."

THE TRUCK SKIDDED to a halt, and Ava threw her hands against the dash to catch herself. He shoved it in park and unlocked the doors. Then he grabbed the pistol, and Ava's heart skipped a beat.

"Get out."

"This is crazy," she sputtered. "People will hear you. Just like they heard you with Molly. Gunshots carry!"

He reached over her with his left hand and popped open the glove box in front of her. Inside was a long hunting knife with a serrated blade.

Ava's throat went dry.

He picked up the knife and pointed it at her. "Out. Now."

She reached her bound hands over to unlatch the door and scooted out of the truck. She landed awkwardly on her injured foot, and pain shot up her leg.

Ava stood beside the truck, darting her gaze around desperately and trying to come up with a plan. They were in the middle of nowhere. Just scrub trees and rocks and prickly pear cacti. She didn't see any people or landmarks, not even the old well he'd mentioned, where he probably intended to dump her body.

He got out of the truck, and she glanced inside as he rounded the front of the pickup. His keys were still in the ignition.

She lunged back inside and yanked the door shut. She

jabbed the door lock button, then turned and pounded the horn.

Pop!

Ava shrieked as glass exploded beside her. She dove to the floor and rolled herself into a ball.

Pop! Pop!

Screaming, she stared at the bullet holes in the seat, then watched in horror as an arm reached through the shattered window and unlocked the door.

She lurched across the truck and scrambled out the other side, landing hard on her knees in the dirt. She cast a frantic look behind her and then made a dash for the trees.

G RANT SPED IN the direction of the gunshots. The truck dipped down, then jerked up as they hit a rut.

Something white streaked through the bushes ahead.

"There she is!" Connor yelled.

Grant stomped the brake and skidded to a stop. He threw the car in park, grabbing his gun from his holster as he shoved open the door.

Another figure darted between the bushes.

"Police! Drop your weapon!" Grant yelled.

A rustle in the trees.

Connor was behind his door now, his weapon aimed at the big rock where the man was hiding.

"Drop your weapon!" Grant yelled again.

Pop!

The bullet pinged off the side of the truck, and Connor looked at Grant in disbelief.

"Fucker's crazy."

Grant scanned the area for Ava, urgently hoping she was just lying low right now, not hit.

"Cover me," he snapped at Connor.

Grant ducked down and sprinted from the truck to a large oak tree.

Pop!

Pop pop pop!

The staccato of gunfire came from different directions as Grant ducked behind the tree trunk. From there he had a better angle. Gripping his weapon, he eased around the tree until he caught a glimpse of the shooter. The man crouched low to the ground with his back pressed up against the rock. He had a pistol clutched in both hands and a hunting knife clamped between his teeth. His eyes looked wild. Desperate.

Connor was right. He had to be crazy to shoot at two cops, knowing more were sure to be on the way.

But where the hell were they? Their backup should have been here by now.

Grant inched around the tree until he had a better angle on the shooter. He took aim.

The man bolted for a giant oak tree. Grant and Connor fired in unison, but they must have missed because he didn't go down.

Suddenly, the man burst out from behind the tree and made the short dash to his truck.

Connor sprang out and tackled him from behind. Grant sprinted over and grabbed the loose gun off the ground as Connor wrestled the man's hands behind his back. Grant tucked the gun into his belt and kicked the knife away, then helped Connor get the man under control as he cursed and flailed.

"You're under arrest, motherfucker," Connor said, holding his hands as Grant slapped on the handcuffs.

Grant noticed the blood on Connor's arm.

"Con, you're hit, man."

He shook his head. "Just a scratch."

There was blood on the ground, too, but it looked to be coming from the shooter. He'd split his lip open when Connor tackled him.

"You got him?" Grant asked Connor.

"Yeah."

He stood and looked around, his chest constricting as he scanned the trees for any sign of Ava.

"Ava!"

No answer.

Grant sprinted to the bushes where he'd seen her run. Nothing. He whirled around, doing a full 360. He kept going, jogging through scrub brush, swiping at branches as he searched the ground.

A soft hiccup came from close by. Grant rushed to a nearby juniper. He found her crouched at the base of it, her back pressed flat against the trunk.

She watched him, wide-eyed, clutching her shoulder as he dropped to his knees beside her.

"God, you're bleeding. Are you hit?"

She sucked in a breath, then shook her head.

He cupped his hand over her bloody fingers. "Ava—"

"It's just"—*hiccup*—"glass."

"Let me see."

She made another hiccuping sound as he carefully pulled her trembling hand away from her arm. Dots of blood and little chunks of glass covered her sleeve.

"He shot"—*hiccup*—"the window. Not me."

Her entire body was shaking uncontrollably. He circled his arm around her shoulder, and she tipped against him.

"Is he"—another hiccup—"dead?"

"No." He eased her head against his chest. "But we got him."

CHAPTER
TWENTY-NINE

CONNOR SPOTTED GRANT as he exited the hospital.

"How's your arm?" Grant asked, stopping on the sidewalk beside the door.

"Fine. It's just a flesh wound."

"Caused by a bullet. You sure you're okay?"

"It just needed a couple stitches."

Grant looked past him at the empty waiting room. "Is Ava still back there?"

"I think she's almost finished," Connor said. "How's it going at the crime scene?"

Donovan had sent Connor to get his arm looked at just as investigators from a host of different agencies descended on the ranch to sort out what had happened.

"Peter Shelton's being booked right now," Grant said, stepping into some shade near the door. It was hot as hell still, even though it was after six. "Willow Shelton is in custody, but still no sign of her husband."

"Damn, he really fled?"

"Apparently so."

They'd been wrong about Trent Gilchrist, obviously. It no longer looked as though Molly Shaw was murdered by an ex-lover who couldn't take rejection.

"So, what's your take now?" Connor asked.

"It's looking like Molly was killed because she was a threat to the Sheltons. That's why they went after Ava, too."

Grant cast another look over Connor's shoulder at the waiting room. Connor had never seen him so tense.

"A threat of what? Exposure?" Connor asked.

"Yeah. Their operation at the ranch has been making money hand over fist, probably illegally. I think Molly figured out the whole thing was a con. They worried she could expose them, so she had to go." Grant shook his head. "Ava's been digging around the same evidence, asking questions, so she was a threat, too."

"And the hiker they just found?"

"Same. I talked to Mel Tyndall. She told her rescuers she had felt like she was being followed by someone during her first afternoon in the park. So after she made camp, she slipped off to hide in a cave, hoping whoever it was would move on. When she went back, all her gear had been stolen and she was almost out of water."

"She could have died out there."

"Seems like that was the plan. And it would have looked like natural causes."

The doors behind them parted, and Special Agent Woods walked out. She wore a navy pantsuit and had her hair up in a tight bun.

Her expression turned wary when she noticed them standing there. She had to know that the sheriff's office wasn't exactly happy with her right now. But she stepped over to talk to them anyway, so Connor had to give her credit.

She nodded at them. "Detectives."

"Is Ava Burch still being treated in there?" Grant asked.

"It looked to me like they were about to finish up."

Grant shot Connor a look. "I'll call you later."

"Later."

He disappeared into the hospital, no doubt to go see whether Ava was still as dazed and shocky as she'd been earlier when he'd insisted that she let a deputy take her to get treated.

Connor turned his attention to Woods. He'd seen her interviewing Ava in an exam room as a resident sutured his arm.

"So, what aren't you telling us?" Connor asked.

"I beg your pardon?"

"Last I checked, this wasn't your case. You're investigating Brittlyn Spencer, not Molly Shaw. So, what's the link? You guys have been hiding leads this whole time."

She didn't try to deny it, and again, he had to give her some credit. But not much.

She sighed. "Until this morning, we didn't have very many leads."

He raised an eyebrow.

"You may not believe that, but it's true."

"What happened this morning?" he asked.

Another sigh. "Yesterday, we learned of the disappearance of another hiker, who also happened to be employed at Whitehorse Ranch. I already suspected that Brittlyn Spencer might have worked there, based on information provided by Brittlyn's mother. This morning, I tracked down a former ranch employee, someone on their kitchen staff, who recognized Brittlyn's photograph."

"Recognized it from what? The news?"

"No. This man lives in California. I found him on social media. He left the ranch before Brittlyn went missing and didn't see all the publicity. But I shared a photo today, and he told me he recognized her." She checked her watch, as though she had to be somewhere. She was a hotshot FBI agent, so most likely she did. "I think what Ava Burch uncovered is just the tip of the iceberg. James and Whitney

Shelton have been posing as owners of the ranch, but the real owner is in a nursing home. Molly Shaw likely found out about it, so they killed her. Brittlyn may have found out, too."

"So, I take it you think Brittlyn—"

"Yes," she said grimly. "It's unconfirmed, at this point. I'd like to ask Peter Shelton about it, but he's not talking. And neither is his sister-in-law."

"And his brother is on the run," Connor said.

"Correct."

"That's some loyalty for you right there." Connor shook his head. "He left his pregnant wife and his brother twisting in the wind. Maybe y'all can use that to your advantage."

Woods smiled slightly.

"Oh, don't worry. We will."

A VA STARED OUT the window, watching the fence posts race past. The closer they got to home, the more anxious she felt, and she wasn't sure why.

Her head throbbed as the day's chaotic images tumbled through her brain—the drive across Whitehorse Ranch, the duct tape around her hands.

The serrated hunting knife pointed at her throat.

No gunshots. That had been the plan. It would have been messy but quiet, and he might have even gotten away with it.

The McCulloughs' gate came into view.

"Oh, we need to go to the main house first." She turned to look at Grant. "I need to pick up Huck."

"Jenna took him to your place."

"She did? How do you know?"

"I called and asked her to. I thought you'd want to see him."

Ava stared at him. A hot lump clogged her throat, and she looked away. "Thank you."

"Sure."

Grant turned onto the driveway leading to her cottage. The sun was low now, and the cottonwoods cast shadows over the house. Huck would be waiting by the door, having heard Grant's truck the instant it turned onto the drive.

He parked beside the tree, the spot where she usually parked. Her car was still in town, but she couldn't worry about that now. She just wanted to be home.

"Here, wait a sec." Grant jumped out and walked around the front of the truck.

Ava pushed open her door and slid out, careful not to put too much weight on her foot. They'd x-rayed it at the hospital and determined that she didn't have a fracture. But now her ankle was sprained even worse than before.

Grant slid his arm around her waist. "Want me to carry you?"

"I got it."

She leaned against him as she made her way to the house. Huck barked and scratched on the other side of the door as she dug her key from her purse.

"Here." Grant took it from her and undid the lock as she held the doorframe and braced herself for seventy-five pounds of furry exuberance.

Huck jumped all over her as she limped into the house.

"Hello, sweet boy." She sank into the nearest chair and rubbed his ears. "I missed you. I missed you so much!" She scrubbed his head as he licked her face and hands. He darted over to Grant as Ava watched him, smiling. Then he ran back. He couldn't seem to decide who was more worthy of his drool and attention.

She looked at Grant. "Thank you."

"For what?"

For knowing she needed to see her dog tonight. For understanding how fragile she felt. For treating her somewhat normally, even though today had been the strangest and most terrifying day of her life.

She got up and stepped into the kitchen as Grant set his keys on the counter. Just the sight of his big presence in her tiny kitchen made her feel better about her insistence on being here tonight. He'd invited her to his place, but she'd wanted to be home.

He picked up a note from the counter. "'Huck is fed and dinner is in the oven. Love, J.'"

Ava's eyes welled with tears. Their argument seemed like a lifetime ago, but it had been only a few hours. Everything felt hyperreal and yet totally *unreal* at the same time.

Grant was watching her with that look of concern. He stepped over and rested his hands on her waist as Huck circled them excitedly.

"Sorry." She brushed a tear from her cheek.

"Don't be. What can I do?"

She glanced around her kitchen, as if she might see an answer. There was nothing for him to do; she simply felt anxious.

"I just need to . . . rinse the day off." She looked up at him. "I need a few minutes."

"How about I walk Huck? Take as long as you need."

She nodded, grateful that he seemed to know exactly how to help her, even though she had no idea.

He reached for the lead on the counter, sending Huck into a fresh fit of excitement. "I'll lock up," he said, grabbing her key chain.

When they were gone, she breathed a sigh of relief to be alone in her quiet house. She hobbled to the bathroom.

The sight of her face made her gasp.

"Oh my *God*." She leaned toward the mirror. She'd known she looked bad, but she didn't realize the extent of it. She touched the bruise on her cheek where Peter Shelton had clocked her. A wave of outrage washed over her. It was just a punch. It would heal. He'd wanted to *kill* her with a hunting knife, so compared to that, this was nothing. But just the sight of the purple bruise made her furious.

She turned the shower to hot and peeled off her clothes. Everything was going straight into the trash. She never wanted to see any of it again.

As the bathroom turned steamy, she unwound the bandage they'd given her at the hospital and placed it on the vanity, then cautiously stepped into the shower. She shampooed her hair twice and heard little *clinks* as chunks of glass hit the tile. She collected the chunks and dropped them into the soap dish.

By the time she dried off and combed her hair, she felt slightly more like herself again. She rewrapped her ankle, then dressed in cutoff shorts and a tank top and made her way back to the kitchen as Grant and Huck returned. It was getting dark out now, and she switched on the light over the sink.

"How did it go?" she asked, leaning back against the counter.

"He chased a roadrunner."

"That's Looney. He loves to chase him."

Grant knelt beside Huck to check his paws for sticker burrs, and Ava's heart melted.

He looked up. "How'd the shower feel?"

"Good. You didn't tell me I looked like a freak."

"You don't." He stepped over to her and planted a kiss on her forehead. "You look beautiful."

She laughed. "Are you *trying* to make me cry?"

"God no."

He kissed her again, on her mouth this time. Ava eased back to look at him. How many beaten-up women had Grant seen through his job over the years? It was a depressing thought.

She turned away and opened the oven to peek at the dinner Jenna had brought over.

"Smells good," Grant said.

"Chicken enchiladas. It's Jenna's mom's specialty." She switched on the oven to warm them.

"There's a plate of brownies here, too," Grant said.

Ava peeled back the foil and sighed.

"What?" he asked.

"All this food. It's her way of nudging me."

"Nudging you to what?"

"Invite you to spend the night here."

He raised an eyebrow. "Are you going to?"

"Do you want me to?"

"Yes."

"I guess the better question is, Can you?"

Irritation flashed in his eyes. "Yes."

He kissed her again, and there was an edge to it now, as if he wanted to prove something to her. She slid her arms over his shoulders and eased into him. He tasted good. Like himself and something else, too—something sharp and sexy that made her think of being skin to skin with him.

She wanted him to stay. She *needed* him to, even if he had to leave in the middle of the night. Or in an hour. His time didn't really belong to him, and she knew that, but she didn't care right now. She'd take what she could get.

"Hold on to me," he whispered.

She clutched his neck as he slid his arm under her legs and scooped her up. He carried her to the sofa and settled her on the cushions. She scooted over to make room for him, and he leaned over her and resumed their kiss. It was long and gentle, and when he eased back, she knew her cheeks were wet.

She still couldn't get her head around everything. Grant had found her. Just in time. A minute more, and it would have been too late.

"Thank you," she said.

"For what?"

"Coming for me. A few more minutes and—"

He silenced her with a kiss. "I know."

"Sorry I'm so rattled right now."

"It's okay." He stroked the back of his finger along her jaw. "I'm rattled, too. This was one of the worst days of my life."

Her heart skittered. She gazed up into those bottomless brown eyes and knew that he meant it. Emotion welled inside her, and she pulled him down for another kiss. It was long and deep, and she tried to show him all the feelings inside her even though she didn't have the words.

He got it. She knew. They were communicating perfectly with just their mouths and their hands.

His fingers slid beneath her tank top, and nerves fluttered through her—the good kind. The fizzy, sexy kind she felt when she got really turned on. He kissed her hotly as his hand cupped her breast, and she arched against him.

He pulled back and gazed down at her.

"Are you hungry?" he asked.

"Not yet. You?"

He traced his fingertip over her breast beneath her shirt. "I'm completely, totally starving." He sucked her nipple through the fabric, and desire jolted through her. "Let's go to bed."

A VA'S CAR WAS parked outside McCullough & Burch, along with a dark red pickup that Grant didn't recognize. He mounted the steps to the office, and a cowbell clattered as he opened the door.

The conversation halted as he stepped inside. Ava and Jenna stood at the reception counter, and Grant would have bet money they'd been talking about him.

"Hi," Ava said, obviously surprised.

"Hey there." He took off his sunglasses. "Hi, Jenna."

"Hello, Grant. How nice of you to come see us on this sunny afternoon." Something about her smug smile told him he'd been right.

He looked at Ava. He had left her house at five thirty this morning and hadn't talked to her all day. He didn't know if she was pissed at him.

"You have a minute?" he asked.

"Sure."

She led him into her office and watched him with a frown as he closed the door with a soft *click*.

"Grant, what's wrong?"

"Have a seat."

She lowered herself onto the arm of the sofa. She wore a denim skirt today and a loose button-down blouse. No shoes at the moment, and her injured ankle was still wrapped in a beige-colored bandage.

"It's been a busy day," he said. "I meant to call you, but I couldn't."

She just watched him.

"I was at Silver Canyon park all morning." He held her gaze, wanting to see if she knew where he was going with this. "We had a recovery operation."

Her eyebrows shot up. "How come I didn't hear—"

"We kept it under wraps."

"Oh God." She pressed her hand to her chest. "Brittlyn?"

He nodded.

"You're sure?"

"They confirmed the ID with dental records." He stepped closer, not sure whether she wanted him touching her or not.

"Oh my God. Poor Rachel. Does she know?"

He shook his head. "I'm heading over there now. I came to see if you might want to come."

"Yes. Of course." She stood up and looked around. "I just need my shoe. Oh my God. I hope she doesn't hear on the news. Or social media."

She slid her foot into a sandal and grabbed her purse on the desk. Grant followed her out of the room. Jenna had taken off, apparently, and her office was dark. Ava flipped the window sign to **CLOSED** and locked the front door as they left.

Grant held her arm on the couple of stairs to street level and helped her into his truck.

"Is she still at that motel in Henley?" Ava asked as they got moving.

"Last I heard." She'd been camped out there since the first whisper of news about a body in Silver Canyon State Park.

Ava shook her head and looked out the window. "I really hope she doesn't see it on TV."

"We've done our best to keep a lid on it. It was sheriff's office only, plus the ME's people and Mel Tyndall."

"Still, things leak."

"I know."

Ava looked at him. "Where did you find her?"

Grant thought about how to answer that. It was an ongoing investigation, and she wasn't a cop. On the other hand, she was on an SAR team and the details would make their way through the grapevine eventually.

"You can't tell me, can you? Forget I asked."

"I can tell you some." He cleared his throat. "You know, they had teams combing the park for two days looking for Camila. One of the search dogs alerted on some bones in the southwest corner of the park."

"How'd she get there? She was last seen in Big Bend."

"We don't know. We think possibly Shelton kidnapped her or offered her a ride, then killed her and dumped her body in the state park. Some scattered bones were found near the entrance to an old mine shaft."

Ava shuddered. "When did this discovery happen?"

"Yesterday afternoon. Right around the time they found Camila. Donovan was able to get a cadaver team out here early this morning to confirm the find." Evidently, cadaver dogs knew the difference between human and non-human bones.

"That explains this morning."

He looked at her. "What's that?"

"This morning. You had your alarm set for five fifteen, and I didn't know why. You knew about this last night?"

"I knew Donovan had a canine team lined up."

And in his heart, he knew what it would find. But Ava had had enough to deal with last night, and he hadn't wanted to burden her with this, too.

"So . . . Peter Shelton's not talking yet, but the evidence is piling up." He glanced at Ava. "The FBI hauled away a bunch of evidence from the ranch, including some computers. And I saw them processing his truck. There was a snake hook in the back."

Ava bristled. "I *knew* it! He tried to kill Huck."

And her, too. But Grant didn't need to point that out.

"I'll never understand—" She shook her head.

"What?"

She shook her head again and looked out the window, and he figured he knew what she was thinking. The utter cruelty of some people was hard to comprehend. Grant saw it over and over again in his job, but the Sheltons ramped up greed and selfishness to a whole new level.

Silence settled over them as the arid landscape whisked by. How many times had Rachel Spencer driven this same lonesome stretch of highway in her twelve-month quest to find her daughter? The woman had scoured hundreds of miles of park trails, and blanketed towns with flyers, and slept in her car in Big Bend when it was too rainy to camp. She'd learned the name of every badge in four counties and their phone numbers, too, and she wasn't afraid to show up at station houses and get in people's way.

Rachel had caught wind of the search for Camila even before the local media did, and she'd immediately put herself in charge of the volunteer effort. Besides combing the park on foot, she'd helped direct traffic and passed out water bottles and Kind bars from the back of her car.

"What about that agent?"

He looked at Ava. "Special Agent Woods?"

"Yeah, isn't this her case?"

"We decided I should talk to Rachel Spencer. She knows me better, so." Grant shrugged.

"In other words, you asked for this."

"Yeah."

They neared Henley and passed a series of cheap motels: the Sunrise Inn, the Desert Rose, the Henley Motor Lodge. Grant drove by a string of gas stations and burger places and finally swung into the parking lot of Rachel's motel. Her blue SUV was parked where it had been last time.

Grant pulled into a space and looked at Ava. This was the single worst part of his job, and now he regretted asking her to come. She had a sprained ankle and a bruised face, and barely a day ago she'd almost been killed.

"You don't have to do this," he said.

She pushed open her door. "Let's go."

They crossed the parking lot, and his dread grew heavier as they neared the door to room 103. Grant's throat went dry. This was irrevocable. Once he took her hope away, it was never coming back. He glanced at Ava. She stood straight, with her hands clasped in front of her.

Before he could knock, the curtains on the window shifted and then the door swung open.

Rachel took one look at him, and her face went slack. She turned to Ava with a question in her eyes.

Ava stepped forward. "I'm so sorry, Rachel."

She fell into Ava's arms.

CHAPTER
THIRTY

Six weeks later

"ENSENADA, MEXICO."

"What's that?" Connor asked over the phone.

"A town down in Baja, right on the Pacific," Grant said. "Looks like James Shelton is hanging out down there. The feds are zeroing in on the place now."

Connor exited the sandwich shop with the meatball sub he planned to have for dinner. "So, you got this from Woods?"

"Yeah. I just got off the phone with her."

Over the last six weeks, the FBI had slowly but surely taken over their entire case. The Sheltons had been running a four-year operation that—in addition to murder—involved a long list of white-collar crimes. Agent Woods had been to visit Eleanor Bennett in a nursing home near Dallas and learned that she knew very little about the young couple who'd befriended her in recent years and offered to "stay at her ranch and look after the place." They'd been paying five hundred a month in rent. But Eleanor had no idea they'd taken out loans in her name and built guest cottages and erected a meditation pavilion. Her tenants had neglected to mention they were raking in millions a year from people desperately seeking weight loss and infertility cures and spiritual enlightenment.

"So, what now?" Connor asked.

"Woods hinted that they've got something in the works. I think they plan to have him arrested and extradited."

"Good."

"And get this, he's not alone. He's down there with a girlfriend."

"Seriously?"

"The feds found records of him communicating with this woman in the months before he became a fugitive. They think she helped him leave the country."

Connor neared his truck and popped the locks with his key fob. "Does his pregnant wife know all this?"

"Not yet. Woods wants to interview her again and see if she might have more to say about her husband once she finds out he's down in Baja with another woman while she's up here facing charges and about to have his baby."

Connor stopped by his truck as he spotted a familiar white Camry parked down the street. He glanced around.

"Listen, I've got a call coming in," Grant said. "I'll tell you the rest tomorrow."

"Sure. Later."

Connor spotted Jenna coming out of a bakery with a big white box in her arms. He dropped off his dinner inside his truck and walked over. Today she wore a skirt and heels, which made him think she'd come from the courthouse. She shifted the box in her arms as she tried to dig her keys from her purse.

"Need a hand?"

She glanced up. "Oh. Hi." She looked flustered as she juggled everything and unlocked her car with a chirp.

Connor opened the passenger door and stood aside.

"Thank you." She bent down and settled the box on the

floor. Then she stood and looked at him, hitching her purse onto her shoulder. She seemed uncomfortable. He hadn't seen her since the morning in June when he'd driven her home.

"How's it going?" Connor asked.

"Fine. Just picking up a birthday cake."

"For Lucy?"

"No, for Samantha, our receptionist. It's her birthday tomorrow and she loves the cheesecake here."

Connor closed the car door and tucked his hands into his pockets.

"So . . . I'm glad I bumped into you," Jenna said. "I've been meaning to call you." She crossed her arms. "I wanted to apologize."

"For what?"

"Snapping at you that morning. That was uncalled for."

"Forget about it. How have you been?"

"Okay." She dropped her hands. "Busy. I'm on my way to get Lucy at gymnastics." She looked at her watch. "I'm running late, actually."

He nodded and waited for her to walk away, but she just stood there looking at him.

"I'd better go."

"Would you like to go out?"

Her eyebrows arched with surprise.

"We could have dinner or something," he added when she didn't answer.

"Why?"

He smiled. "Um, because it might be fun?"

She looked away, clearly uneasy with this topic. "That's probably not a good idea."

"Why not?"

She turned to look at him. "Because. As you're obviously aware, my life's kind of a mess right now. I'm taking care of my parents and my daughter, and I'm not doing a very good job of either."

"It's going to get worse."

"Excuse me?"

"I hate to tell you that, but it's true," he said. "My grandfather had Alzheimer's, and my mom took care of him for years. It's progressive."

"I know that. You're kind of making my point for me."

She looked away again, and the pained expression on her face put a pinch in his chest.

"So, are you just planning to put your life on hold?" he asked.

She turned toward him. "What did your mom do?"

He stepped closer. "She took it one day at a time. That's all you can do."

She stared up at him, and he could see the conflict in her eyes.

"Give yourself a break once in a while." He smiled. "Come on a date with me. We'll have fun."

She looked skeptical. "Where would we go?"

"Anywhere you want. Dinner. A movie."

"I don't know."

"We could play putt-putt. You could bring Lucy."

She didn't respond.

"Say yes."

Her gaze narrowed, and he knew he'd gone too far.

She glanced at her watch again. Then she walked around the car and opened her door. She looked at him over the roof.

"I'll think about it."

He smiled.

"That's not a yes, that's a maybe," she added.

"I know."

AVA ARRIVED AT Grant's, but he wasn't there. He'd been working crazy hours all week, going in early and staying late. He wouldn't tell her what was going on, but she'd gleaned enough to know it had to do with the Shelton case. Something big was afoot, and Grant was involved, even though the FBI seemed to be taking the lead.

Ava scooped the FedEx box off the front seat, along with her computer bag. She walked to the garage and tapped in the code. As the door lifted, she could hear Huck barking excitedly inside the house.

She let herself in, and he greeted her with what seemed like extra enthusiasm. She'd needed to be at the courthouse most of the day, so she'd decided to leave him at Grant's so she could pop over and let him out during the afternoon. As she entered the quiet cabin, she scanned the floor for any sign that he'd eaten or destroyed anything since she'd last seen him.

She set her package on the kitchen counter and slipped off her heels.

"You hungry, boy? Me, too."

Ava padded barefoot into Grant's bedroom. She changed into shorts, a T-shirt, and flip-flops before going to the kitchen to find Huck waiting eagerly by the door.

He wanted a walk more than he wanted dinner, apparently.

Ava skimmed the astronomy article she'd been reading on her phone earlier, then checked the time. It was almost nine. She got a bottle of water from the fridge, then grabbed the folded Mexican blanket from the hall closet before heading out the back door with Huck.

He raced down the stairs and sniffed around the yard.

"Come on," she said, switching on her phone flashlight and leading him past the fire pit into the wide-open space. Darkness was falling over the canyon, and she could see Venus already near the western horizon.

Ava's phone chimed. To her disappointment, it wasn't Grant calling to tell her he was on his way home.

"Hey," she said to her sister.

"I saw your text. So, you got the package?"

"Yes, thank you." Ava took a deep breath. "You were right."

For a moment Abby didn't say anything.

"So, you're not mad?"

"Why would I be mad?" Ava asked.

"I don't know. You've been pretty prickly about everything. And you sounded so adamant about Dad's stuff. But I thought you'd change your mind when you saw it."

"I did."

After spending several Saturdays going through their storage unit, her sister had mailed her a box of mementos, including drawings and Father's Day cards and a hideous clay bowl that Ava had made at camp when she was seven. Her dad had saved all of it, and the sight of everything had opened the floodgates.

"Well, I hope you didn't open it at work," Abby said.

"I did."

"Oh, damn. I'm sorry. I shouldn't have mailed it there."

"It was no problem. I was alone."

"Did you recognize the pendant?"

The package had included a Saint Anthony pendant with the name of their childhood dog engraved on the back.

"It was Buddy's," Ava said. "Of course I recognized it."

"I figured Huck could wear it."

Huck already had one, but Ava didn't mention that. It was a sweet thought.

"Thanks, Abs. Really. You were right about the stuff." Ava stopped walking and gazed up at the starry sky. "You were right about a lot of things. I've been thinking about all this anger I've kept pent up. I realize it really hasn't been about him hurting mom or being absent from our lives all those times."

"No?"

"I mean, yeah. That's some of it." Ava tossed the blanket to the ground and sank down onto it. "I think the thing that's *really* been bothering me was the end. How he shut us out until it was too late. That was such a shitty thing to do." Ava swallowed the hot lump in her throat. "He wouldn't let us help him. It's hard to forgive him for that."

Her sister didn't respond, and Ava's chest ached.

"I know what you mean," she finally said.

Huck trotted up to her, and Ava stroked his ears. Then he dashed away.

"I felt that way, too, at first," Abby said. "But now I think I had it wrong. I don't think he was trying to shut us out. Not in a malicious way. I think maybe . . . I don't know, he was trying to protect us. There was nothing we could really do anyway, so maybe he thought it would be easier for us."

"Yeah, well, it wasn't."

"I know."

But maybe his heart had been in the right place. Abby was probably right. She was the younger sister, but somehow she seemed so much wiser about everything. Emotionally, she'd been way ahead of Ava this whole time.

"Well, I'm glad you got the box," Abby said.

"Thank you. It means a lot."

"Sure. Talk to you soon, okay?"

"Sounds good."

They hung up, and Ava gazed down at the phone glowing in her hand. They *would* talk again soon. Ava would make sure of it. Over the past six weeks, she'd made an effort to get back into regular communication with her sister and her mom. Until she'd started talking to them again—really *talking*—she hadn't realized how much she'd missed her family. Grief was hard enough without trying to get through it alone.

Ava stood up and spread the blanket out. She sat back down and checked her phone again. Still nothing from Grant, which probably meant he had to stay late again tonight.

She gazed up at the stars and waited for the resentment

to come. But it didn't. She didn't feel as hurt by his long hours as she had those first few times that his job got in the way of their plans. For the past six weeks, they'd spent practically all their free time together, and she'd learned a lot about Grant. First and foremost, she'd learned that he was dedicated. She'd also learned that he had an incredible work ethic. He cared deeply about people, even perfect strangers, and didn't hesitate to go the extra mile for them, even if it meant sacrificing his personal time.

The personal sacrifices were challenging because they directly affected her, but that came with the territory. Grant's integrity and his demanding job were two sides of the same coin. She couldn't admire his dedication to others without accepting the downsides, too.

Ava lay back and laced her fingers behind her head as she studied the sky. She found Ursa Minor and tried to locate the Summer Triangle.

Huck barked in the distance, and Ava smiled. Contentment settled over her like a warm blanket as she gazed up at the inky sky and waited.

"Hey, beautiful."

She sat up and turned around. Grant walked toward her, a tall silhouette against the yellow glow of the cabin.

"Hi."

He stopped beside the blanket and handed her a plastic tumbler. Then he reached down to pet Huck.

"Thanks." She took a cold sip. It was her new favorite drink, a mescal margarita. It looked like he'd made himself one, too.

He sat down on the blanket beside her. He'd changed from his work clothes into jeans and flip-flops, which told her he wasn't going back in tonight. At least, he wasn't planning to. He could easily get a call at three in the morning.

He leaned close and kissed her.

She smiled. "You smell like garlic."

"I do?" He combed his hand through his hair. "I stopped at Nino's on the way home and grabbed us a pizza."

"Sounds great."

"What are you doing out here?"

"Stargazing." She settled her drink beside her and lay back down. He leaned back on his elbows.

"There's a meteor shower this week."

"Oh yeah?"

"Northeast sky." She pointed. "Just over that ridge there with the tall tree."

He reached up and shifted her arm to the left. "You're about thirty degrees off."

She dropped her arm and looked at the cloudless sky and the crescent moon. Huck slowed down and began sniffing around instead of darting from place to place.

She turned and studied Grant's profile. He seemed tense tonight.

"What's wrong?" she asked.

He looked up at the sky for a long moment.

"Is it the case?"

"Yeah." He paused. "James Shelton was arrested today."

Ava's heart skipped a beat. "Where?"

"Mexico. It sounds like he's going to be extradited soon."

Ava sat up. "That's great. Oh my gosh. Aren't you excited?"

"Yeah. The feds got his wife to talk, so that's even better news. They're going to have a ton of evidence against him as they build the case."

She studied his face, looking for signs of relief or pride or just plain happiness. But there was something wrong. Maybe he wanted to be more involved in building the case and wasn't happy so much of it was going to the feds.

"Grant, what is it? Something's on your mind."

He looked at her. "Donovan offered me a promotion. Head of criminal investigations."

"*Really*? That's amazing." She leaned in and kissed him. "And well deserved."

"I don't know whether to take it."

She frowned. "Why wouldn't you?"

He sat up and turned to face her. "This affects both of us. I think we should talk about it first."

Her heart thrummed at his words. He usually seemed fairly closed off when it came to his work.

"Well . . . what are you thinking? Is it a raise?"

"A little." He shrugged. "Mainly it's more time. More paperwork. More responsibility."

"Is that what you want?"

"I think I can handle it." He rested his hand on her bare knee. "But I don't want to deprioritize you. Us. You've been through a lot, and I know it's been hard on you with the hours I've been working."

"Yeah." She looked out at the canyon where Huck was sniffing around among the desert plants. "But you know, I've been busy, too. Things have really taken off, and Jenna and I are swamped with work right now."

He looked at her for a long moment. "So, are you saying you want me to take it?"

She reached over and squeezed his hand. "It means a lot to me that you want my opinion."

"Which is what?"

"I think you should do what you want. What you feel is best for your career."

"That's not all I'm thinking about, though." He took a deep breath. "I've been thinking lately about us."

She just looked at him in the dimness.

He took her hand. "What would you think about moving in together?"

"What, you mean here?"

"Have you thought about it at all?"

"Yes." She thought about it all the time.

"We'd spend less time driving back and forth," he said.

"We'd wake up together. Go to bed together. The downside is, you'd be farther from your law firm."

"Not that much farther. And I'd be closer to court."

He lifted an eyebrow. "Does that mean you'll consider it?"

"Well." Her heart was thudding now as she thought about all the implications. She cleared her throat. "It's a big step."

He nodded.

A quiet settled over them, and she listened to the sound of cicadas in the distant trees.

"Ava."

She looked at him.

"I almost got married once. You probably heard about that by now."

"Missy Donovan," she said, relieved that he'd brought it up. She'd been wanting to talk about it, but it never seemed to be the right time. "What happened?"

"She slept with someone else after we got engaged. I found out about it a month before the wedding."

Ava looked at him with surprise. "I heard you got cold feet and left her at the altar."

"Yeah, well. That's how she wanted to spin it. I didn't mind being the bad guy. I was leaving town anyway and didn't care. At the time, I thought I wasn't coming back."

Ava watched him, searching for any clue to how this had affected him. He had to have been hurt and embarrassed and probably angry, too. Ava hadn't experienced that level of betrayal, but Jenna had, and it very much sucked.

"So, why did you come back?" she asked.

He shrugged. "This is home. I invested almost six years in my career in Dallas, and I realized I was investing in the wrong place. So I moved back and applied for a job at the sheriff's office."

"That must have fueled some gossip," she said.

"That didn't matter. The main thing was, I was worried

I could be making a mistake. You know, what if I got back here and realized I'd outgrown it?"

"Had you?"

"No." He paused for a moment. "But I definitely saw it differently. This job makes you jaded about people. About everything." He met her gaze. "This place is beautiful, but it's not perfect, Ava. No place is. No relationship is, either."

She tipped her head to the side. "It sounds like you're trying to warn me."

"I'm not. Or maybe I am." He shook his head. "I just wanted to talk about this up front." He looked at her. "I know we'll have ups and downs. But I want you to trust that I'm committed. I don't know what you heard about my past, but I want you to know that I take my commitments seriously."

The earnestness in his eyes made her chest tighten. "I know that."

He watched her, as though waiting for more of a reaction.

Ava smiled at him in the darkness. Jenna was right about this man. He was totally hot and totally into her. And Ava felt dizzy with disbelief right now that they were having this conversation together out here under the stars.

She lay back on the blanket again and tugged his sleeve. He stretched out beside her and laced his fingers through hers. They held hands and stared up at the sky, and Ava's heart thudded as she thought of the things they might do together.

Huck trotted over and settled himself beside the blanket. He loved this place. She did, too.

"We could sleep out here," she said.

"We have a perfectly good bed inside."

"Yes, but no shooting stars."

He propped himself on his elbow and leaned over her, blocking out what limited light there was from the sliver of moon.

"Come inside, and I'll make it worth your while."

She smiled. "You promise?"

He kissed her. It was long and sweet, and she combed her fingers into the thick softness of his hair as she let it go on and on. Tonight was special, and she wanted to savor this moment with him.

He eased away.

"I love you," she said.

For an excruciating moment he didn't react.

"Damn. You beat me to the punch."

Her heart squeezed. "I did?"

He kissed her gently. "I love you, too. I think I've loved you since that first day."

Her heart swelled with love and joy and nervousness about the future. It was a good sort of nervousness, though— the kind that put a giddy smile on her face.

She reached up and traced her finger over his chin. "What are we going to do?"

"About what?"

"Everything."

"I don't know. We'll figure it out."

She ran her fingertip from his ear to his mouth and then along his jaw. They *would* figure it out. Together.

"It feels good out here," she whispered. "Will you lie with me awhile longer?"

He kissed her forehead, then slid his arm under her shoulders and tucked her head against his chest. "As long as you want."

Keep reading for an excerpt from Laura Griffin's next Texas Murder Files novel,

Deep Tide

THE STARS WERE still out as Leyla drove to work the next morning. Because it was Sunday, she'd rolled out of bed at five instead of four, but the extra hour of sleep had done little to energize her. Between all the relatives in town and the wedding and her first big catering job, the past few weeks had been an emotional roller coaster.

And then there was Sean Moran.

Leyla had gone to sleep buzzed from champagne and wondering whether she'd made the right decision turning him down for that drink.

Of course she had.

She didn't date tourists. Ever. It was her most important rule. Growing up in a resort town, she'd learned quickly where those encounters would lead. She had no illusions about what men wanted when they sidled up to her at a bar with their charter-boat tans and designer shades and offered to buy her a beer.

So why had she asked Sean to meet her for coffee? She didn't know.

Well, she did know. She'd wanted to mess with him a little. She'd wanted to see the look on his handsome face when she basically called his bluff. She'd been curious about how he'd wiggle out of it last night when he realized he wasn't getting lucky, but now he had a platonic coffee date to contend with. Chances were, he wouldn't show up. His being her brother's friend helped the odds a little, but even if he *did* show, he was almost certain to walk in with a handy excuse about how something came up with work and he had to be getting on the road back to Houston soon.

And then there was the other thing, the second reason her mean streak was showing.

He'd lied to her.

She didn't know why, but he had. His story about working vice with Joel in Houston was pure bullshit. Joel had worked property crimes in Houston, full stop. Leyla had thrown that out there because she sensed Sean didn't want to talk about his connection to her brother. Maybe he knew Joel from some context he didn't want to discuss with her. But what? Her brothers weren't saints, for sure, and Owen in particular had been pretty wild in his twenties, but Leyla would have been surprised if Joel had any kind of checkered past he wanted to keep hidden.

But who knew? Her brothers no doubt had secrets they didn't tell their little sister, just like she had secrets from them.

She pulled into the lot and parked in her favorite spot beneath an old oak tree that had been bent and twisted by decades of wind off the Gulf. After cracking her windows so her car wouldn't get too hot, she crossed the parking lot and was surprised to see lights on in the surf shop next door. The mannequin in the window was naked, so maybe they were putting out new inventory today.

Leyla let herself into the café and turned on the lights. The chairs were up, the floor was clean, and the air smelled faintly of the vinegar they used to clean the coffee

machines—all good signs. But several of the syrup bottles
needed filling and a dirty shot glass sat beside the espresso
machine. Also, the steam wand was sticky—her major pet
peeve—and the countertop needed a wipe down.

But first, coffee. And then she had to get her muffins
going so they'd be ready by seven.

She switched on the espresso machine to Warm and
checked her phone as she headed into the kitchen. It was
6:05, so Siena would be awake.

"Hey, it's me," Leyla said. "You up?"

"Absolutely."

"Liar."

"I'm just getting up," Siena said. "Are you at the shop?"

"Yes, and the pastries aren't here yet. Is Rogelio out
sick, too?"

"I don't think so."

The Island Beanery had a sister location at the Wind-
jammer Hotel. Besides giving them some steady foot traffic, the location gave them access to the hotel's kitchen,
which had three big ovens to Leyla's one. Most of their
pastries were made there and delivered each morning.

"He should be bringing the croissants and donuts, plus
cherry kolaches," Siena said. "You're doing the muffins,
right?"

"Chocolate-chip coconut." Leyla grabbed a bag of Ghi-
rardelli chips from the baker's rack. "And lemon poppy-
seed. Our lunch special is tomato-basil soup."

"Okay."

"How are we on coffee beans?"

"I honestly don't know." Siena yawned. "We got a deliv-
ery yesterday morning, but I didn't get a chance to open it
yet. I can do it when I get in."

"Thanks. See you in a few."

Leyla glanced at the clock above the baker's rack before
heading down the hall to the stock room. A full trash bag
sat by the back door, and she felt a surge of annoyance. She

grabbed the bag and hurried out back, where she heaved it into the dumpster behind the café. The sky was brightening but the moon was still out, and she remembered Sean Moran standing in the moonlight on the beach last night.

Anyone ever tell you you're very persistent, Sean?
Yes.

She pictured his sexy half smile as he'd waited for her to succumb to his charm and have a drink with him, which would have turned into an invitation back to his place. He didn't get turned down a lot—of that, she felt sure.

Leyla reached for the door, and movement in the alley caught her eye. She stepped toward it, then jumped back as a large black bird flapped toward her.

She caught her breath and stepped forward, peering into the shadowy alley beside the surf shop. The breeze kicked up, and a stench hit her. There was something dead there. An animal or . . .

She lurched back, gasping.

Not an animal but a *person*.

Leyla's heart seized. She recognized the hair, the shirt, the chunky silver rings on the outstretched hand.

"No. *No no no no.*"

Leyla's breath came in short gasps as she fumbled with her phone and switched on the flashlight feature. She shined the light into the alley, hoping, hoping, *hoping* she was just asleep or passed out.

Leyla's chest squeezed as the beam of light fell over the woman's face. A line of ants marched into her lifeless mouth.

Ready to find
your next great read?

Let us help.

Visit prh.com/nextread

Penguin
Random
House